THE
STOLEN ONES

A graduate of the University of British Columbia's Creative Writing Program, Owen Laukkanen spent three years in the world of professional poker reporting before turning to fiction. He currently lives in Vancouver.

ALSO BY OWEN LAUKKANEN

The Professionals

Criminal Enterprise

Kill Fee

THE
STOLEN ONES

OWEN LAUKKANEN

CORVUS

First published in the United States in 2015 by G. P. Putnam's Sons, a division of the Penguin Group, part of the Penguin Random House Company.

Published in e-book and paperback in 2015 by Corvus in Great Britain, an imprint of Atlantic Books Ltd.

10 9 8 7 6 5 4 3 2 1

A CIP catalogue record for this book is available from the British Library.

E-book ISBN: 978 1 78239 604 8
Paperback ISBN: 978 1 78239 639 0

Printed and bound by CPI Group (UK) Ltd, Croydon, CR0 4YY

Corvus
An imprint of Atlantic Books Ltd
Ormond House
26–27 Boswell Street
London
WC1N 3JZ

www.corvus-books.co.uk

This one's for Stacia

1

ONLY HER SISTER kept her alive.

The box was dark and stank of shit. Sweat, Urine. Misery. Irina Milosovici had lost track of how long she'd been inside. How long since Mike, the charming American, had disappeared with her passport in Bucharest. Since the two stone-faced thugs had shoved her into the box with the rest of the women, maybe forty of them. And Catalina.

Irina had lost count of how many days they'd spent in the pitch-black and silence, sharing stale air and meager rations behind the shipping container's false wall. How many times they'd clawed at the steel that surrounded them, screamed themselves hoarse, as the box lurched and jostled on its terrible, claustrophobic, suffocating journey.

Only Catalina kept her alive. Only her younger sister's warmth pressed against her in the darkness staved off the fear and, above all, the empty, sickening guilt.

> > >

THEY WERE IN AMERICA NOW. For days the box had swayed with the lazy rhythm of the ocean, had shuddered with the ever-present vibrations of a big diesel engine somewhere far below. Some of the women had been seasick, and the smell of vomit filled the box, mixing with the foul stench from the overflowing waste bucket in the corner.

Irina had passed the time telling Catalina stories. "This is the only way into the country for us," she told her. "When we arrive in America, they'll give us showers and new clothes and find us all jobs."

Catalina pressed tight to her in the darkness, said nothing, and Irina wondered if her lies were any comfort at all.

Then the waves calmed. The pitch of the engine slowed. The box seemed less dark, the air slightly fresher. The women had screamed again, all of them, pleading for help as the box was lifted from the ship, the lurching of the crane sending them tumbling into one another, momentarily weightless.

The box touched down again. Irina could hear a truck's engine, and the box rumbled and shook along an uneven road for a short while, maybe fifteen minutes. Then the movement stopped and the engine cut off. A door opened in the container's false wall.

The light was blinding. The women blinked and drew back, shielding their faces. Irina pulled Catalina to the rear of the box, far away from the light and whatever waited beyond.

Two men appeared in the open doorway, big men, their heads shaved nearly to the skin. One had a long, jagged scar across his forehead. The other held a powerful-looking hose. "Get these bitches out of here," he told his partner in English.

"What did he say?" Catalina whispered, and for a moment Irina was angry. Her sister's English was no good. What on earth had possessed her sister to join her?

But then Catalina had always been running to keep up with her older sister, and Irina had baited the hook. She was as guilty as the traffickers, she knew.

The men dragged the women out in pairs, past the stacks of cardboard boxes holding DVD players and cheap electric razors, until the container was empty and the women stood disheveled and weak in the harsh sunlight.

They were in a shipping yard. Irina could smell the ocean nearby, but the stacks of rusted shipping containers prevented her from seeing anything but the box and the two thugs.

The men sprayed out the inside of the false compartment. They dumped the waste bucket out onto the gravel and sprayed it clean also. Then they turned the hose on the women.

The water was cold, even in the warm summer air. Catalina's fingers dug into Irina's skin when the water hit her, spurring her on, tempting her to run. She didn't run, though. She withstood the spray, coughing and sputtering, and then the hose was turned off, and they stood shivering in the yard again.

The thugs began to maneuver the women back into the box. They took one girl aside, a pretty young blonde about Catalina's age. Then the scar-faced man saw Catalina, and beckoned to his partner. "Her, too," he said.

Irina felt suddenly desperate. "No," she said. "Get away from her."

The scar-faced man reached around her, grabbed at Catalina. Irina blocked his way, ready to fight. To claw at him, to hurt him. She would die before she let her sister go.

But the thug didn't try to kill her. He studied her for a moment. "Whatever," he said finally, and moved on down the row of women. "The bitch is too old anyway."

He picked out another girl instead, a black-haired girl even younger than Catalina. Dragged her away from the container, the young blond girl, too, and then the scar-faced man's partner was herding Irina and Catalina back into the box with the rest of the women, confining them in the darkness again.

> > >

THE DOORS HAD OPENED TWICE since the day of the hose. Days passed in between. The box rumbled and lurched, and the girls heard traffic outside, cars and trucks. The box rarely stopped moving. Irina screamed for help, but no help ever came.

The doors opened. The thugs peered in, spoke to each other quickly, unintelligibly, scanning the huddle of women. The man with the scar on his face climbed into the box and chose two girls at random. Another blonde, perhaps twenty, and a very young brunette. He dragged them out of the box by their hair, ignoring their screams, and came back for two more women, and then again, until he'd taken a total of ten. Then the doors closed and were locked, and the box resumed its journey.

The next time the door opened, the scar-faced man took only two women. Irina clutched Catalina and fought with her sister to the rear of the box, desperate to avoid being chosen. She screwed her eyes tight, heard the screams from the unlucky ones, and only breathed again when the men sealed the compartment.

The box rumbled onward. There was more space in the darkness now. The men had taken almost half of the women away. Sooner or later, they would come for the rest. They would come for Catalina.

The men had been careless when they'd sealed the box. The lock on the compartment door had failed to engage properly; it rattled and shook with a promise that hadn't existed before. Irina crossed the compartment and pushed at the door. Clawed at it. Punched it until it swung open to the mountains of cardboard and the rest of the container.

Already the air seemed fresher. Here was opportunity. Let the men do what they wanted to her, but they would not get Catalina. She would get her sister home.

"Come on," she said, pulling Catalina to the doorway. "The next time they come for us, we'll be ready."

2

CASS COUNTY SHERIFF'S deputy Dale Friesen finished his coffee and stepped out through the front door of the Paul Bunyan Diner and into the waning light as another summer day met its end. He stood on the steps for a minute, savoring the still air, the mad rush of campers and city folk all but gone from the 200 highway just across the way, everyone now hunkered down in their tents and cabins, swatting mosquitoes and telling ghost stories and hoping the thunderheads in the distance veered south before nightfall.

Friesen circled around the side of the diner to his Suburban, figuring he'd be happy if the road stayed dry just long enough for him to get back up to Walker, just long enough that he didn't look like a drowned rat showing up at Suzi's door with a bottle of wine after blowing off their big date day to go bass fishing. Shit but he was in trouble.

As Friesen reached his Suburban, a big semitruck pulled into the lot, a nice Peterbilt towing a rusty red container. The guy pulled in and parked behind Friesen, the ass end of his truck hanging out into the driveway, and as the guy climbed out of the cab, Friesen called over to him.

"You're a little long for that spot," he said, thinking, *That's what she said.* "Gimme a sec and I'll pull ahead."

The driver, a big guy with a shaved head and a face like he'd never smiled in his life, looked back down the length of his rig, then back at Friesen. "Yeah," he said. "All right."

"Don't get too many long haulers up here in lake country," Friesen said. "Where you headed?"

The driver glanced into the truck, and Friesen followed his gaze and saw the guy had a partner, another big, bald fella. This guy had a scar on his forehead like he'd lost a fight with a band saw.

"Out of state." The driver had an accent, some kind of European. "Going to I-94."

"I see you boys got the standard cab," Friesen said. "No bunk in the trunk, so to speak. You want a decent motel recommendation? Town of Walker's just up the road, about five miles or so. There's a—"

"We make Fargo tonight." The driver shifted his weight. "Got a schedule."

Friesen grinned. "That's a hundred twenty miles away," he said. "Gonna storm, too. Chamber of commerce would hate me if I let you get away."

"Thanks." The man's voice was flat. "We're making Fargo."

"All right." Friesen gave it up. Something wasn't meshing about these two jokers, but hell, the county didn't pay him enough to play every hunch. Besides, it was his day off. He was turning back to the Suburban, the driver and his buddy more or less forgotten already, when he heard something out the back of the rig. Sounded like banging. "You hear that?" Friesen asked the driver.

The driver shook his head. "I didn't hear nothing."

Friesen studied the truck again. New tractor. No logos. No markings of any kind, except the USDOT registration number and an operator decal. Standard cab, like he'd noted. Meant no beds, no creature comforts. Had to be an original badass to be driving a truck like that in northern Minnesota, a hundred and some miles from anywhere.

"Where you guys coming from, anyway?" Friesen asked.

The driver shifted his weight again, glanced back into the cab at his partner. "Duluth," he said finally. "Look, buddy, I don't have time for this—"

"Deputy, actually." Friesen showed the guy his identification. Kept his smile pasted on as he started toward the rear of the truck. "Look, humor me, would you? Maybe you got a stowaway back there. Couple of rats or something. What's your cargo, anyway?"

The driver hesitated a split second, then followed Friesen to the back of the rig. No markings on the container, just more old USDOT numbers. Ditto the chassis. New Jersey plates, though. "You guys sure are a long way from home," Friesen said. "What'd you say you were carrying?"

The driver just looked at him. "Electronics," he said finally.

Friesen felt his Spidey sense tingling. Slid his hand to his side, slow as he could, and snapped open the holster on his hip. Kept his eyes on the driver, kept his voice calm. "You wanna open her up for me?"

The driver didn't blink. "I think you need a warrant to open up my container."

"Heard something moving around in there," Friesen said. "That's probable cause. Now, you gonna make me phone this thing in, or can we just clear this up before the storm sets in?"

As if for emphasis, thunder rumbled in the distance. The driver pursed his lips. Pulled a key ring from his pocket and fiddled with the back-door lock. That's when things got crazy.

As soon as the lock disengaged, the rear door swung open, knocking the driver backward. Friesen caught a glimpse of a wall of cardboard boxes, DVD players or something, and then a woman came flying out, grungy and wild-eyed, barely more than a girl, yelling something in some crazy foreign language as she launched herself through the open door.

Friesen scrambled back, drawing his sidearm, hollering at the girl to slow down. The girl didn't listen. Probably couldn't even hear him. She knocked the driver to the ground as another girl appeared in the container doorway. Even younger. Just as dirty. What the hell was going on?

Friesen holstered his gun and grabbed at the first girl, couldn't hold her. She fought free of his arms and ran, bolted to the edge of the parking lot, and the woods that butted up against the back of the Paul Bunyan. The driver pulled himself off the ground. Made a run at the second girl, who'd dropped down to the dirt. Tackled her from behind as she ran after the first girl, wrenched her back toward the box.

"Jesus." Friesen had started after the first girl. Now he stopped. The second girl was screaming, fighting in the driver's arms, crying and clawing. The driver picked her up like she was paper, dragged her back to the box, and Friesen just stood there and watched like the dumbest kid in class, his mind struggling to piece the whole scene together.

The driver threw the younger girl into the container and scanned the lot for the older one. She'd disappeared into the forest somewhere, out of sight, and the driver hesitated for just a moment before he slammed the door closed, and locked it again. Finally, something triggered inside Friesen's head. He drew his sidearm again. "Wait a minute," he told the driver. "Just hold your damn horses."

The driver ignored him. Started across the parking lot, toward the girl in the forest. Friesen followed. Was about to reach out and grab the guy when he felt something behind him.

It was the other guy from the truck. The guy with the scar, and he was holding a big goddamn gun.

"Shit," Friesen said. "What—"

Then the guy pulled the trigger.

3

IRINA RAN INTO the woods as fast as her weak legs would carry her, into the underbrush, fallen trees, and tangles. Somewhere nearby, lightning flashed and thunder rolled. The first drops of rain began to fall.

Catalina wasn't behind her.

The realization came suddenly, like hitting a brick wall at high speed. She was alone in the forest. Her sister was gone.

Heart pounding, panic in her throat, Irina hurried back through the woods, toward the patch of parking lot, the truck. She was almost at the clearing when she heard the gunshots.

Three fast shots, then silence. Voices—the thugs, arguing with each other. They sounded frustrated, their tones urgent. Irina heard doors slam, and the truck rumble to life.

Irina forced her way through the last of the forest. Burst out onto the edge of the parking lot, where the big truck was pulling away from the restaurant, where the third man lay dead in the mud. There was no sign of her sister. The two thugs were leaving. They were leaving her here. And they were taking Catalina with them.

Irina hurried across the lot to the third man's body. He'd dropped his gun in the struggle with the thugs, and she picked it up, fumbled with it. Aimed it at the truck and fired.

The truck didn't slow. Irina fired until the gun was empty and the truck had disappeared. The men and Catalina were gone.

It was raining now, steady. Thunder and lightning like an artillery barrage. Irina looked around the parking lot. Saw mud, forest, nothing that looked like home. She dropped the gun beside the dead man. Then she sat down next to him and cried.

4

"PLEASE, DAD, CAN we go somewhere with cell reception next year?"

Kirk Stevens swapped an exasperated glance with his wife as, from inside the doorway of her tiny tent, his sixteen-year-old daughter stared at her new iPhone, searching in vain for a signal.

"What do you need reception for?" Stevens said. "This is nature, Andrea. The storm's passed. Come on out and help me build a fire."

Andrea swatted a mosquito and made a face. "It's dark and muddy out there," she said. "I *hate* nature."

Stevens watched his daughter zip the tent closed behind her. He sighed and dried a spot on the picnic bench next to his wife. "I don't get it," he said. "Last year, she was begging to go camping. What happened?"

Nancy Stevens looked up from her novel. "She's growing up, Kirk. It happens."

"Not like this," Stevens said. "This isn't maturing. This is *Invasion of the Body Snatchers*. This isn't the same girl."

"Sure it is." Nancy turned her flashlight toward the lakeshore, where ten-year-old JJ chased fireflies with his dog by the water. "She's just getting older. Her priorities are changing."

"So now her priority is a stupid cell phone."

"Not the phone, Kirk." Nancy gave him a sly smile. "It's the boy on the other end of it."

Stevens frowned. "A boy."

"Uh-huh."

"Andrea has a boyfriend?"

Nancy turned back to her book. "You didn't hear it from me."

Stevens considered his daughter's tent again. The light from her phone shone through the thin nylon walls. Every minute or so, those walls shook, accompanied by a slap and a groan as Andrea swatted another mosquito.

A boyfriend, Stevens thought. *Already?*

> > >

AS LONG AS STEVENS COULD remember, his daughter had loved the family's annual summer vacation in the woods. Every year, he and Nancy would pack up his old Cherokee with tents and coolers and inflatable rafts and take the kids north from Saint Paul into some real terrain—well, mostly just family campgrounds on one of Minnesota's famous ten thousand lakes, but if you got a quiet campsite and were willing to pretend, you could almost imagine you were Louis Hennepin or Pierre-Charles Le Sueur, venturing into uncharted wilderness.

This year, more than ever, Stevens needed a break. A special agent with the state's Bureau of Criminal Apprehension, he'd worked the spring months on a blockbuster case, another Carla Windermere special. In the three years that he'd known his beautiful FBI counterpart, Stevens had helped Windermere put down a kidnapping ring, a violent bank robber, and, this past April, the ringleader of an online contract-killing operation called Killswitch. It had been another exhausting, exhilarating ride, and as soon as the case was closed, the paperwork was stamped and signed, and JJ and Andrea were out of school for the summer, Stevens had filled up the Jeep with family, dog, and provisions, and pointed it north for a couple well-deserved weeks off, away from the BCA, Windermere, and any cell phones.

This summer's destination was Itasca State Park, the headwaters of the Mississippi River, some two hundred miles northwest of the Twin Cities. Stevens had been looking forward to exploring the park with his family, hiking, fishing, swimming, and maybe checking out a few of the pioneer landmarks in the area. Usually, his daughter was an enthusiastic sidekick. This year, though, Andrea was treating her vacation like a prison march.

Stevens looked around for the matches. Found them beneath one of Andrea's teen-heartthrob magazines. Both the magazine and the matches were soggy; the storm had kind of surprised the Stevenses in their campsite.

Stevens held up the matchbox. "Not going to have much luck cooking dinner without a fire," he told Nancy. "Maybe I'll take lover girl to town with me, get some more matches."

> > >

"SO WHAT'S SO IMPORTANT THAT you can't spend a couple weeks in the wilderness with your old dad?" Stevens asked his daughter as they drove away from the campground toward the Lake Itasca townsite. It was fully dark now, the headlights of Stevens's Cherokee lighting up the dirt road and the forest beyond, the moths and mosquitoes and the odd pair of eyes from a creature in the woods.

In the passenger seat, Andrea rolled her eyes. "Nothing, Dad. Don't worry about it."

"You used to love this stuff, kiddo. Now you fiddle around with that phone all day. You haven't even gone swimming."

"The water's too cold," Andrea said.

"Never used to bug you before." Stevens grinned at her. "Your mother says you might have a new friend back in town."

"*Dad!*" Andrea went bright red. "She *did not* say that."

"I think the term she used was 'boyfriend.'"

"*Oh. My. God.* Not even." Andrea shook her head furiously and turned to look out the window. "We're just friends. I can't believe Mom told you that."

"He have a name, this guy?"

Andrea hesitated. "Calvin," she said.

"As in *Calvin and Hobbes*? He come with a tiger?"

"What?"

"Before your time," Stevens said. "Look, here's the townsite. Maybe you'll get some reception."

Andrea pulled out her phone as the lights of the townsite—barely more than a hostel and a corner store—came into view. To Stevens's surprise, though, it was his own phone that began to buzz. Three missed calls, all from Tim Lesley.

Strange, Stevens thought. Tim Lesley was his boss, the Special Agent in Charge of Investigations at the Minnesota BCA. And even though Stevens was on vacation, pending a new assignment on a joint BCA-FBI violent crimes task force, something was bothering Lesley enough to call his star agent in the middle of the woods.

Stevens glanced at his daughter. "Any luck?"

Andrea fiddled with her cell phone, held it aloft, and made a face. "No," she said.

"Tough beans." Stevens sighed as he dialed Lesley's number. "Wanna trade?"

5

THE BARBECUE WAS winding down when Andrei Volovoi's phone began to ring. Instinctively, he stiffened in his seat, scanned the backyard as, in her lawn chair beside him, Veronika giggled

"What kind of ringtone is that, Uncle Andrei?" she said as the phone continued to ring in his pocket. "It sounds like your phone is from 1980."

Volovoi smiled back at his niece. "It's a genuine antique, Veronika," he told her. "I bought it when I was your age."

He excused himself from the table, stood, and wandered into his sister's backyard, where darkness had fallen fully and mosquitoes swarmed. He removed the phone from his pocket, a cheap, corner-store throwaway, and checked the number on the screen. Bogdan Urzica, one of his drivers. He would be calling from the road, probably Minnesota.

Volovoi glanced back at the table, made sure none of his family could overhear. Then he answered the phone. "Bogdan."

"We have a problem, Andrei."

Even from fifteen hundred miles away, Bogdan Urzica's voice made Volovoi nervous. The driver and his partner, the idiot Nikolai Kirilenko, were at this moment delivering another cargo of Volovoi's women to their buyers. Any problem Bogdan might have was bound to be serious.

Volovoi retreated farther into the backyard. Watched his sister gather his two nieces, Veronika and little Adriana, and herd them toward the house. In the distance, Volovoi could hear traffic on Ocean Parkway, happy laughter, the sounds of another Brighton Beach summer night. Inside, though, he felt cold, despite the humid air. He turned away from the house and spoke quietly into his phone. "What kind of problem?"

"A girl escaped the box," Bogdan told him, "in northern Minnesota, just now. There is a dead man. A police officer. We had no choice."

Volovoi closed his eyes. He trusted Bogdan Urzica. If the man was not a friend, he was a good acquaintance anyway. He was a hard worker. He was cautious. He avoided problems. He was a man Andrei Volovoi could respect. If Bogdan Urzica had killed a police officer, he'd had a good reason to do so.

Still, the thought made Volovoi's stomach churn.

"We are safe," Bogdan told him. "We escaped with the rest of the cargo. If you have no hesitations, Nikolai and I will continue our deliveries."

Volovoi forced himself to exhale. Relax. It was not the first time a girl had escaped from the box. It was not the first time the drivers had been forced to kill someone.

In any case, the girl probably didn't speak English. Most of them didn't, but they still bought the dream that Volovoi's pickers sold them. A new life in America. Supermodel. Actress. Fame and fortune.

Hell, Volovoi thought, *any woman dumb enough to fall for the trap deserves the box and whatever comes after.* Generally, though, he tried not to think about the women. He was too busy keeping his business afloat.

Bogdan Urzica cleared his throat. "Boss?"

It was troublesome that a girl had escaped. It was bad, very bad, that a police officer was dead. But these things happened when you made your living selling women. There were always going to be risks, no matter how fervently you fought to contain them. No matter how often you tried to preach prudence.

This was not a disaster, Volovoi decided. Therefore, there was no reason to mention it to the Dragon.

He crossed the backyard to where Veronika watched him from the doorway, her blond hair falling in ringlets across her face. Volovoi waved at her, watched her face light up as she smiled back at him. He exhaled again, felt the tightness in his chest dissipate.

"Everything will be fine," he told Bogdan Urzica. "Carry on with your deliveries as planned."

6

"IT'S JUST FOR the day," Stevens said. "We'll check out Leech Lake, have a nice dinner. Maybe get a hotel room for the night."

Andrea pumped her fist. *"Yes,"* she said. "Mom, can we?"

"I just don't understand why Lesley can't find someone else," Nancy said from across the campfire. "You're on vacation, Kirk."

Stevens pulled his marshmallow away from the fire. Even, golden brown. He reached behind him for a Hershey bar and a couple of graham crackers, assembled the perfect s'more, and handed it off to JJ. "There you go, kiddo," he said. "Make sure Triceratops doesn't get any of that chocolate, right?"

Triceratops, JJ's big German shepherd, fixed Stevens with a mournful expression. Stevens scratched behind the dog's ears. "It's forty miles away," he told his wife. "I'm closer than any other agent. He said it's an open-and-shut kind of deal. The sheriff's department just wants someone there to oversee the procedure. Make sure every *i*'s dotted, that kind of thing."

"And it has to be you," Nancy said.

"Sounds like it," Stevens said. "On the bright side, Cass County's springing for motel rooms." He grinned at her. "Two of them."

> > >

IN TRUTH, STEVENS WAS A little miffed that Tim Lesley had decided to interrupt his vacation for some kind of procedural exercise. Yes, Itasca State Park was less than forty miles from the Cass County Sheriff's Office in Walker, but so was Bemidji, where the BCA's forensics team was based. Surely someone could spare the drive.

The case itself was kind of a head-scratcher. A sheriff's deputy, headed back to Walker from his favorite fishing hole, stops at a local diner for a cup of coffee and a slice of pie before the rain sets in. Finishes the pie, wanders out into the parking lot, and gets himself shot. When the deputy's colleagues arrive, they find a hysterical young woman holding the guy's personal Smith & Wesson, the mag empty.

Gunpowder residue on her hands. Three holes in the guy's chest and forehead.

"Easy-peasy," Lesley had said. "Sheriff's office just wants some outside oversight. They don't get too many homicides, so want to make sure they're doing this one right."

"Who's the woman?" Stevens asked.

"Nobody's sure yet," Lesley said. "She didn't have ID on her, and best anyone can tell, she wasn't speaking much English."

"So why'd she kill this guy Friesen?"

"Who knows?" Lesley replied. "Like I said, she's not saying much."

A mystery woman. No ID. No English. No clue how she got to the truck stop, or how she got her hands on that deputy's piece. *Maybe the sheriff's department has a better line on her,* Stevens thought, surveying his family across the campfire. *The last thing I need is another blockbuster.*

7

HOWEVER SHE FELT about the rest of Derek Mathers, Carla Windermere had to admit that the junior FBI agent was pretty damn good in bed.

And a good thing, too. Windermere had almost given up on sex after Mark had walked out on her and moved back to Miami two and a half years ago. She had pretty well resigned herself to living alone, avoiding complications. People were overrated, she'd decided. Relationships got messy, and Windermere liked her life clean.

She sat up in bed and studied Mathers, all six-plus feet of goofy corn-fed Wisconsin farm boy tangled up in her new cotton sheets, smiling that dumb smile that, despite her best efforts, always seemed to worm its way past her defenses.

"Goddamn it, Carla," Mathers said. "I think we're onto something here."

She'd have bet money he was wrong a few months back, after they'd hooked up the first time in a Philadelphia Four Points, middle of the last case. She'd figured the big lug would make a decent stress reliever, that a guy with his looks and easygoing personality would have no trouble buying in for some no-strings-attached action.

Hell, he'd told her he joined the FBI because he wanted to be like Keanu Reeves in *Point Break*. At the time, Windermere figured the guy had a whole harem of badge bunnies waiting for him back in Minneapolis.

But Mathers had surprised her. He'd pursued her once the case broke, and when she finally relented and agreed to see him again, she found he wasn't just the dumb lunkhead he liked to pretend to be. He'd traveled. He read books. He was a terrible dancer, but he was willing to try salsa, willing to laugh at himself when he sucked at it. And when Windermere needed her space, he didn't get needy, or whiny, or start brooding, didn't sulk the way Mark had always done.

And moreover, he was dynamite in bed—not that Windermere would ever let him hear that. She stood, pulled on a hoodie, and drew open the curtains of her downtown Minneapolis condo, letting the morning light into the bedroom.

"Yeah," she said. "Whatever. That was okay, I guess."

"'Okay'?" Mathers sprung up from the bed and was instantly beside her, his arms wrapping her up and drawing her close. He was so big and strong and relentlessly enthusiastic that she felt herself caving, as always.

Just like a damn girl. Some lovestruck teenager.

"Just 'okay'?" Mathers asked again, his chin resting on her shoulder, his breath on her neck. "You were singing a different tune a couple minutes ago, lady."

"A couple minutes, yeah," she said. "Next time, try for five. Maybe you'll get more of a reaction."

Mathers laughed and picked her up, carried her back to the bed. Tossed her down and pinned her with those piercing blue eyes of his. Windermere let him kiss her, then shoved him away. "Okay, you big lug," she said. "We're going to be late."

"You know you like me," he said, releasing her. "No matter how much you try to play badass."

She walked to her closet, started picking out an outfit. "I don't have to *play* badass, Mathers," she said. "But, yeah, maybe I like you just a little."

"Good enough for me." Mathers padded to the kitchen. She heard him fiddle with the coffeemaker, and then the TV came on. She ducked into the bathroom, started the shower.

"Want some company?" Mathers called.

Yes, please, Windermere thought, but she was running late already, and not for the first time she cursed the FBI and its damn heightened-security concerns. Up to about a year ago, the Bureau's regional headquarters had been located in downtown Minneapolis, just a few blocks from Windermere's Mill District condo. Last year, though, the entire circus had moved north, way north, to a brand-new, high-security compound on the outskirts of town. Totally screwed up her commute.

"No time," Windermere called back. She closed the bathroom door and locked it, lest he get any funny ideas. Showered, she did her makeup, and when she came out of the bathroom, Mathers was in the living room, watching the news.

"You see this?" he said. "Sheriff's deputy shot somewhere up north. Some girl did it, they figure. Only, she doesn't speak any English."

Windermere studied the TV. Footage of the tiny sheriff's office in Walker, Minnesota, a couple of cruisers and a young woman being ushered inside. She was tall and incredibly thin, with long brown hair and dark, haunting eyes.

"No ID on her, either," Mathers said. "Nobody can figure out where she came from."

"Walker." Windermere poured herself a cup of coffee. "Where the hell is that, anyway?"

"Up north somewhere. Leech Lake, or something? Mississippi headwaters, thereabouts. Lake country."

"Huh." Windermere sipped her coffee. "I wonder if . . ."

"Yeah?"

She shook her head. "Just wondered if it was anywhere near Stevens, I guess."

Mathers's expression clouded briefly at the mention of the BCA agent's name. Then he shrugged. "Could be," he said. "Who knows? You said he was camping up there somewhere, right?"

"Could be anywhere, Mathers," Windermere said. "The hell do I know about this miserable state?" She picked up the remote and shut off the television. "Put some pants on. We're going to be late."

8

STEVENS FIGURED OUT pretty quick that Dale Friesen's murder
was more than just open and shut

The Cass County Sheriff's Office was located around the side of
the county courthouse in Walker, across the 371 highway from a
crowded Dairy Queen and a couple blocks from the lake. Stevens
dropped Nancy and the kids at a picnic table by the water and drove
up to the courthouse, where the sheriff himself met him in the parking lot.

"You're the BCA guy, right?" Ed Watkins was middle-aged and
slightly paunchy. His handshake was firm. "Appreciate you coming in."

"Not at all," Stevens said. "Anything I can do. Gotta be tough for
you guys right now, I know."

"Dale was a good man," Watkins said, and he squinted as his eyes
looked out across the parking lot. "Just seems, you know, senseless.
Would be nice to get to the bottom of it."

"My SAC said you have a suspect in custody," Stevens said. "A
woman."

"Betty Horst found her," the sheriff said. "She runs the Paul
Bunyan down there at the junction. Said the girl was just sitting in
the mud beside the body—beside Dale—in the pouring rain, gun at
her feet. Said she figured the first three or four shots were thunder
before she came to her senses."

"And the woman," Stevens said. "You don't have a name for her?"

"Don't have anything. No ID, nothing. I guess she was saying something when Betty found her, but Betty says it didn't sound like English. Anyway, she sure clammed up when my men arrived."

"Didn't say anything?"

"Not a word. Eyes all wide and panicky like she was thinking about running. Like she knew she was in for it now." Watkins whistled, low. "She's a looker, though, I'll tell you that. But dirty as all hell. Reeked something rotten when we put her in the truck."

"And you make her for the shooting?"

"Best as we can figure, yeah," Watkins said. "She had Dale's Smith and Wesson at her feet and residue on her hands. Seems like the simplest explanation."

Stevens mulled it over. Looked across at the Dairy Queen, the line for ice cream cones four kids deep. "I heard the mag was empty."

"You heard right," Watkins told him. "Betty Horst said she heard a whole pile of shots out there. We found casings in the muck all over the place."

"And Friesen was shot, what, three times?"

"Twice in the chest, once in the head. Like a goddamn execution." Watkins's gaze went distant. Then he straightened. "Why don't I take you inside, Agent Stevens, show you around?"

> > >

STEVENS FOLLOWED WATKINS INTO THE sheriff's office. Smiled at the secretary, shook hands with a couple deputies. Got the sense that everyone was staring at him, waiting for him to say something profound.

He wondered if his reputation had made it north to Cass County. After the first case with Windermere, the kidnappers, there'd been news coverage. Sensational stuff. A little more after the next couple cases, too. *I hope these guys aren't looking for some big-city crime-fighter tricks,* he thought. *That's Windermere's department.*

Still, there were a couple questions that jumped out at him, right off the bat, though he waited for Watkins to give him the grand tour before he asked them. The sheriff showed him around the department's modest headquarters, then led him into lockup and showed him the suspect.

"Here's our shooter," Watkins said, gesturing into the holding cell. Inside was a very thin, very young, very miserable-looking woman, clad in an oversized WALKER, MINNESOTA sweatshirt and jogging pants. She was huddled at the back of the cell, hugging herself, shivering, as far away from the bars as she could get. She didn't look at the men, but stared at the floor instead, her eyes dark and hollow, her hair stringy and limp. She was a couple years older than Andrea, probably, a couple years at most.

"And you can't get a word out of her," Stevens said.

"Won't talk, won't eat, won't even look at you," Watkins said. "Every time we come near her, she shies away like a dog that's been kicked one too many times."

The girl looked haunted, Stevens thought. Scared. More like a victim than a killer.

"The rest of the bullets in the magazine," he said, following Watkins back into the departmental offices. "Where'd she fire them? Into the ground beside the decedent?"

Watkins rubbed his chin. "No, sir," he said. "To be honest, we're not really sure where she fired them. Seemed to just kind of shoot them at random."

"You said Betty Horst heard the shots?"

"Like a hammer, she said. Like someone pounding nails."

"Sure," Stevens said. "So we have the suspect blasting off the full magazine, pretty much nonstop. But the decedent—Deputy Friesen—takes a couple shots to the chest and another to the forehead. Pretty precise, you said."

"That doesn't exactly make sense, does it?" Watkins said.

"No, it doesn't." Stevens found a coffee machine, poured himself a cup, realizing that his family's camping adventure was probably over. "So what the heck was she shooting at?" he asked Watkins.

"Wish I knew," the sheriff replied. "You want to check out the crime scene?"

Stevens thought of the suspect again. Couldn't shake the feeling of unease as he pictured her in that cell. The young woman was small, lost, and terrified out of her wits. And somehow she'd wound up the prime suspect in a murder.

Stevens shook his head clear. Straightened. "Sure," he told Watkins. "Let's go."

9

IRINA MILOSOVICI CURLED up on the hard prison bunk and forced herself to lie still, staying as far away from the cell door as she could until the men disappeared, and the courthouse was quiet again.

There were men everywhere. Big men, leering men. Rough men. They'd wrenched her away from the dead man's body. She'd felt their hands on her skin, through her ragged clothes, as they dragged her into their police car, and then out again and into the cell. She'd felt their eyes on her, read the hunger. They were tough, violent men, and she was nothing but prey, no matter the badges on their chests or the guns at their waists.

The men wanted her. She could tell from their eyes. They would come for her, too. It was only a matter of time.

Irina gathered that the Americans believed she'd killed the young man. She'd tried, frantically, to tell the first woman, the large woman from the diner, about Catalina. Tried to tell her the whole story, but her English wasn't good enough. Glossy American magazines didn't teach the right vocabulary words for situations like this. And then the men had arrived.

The men had replaced her clothing when they'd put her in the cell. They'd forced her to bathe, too, but Irina still felt the stink of the box, a maddening filth on her skin, in her hair, inside her body. She knew how awful she must appear, her long hair—her pride and joy—tangled and unkempt, her eyes sunken, her cheeks gaunt. A pitiful little vagabond in the wilderness.

Not that it mattered what she looked like. The men still consumed her with their eyes. And Catalina was gone. Still in the box probably. Or maybe with the thugs, enduring horrible things. Or maybe she was already dead.

> > >

IRINA HAD RUN AWAY FROM her family once, as a child. Spent the night in the forest on the outskirts of her little town. She'd decided that she would disappear into the woods, carve out her own civilization, live free from her parents and her sister and the other girls at school, the girls who laughed at her dresses and unfashionable shoes, who tripped her and pulled her hair.

She hadn't realized the woods would be so unpleasant. Brambles caught in her clothes. Branches raked her face. Very quickly, her shoes and stockings were soaked through with mud. Within an hour, she'd eaten the one sandwich that she'd brought. She'd imagined—foolishly—there would be berries to pick, and wild animals she could hunt. She'd imagined she would be queen of the forest, told herself she needed no one but herself.

Catalina had found her at sunset. Irina could still remember her little sister trampling through the woods, loud as a bear, calling her name and dragging her big suitcase behind her. At first, Irina had hid, desperate to be alone, to make a point to her parents, her classmates, the entire world, that she didn't need anybody.

She'd hid well. Catalina had passed her, wandering deeper into the forest, unfazed by the setting sun, the shadows, the temperature dropping. Irina had waited until Catalina was almost out of sight before calling to her.

"What are you doing here?" she asked when her sister had turned around and dragged that big suitcase back to the crook of the root where Irina had hidden herself. "Why are you following me?"

In response, Catalina tipped the suitcase over on the ground, fumbled with the catch. "I brought chocolate," she said proudly. "Matches to start a fire. Magazines, in case we get bored."

"I have matches," Irina said. "Anyway, the wood is damp."

"So we can burn the magazines."

Irina stared at her sister. Felt frustration like an itch. *This is my story,* she wanted to say, *my tragic escape. Why do you always have to be such a tagalong?*

Catalina seemed to read her mind. "I won't stay if you don't want me to," she said, smiling wide. "I won't tell them where you are, either."

She stood, set out again in the direction of the village. Irina watched her go.

She felt lonely suddenly, stupid for running away. "Wait," she called out. "Catalina."

> > >

SHE'D MADE THEM SPEND THE night in the forest out of principle. It was a long night, cold and restless. Irina had huddled close to her sister, shivering and afraid, thinking of her parents, hating Catalina for finding her, and loving her all the same.

Catalina had always followed her. Stolen her clothing and makeup and glossy American magazines, tagged along with her friends to movies after school. Of course she'd followed Irina to the United States.

Irina had bragged to her little sister incessantly about Mike, about America, the places she would visit, the people she would meet. She had conjured a magnificent fantasy. Was it any wonder, then, that on the day she was to meet Mike, she'd found Catalina at her door?

"What are you doing?" she'd asked her sister, staring at her battered suitcase, her inexpert makeup. "What about school? Mom and Dad will kill you."

Catalina had laughed and pushed past her into the dingy apartment. "It's summertime," she'd said. "They'll forgive me. Soon as we become movie stars."

Movie stars. Irina pulled the thin blanket around herself and tried to find comfort on the hard mattress. She was tired, but she dared not close her eyes. Could not let her guard down. The men could come back for her at any minute.

And if she slept, she would only dream of Catalina, and the American men who would devour her like monsters.

10

STEVENS CALLED NANCY from outside the Paul Bunyan Diner, five miles east of Walton. "I'm going to have to call in a tech team from Bemidji," he told her. "Try and process what's left of this crime scene, get an autopsy done. You might as well check into the motel and scrounge up some food for the kids."

There was a pause, and Stevens braced himself. But Nancy surprised him. "This is about the girl, isn't it?" she said. "And the sheriff's deputy."

"Well, yes." Stevens scanned the muddy parking lot. The rain had come and gone quickly, but the lot was uneven and there were still puddles everywhere. He was standing at the front door of the diner, to save his shoes. "How'd you know?"

"Read about it in the paper," Nancy said. "Heard about it all over town. Watched it on the local news in the restaurant at lunchtime. Everyone's talking about it. Have they brought in a translator for that poor girl yet?"

"Working on it," Stevens told her. "She's not speaking, though, not at all anymore. They're having kind of a hard time figuring out where she's from."

"Jesus." Nancy muttered something, and Stevens could imagine his wife, a Legal Aid lawyer and perennial champion of the underdog, shaking her head in disgust. "At least make sure they're feeding her, Kirk. That girl looks like she hasn't eaten a solid meal in weeks."

"Sheriff says she's not eating," Stevens said. "They'll keep trying. Anyway, I'd better get back to it. I'll hook back up with you all in a bit."

"Make sure they treat that girl right, Kirk," Nancy said.

"I promise they'll treat her as right as any suspect in a murder investigation has ever been treated," Stevens told her. "Tell the kids I say hi."

He ended the call and pictured his wife on the other end of the phone, gathering material about the mystery girl. Wondered if the staff at the Cass County courthouse was ready for her. Then he stepped away from the diner and out into the mud. Behind him, Sheriff Watkins hurried to follow.

"Dale's Suburban was over that way," he said, pointing around the edge of the lot. "Guess Betty said it was kinda crowded when he came in."

"Cleared out by the time he left, though?" Stevens asked.

Watkins smiled. "Dale was a talker, that's for sure," he said. "Figure a cup of coffee and a slice of pie'd take him on average two hours to consume, factoring in all the bullshitting."

Stevens wandered over to where Friesen had parked his Suburban. Stared back across the mud to where Highway 200 paralleled the lot and, a hundred yards down, met Highway 371 headed south.

"Clear view of the lot from those windows," Stevens said, pointing back at the diner. "Anyone inside would have seen. Anyone on the highway, too."

"Sounded like Betty was in back," Watkins said. "And I guess

Dale decided to go and get shot the one time that highway's been empty all summer."

"Bad luck."

"You said it."

Stevens wandered along the edge of the parking lot to where the driveway turned in from the highway. "You said about here's where the body was found?"

"That's right," Watkins said. "Flat on his back, right there."

About eighty feet, give or take, from where the Suburban had been. Nowhere near the diner's front door. Friesen would have had to walk out a ways. Something had caught his attention. "And you say your guys found shell casings in this muck?"

"Eight or nine," Watkins said. "We figured there were more out here. Just didn't have the manpower to dig up this whole mud pit and find them."

Stevens could see his point. The lot was torn up with tire tracks and mud puddles; the place was a shoe swallower. "How many shells were in Deputy Friesen's magazine?"

Watkins said, "If memory serves, Dale had a forty-cal Smith and Wesson, tricked out for a .357 SIG shell, fifteen-round magazine. Didn't have a bullet left when we took the gun from the girl."

"Sure," Stevens said, thinking, *If the girl shot off a full mag, there's at least six more casings in this mud.* Thinking, *Let's start digging.*

11

THE DRAGON WAS waiting in Andrei Volovoi's home.

The loft was a mess. It reeked of marijuana and dirty laundry and burnt fish, and it was filled, as always, with idiots.

Volovoi felt the tension as soon as he walked in the door. A couple of foot soldiers sat on his leather couch, their women beside them. Normally, the soldiers would be playing video games, sharing a joint. The women would be bored as corpses. Today, though, the women sat as rigid as the soldiers. They weren't speaking to one another. The TV played sports highlights on mute.

One of the soldiers gestured out at the balcony. "He's out there."

Shit. Volovoi followed the man's eyes to the windows. Couldn't see anyone in the darkness outside. Knew, though, instinctively, who the soldier meant.

The Dragon was here.

> > >

ANDREI VOLOVOI HAD NOT MEANT to go into business with the man his men knew only as the Dragon. He'd never intended to partner with anyone when he'd started importing women from the Old Country. He'd been a petty thug, a lowlife like the idiots on his couch, a new arrival in America tempted by music videos and flashy action movies. He'd struggled and starved for years before he'd hit upon his idea.

His idea was women. America was a country full of men accustomed to buying whatever they pleased, be it land, luxury cars, or political influence. Why should sex be any different? In Romania, Volovoi knew swarms of eager, starry-eyed young women, as desperate as he to make a mark on the New World. In America, he saw opportunity, an ocean of wealth and a dwindling morality.

He'd imagined the scheme would be easy to execute. A shipping container full of fresh product, all of them imagining they were destined for happy, glamorous, American lives. They would arrive terrified, disoriented, helpless, and he would sell them to pimps and brothel owners at a terrific markup. Sex was a commodity. Young women were currency. Andrei Volovoi would import them and make himself rich.

It was not, as it turned out, that easy. No matter how dumb and impressionable the young women may have been, they still had eyes and ears. They still saw and heard and remembered, and sometimes they escaped. Sometimes, the police raided brothels. Sometimes, the women told their stories.

Volovoi had not been aware how close he was to disaster until the Dragon found him. Until he saw, in disturbing detail, how near the American authorities were to closing down his operation.

"You cannot simply ship boxes of women, Andrei," the Dragon had told him, smiling his devil smile. "Sooner or later, somebody will notice. And if you haven't taken the steps to protect yourself"—the Dragon mimed a knife to his throat—"you will not be in business very long."

The Dragon brought capital, enough money to expand Volovoi's operation tenfold. He also brought expertise, culled from years of ruthless, back-alley dealings and criminal enterprise.

The Dragon helped Volovoi hide his operation under layer upon layer of shell corporations and false fronts, behind byzantine trails of corporate ownership, anything to bypass the Americans and their laws. He was as good as his word. Volovoi's basement operation soon blossomed into a flourishing business; revenue soared, and the authorities lost the trail. Volovoi bought a Cadillac, moved into a swank penthouse loft. And the women kept coming in their boxes.

But the Dragon's knowledge didn't come cheap. Even as the boxes multiplied and the customer base grew, Volovoi struggled to make a profit. The Dragon wanted royalties on his investment. Percentages on every dollar. And Volovoi, loathe as he was to admit it, could hardly keep up.

Business was booming. Profits were not. Still, the Dragon wanted to be paid. And now that Bogdan Urzica had killed that police officer, Andrei Volovoi had one more thing to add to his list of worries.

> > >

VOLOVOI PAUSED FOR A MOMENT at the balcony door. Then he pushed the door open and stepped out into the night. It was warm again, humid. The day's heat wafted up, as if from a furnace, from the city streets below, but still the figure at the railing wore an overcoat, long and black and punk rock. Volovoi had rarely seen the Dragon without the coat; it complemented his spiky hair and coarse, wiry black beard, and made the gangster look like some kind of heavy metal rock icon or something—assuming you didn't notice the long, wicked knife at his belt.

The Dragon grinned as Volovoi approached, that devil smile, wide, all teeth and barely disguised menace. "Andrei," he said. "Here you are, at last."

Volovoi hesitated. Then he shook the gangster's hand. "To what do I owe the honor?" he asked.

"You are behind on your payments." The Dragon kept his tone conversational, but Volovoi felt the danger in the man's voice, regardless, like the blade of a knife to his throat. "What's going on, Andrei?"

Volovoi tried not to betray his fear. His business partner had not earned his mantle through acts of kindness and decency. No, he was named after the *balaur*, the fearsome dragon of Romanian mythology. He'd earned his nickname peddling weapons and women during the insurgencies in the Baltic states, where his appetite for blood and his relentless greed made a natural pairing. The Dragon was still spoken of in hushed tones in the Old Country. Volovoi did not relish the thought of owing the man anything.

"I apologize to you sincerely," Volovoi told the gangster. "Our profits are down, but I have been trying to reduce overhead. Streamline the operation. You will get your late payment as soon as this latest shipment is fully delivered."

"And the next payment, Andrei?" the Dragon said, his lips pursed. "When will *it* come?"

"I am ordering more women from our supplier," Volovoi said. "My buyers are lined up and ready. Business is growing. It is only a matter of time before our profits catch up."

The Dragon didn't answer for a moment. Left Volovoi hanging, wondering, his eyes drifting down to the knife on the gangster's belt.

"Your business isn't the problem," the Dragon said, finally. "It's your buyers, Andrei. They're too small for our operation."

"So you have said," Volovoi replied. "But as our reputation grows, so does our reach. We have nearly thirty clients ready to buy women from us. They are—"

"They are nobodies," the Dragon said. "They are small-town operators. They are where, Andrei? Duluth, Minnesota. Chicago, Illinois. Pittsburgh. Saint Louis. Reno, Nevada. They are nowhere, Andrei, nowhere that matters."

Volovoi followed the man's eyes. "You still think we should expand to New York."

"I don't just think it, Andrei," the Dragon said. "I have clients willing to pay ten times what your buyers pay for a woman now. They're all stinking fucking rich, and they're desperate to buy. We could drown ourselves in money if we tapped into the market."

Volovoi said nothing. He'd had this conversation with the Dragon before, and he knew what the gangster's wealthy friends expected for their money: not women, but girls, the younger the better. The Dragon's Manhattan friends were perverts and pedophiles—wealthy, yes, but still the scum of the earth—and every time Volovoi considered expansion, he thought about his young nieces and felt his stomach turn.

"I am not ready to expand to this market," Volovoi said finally. "I will streamline my business. You will be paid."

The Dragon shrugged. "Someday you'll see things my way, Andrei," he said, and smiled that unpleasant smile again. "At least I hope you do. I would hate to have to terminate our partnership over something so stupid."

Volovoi was careful to keep his face expressionless, but he couldn't chase the chill that coursed through his body. The Dragon was not known for his patience, or his mercy. If he terminated the partnership, he would terminate Volovoi with it.

Volovoi had resisted the Dragon's Manhattan overtures thus far. He did not intend to give in.

All the same, he'd recently instructed his thugs to stockpile the youngest-looking girls from each new shipment of women, just in case. Just in case profits continued to suffer, and things became desperate.

Successful businessmen planned ahead. They made sure they had options. Volovoi tried to emulate that mentality. Still, he could see little fun in crawling further into bed with the Dragon. He hoped fervently that things wouldn't become desperate.

He eyed the Dragon again, thought of Bogdan Urzica and the missing girl. Wondered how in the hell he was going to sleep at night now.

12

THE TECHS SHOWED up around four. Three of them. The lead was a young guy, Nazzali. "Heard they ruined your vacation for this," he told Stevens. "Or did you get bored of the camping?"

"Wife and kids are at the motel," Stevens told him. "I'm just trying to close this and salvage some family time."

"Yeah?" Nazzali squinted across the lot at the Paul Bunyan. "And how's that going so far?"

Stevens looked down at the mud. "Ask me when we've dug up this lot."

Betty Horst hadn't been thrilled when Stevens explained to her that he wanted to tear up the parking lot to search for more casings. "Ed said they found a bunch of casings already," she told Stevens.

"Sure," Stevens said. "But I'm thinking we could be missing a couple. I'd like to do a little more looking."

The diner owner contemplated her parking lot, as if already seeing the diggers in action. "Well, okay," she said, sighing. "If you think it'll help, dig away."

> > >

STEVENS WENT FOR A WALK while the techs did their thing. Checked out the gas station down the road from the Paul Bunyan, and the marine shop next door, your typical vacationland toy store. He browsed around the lot for a while, gaudy powerboats with monstrous outboard motors, Jet Skis, pontoon boats with patio tables and deafening sound systems. Imagined, briefly, being the kind of family that could afford toys like this. *Maybe if Nancy worked corporate,* he thought. *Or we robbed a couple banks.*

He chased the thought from his mind, left the boats, and started back toward the diner. Was almost there when Nazzali stood up and waved. "Come see this, Agent Stevens."

Stevens hurried over, slogging through the mud. Found Nazzali holding six bullet casings in his open palm.

"Check this out," he said. "We found these in this puddle here, a couple feet from where you guys said the decedent was found. Kind of buried in a tire track and sunk in the mud."

"Six casings," Stevens said. "That makes, what, fourteen total?"

"Fifteen." One of the techs poked her head up from the mud. "Just found another one, Ramze."

"Fifteen," said Nazzali. "And counting."

"Here's another one," said the tech. "That makes sixteen."

"Sixteen," Stevens said. "My guy had a fifteen-round mag."

Sheriff Watkins had wandered over from his truck. "So, what?" he said. "Are we thinking the girl reloaded?"

"I don't think so," Nazzali said. "Those casings you found earlier, they were .357 Sigs, right?"

Watkins nodded. "That's right. That's what Dale was shooting."

Nazzali held up a couple more casings. "We found a bunch more . 357 casings in the muck here, Agent Stevens, but we found these, too," he said. "These here are for nine-millimeter rounds."

Stevens frowned. "Two guns."

"Sure looks like it."

"Well, shit," Watkins said. "Makes you kind of wonder which gun killed my deputy, doesn't it?"

The sheriff's words lingered in the air, and Stevens let them echo, feeling his wholesome family vacation in the woods come to a final crashing halt.

"Two guns," he said. "Damn it. So where in the hell is our second shooter?"

13

CATALINA MILOSOVICI FELT the truck slow, and wondered if this would be the stop where the men dragged her finally from the box. She knew she should be afraid. But she felt nothing. She felt numb.

A part of her had known, all along, that Irina's big American scheme was just madness. Her older sister was a dreamer, a hopeless romantic. She'd gushed about Mike, the charming, handsome American, relayed his promises to her.

"He says he'll make me a model, Catya," Irina had told her. "He says I have the right look for a magazine cover."

It was fanciful. It was fantasy. It was plain foolishness, but Irina had been too caught up in the illusion to really understand. And Catalina had let herself be convinced, too. She'd seen pictures of Mike, and he really was handsome. Wholesome-looking. American. He didn't look like any criminal Catalina had seen.

Still, she must have known somehow, deep down inside. Why else would she have run away and joined Irina? It wasn't like Catalina wanted to be famous. She didn't even really want to visit America; had barely ever left Berceni, the little village south of Bucharest where her mother and father lived. But just as she'd trooped after Irina that day her ridiculous sister had run away into the woods, she'd followed her to America, her trusty old suitcase packed with snacks and clothing and toothpaste, always the practical sister while Irina pranced about with her head in the clouds.

And now it had all gone to shit. Irina was gone, run off into the woods somewhere. With any luck, she had escaped. Catalina held out little hope that her big sister would come back for her. How would Irina find her in this vast, foreign country? And even if she did, Catalina had seen the size of the thugs who drove the truck. They were ruthless killers. Irina would have no chance against them.

So now the truck was slowing again, and the men would appear at the door, and they would drag out more women until all of the women were gone. And maybe this time they'd choose Catalina, and who knew what they'd do to her then? Something perverted, no doubt, and she'd never even kissed a boy.

She pushed the thought away, tried not to think about it. Let them do what they wanted. Irina was free. Catalina had saved her big sister yet again, and wasn't that enough?

The thought was cold comfort, but it would have to do. The truck had stopped, and the men were unlocking the door. Catalina stood in the gloom and prepared to meet her fate.

But when the men opened the door and searched the mass of huddled women, their eyes seemed to skip past her, unseeing. They took more women—ten of them, maybe—dragging them out of the box, screaming, and locked the door again.

The box began to move. The women around her said nothing. Catalina sank into a gloomy corner, resigned to more boredom and terror, as the truck and its cargo continued the journey.

14

NANCY STEVENS PUT down her paperback and cast her eyes around the motel room. It wasn't a bad little room, as these things went, and truth be told, she was secretly a little grateful for the hot shower and comfy mattress that Kirk's unplanned vacation from vacation had provided, but still. Kirk wasn't here, and as charming as the town of Walker was, she figured she'd pretty much shown the kids all of it. Now it was evening, the sunlight was waning, and Nancy needed something to do.

No fair that Kirk gets to work while I can't, she thought. *It's not like I don't have a mountain of paperwork I could be working through while he's off playing cowboy again.*

She stood and walked to the window, looked out across the motel lot toward downtown Walker, the shadows creeping across the pavement like fingers in the evening light. "I'm bored," she said, turning back from the window. "Who wants to go for a walk?"

On the bed, JJ didn't even bother to look away from the TV, some shoot-'em-up action movie, no doubt completely age inappropriate. Andrea had curled herself into an easy chair and was texting incessantly, her iPhone tethered to a wall outlet and her eyes on the screen. Neither kid responded.

Triceratops, though, knew a good thing when he heard it. The dog had scrambled to his feet as soon as she'd said the W-word, and had bounded to the door, where he stood, whining, tail wagging, his big eyes pleading with her. "Well, fine," Nancy said, reaching for the leash. "Just you and me, dog."

> > >

SHE CLIPPED THE LEASH ON the dog and told the kids to behave, walked Triceratops down to the lake, and stared out over the water and missed Kirk, hoping he would finish his case and come back to them. And as she thought about Kirk, she thought about his case, about the thin, beautiful girl who'd shot the sheriff's deputy. She wondered if the girl was eating yet, where she'd come from, and if she was scared. And before Nancy knew it, she was leading Triceratops up from the lake, toward the county courthouse where the girl was being held, walking without a plan besides the vague idea that she might as well try and do something useful.

"Nancy Stevens," she told the deputy at the front desk of the sheriff's office. "My husband's the BCA guy. I was just out walking the dog and thought I'd check in on him."

Behind the deputy, the department was empty. "I think they're all still out at the Paul Bunyan," he said. Then he gave her a sheepish smile. "Did you say you brought the dog?"

Turned out the guy was a bit of a dog lover. Nancy brought Triceratops into the small lobby. The dog gave the deputy a good minute and a half of tail wagging and tongue slobbering, then put his nose to the ground and set about sniffing out his new environment.

"Probably smells dinner," the deputy told Nancy. "I was just about to bring some in for the prisoner, see if she'd decide to eat this time."

"She's still not eating?" Nancy asked.

"She's not doing much of anything," the deputy told her. "She just crawls back to the corner of her cell and looks at us like we're coming to kill her whenever we step near the door."

Nancy surveyed the empty department. "Sometimes it takes a mother's touch," she told him. "Tell you what, you watch the dog and I'll deliver the meal."

The deputy winced. "Probably breaking all kinds of rules."

"What am I going to do," Nancy asked him, "break her out?"

The deputy looked at her. Looked at the dog. Like the perfect accomplice, Triceratops bounded over. Nuzzled and slobbered on the guy until he laughed, and Nancy knew she had him.

"Fine," the deputy said, taking the dog's leash and leading them both deeper into the department. "Come on. Just make it quick, okay?"

15

"SHE'S ROMANIAN," NANCY told Stevens. "She speaks a little English, but I got you a translator anyway."

Stevens met his wife's eyes across the motel room and couldn't help smiling. "Why am I not surprised?"

"You're not the only big-city hotshot in this town, Agent Stevens,"

Nancy said. "I conned my way into taking the girl her dinner. Bribed a deputy and all. I was right, Kirk, she's starving. Emaciated. God knows when's the last time she'd eaten."

"Bribed a deputy," Stevens said. "Of course you did."

"Someone had to do it, Kirk," she said. "Those people would have just let her waste away before they found someone who could speak her language."

"She wouldn't talk to them," Stevens said. "Hell, the girl was damn terrified. Watkins said she seemed like she was ready to bolt every time the deputies came near. How'd you get through to her?"

"Easy." Nancy said. "I talked to her."

Stevens stared.

"I talked to her, Kirk. She wasn't going to just burst open and tell me her life story, but I talked to her anyway. Just so she'd feel like a human again."

"What'd you say?"

"I told her she was safe now. She was going to be fine. That whatever happened, my action hero husband was going to get to the bottom of it." She crossed the room to him, hugged him. "And you will, Kirk. Whatever happened, this girl's not just some murderer. Something brought her to Walker, something bad."

Stevens let his wife wrap her arms around him. "We'll see, Nance," he said. "She's still the main suspect in a murder investigation. I'm not sure I'm ready to just spring her right yet."

He was thinking, *Slow down, Nancy*. Thinking how awkward it would be if it turned out the girl had killed Dale Friesen after all.

But he was also thinking how Nazzali had found those 9mm casings at the Paul Bunyan, how there was probably another shooter.

Thinking, whatever the girl did, there was a hell of a lot more to the story than one dead sheriff's deputy.

"So, okay," he said. "You talked to her."

"Honestly, I just babbled," Nancy said. "She didn't look at me, say anything, nothing. But then she finished her meal and she pushed the tray back at me and she said, really soft, *'Mulțumesc.'*"

Stevens blinked. "Mult-zoo what now?"

"It means 'thank you' in Romanian, Kirk. I had Romanian neighbors growing up. My mom used to make me bring them casseroles and cakes and stuff. They'd always say that to me, *'Mulțumesc mult.'* Thank you very much."

"Hot damn," Stevens said. "You're unbelievable."

"That's not the end of it, Kirk," Nancy said. "I went to take her tray back and she stopped me. Just grabbed my arm and held me."

"Just held you." Stevens frowned. "Did you call for the deputy?"

"It wasn't like that," Nancy said. "It was—I've never seen anyone look so scared. 'Please,' she said. 'My sister.'"

"Her sister," Stevens said. "What does that mean? Was she calling you her sister?"

"I don't think so, Kirk. I think she was talking about somebody else, somebody real." Nancy drew back, looked at Stevens. "Kirk, there's something going on here. Something more than just a murder."

.Stevens nodded. "I know, Nance," he said. "Let's see what happens when the translator gets here."

> > >

STEVENS CHECKED IN ON THE kids in the adjoining motel room, found JJ and Triceratops watching TV while Andrea texted, furiously, on her iPhone. He sat down beside his son, scratched the dog's belly. "You guys have a good day?"

Andrea grunted something noncommittal from the other bed. JJ rolled his eyes. "She's been on that thing all day, Dad. I don't think she even knows where she is."

"I swear to God, JJ." Andrea put down the phone and scowled at him. "Can you mind your own business, *please*?"

"Okay," Stevens said. "Everybody calm down. You getting decent reception, Ange?"

"It's fine." Andrea's phone buzzed, and Stevens watched her type something, a smile on her lips and her eyes suddenly alight.

"What about you, kiddo?" he asked JJ. "How was your day?"

"It's okay." JJ rolled over onto his back. "Dad, this place is boring. Can we go back to the lake tomorrow?"

Stevens could sense his son's restlessness, and no wonder. The motel room was dingy, kind of plain. Nothing like the open wilderness. "I dunno, Jay," he said, sighing. "This case isn't turning out as easy as it was supposed to."

"Does that mean we get to go home?" Andrea asked.

"We were supposed to go canoeing again," JJ said.

"I know," Stevens told him, "I know, guys. I'm working through this as quick as I can."

16

THE TRANSLATOR ARRIVED just after breakfast. She was an older woman, in her late sixties probably, a shock of white hair and a stern expression.

"Maria Zeklos," she said, shaking Stevens's hand as she climbed from her car. "Where is the girl?"

"She's inside," Stevens told her. "Listen, thanks for coming on such short notice. We—"

Zeklos waved him off. "Never mind," she said. "Shall we talk to your suspect?"

Stevens and Nancy swapped glances as they followed her to the front door of the sheriff's department. "Where'd you find this woman, anyway?" Stevens whispered. "I feel like she's about to put me in detention."

Nancy laughed. "She runs some kind of Romanian language school in Saint Paul," she said. "Came up on a list of available translators. Through *your* office, I might add."

"Well, okay," Stevens said. "Then I guess she's *my* problem."

He kissed his wife good-bye, and promised to keep her updated. Then he walked into the sheriff's department and nearly collided with Maria Zeklos at the secretary's desk, where she was refusing Ed Watkins's offer of a fresh cup of coffee.

"I was told this girl killed a deputy," she told Stevens. "And that she doesn't speak any English. I believe we can save the coffee until after we've talked to her, don't you?"

"Fine by me," Stevens replied. "Save the coffee. I'd kind of like to hear what the suspect has to say myself."

> > >

IF THE YOUNG WOMAN'S CONDITION had improved overnight, it was minimal at best. Nancy had sworn she'd seen the girl eat, but even though Stevens could see a little more color in her cheeks, the girl was still rail thin, her eyes sunken and lifeless. She sat opposite Stevens and Zeklos in the little interview room, as far away as she could, hugging herself and staring down at the floor. She looked like she hadn't slept a minute.

She was trembling, Stevens realized. She was still so afraid.

"We're not here to hurt her," he told Zeklos. "Would you tell her that, please?"

Zeklos studied Stevens as though she were gauging the truth in his statement. Finally, she leaned down and spoke softly to the girl. The girl didn't answer. Didn't look up.

Stevens cleared his throat. This was a first for him; over his nearly twenty years in law enforcement, he'd never needed a translator. So he paused, aware of the sheriff's eyes on him through the room's two-way mirror. "Maybe she'd like some coffee," he told Zeklos. "Or some water?"

Zeklos relayed the question. Again, the girl didn't respond. She looked small, frail, traumatized, and Stevens felt a twinge in his heart as he looked her over. Whether she'd killed Deputy Friesen or not, this young woman's problems were serious. If he could only convince her to talk to him.

"Tell her we're here to help her," Stevens told the translator. "She's safe now. We just want to know what happened."

Zeklos translated. Still the girl said nothing. She was crying, he saw. Silently shaking. He watched a tear slide down her cheek. Then she mumbled something without lifting her head.

"What did she say?" Stevens asked.

"She wants us to go," the translator said. "Leave her alone."

The girl whispered. *"Please."*

"We should go," Zeklos said. "She is in no shape to talk."

Stevens looked at the girl. Looked at the two-way mirror where the sheriff stood, watching. Looked around the tiny interview room and then back at the girl.

He stood. "I guess you're right," he said. "We'll try again later."

17

"WE KNOW SHE knows something," Stevens told his wife. "We just don't know how to get her to tell us what it is."

Nancy Stevens unwrapped a sandwich and passed it to her husband. Dug in a paper bag for a carton of fries. She'd dropped by with lunch, and to check in on his progress, and Stevens had to admit he was grateful for the break.

He'd spent a few more fruitless hours in the interview room with the mystery girl and Maria Zeklos, trying in vain to convince her she was safe. The girl had stayed silent. She hadn't responded. She'd huddled up in her chair and begged Stevens to leave her alone.

"She's afraid," Stevens told his wife. "I can't come within fifteen feet without her tensing up."

Nancy Stevens took a bite of her own sandwich. Chewed. "You said this poor girl was filthy."

"That's right," Stevens said.

"She hadn't eaten. Doesn't speak any English."

"Uh-huh."

Nancy looked around the sheriff's department. Watkins sat in his office, eating his own lunch from a brown paper bag. The deputies lingered by the coffee machine, talking baseball. "Let me talk to her," Nancy said.

Stevens blinked. "What?"

"All this poor girl's seen are men, Kirk," she told him. "Big, burly policemen. She's probably terrified. She opened up to me earlier, a little bit. Let me try again."

"You want to try to interview her."

"She could stand to talk to a woman, Kirk," Nancy said. "You see any others around?"

18

IRINA MILOSOVICI LOOKED up as the interpreter let herself back into the interview room. This time, she did not bring the kind-faced policeman with her; instead, she brought the woman who'd delivered Irina her dinner last night. She was beautiful, tall and blond, the kind of all-American woman who filled the pages of Irina's glossy magazines.

The woman sat beside the interpreter. She glanced at the big mirror on the wall, behind which no doubt sat the rest of the American policemen. Then she smiled at Irina and spoke to her in English.

The interpreter translated. "She says her name is Nancy Stevens and she is not a police officer," she told Irina. "She is a lawyer, and she's here to help you."

Irina said nothing. She did not look at Nancy Stevens. After a moment, Nancy spoke again.

"She says the man who talked to you last is her husband," the translator said. "His name is Kirk Stevens, and he is a good man. A police officer. He's not going to hurt you."

Irina thought about the man, the big policeman with kind eyes. He'd spoken to her gently, she remembered. He hadn't leered at her. But he was still a man, and he still had her locked up in this terrible place.

The interpreter cleared her throat. Nancy Stevens's eyes shifted to the mirror again. Her smile wavered a little, and she looked down at the table as she asked her next question.

She's nervous, Irina realized.

"She wonders if you'd tell her your name," the interpreter said.

Irina didn't answer.

"She's here to help you," the interpreter told her. "This woman, and her husband, and the policemen. They are all here to help you."

They are not, Irina thought. *They are here to consume me.*

Nancy Stevens spoke again. Softly. Patient. "She wonders if you'll tell her about your sister," the translator said.

Irina felt her breath catch. Closed her eyes and saw Catalina. She opened her eyes again, quickly, and found herself in the little interview room once more. Nancy Stevens met her eyes. Smiled.

Irina realized, suddenly, that she feared for Catalina more than she feared the leering men on the other side of the mirror. She realized that her sister's only hope was through this friendly woman. The woman could betray her, as Mike had. She could throw her back to the ravenous police officers.

But she could also save Catalina.

Nancy Stevens said something. "The deputy," the translator said. "Do you remember what happened to the deputy?"

Of course she remembered. What a stupid question. Irina closed her eyes, saw the truck pulling away, great plumes of black smoke shooting into the air as the bald-headed driver made his escape.

Of course she remembered. She remembered running back for the dead man's gun, firing at the truck until the gun was empty. Remembered the panic and helplessness and frustration when the truck didn't slow. She remembered Catalina, the other women. Of course she remembered.

"Tell us what you remember," the interpreter said. "Tell us about your sister."

All of a sudden, Irina was crying. Like whatever wall she'd built and hardened inside herself had cracked and collapsed. Nancy Stevens was still watching her. Irina looked away. Swore under her breath.

"*The box*," she said. It was barely a whisper. It was capitulation. "My sister is inside the box."

19

"I *TOLD* YOU." Nancy hugged her husband. "Didn't I tell you, Kirk?"

Stevens hugged her back. "This is big, Nancy," he said. "It's huge."

Twenty minutes had passed since his wife had emerged from the interview room, and Kirk Stevens still wore an expression of disbelief on his face. Nancy supposed she couldn't blame him. She'd known the girl was into something more than simple murder, that Kirk's open-and-shut case was more complicated than he would admit. Even she hadn't been prepared for this, though.

If that girl in the interview room was telling the truth, if she and her sister had indeed been kidnapped from their home and shipped to America in a cargo container with thirty or forty other women, if they had wound up in tiny Walker, Minnesota, by bad luck, random happenstance, and a young deputy's fatal curiosity, well . . . it boggled Nancy Stevens's mind.

The girl in the interview room, Irina Milosovici, was twenty years old. Her younger sister was *sixteen,* the same age as Andrea, who was caught up in young love, her first boyfriend, the trials of the average American teenager. Meanwhile, Irina's sister was imprisoned in a shipping container somewhere. Or worse. Nancy had worked with battered women before, with new immigrants to America, trapped in abusive marriages without any kind of support network. She'd worked with sex abuse cases, assaults. She had never seen anything like what Irina Milosovici had described.

"We need to find that truck," Nancy told her husband. "Track it down and rescue the sister and the rest of the women inside."

"A red truck with a plain red shipping container," Stevens said. "It won't be easy."

"There are women inside, Kirk. Girls. Teenagers."

Stevens looked at her. "I know. I'll get a BOLO out to local law enforcement, get their eyes peeled. Maybe somebody gets lucky and spots it."

"Hell, who knows how many more of those containers are out there?" Nancy was aware she was practically yelling but didn't care, ignoring the looks from the sheriff and his deputies. "You can be sure this isn't the first time these guys have done something like this, Kirk. Who knows how many women they've taken?"

Stevens nodded. "I *know,* Nancy."

"So what are we going to do about it?" she said. "How do we track down that truck? How do we get those girls back?"

Stevens rubbed his chin, thinking. The sheriff and his deputies watched him.

"Irina said the truck drove away west," he said. "She can give us descriptions of everybody she saw—the driver, the shooter, this Mike guy on the Romanian side. The women, too. Catalina. We put their faces on the wire in North Dakota, Montana, hope somebody recognizes them."

"We have to work fast, Kirk," Nancy said. "These women are at risk. If these guys figure out we're onto them . . ."

"We can track them backward, too," Stevens said. "Try and pinpoint the box's point of entry and figure out who brought them into the country. Work both sides of the supply chain."

"You can't do this by yourself," she said.

He met her eyes. "Let me make a phone call," he said.

20

WINDERMERE WAS UNPACKING boxes in her new office when the phone rang, scaring the crap out of her. The damn thing had been hooked up, what, an hour tops, and already it was hollering for attention.

She let the thing ring a minute. Looked around the room. Since she'd transferred up from Miami four years ago, Special Agent in Charge Drew Harris had been promising her a private office. Now, after three blockbuster cases and the Bureau's big move, her boss had finally made good on his promise.

Not that it had much to do with Windermere. If Kirk Stevens hadn't tabbed her to join the joint BCA-FBI major crimes task force he was putting together, she'd still be at a cubicle somewhere in the middle of the Criminal Investigative Division, slowly losing her mind in the chaos of the bullpen.

Derek Mathers appeared at the door. "You going to answer that phone, or what?"

"Thought you were my secretary, Mathers," she replied. "Isn't that why they keep you around?"

The junior agent pretended to pout. "Always doing your grunt work." He crossed into the office, and before Windermere could stop him, picked up her phone and held it out of her reach.

"*Carla Windermere's office,*" he said, his voice syrupy sweet. Then his smile disappeared. "Yeah," he said. "Yeah, sure. She's right here."

He handed the phone to Windermere, wordless. Windermere cocked her head at him as she took the handset. "Agent Windermere."

"Carla."

Stevens. Windermere let her breath out. The BCA agent had a maddening ability to knock her off her game, even after three cases together. "Kirk," she said. "Thought you were on vacation. Communing with nature or something."

"I was." There was something to his voice, an electricity that automatically got Windermere's heart pumping faster. "Got called in to do a little day work. That sheriff's deputy up in Walker, you see that?"

"The shooting?" Windermere replied. "Yeah, I saw. Some girl did it, right?"

"That's what they thought anyway. What we *all* thought, in fact." He cleared his throat. "Listen, how's your caseload right now? You working on anything big?"

"Kinda killing time, to be honest," Windermere said. "After that Killswitch ordeal, I'm pretty much pushing paper. Why?"

"I have something here, Carla," Stevens said, and she could sense that same urgency in his tone. "Something major. I could really use your help."

21

"TRAFFICKING." SAC DREW Harris tented his fingers. "And what does Stevens intend to do with this girl?"

Across the desk, Windermere met her boss's eyes. "He's hoping we'll take her," she said. "Bring her into protective custody while we search for her sister and the others."

"We," Harris said. "You and Stevens?"

"And whoever else we can spare," Windermere said. "If this thing is as big as the girl says, we're going to need help. Homeland Security, State Department, Customs and Border Protection, whoever we can find."

Harris held up his hands. "Let's not get ahead of ourselves," he said. "I don't want to be calling in a task force when we haven't even heard this girl's story."

"Yes, sir," Windermere said. "Of course."

"I don't have the resources to be chasing this thing down, you understand? Not as long as antiterrorism is top priority around here. Let Stevens and the BCA have the ball in the short term. Bring the girl in and we'll hear what she has to say. Then we'll evaluate, okay?"

"Yes, sir," Windermere said. "I'll get her down here ASAP."

"Good stuff." Harris grinned at her. "Kirk Stevens again, huh?"

Windermere stood. "Yes, sir."

"Guy can't seem to stay out of trouble." Harris winked at her. "Have fun."

22

VOLOVOI WAS WORKING late when his phone rang. The burner again. The business line.

The Dragon.

He looked up from his computer, surveyed the empty loft. He'd kicked the idiots out earlier, ruined their party. Sent them out into the streets to get their thrills elsewhere, told them to be happy they still had jobs. Then he sat down in front of his computer, opened up the accounting software he was trying to learn to use, the small business textbooks, and settled in for another long night of headaches and tough decisions.

The trick was finding redundancies, he knew. And in his business, like most, there were plenty of redundancies. Those idiots, for one thing, spent most of their days sitting on their asses, getting high. It was only when new shipments came in that Volovoi really needed all of them. Still, he paid them whether they worked or not.

Switch them from salaried employees to independent contractors, he thought. *Pay them when you need them. You'll sacrifice loyalty, but you'll save money.*

It was an idea. But it wasn't a good idea, to Volovoi's way of thinking. He paid his idiots a day wage because he wanted them happy and out of trouble. Because he didn't want them getting bored and getting popped for some dumbfuck break-and-enter, some assault charge, and ratting him out to save themselves a couple years in a cell. He'd never made decisions based on money before. He'd always taken the safest path.

So, he would keep the idiots. He could sell the Cadillac. Move out of the loft and find something smaller, a little more practical. But then, what was the point of becoming a crime boss in America if you couldn't enjoy the trappings of success?

The real problem, Volovoi knew, was the Dragon and his ridiculous percentages. His royalties crippled the whole operation.

So they do, Volovoi thought, *but you can't get out from under him now. You don't have nearly the capital to buy out his partnership, and if you simply stop paying him, he'll destroy you. You're stuck.*

No, you're not.

New York. Volovoi knew the Dragon was right, knew the city was awash in easy money, if you could provide the right product. And Volovoi knew his supplier in Europe could find younger women for sure. Anything the market wanted, Mike could deliver. And the profit from one box of Manhattan-grade product would trump six months' worth of women at Volovoi's current rates.

Still, he held out. The Dragon terrified him, and this current business venture had caused Volovoi nothing but sleepless nights and paranoia. He would find the Dragon's money somewhere else. He didn't need New York.

Then why am I stockpiling young women, just to be on the safe side?

The phone was still ringing. Volovoi checked the number again, made a face, answered anyway. "If this is about your expansion, I haven't reconsidered," he said. "I am happy enough doing business my own way."

"I am sorry to hear that, Andrei." The Dragon's voice was syrup smooth. "But this isn't about New York."

"No?"

"Do you have something you want to tell me?" the Dragon said, and Volovoi could imagine him licking his lips. "Is everything okay with the last shipment? Anything your business partner should know about?"

The girl. The Minnesota girl. Volovoi cleared his throat. "It is nothing," he said. "A little speed bump. This is no cause for concern."

"I hear through my connections that a police officer is dead," the Dragon said, still deathly calm. "The FBI is involved, Andrei. They are bringing your missing girl to Minneapolis."

This was news to Volovoi. Earlier in the day, he'd checked on the story. Found that the girl was in custody in a little town in northern Minnesota, the state police investigating. Details were scarce, though. Nobody knew much.

"I heard also," the Dragon said, "that the girl has a sister. A younger sister, Andrei."

Volovoi thought, involuntarily, of his little nieces. "A younger sister," he said. "I had not heard this."

"She is still in the box," the Dragon said. "The eldest sister escaped, but the younger remains. She is still ours, assuming your idiot thugs haven't sold her already."

"She is probably gone," Volovoi said. "The drivers are near the end of their delivery. The odds are she has been sold already."

"I want her, Andrei." The edge was back in the Dragon's voice. "We will use her to teach her sister a lesson. To teach the world not to fuck with the Dragon. We will kill her." He paused, and Volovoi could hear his breathing. "*I* will kill her. Have your drivers bring her to me."

"That will be difficult," Volovoi said. "If she is already sold—"

"They will have to retrieve her," the Dragon said. "You have already disappointed me once this week, Andrei. Please don't do it again."

He ended the call. Left Volovoi listening to dead air. Volovoi sat there, struck stupid for a moment. Then he took the phone from his ear and dialed another number.

"Bogdan," he said when the driver picked up. "Listen to me very carefully."

23

BOGDAN URZICA PUT down the phone. "Pull the truck over," he told his partner. "I need to get in the back."

From behind the wheel, Nikolai Kirilenko raised an eyebrow. "What for? Are you horny, Bogdan? Do you want a fuck?"

"*Those* filthy bitches?" Bogdan shook his head. "Andrei has new instructions for us. The Dragon has a special request."

Nikolai grimaced. "A special request." He pulled the truck onto an empty side road. Cut the engine. "So what does the Dragon want with us now?"

"The girl who escaped," Bogdan said. "She has a sister in the box. The Dragon wants us to bring her to him."

"The poor girl." Nikolai looked across the cab at Bogdan. "So, what are you waiting for?" he said. "You want me to show you where your *pulă* goes?"

Bogdan climbed from the cab and slammed the door. Crossed around to the rear of the box and scanned the road, both directions. Deserted. Almost completely dark. Perfect.

He drew his pistol as he unlocked the rear doors. Hoped that none of the bitches had any more cute ideas. Hoped the damn lock on the false front had stayed shut this time.

No women leapt out of the truck at him. The door to their compartment was locked and secure. Bogdan set his gun on a stack of boxes, unlocked the compartment. Switched on a flashlight and shined it into the darkness. *"Soră."* Sister. He didn't know the girl's name. Didn't care.

A pause, a rustling, and the girl emerged from the gloom. She was as dirty as the others, as pale and as gaunt. He supposed she'd been pretty, back when she was clean. She was young, though. Very young. He remembered her now. Remembered her sister.

The girl stared at him. Behind her, her companions rustled in the darkness. Bogdan shone the flashlight in her eyes. Removed his cell phone and pointed it at her. "Look at me," he told her in Romanian.

The girl looked at him. He pressed a button on his phone, took her picture. "Good," he said. "Go away."

The girl didn't move. "I'm hungry."

"I bet you are," Bogdan told her. "You'll eat tomorrow."

"I'm hungry now," the girl said. "We all are."

She fixed her eyes on his, defiant. "You'll eat tomorrow," Bogdan repeated. "Now disappear. Don't make me tell you again."

Wordless, the girl backed into the stinking compartment. Bogdan closed the door and locked it. Retrieved his pistol and replaced the boxes that hid the door. Closed the outer door to the box and turned off his flashlight, locked the box closed, and circled the truck to the cab, where Nikolai waited.

"So?" Nikolai said when Bogdan had climbed back into the passenger seat. "Is she pretty at least?"

"As pretty as the rest," Bogdan told him, "but she belongs to the Dragon now. So keep your hands off of her."

Nikolai smirked. "It's not my *hands* I'm thinking about," he said, and he laughed, an ugly noise that echoed in Bogdan's ears, harsh and grating and incessant, as his partner fired up the truck and pulled out onto the road once again.

24

THE PHONE WAS buzzing. The Dragon reached for the nightstand. A text message. A picture. A grimy little girl: Catalina Milosovici.

Perfect.

The Dragon forwarded the message to his contact in Romania.

Then he dialed his number. "Find this girl's family," he told him. "Teach them a lesson."

The Dragon examined the picture of the little girl, the sister, and felt his heart start to race. She was pretty, this girl. He would take his time with her.

He leaned over to the bedside table, to the cocaine he'd piled beside the phone. Dove in and inhaled, saw fireworks behind his eyes, the little urchin from the box, the knife hanging from its scabbard on his belt.

Yes, he thought, studying the long blade. He would savor the wench before he ended her sorry life.

25

AT ONE POINT in his life, Kirk Stevens had been terrified of flying. Three cases with Carla Windermere had all but cured him. Still, he felt no small relief when the BCA's chartered King Air touched down in Minneapolis. The flight had been smooth, the pilot calm and confident, but nothing could shake the funny feeling in the back of Stevens's mind.

They'd moved Irina Milosovici out that morning. Driven her to the little airfield north of Walker in a convoy—the sheriff's pickup and a couple of cruisers—Stevens's eyes searching the road for threats the whole way. Probably just paranoia, he figured, but anyone who shipped a bunch of women across the ocean in a box was bound to be a little bit ruthless, as Dale Friesen might have attested, were he able.

Nancy was going to drive down with the kids and Triceratops later in the day. They'd packed up the Cherokee together, and he'd caught Nancy looking at him.

"Make sure she's okay, Kirk," Nancy had told him. "She's still going to be scared of you and the deputies. Treat her gently, okay?"

Stevens had thought about Irina, how she'd shivered when she'd seen him, as if a light breeze could blow her over. Felt that same twinge in his heart again. "I will," he said. "I'll make sure they go easy on her."

He gave his wife a kiss. Held her for a moment. Then he kissed his daughter's forehead and ruffled his son's hair. "Gotta go," he told them. "I'll see you back in town tonight, okay?"

Andrea looked up from her phone. "Is everything okay?"

"Everything's fine." He forced a smile. "Duty calls."

"Daddy."

She studied Stevens, wide-eyed and serious, and he felt a pang of sudden tenderness toward her. Andrea had been a hostage, briefly, in one of Stevens's earlier cases, and since then had viewed her dad's job with a kind of worldly concern. She wasn't going to buy his reassurances, Stevens knew. Not now that she'd seen what cop life was really like.

Stevens bent down, wrapped his daughter in a hug. "We're going to be fine," he told her as Triceratops licked at his ear. "We have a woman in custody, and we figure she's in a little bit of danger, so she'll be safer off with Agent Windermere in town. That's all."

Andrea let him hold her. "Just be careful."

"I will," Stevens said. "You be careful, too. Help your mother take care of JJ, okay?"

She hugged him tighter. "Okay."

He held her a minute or two longer. Then he kissed Nancy again, waved about fifteen good-byes, and walked the couple blocks to where Irina and the translator waited with Sheriff Watkins, ready to get the heck out of Walker.

Irina Milosovici didn't say much the entire flight. Stevens had the translator explain the situation, watched Irina's brow cloud over.

"My sister," she said.

Stevens nodded. "We're working on it," he told her. "We'll get her back for you. We're just going to need a little more help."

Irina studied his face. Didn't react. Turned away to stare out the airplane's window and watch as Walker disappeared beneath them.

The flight took a couple of hours. Terminated at Crystal Airport, a small public facility northwest of Minneapolis. Stevens checked his phone, found a text message from Nancy. *On the road,* it read. *See you tonight. xoxo.*

He wrote a quick text back—*Made it to Mpls. Hurry home. Love, K.*—then put the phone away. Followed Irina off the plane and found Carla Windermere waiting on the tarmac.

Even now, three years after their first meeting, the sight of her made him pause. She was a beautiful woman, tall and slender, looked more like a movie star than a badass FBI agent. But she *was* badass, the toughest partner Stevens had ever had, and as he stepped off the plane and walked toward her, he felt his nerves suddenly calm, as if Windermere's mere presence could deter Irina Milosovici's kidnappers.

"Stevens." Windermere was smiling, sly, those deep chestnut eyes fixed on his. "Even on vacation, you couldn't resist me."

26

IT WAS GOOD to see Stevens again.

Even with Derek Mathers in her life, Carla Windermere still held a soft spot for the BCA agent, whose unassuming looks belied, she believed, dynamite cop instincts and an extraordinary calm under pressure.

Except this case was shaking her partner, she could tell, as they brought Irina Milosovici through the myriad security checkpoints outside the FBI's new Brooklyn Center offices. The place was a fortress, built to withstand the kind of attacks that had destroyed the Alfred P. Murrah Federal Building in Oklahoma City, and sometimes Windermere caught herself thinking the new security measures were overkill. Not today, though. Not with one cop already dead on this case.

Windermere and Stevens shepherded Irina Milosovici and her translator through security and up into the Bureau's Criminal Investigative Division. Found a conference room with a couch and a coffeemaker and waited as the two women made themselves comfortable.

"Okay," Windermere said, glancing at Stevens and Agent Harris, who'd slipped into the room to listen in. "So let's hear what we're dealing with."

> > >

BUT IRINA'S MEMORY WAS HAZY.

"It was very bright," she told Windermere and Stevens. "Every time the door opened, I hid my face. The men were taking women out. We all tried to hide. I tried to hide Catalina so they wouldn't take her."

"You were put in the box in Bucharest, right?" Windermere said. "What do you remember about where you came out?"

Irina furrowed her brow. "I remember the ocean," she said. "The smell of it, the salty air."

Stevens made a note in his notebook. "This was days later," he said. "You thought you'd been on a boat?"

"Yes," Irina said. "First we were on a truck, I think. Overnight, maybe. Then they put us on the boat. I could tell when the crane was lifting us. And then the ocean—some of the girls got seasick."

"But you didn't see anything when you came out?" Windermere asked.

"We were on a truck again, briefly," Irina told them. "A quarter of an hour, maybe. Then the doors opened. It was a yard full of boxes like ours. I heard gulls in the distance. The two men were there. They—" She shuddered. "They tried to take Catalina."

"But they didn't, though," Windermere said. "They took a couple other girls, and Catalina went back into the box with you, correct?"

"Correct," Irina said. She opened her mouth. Then she faltered. "She went back into the box, and I abandoned her there."

"You were scared," Stevens said. "You were trying to escape."

Irina looked at him sharply. "I left her," she said, her voice cracking. "I left her there to die."

Windermere watched the girl dissolve into sobs. Violent and uncontrollable. Watched the translator try in vain to console her. Felt utterly helpless. Couldn't imagine how the girl was feeling, her little sister gone and, face it, probably dead. Couldn't imagine the guilt.

Personally, she felt anger more than anything. Irina Milosovici was barely more than a kid herself, and her little sister was barely too old for Barbies, for Christ's sake. Somewhere, there were men who'd stolen these girls, sold them. Somewhere, there were men who would buy them.

Stevens touched her shoulder. "Let's give her a second," he said. "Take a breather."

Windermere wanted to complain. A breather was the last thing she needed; she had about a million more questions to ask Irina Milosovici. Was aching to saddle up and get the case underway. But the girl was still sobbing, pretty much a wreck, and Windermere realized Stevens was right. She followed him out into the hallway, held the door open for Harris coming out behind her.

"These guys," Harris asked Stevens. "These traffickers, who are they? Do you have any leads?"

"We're still putting the pieces together," Stevens said, "but obviously, these guys are major. They didn't hesitate to kill that deputy to keep their shipment moving. It's only blind luck they didn't shoot Irina."

"Well, you got her here safe," Harris said. "And she's not leaving until we track these guys down."

"Yes, sir," Stevens said.

"I told you we needed to wait," Harris told Windermere. "Evaluate the situation and come up with a plan."

"Yes, sir," said Windermere. "You did."

"The time for waiting is over, Agent Windermere. Consider that woman's case your priority. I can't promise you a task force, but I'll do what I can to get you the resources you need." Harris fixed his eyes on hers. "Just track these bastards down, understand?"

Windermere nodded. "Yes, sir," she said. "We're on it."

27

THE AMERICAN KNOWN as Mike peered through the windshield of the battered Škoda at the lights of the village of Berceni. He'd borrowed the car for the short drive south from Bucharest; his own Audi would have attracted attention in such a tiny farming town.

It had not been easy to trace Irina and Catalina Milosovici back to this shitty little place. The sheer volume of women Mike processed for Andrei Volovoi made remembering any single one of them difficult. In the weeks after he'd secured these particular girls in their container, Mike had traveled to Budapest, Bratislava, and Zagreb, sowing the seeds for more shipments west. The Dragon's call had surprised him, pulled him away from his task, and why? Because some lunkheads had let the older sister get away.

Mike idled the little Škoda through the village, pausing beneath a streetlight to glance at the address on the map he'd printed back in Bucharest. Found his way to a narrow road, a little cottage backing onto farmers' fields and darkness.

This was the house that the Milosovici sisters had come from. Single-story, ramshackle, an unkempt front lawn. Some clunker of a Soviet-era vehicle sat rusting in the car park; a mutt lay asleep on the doorstep. Considering the state of the house, it was not hard to imagine why Irina Milosovici and her little sister had yearned to run away. America would seem like a paradise compared to Berceni.

He climbed from the car and crossed the road to the yard. The dog stirred, woke, rose on its chain, its tail wagging as he approached. A friendly dog. All the better.

From his pocket, Mike removed a computer printout. A picture of Catalina Milosovici, and a short, simple note. A warning. A message to the family and the town, to all of Romania: Don't fuck with the Dragon. The Dragon will destroy everything that you love.

The dog reached the end of its chain. Whined and yelped as it leapt at Mike, again and again. Mike watched the dog. Its tail wagged furiously. It licked and slobbered and choked on its chain.

Mike reached for the knife on his belt.

28

"SO, OKAY," WINDERMERE said. "I've never taken down a bunch of human traffickers before. How do we approach these guys, Stevens?"

Stevens watched her move. She was pacing, jumpy, unable to sit still. She had peppered Irina Milosovici with questions until she couldn't think of any more, then dragged Stevens into an adjacent conference room and still couldn't stop moving.

Windermere had asked Derek Mathers to put in a call to the FBI's Organized Crime division to dig up whatever they could find about known trafficking outfits with ties to Eastern Europe. She'd also asked Mathers to put sketches of Dale Friesen's killers out on the wire, to get people talking, in the hopes that some law enforcement agency somewhere would recognize the faces.

Windermere was excited, Stevens could tell. His sometime partner lived for the big cases, thrived on excitement and danger and jet lag. She was every bit the glamorous FBI agent, while he, on the other hand . . .

Well, if he was honest, he felt a little bit daunted. A little scared, even. Every time he closed his eyes, he saw Irina Milosovici in tears. Saw Andrea, for heaven's sake. These were professional-grade criminals. They trafficked in human life. Who could guess how many women they'd stolen?

But Windermere was waiting, and she wanted a plan of attack. Stevens tried to forget about his misgivings.

"We've got a box full of women on the back of a truck," he said, straightening. "According to Irina, the truck was heading west. We track down that truck, odds are we find Catalina."

Windermere stopped pacing. "Yeah," she said slowly. "About Catalina . . ."

"Yeah?"

She sat down across from him, looked him in the eye. "Okay," she said. "This is going to sound harsh, Stevens, but bear with me."

"Sure," he said.

"I think we need to accept, first and foremost, that we might never find Catalina Milosovici," she said. "The girl might be dead already, or so far underground that she never turns up. If we go into this case trying to rescue one little girl, we're going to drive ourselves crazy."

Stevens felt suddenly hollow. "Jesus, Carla."

"I know," she said, "but think about it."

"That girl is Andrea's age."

"You're right," she said. "But so are half the girls in that box. And who the hell knows how many more boxes there are? This is a broad-scope situation, Kirk. We need to cut the head off this monster. Find the source."

Stevens didn't say anything, and Windermere's eyes softened. "We're not going to get anywhere looking for a red container truck headed west," she said. "The more we can learn about these assholes, the better the chance we have of tracking down Catalina Milosovici alive. So where do we start, Kirk?"

Stevens rubbed his eyes. Knew she was probably right, even if admitting it made him feel like a monster. "Irina said she was kid-napped from Bucharest roughly two and a half weeks ago," he said. "She crossed the Atlantic in that box, and her next breath of fresh air came in a container yard when the ship docked. So we know how she came over here, and we know basically when. How many ships made that crossing over the last couple of weeks?"

"Good question," Windermere said. She walked to the door, poked her head out, and hollered, *"Mathers."*

There was movement outside as Mathers came to the door, and

Stevens felt the familiar pangs of jealousy when he caught sight of the kid, a big Wisconsin farm boy with a wide, easy smile. Windermere had hooked up with Mathers on the last assignment, and the two were some sort of an item now.

"More research," Windermere was telling Mathers. "We need transatlantic shipping schedules, from anywhere within a day's drive of Bucharest to any port on the East Coast within the last week or so. Vessel names, ports of entry, the works, okay?"

Mathers nodded. "Got it," he said, tossing Stevens a sheepish grin before disappearing from the doorway.

Stevens watched him go. "Your minion?" he asked Windermere.

She shrugged. "Sounds better than 'boyfriend,' doesn't it?"

"Is he—" Stevens frowned. "Are you guys—"

"Who knows, Stevens?" she said, shaking him off. "Focus on this case. What else have we got? The clock is ticking."

29

BOGDAN URZICA AND Nikolai Kirilenko sold the last of the women to the buyer in Reno, emptying the box of every last little tramp but the Dragon's special princess.

"So now what?" Nikolai asked Bogdan as they returned to the truck. "What do we do about her?"

Bogdan regarded the box. Normally, at this point, he and Nikolai would allow themselves a little time to decompress, have a drink, a nice meal, maybe check into a motel for a decent night's sleep for a change. Not this time, though. Not with one girl left to go, and the Dragon waiting for her arrival. Bogdan had heard stories about people who'd disappointed the Dragon. They didn't tend to survive very long. Neither did their loved ones.

"I guess we should feed her," Bogdan said. "Clean out the box. That waste bucket is probably overflowing at this point."

Nikolai made a face. "I think I'll let you handle that," he said. "I'm too tired to be slopping around shit."

"You're just going to leave me to it?"

"You let the little bitch's sister escape, Bogdan," Nikolai said. "You earned yourself that bucket of shit."

> > >

BOGDAN CLEANED THE TRUCK. FOUND a 7-Eleven and bought the little sister a frozen burrito and a bottle of water. Locked her away in the box again and caught up to Nikolai at the Peppermill Casino in Reno. Had to drag him away from a cocktail waitress beside the craps tables. "What are you doing?" Nikolai protested. "She *liked* me."

"What an unfamiliar feeling that must have been for you," Bogdan told him. "We have to get moving."

Bogdan was in no mood for his partner's antics. The Dragon was waiting for his delivery. The job wasn't finished, not by nearly three thousand miles.

He followed Nikolai to the truck, where his partner, with one last mournful glance back at the Peppermill, tossed him the keys. "Your turn to drive," he said. "I want to dream about what I could do to that waitress."

"You embarrass yourself," Bogdan told him. "She was hustling you for tips."

"Everyone's a prostitute, Bogdan." Nikolai climbed into the cab. "Whether they admit it or not."

Bogdan stepped up to the driver's seat. *Let's get out of here,* he thought, shifting the truck into gear. *Deliver the little girl and forget about the Dragon for a while.*

30

STEVENS AND WINDERMERE worked through other possibilities while Mathers studied up on the transatlantic shipping trade.

"Irina said the truck made a couple of stops before she wound up in Walker," Stevens said. "Both times, the drivers dragged a bunch of women out."

"Deliveries," Windermere said. "Like fucking UPS. So who's buying these women, Stevens?"

Stevens brought up a map of the country on his computer. "That truck wound up in northern Minnesota," he said. "The highway she was on when they found her, the 200—it's pretty much a straight shot from Duluth."

"A hundred and thirty some miles from Walker. That's a couple of hours on the road. Irina said the truck's last delivery came a couple hours before she escaped."

"And it's the easiest path across the state from Duluth," Stevens said. "If they had a cargo of more women, they were probably headed to hook back up with the interstate around Fargo, head west."

"So where's their next delivery? And where'd they stop before Duluth?"

Stevens studied the map. "Could be south, could be east. Could be Canada. Pretty easy to slip across the border up there in the wilderness."

Windermere stuck her head out the door and hollered for Mathers again. The kid showed up quick, Stevens noticed. And he showed up with that same unflappable smile, didn't blink when Windermere asked him for a progress report.

"It's tough sledding," he told Stevens and Windermere. "Plenty of ships make that transatlantic run, and they call in up and down the coast, from Halifax to Miami and everywhere in between." He exhaled. "Even if I can narrow it down, those ships carry thousands of boxes apiece. It'll be a needle in a haystack trying to figure out which container held the girls."

"We crush the needle in the haystack game, Mathers," Windermere told him. "Keep working."

Stevens watched the kid disappear down the hall again. Wished he shared Windermere's good spirits. He considered the map some more, zoomed out to the entire Eastern Seaboard. Halifax. Boston. New York. Baltimore.

"The kid is right," he said. "Every major city has a container terminal. They could have come in anywhere."

Windermere caught the expression on his face. "Cheer up," she said. "I have an idea what we can do while we wait for Mathers to find us our haystack."

"Oh yeah?"

"Yeah." She winked at him. "You know folks in Duluth, don't you?"

31

"IT'S DONE," MIKE told the Dragon. "The message is sent."

The American sounded groggy. It was nearly dawn in Romania, and Mike had been running the Dragon's errand all night.

"Excellent," the Dragon said. "And the message was clear?"

"Oh, it's clear," Mike replied. "Nobody in that pissant town will mess with you again. And if big sister calls home, she'll lose her fucking mind."

The Dragon smiled to himself. "Perfect," he told Mike. "You've done well, Mike. Thank you."

"Yeah," Mike said. "Maybe you can pass the good news on to that partner of yours. Maybe he stops worrying so much."

"I'll tell him," the Dragon said. "I'm sure he'll be very pleased."

"You can tell him his next shipment's on the way, too," Mike said. "The *Atlantic Prince*. Give it four or five days."

"You made the changes to the order as I instructed?"

"Sure did. Swapped out any girl over eighteen, put together a box full of the prettiest teenage product you ever laid eyes on," Mike said. "I guess that means Andrei finally agreed to go in with you on the New York thing, huh?"

"Not yet," the Dragon said. "But he will."

32

IRINA MILOSOVICI LOOKED around the little conference room where the FBI had decided to keep her. It was comfortable enough; there was a couch and a big TV, and somebody had run out for sandwiches, but it was still a prison. The police were everywhere, the famous FBI. An army of strange men, just outside the door, studying her with prying, curious eyes.

Irina had decided that she trusted Agent Stevens, and his wife. She trusted the beautiful black woman who seemed to be friends with Stevens. The other agents, though, the quiet men, Irina did not trust.

Probably most of the other agents were good people. Kind men, and brave. Undoubtedly, though, a few of them were bad. They would watch her like predators. They would hurt her if they wanted, and she could do nothing to stop them. She could not even pick out the bad men from the good.

She did not want to be around any man right now, she decided. She didn't want to take the risk. She would tolerate Kirk Stevens because he would help her find her sister. Because he had been kind to her. Because she trusted him.

She would not trust anyone else.

The translator, Maria, sat in an office chair at the conference room table, eating a croissant and watching a bottle blonde cling to a chisel-faced man on the TV set. The blonde was weeping, and the man was pouting. He was wearing hospital scrubs. Irina didn't recognize either of them, and she knew most of the American movie actors.

A soap opera, then, and a bad one, judging by the melodramatic soundtrack and the woman's ceaseless sobbing. Irina stood from the couch and walked to the window, gazed out over the high iron fences, the security guards by the parking lot, the roadway and the flat fields beyond. Yes, this was a comfortable prison, but it was still a prison.

Still, it's better than what Catalina has.

Irina watched cars pull in and out of the parking lot, heading out into the flat land beyond. The countryside resembled Berceni—not a lot, but just enough that Irina felt suddenly, terribly homesick.

Her parents must be worried sick. She hadn't talked to them in weeks, maybe a month. And Catalina had gone missing, too. They would be out of their minds with fear.

You stupid cow. Never thinking of others. Only thinking of yourself.

The guilt washed over her, threatened to knock her down. She turned away from the window, from the flatland beyond. Maria was still watching that insipid soap opera. Irina walked over to the TV, turned down the volume. Caught Maria's eye when she looked up, surprised.

"I'm sorry," Irina told the translator, "but I would like to talk to my parents."

33

WINDERMERE HAD ONE missed call when she and Stevens landed in Duluth. Mathers, back at the office. She glanced at Stevens, almost reflexively, and then dialed Mathers's number.

"Yo," Mathers said when he picked up the phone. "How's Duluth?"

"Just landed," Windermere said. "Do you answer the phone like that because I'm black, Mathers?"

"What?" Mathers coughed. "Um, wait. Carla. No—"

"I'm messing with you," she said. "What do you want?"

"Jesus." Mathers exhaled. "Sometimes you scare me, Carla."

She met Stevens's eye. "Anyway."

"*Anyway*, Irina wants to call her mother. Wants to tell her parents about her sister, the translator says."

Of course Irina wanted to call her family, Windermere thought. Her folks were probably terrified out of their minds. But Windermere wasn't sure she wanted the girl calling anyone at this point in the investigation.

"Tell her to wait until tomorrow, at the earliest," Windermere said. "Me and Stevens should be back around midafternoon. We can set something up then."

A beat. "You brought Stevens?"

"To Duluth? Yeah, Derek, we're working the case together. Is that a problem?"

"No." Mathers went quiet. "Just, no."

"We'll talk about it when I get back," Windermere said, and ended the call. She wished Mathers would man up a little. Apparently he still had some jealousy issues, which made no sense at all—except it made plenty of sense. It had been partially to get back at Stevens, happily married Stevens, that she'd hooked up with Mathers in the first place. She'd always felt a spark, stupid and unexplainable, with the BCA agent, and though she'd never been close to acting on it, she knew Mathers could tell it was there.

Gah, she thought. *This better not get messy.*

Then she pushed Mathers from her mind and hurried to catch up with Stevens, who was standing beside the baggage claim, talking to a tall, rather stout woman. "Carla," he said, "meet Detective Donna McNaughton, the pride of Duluth."

McNaughton shook Windermere's hand, a firm grip. "Good to meet you," she said, a twinkle in her eye. "Understand you're in town for a little sex tourism."

34

"SO LET ME get this straight," Stevens said to the woman. "You're a hooker, and Donna—Detective McNaughton—is cool with it?"

McNaughton had claimed ignorance of the local sex trade, begged off any knowledge of underground brothels or shady strip clubs, anywhere a bunch of gangsters would try to sell women.

"I can't say I know anything about any beautiful young women at all, Kirk," she'd said with a smirk. "Vanessa gets jealous if my eyes start to wander." She'd cocked her head. "But maybe I can hook you up with somebody who knows this kind of thing."

She'd driven them to a condo building in downtown Duluth, buzzed them up to a swanky unit with a view of the lake, where a pretty blonde twenty-something greeted them in horn-rimmed glasses and yoga sweats and ushered them in for tea.

The girl—Shannon Spenser, she said her name was—glanced at McNaughton. "Escort," she said. "Not a hooker. There's a difference."

"You have sex for money, though," Stevens said. "What's the difference?"

"I provide companionship," Spenser told him. "Whatever happens above and beyond that is between two consenting adults." She turned to McNaughton again. "Look, am I going to need my lawyer for this?"

"I just don't understand," Stevens said, before McNaughton could answer. "Prostitution is illegal in this state, is it not?"

"Sex for money is illegal," Spenser replied. "I run a registered business for men who want female company. Like I said, if a client and I decide we want to do anything more than hang out with each other, it's our business, legally and—" She looked at Stevens. "—morally, too."

Semantics, Stevens thought. *A legal loophole.* He was fully aware that high-dollar escorts used the argument that they were being paid for their time and not for sexual activities, even in states like Minnesota, where prostitution was harshly punished. It was still sex work, cut-and-dried, and as the father of a teenage girl, Stevens couldn't figure out why everyone in the room—McNaughton and Winder-mere included—seemed so blasé about the situation.

"We met at the charity Fun Run last year," McNaughton explained. "Vanessa's got me getting out, getting me in shape. I nearly died."

Spenser laughed. "She made it to the finish line. We ran together."

"I held you back."

"Whatever." Spenser rolled her eyes. "Anyway, I convinced Donna to come to my friend's yoga studio."

McNaughton groaned. "All that bending and twisting."

"Anyway," Windermere said. "How long before you found out—"

"About my job?" Spenser shrugged. "I guess it was about the time I found out Donna here is a cop."

"And it wasn't weird?" Stevens asked.

"Why should it be? In the eyes of the State of Minnesota, I run a legit business." Spenser picked up the empty teacups and took them into the kitchen. "What do the FBI and BCA want with an escort, anyway?"

Stevens looked around the condo. Then he cleared his throat. "We're looking for information on the sex industry up here," he said.

Spenser poked her head out from the kitchen. "I'm not ratting anybody out," she said. "Donna knows this. People think sex workers are all exploited and abused, but I—"

"These girls *are* exploited," Windermere said. "We're talking about girls who've been brought in from Europe as slaves." She explained Irina Milosovici's situation as Spenser came out from the kitchen and listened. "What we're hoping you can help us with is pointing us toward a particular brothel or club that might help house these women."

Spenser frowned. "Jesus," she said. "Yeah. Let me think."

She walked to a computer in a small cubby of an office. Fired it up and typed something into an Internet browser. "A couple of my guys mentioned something," she said. She looked pointedly at Stevens. "You're not getting their names, not ever, by the way."

"Fine," Stevens said. "Whatever you can give us."

"There's this club, Heat, in the south end," Spenser said. "A strip joint, but my guys said the rules are pretty lax. You have the money, you can do whatever you want."

"These guys are your clients?" Windermere asked.

"*Former* clients. Guys like that aren't exactly in my league, Agent Windermere. I cut them off pretty quick."

Stevens watched the way Spenser looked at Windermere, noticed the way she made sure to call her by name. She wasn't flirtatious or solicitous, but she certainly played attentive well. Stevens figured she had no trouble finding well-heeled men to pay her for that kind of charm.

Windermere, though, seemed impervious to it. "Heat," she said. "Okay. So what makes you think this place is our spot?"

"My guys both mentioned a language barrier," Spenser told her. "Said the girls were beautiful, every one, but none of them spoke much English. They had to negotiate with some guy to get what they wanted."

"And what did they want?" Stevens asked.

"You know. Sex. A blowjob. Nothing crazy, I don't think."

"You didn't think about reporting this?" Windermere asked.

"Look, I take sex crimes as serious as anyone," Spenser said. "I don't want to see any woman abused. How was I supposed to know these women were being trafficked? It's not like there aren't tons of Eastern European chicks working legit in this country, you know?"

Stevens stood. "Thanks for the tea," he said. "You have an address for this Heat place, by chance?"

Spenser scribbled something on a notepad. "I would have phoned it in if I'd known," she told Stevens as she walked them to the door. "I'm not a bad person, you know."

Stevens studied Spenser, her wide, concerned eyes, her yoga sweats, her comfortable condo, Kafka on the end table. Figured the girl was about as far away from Irina Milosovici as she was from Hillary Clinton. Figured it wasn't women like Shannon Spenser who were shipping boxes of women into the country.

Still, though. If Andrea ended up like this . . .

Stevens shook his head. "Maybe not," he told Spenser. "But still."

35

FROM THE OUTSIDE, Club Heat was small and dirty and depressing, a windowless box surrounded by warehouses, train yards, and a gravel parking lot a quarter full, with mostly rusty old pickups and beat-up American econoboxes.

The interior wasn't much better: dim lighting and a dank, pervasive odor; cloudy mirrors and well-polished brass poles; track lighting and a large disco ball. A pretty blonde stood on the main stage in a pale yellow bikini, staring at her reflection above the bar as she swung her hips more or less in time to the music.

"It's not exactly the sultan's harem is it?" Stevens said, surveying the room—the girl on the main stage, the off-duty dancers working the floor, the furtive men who sat, alone or in small, grim-faced groups, watching the show. "Hardly seems like the kind of place where your every fantasy gets fulfilled."

Beside him, Windermere snorted. "Truth never lives up to fantasy, Stevens," she said. "Anyway, it *does* seem like the kind of place that would buy a truckload of women, wholesale."

Across the room, a large bouncer guarded a velvet-curtained doorway. Another big man tended bar. And a third bouncer was now approaching them, his eyes roving hungrily over Windermere's body. "Evening, folks," he said. "Two-drink minimum."

Windermere had her badge out before Stevens could react. "No drink minimum," she said. "Who's running this place?"

The bouncer's jaw worked as he studied the badge. He studied it a long time. Stevens slid his hand around to his holster, hoping McNaughton and her Duluth PD cronies outside would move fast if the whole plan went sideways. Then the bouncer straightened. "You want Jimmy," he said. "In the back."

> > >

STEVENS COULD FEEL THE BOUNCER watching him as they crossed the room toward the red velvet curtain. The bartender, too. "I don't think these guys like us," he said.

Windermere snorted. "What was your first clue?"

They walked between the dark tables, dodged a couple of girls hustling lap dances. Stevens overheard a brief, stilted exchange, a heavy accent, halting English. A dark-eyed brunette met his gaze, and for a moment, he saw her eyes cloud with fear. Then, quickly, she looked away.

"You seeing these women?" Stevens asked Windermere. "If they're here by choice, they don't exactly seem happy about it."

Windermere nodded. "Very least, they're drugged out of their minds."

They walked up to the bouncer at the red curtain. The bouncer looked past them, got a signal from his friend at the front, and stepped aside, pulling the curtain with him. Beyond the curtain was a hallway, more curtains on either side: private booths. *You have the money, you can do whatever you want.*

"All the way back," the bouncer said. "Where the office is."

Stevens followed Windermere down the hallway. Some of the curtains they passed were open to empty booths, banquettes, knee-high private stages. Some were closed, and Stevens could hear noises from within, some identifiable, some not. Windermere's eyes were dark. "I feel an ass-whooping coming on, Stevens."

They reached the end of the hallway, and a flat-gray steel door. Another bouncer. Another hallway, this one drab and sparse. The back of the club. A tiny office, a little man behind a cluttered desk.

The man scrambled to his feet as Stevens and Windermere entered the room. "Who the hell are you?" he said, his face red. "Who let you back here?"

"FBI, chief," Windermere told him. "Had a couple questions about that two-drink minimum."

The guy stared at her. Then Stevens. His eyes were wired, his movements jittery. "FBI," he said. "Christ."

"Jimmy, right?" Stevens stepped toward the desk. "You run this place?"

The guy looked at them both again. Swallowed. "I want my lawyer."

"You doing something wrong, Jimmy?" Windermere said. "Why don't you sit down and we'll talk."

Jimmy didn't sit. "What's this about?" he said. "You can't be— That two-drink thing is standard. Everybody does it. What does the FBI care about—"

"It's not the drinks, Jimmy," Windermere said. "It's the girls."

"Oh, shit." Jimmy's eyes went wide. He didn't wait to hear the punch line, just ran: half hurdled the desk, pushing papers everywhere, scrambling for the door. Threw a fist at Windermere, quick and off balance, then shoved her aside and ran into the dingy hallway.

"Round 'em up, Cole," he called to the bouncer. "Get the girls out of here, right fucking now."

"Don't you *dare*." Windermere drew her Glock and trained it on the bouncer. "Don't you fucking move, Cole. You keep those girls where they are."

Cole froze. Jimmy didn't. He bolted the other way down the hall. Stevens chased after him. Followed Jimmy through an exit door and nearly landed on top of the little man where he lay on the gravel beside the back step, grabbing his ankle, moaning. *"Shit."*

Stevens drew his gun, covered the club owner. Watched McNaughton roar up in an unmarked sedan. "You said it, pal," he told Jimmy. "You're in the shit now."

36

"I SWEAR TO God, I don't know anything."

Jimmy Callaway was sweating, a lot. It was oven-hot in the Duluth PD's interview room, where Donna McNaughton had taken the club manager while Stevens and Windermere tore Club Heat to pieces.

They'd found enough to validate Shannon Spenser's assertions about the place. Jimmy Callaway had kept meticulous records for each of his dancers, everything from tips earned to clients entertained to the price he'd paid to purchase the girl in the first place.

Windermere had studied the manager's logbook for a long time. "Goddamn it," she told Stevens. "This guy has dates of delivery for each girl, starting a couple years back, one girl at a time. Paid thirty grand a head, until he started buying in bulk."

"'In bulk.'" Like buying steaks at Costco. Stevens felt his stomach turn.

"I guess he wanted to see how long it took for each girl to earn back her purchase price," Windermere said. "Looks like a lot of lap dances."

Shannon Spenser charged her clients two hundred dollars an hour, Stevens remembered. She'd have to work a hundred fifty hours to earn thirty grand. At Club Heat, though, Stevens figured the girls would be lucky to earn ten percent of what Shannon Spenser was making.

He'd left Windermere to the logbook and concentrated on cracking Jimmy Callaway's safe. The thing was locked, but Stevens found a scrap of paper taped to the underside of Callaway's bottom desk drawer, the one with the stack of *Hustler* magazines and the fifth of rum.

"Bingo," Stevens said, examining the string of numbers on Callaway's note.

Windermere looked up from the logbook. "'Bingo'?"

Stevens worked the safe's combination, felt the lock disengage. Swung the door open and laughed out loud. "Oh yeah," he told Windermere. "Bingo."

> > >

NOW STEVENS AND WINDERMERE STOOD in the Duluth PD interview room, watching Jimmy Callaway sweat and stammer his way through a clumsy alibi.

"I don't know anything," the club manager told them. "I thought they were just normal working girls. I'm as surprised as you are."

"We have your logbook showing purchase prices, Jimmy," Windermere said. "And Stevens here had a peek in your safe."

Callaway blinked. His face went pale.

"That's right," Windermere said. "I gotta say, we'd be a lot more inclined to believe your bullshit if you didn't have fifteen of your dancers' passports stashed away in there."

"Romanian, Bulgarian, Polish." Stevens ticked off his fingers.

"Hungarian, Croatian . . . Where'd you get all those passports, Jimmy?"

Callaway ran his hands through his hair. Stared down at the table. When he looked up again, his face was ashen. "He'll kill me," he said.

Windermere sat down across from him. "Not if you help us, he won't."

"I don't even know that much," Callaway said. "I just took delivery."

"Who is this guy?" Stevens said. "What do you know about him? How'd you get involved in all this in the first place?"

Callaway gave himself a moment to resist. Then he seemed to deflate. "I was running girls," he said. "*Real* girls. Streetwalkers, but legit."

"You were a pimp," Windermere said.

"Pretty much, yeah." He shrugged. "I did okay at it, too. I mean, not great, but I was eating. So, one day this guy pulls my card, tells me he has a deal for me. Says he can set me up so I'm running my own show, making insane money. He showed me some figures, man, and it was unreal."

"So you went for it."

"Wouldn't you?" Apparently Callaway thought the question was rhetorical. "Yeah, man, I went for it. The girls weren't cheap, but they worked for it. Long as you kept them in line, anyway."

Stevens felt his stomach churn. His fists clench at his sides. He cleared his throat. "You had, what, fifteen girls? Where'd you keep them?"

"Rented a couple townhouses a mile or so from the club. Three bedrooms each, three girls to a room," Callaway said. "It worked fine. They never tried to escape. Hell, they were terrified, and where the fuck would they go? You saw how we kept their passports."

"Uh-huh," Windermere said. "And you got a delivery from where?"

"East Coast somewhere," Callaway said. "Nobody told me anything. I called the number they gave me and told them I wanted a couple girls. A few weeks later a truck showed up with a couple girls in it."

Windermere pushed him a pad of paper and a pen. "Write down that number, Jimmy."

"They switch phones all the time, though," Callaway said. "Sometimes I have to wait for them to call me, just so I know how to get in touch again."

"Let us worry about that," Windermere told him. "Just give us the last number they gave you and we'll take it from there."

Callaway looked a half second from puking, but he scribbled something down. Windermere passed the paper to Stevens, who couldn't place the area code off the top of his head. "This guy who approached you, you dealt with him the whole time?" he asked.

"That's right."

"And he's the guy bringing the girls into the country."

"No." Callaway swallowed. "*That* guy, he's the main guy. The guys I was dealing with were some lower-level guys. I think they were just, like, the drivers."

"Show him the sketches," Windermere said.

Stevens brought out the sketches the FBI artist had made. Callaway sucked his teeth. "Fuck," he said. "I fucking knew this thing was too good to be true."

"The contact, Jimmy. Tell us what you know."

Callaway studied the sketches. "Yeah," he said. "These are the guys." He pointed to the thug with the scar on his face. "I remember the scar. Like he'd face-fucked a screwdriver."

Windermere looked at Stevens. "Same guys as killed the deputy." She turned back to Callaway. "What are their names, Jimmy?"

"Names?" Callaway laughed, incredulous. "You think these assholes ever told me their names?"

"Okay," said Stevens, "What the hell did you call them?"

"'Hey, you,' and 'Yes, sir,'" Callaway said. "I didn't need to know anything more than that." He shrugged. "Sorry, guys. My line of work, you don't ask too many questions you don't need to know the answers to."

37

WINDERMERE'S PHONE RANG just after dawn.

"Carla." It was Mathers. "I wake you?"

Windermere sat up in bed, looked around the motel room. She'd fallen asleep barely four hours earlier, her laptop open, the TV playing reruns on mute. She and Stevens had run down the phone number Jimmy Callaway had scribbled out for them, traced it to Newark, New Jersey, some corner-store disposable, paid for in cash. If the traffickers were as careful as Callaway thought, Windermere figured she probably wouldn't find much when she tracked down the phone records, but she'd made a note to put Mathers on the trail anyway. Then she and Stevens retreated to the local Super 8 to catch a few winks, planned to start interviewing Jimmy's girls in the morning. The *late* morning.

"Carla?"

"I don't sleep, Mathers," Windermere told him. "You know that. You calling because you miss me?"

"Actually, yeah," Mathers said. "I didn't really know what to do with myself last night, without you chirping at me and hogging all the blankets."

"Sounds like you had it pretty good," Windermere said. "I met a high-class call girl and a degenerate strip-club boss. And," she said, eyeing her unopened suitcase, "I fell asleep in my makeup."

"You get all the fun assignments," Mathers said. "If I want to see strippers, I have to pay the cover charge."

"As if you need a strip club," Windermere said. "I don't even stick you with the two-drink minimum."

"You keep running away with Stevens, I might just pony up."

"Yeah, yeah." She went into the bathroom, splashed water on her face. "You call me up just to flirt, Mathers, or do you have something to talk about?"

"Depends." She could hear the smile. "What are you wearing?"

"My chastity belt. Now spill."

Mathers sighed. "Fine," he said. "If I can't get you hot and bothered, maybe this will do the trick. The *Ocean Constellation*."

Windermere shook her head. "Nope, not feeling anything."

"Wait for it," Mathers said. "The *Ocean Constellation* is a thousand-foot container ship running the Mediterranean trade route to the eastern United States. It left Trieste three weeks ago and arrived in the port of Newark, New Jersey, around the same time we think Irina Milosovici arrived on American soil."

Instantly, Windermere was awake. "Hot damn, Mathers. You *do* know how to get a girl's attention." She told him about Callaway, about the burner phone with the Newark area code. "But why Trieste?"

"Closest major container port to Bucharest," Mathers said. "Irina didn't seem to think the box was moved more than once between Bucharest and America. They must have trucked it overland before they loaded it on the *Ocean Constellation*."

Windermere turned on the shower. "It's perfect," she said. "Let's say the *Ocean Constellation* is our ship. Now we just have to figure out who sent the container."

"I'm working on it," Mathers said. "One more thing."

"Uh-huh?" Windermere said.

"The *Ocean Constellation* off-loaded in Savannah, Georgia, and Charleston, South Carolina, after Newark," he said. "It's supposed to head back to the Mediterranean in a day or so, but they have an out-bound stop in Newark scheduled for tomorrow. If you haul ass, you might be able to get on board, talk to the crew."

"Dynamite," Windermere told him. "Call Newark and tell them to prepare for my arrival. Don't let that ship set sail before Stevens and I get a good look at it."

"Roger," Mathers said. "Any shot I can let Irina call her family? Her translator's getting pretty worked up about it."

"Negative," Windermere said. "Wait for me to get home."

"You know, we're supposed to let her talk to her people, Carla," Mathers said. "Legally, I mean. We can't just keep her locked up for-ever. And I don't know if you noticed, but that translator is kind of scary."

Windermere knew he was right. Still, something made her reluctant to let the girl do much without her direct supervision. The case was too fragile.

"Just a little longer, Derek," she told Mathers. "See if you can keep her in check for another day at least."

"Okay," Mathers said. "I'll try." Then he brightened. "Hey, since you're not coming home, can I have the name of that call girl you talked to?"

"You can't afford her," Windermere told him. "I'm getting into the shower now. Think about that while I'm gone."

38

"FUCKING FBI INSECTS."

The Dragon smiled at Volovoi, clucked his teeth in commiseration. Beside him, Volovoi stared out the town car's smoked windows at the Manhattan skyline across the river, the twin humps of Midtown and Lower Manhattan, the Empire State Building, the Chrysler Building, the Citigroup American International buildings, the new World Trade Center—the Freedom Tower, they were calling it—the Dragon's city. He knew it was no accident that the Dragon's driver had taken this route.

The FBI had raided Club Heat in Duluth. Volovoi had learned of the disaster this morning. The women were freed. The club owner imprisoned. Shortly after he'd heard the news, the Dragon had called.

"Insects," the Dragon said, smiling again at Volovoi, a bad approximation of sympathy. The gangster couldn't hide his delight. With the Duluth club out of business, Volovoi was down a buyer. Out thousands of dollars in revenue, money he'd been counting on to pay back the Dragon.

Shit, Volovoi thought, *it wouldn't be so surprising if the Dragon was behind the raid at Club Heat himself.*

Sure enough, the Dragon turned away from Volovoi to watch the Manhattan skyline. "You will need a new source of income," he said, as though the thought had just occurred to him. "Perhaps now is the time, Andrei, to consider my New York offer."

"Now is not the time," Volovoi replied, sinking back in his seat. "The FBI has picked up my drivers' trail. They will be searching for traffickers, picking at threads. Now is the time to lay low and be cautious."

"Caution never made a man any money, Andrei," the Dragon replied. "And surely you'd agree that now, more than ever, you're in need of a profit. You have a new shipment coming in a couple of days. Where will you send it?"

Volovoi didn't answer. There was money in Manhattan, he knew, enough to push the Dragon off his back forever. But there was also heavy risk. And the Dragon wouldn't go away easily, even after the Manhattan project took hold.

If he were a smart man, he would ditch the next box, now that the FBI had begun to trace the big sister's trail. A cautious man would not attempt to sell any more women. He certainly would not employ Bogdan Urzica and his idiot partner, not with police drawings of their faces on every news channel in America.

But he couldn't just quit. The Dragon wouldn't allow it, would chase him if he ran. Would hunt down his family, his sister, her children. The Dragon would demand payment, one way or the other.

"Just a small meeting with my New York friend, Andrei," the Dragon said. "You don't have to agree to anything, no obligation. Just allow us to lay out our proposal."

The driver turned the town car away from the river, and Manhattan receded in the rearview mirror, replaced by grimy, soul-crushing New Jersey. Volovoi closed his eyes, imagined the FBI insects tearing down his operation. Imagined severing ties with the Dragon, the havoc it would wreak. He'd come to America for glamour and sensationalism. Such things required a man to make difficult decisions. Sometimes a man had to take risks.

Volovoi knew there was only one answer. He opened his eyes. "One meeting," he told the gangster. "No obligation."

The Dragon smiled back. "No obligation, Andrei," he said. "None whatsoever."

39

"NEWARK, NEW JERSEY," Stevens told his wife over the phone. "We're wheels-up in about half an hour. Hopefully, someone on this ship saw something we can use to start following the trail to the bad guys."

"This is the same ship that brought Irina and her sister over?" Nancy said. "It's back in Newark already?"

"It's an outbound stop," Stevens said. "It docked in Newark last week, its first stop in America. Went down the Eastern Seaboard dropping off boxes and then turned around to pick up a few more in New Jersey before it crosses the Atlantic. Lucky us, I guess."

"Have to be good to be lucky," Nancy said. She let her breath out, weary. "We almost had World War Three around here last night."

"Oh no," Stevens said. "What happened?"

"I worked late," she said. "Left Andrea to handle dinner for JJ. I got home and he's starving, and your daughter is nowhere to be found. She straggles in a half hour later, says she went to McDonald's with her friends."

"Friends," Stevens said.

"One friend in particular."

"Calvin." Stevens rubbed his eyes. "That guy still around?"

"She left JJ alone for an hour, Kirk. I don't care about her little blossoming romance. It's not acceptable."

"Of course not," Stevens said. "So what happened?"

"Nothing," Nancy said. "She stomped off to her room, and I made JJ spaghetti. You're going to have to talk to her, Kirk. She won't listen to me."

"Maybe if we texted her."

"Ha-ha," Nancy said. "Hurry back, would you?"

"I will," Stevens told her. He ended the call and hurried out of the motel to where Windermere stood beside a waiting cab. She raised an eyebrow at him as he approached.

"Andrea has a boyfriend," Stevens told her. "For once in my life, I'm glad I'm not home to deal with it."

"Say no more," Windermere said, climbing into the taxi. "I'd take Romanian mobsters over a moody teenage girl any day."

Stevens laughed. "You and me both." He slipped in beside her, slamming the door as the cab motored out of the motel parking lot toward the airport. Somewhere in the distance, the *Ocean Constellation* waited.

40

IRINA PACED THE conference room. "My parents," she told Maria. "No doubt they are frantic with worry. How long do I have to wait before I can call?"

Maria looked up from the television. "Agent Mathers said you could call today," she said. She checked her watch. "With the time difference, it's already nighttime in Romania."

"Forget about that," Irina told her. "I'll wake them up if necessary. I need to contact them as soon as possible."

She'd been pacing all day, wracked with guilt that she hadn't contacted her parents sooner. They'd no doubt been panicking since the day Catalina had disappeared, weeks ago now. Irina was dreading the call, knew what she had to tell them was as bad as anything they'd imagined. But the thought of waiting even one more night to speak to them seemed even more like torture.

"As soon as possible," Irina told the translator. "Please."

Maria glanced at the TV again. Then, wearily, she pushed herself to her feet. Walked to the door and beckoned to the young FBI agent. Irina shrank away as the man approached. He was big, tall, and broad-shouldered, and he walked with a power and purpose that scared her. If the young agent wanted to, he could break her like a piece of dry spaghetti.

> > >

"WE HAVE TO WAIT UNTIL Agent Windermere gets back," Mathers told the translator. "Shouldn't be more than a couple days."

"A couple days?" The translator gestured to Irina Milosovici. "Her sister has been kidnapped. Her parents have no way of knowing either girl is alive."

Mathers followed the translator's eyes to where Irina sat huddled in a corner, hardly daring to lift her head from her chest. He knew the translator was right. Knew his own mother would have worked herself into a panic by this point, and she lived the next state over.

"It's just cruel to keep her isolated like this," the translator was saying. "Not to mention, it's illegal. This woman has rights."

Mathers said nothing. He knew that, too. He'd done a little research on human trafficking cases, found out that a victim like Irina shared the same rights as an American citizen. Hell, if she wanted to, Irina could walk right out of the building, and it wouldn't make much difference what the FBI had to say about it. A phone call, Mathers figured, was the least of his worries.

The translator was watching him. "You know what I'm saying is true," she said. "And I mean it. You let this woman call her parents, or I'll start calling lawyers."

Mathers looked at her. Looked at Irina, who shied away, hid her eyes like he was some kind of boogeyman or something. A monster, like the assholes who'd put her in the box in the first place. Mathers felt his resolve weakening. What was one little phone call, anyway? Hell, it was the decent thing to do.

Still, Windermere—

"Do it," the translator said. "Tonight."

Mathers sighed. "Carla's going to kill me," he said.

41

THE *OCEAN CONSTELLATION* towered over the pier like a skyscraper, dwarfing the FBI sedan as it pulled alongside the ship's massive blue hull. At a thousand feet long and over five stories high, the thing was a behemoth, the biggest moving object Stevens had ever seen. Brightly colored containers covered every inch of deck space, stacked four and five high like Legos, and for the first time, Stevens began to comprehend what an impossible task the Customs and Border Protection guards faced in stemming the flow of contraband—be it women, drugs, guns, or anything else—into the country.

He and Windermere had landed in Newark a little before two. Met a special agent from Newark's Organized Crime division, a fair-skinned, solid guy named LePlavy, and by three, they were on the pier, driving through a customs checkpoint and navigating the chaotic mess of trucks and trains and dockworkers scattered beneath the giant orange gantry cranes that loaded the ship.

There were ships everywhere. Containers by the thousands. There was no way that anyone could check every box that came into the country, Stevens decided. Hell, even checking one container in five would be an impressive feat.

Beside him, LePlavy seemed to read his mind. "I did a little research on this ship of yours," he said, pulling the car to a stop beside a spindly gangplank hanging from the *Ocean Constellation*'s flank. "Apparently she off-loaded over a thousand boxes in Newark last week. Almost half of those came from Trieste."

"Any chance you got a list of the cargo in those boxes?" Stevens asked him.

"I did. None of them said 'women.'"

Stevens glanced at Windermere. "Needle in a haystack territory again," Windermere said. "Even if nothing on the manifests raised any flags, maybe we can isolate single boxes, work through every shipper individually. Maybe something jumps out at us."

"Five hundred boxes at least," Stevens said. "That's a lot of digging."

Windermere nodded. "Sure is," she said, reaching for the door handle. "So let's hope one of these sailors can give us a clue."

42

THE BIG AMERICAN agent led Irina into a small office, sat her behind the desk in a comfy leather chair, and gestured to a telephone. Irina felt a tightness in her chest as the agent dialed her parents' number and the phone began to ring in her ear. Anxiety.

She wondered how she would tell her parents what had happened, how she would explain that she had lost them their youngest daughter. She wondered how she could dare to speak to them at all, and she reached to hang up the phone as her guilt overwhelmed her.

Before she could hang up, though, her father answered. She hesitated, closed her eyes, and began, haltingly, to explain. She was afraid of his anger when he found out how she'd failed him.

But her father already knew about Catalina. Her father, she realized, was *crying*.

"They came to the house," her father told her through his tears. "Someone, in the night. They left a picture of Catalina, a warning for us. For the whole town."

Irina felt sickness in her stomach. Felt like she was going to puke.

"They slaughtered Sasha-dog," her father said, and Irina pictured Catalina's little mutt and felt a dam burst inside of her, began to cry as her father choked back his own sobs. "They warned us that if we contact the authorities, they will do the same to Catalina."

"I'm sorry," Irina told. "I'm so sorry, Papa."

Over the phone line, her father wept bitter, helpless tears that scared Irina almost more than anything she had endured. If the devil-faced man could turn her father into this kind of terrified mess, what would he do to Catalina?

Then her father regained control. She could hear him blowing his nose, and when he came back his voice was clear again. "These people are evil, Irina," he told her. "There is nothing you can do to stop them. Come home and help us pray for Catalina's sake."

> > >

IRINA PUT DOWN THE PHONE. Felt suddenly claustrophobic in the tiny office, suffocated by fear. Her sister was in danger. Irina was in danger, too, imprisoned here with these men.

She would not go home, she decided. Going home would accomplish nothing. But staying here, sitting and doing nothing, would be just as stupid. Every minute she waited was another minute of Catalina's life wasted. Catalina didn't have much more time to waste. And it wasn't like the police were finding her anyway.

Maria was watching her. So was the young FBI agent. Irina swallowed. Welled up her courage and looked at the translator. "I want to leave this place," she said. "Please. I will find my sister myself."

43

BY NIGHTFALL, WINDERMERE was sure that somebody on the *Ocean Constellation* knew something about Irina Milosovici's container. She just wasn't sure how to get the crew to talk.

She and Stevens left LePlavy on the pier while they boarded the ship. The captain, a Dane named Pedersen, met them on the bridge, where he was supervising the loading of eight hundred more containers onto the ship. He was middle-aged, handsome, and clean-shaven, and he smiled apologetically as he shook their hands.

"I'm sorry," he told them. "I'm not sure what you're hoping to find here. This ship has a crew of twenty, and a capacity of almost twenty-five hundred forty-foot containers like the box you're describing. It would be impossible for anyone to know what was inside each box."

"Sure," Stevens said. "We're just wondering if anyone heard or saw anything out of the ordinary."

"This box had forty women in it," Windermere said. "Maybe somebody heard something they weren't sure about. We can jog their memory."

"I can say almost for certain that the officers wouldn't have heard anything," Pedersen told them. "We don't spend much time on deck during a voyage. And the rest of the crew is from all over the world—mostly the poorer parts. In my experience, they don't speak English very well at all."

"Can't hurt to try, though."

Pedersen hesitated. "Very well," he said finally, glancing out the bridge window to where a giant gantry crane was depositing another long container. "But hurry, please. This ship sails at slack tide. I have a schedule to keep."

> > >

"SO HE DOESN'T KNOW ANYTHING," Windermere said to Stevens, as they descended in the ship's elevator toward the deck. "Does he?"

Stevens shook his head. "I don't think he was lying," he said. "That leaves us the crew."

Captain Pedersen had his third officer gather the crew in the mess, a low, utilitarian room with the long cafeteria tables and flat beige walls of a hospital—or a prison. The crew hailed mostly from the Philippines, and they were entirely men. They spoke halting English, but they seemed to understand what Stevens and Windermere represented; they stiffened, avoided eye contact, answered in single syllables. Whether they knew anything or just feared the police, though, Windermere couldn't tell.

One man, however, gave Windermere a funny feeling. He was a short, bearded man, nondescript, kept trying to edge his way to the back of the mess and out of sight. He froze when her gaze caught him, avoided her eyes when she called after him.

"You there," she said. "What's your story?"

The man didn't look at her. Didn't answer.

"This box with the women," she said. "What do you know? Did you hear something, see something? What can you tell us?"

The man finally spoke. "I didn't see anything," he said, his accent heavy.

"A red shipping container. Forty women inside. Maybe you heard something. Come on."

"I can't help you," the man said. "I'm sorry."

"'Sorry.'" Stevens stepped forward. "Why are you sorry?"

The whole room was quiet. Nobody looked at Stevens and Windermere. Nobody looked at the man they'd cornered.

These people know something, Windermere thought. *They have to know something.*

"Why are you sorry?" Windermere said. "What do you know that you're not telling us?"

The man stayed silent. Kept his eyes downcast and seemed to be fighting a battle with himself. *Attaboy,* Windermere thought. *You can do it.*

Then the man slumped. "I'm sorry," he said. "I just—I cannot."

"Sure you can," Windermere said. "Just tell us what you know." She started toward him, pushing between the rows of the sullen-faced crew. Not a man cleared a space for her to pass.

Before she could reach the man, though, she was interrupted by a knock at the door. The third officer, wearing the same apologetic smile as Captain Pedersen. "I'm afraid we must prepare to be sailing," he told Stevens and Windermere. "The company has a strict schedule to keep."

"Just a couple more minutes," Windermere told him. "We're getting somewhere. Please."

The third officer tapped his watch. "We really must be getting underway," he said. "I'm very sorry."

44

WINDERMERE STOOD BESIDE LePlavy's Crown Victoria and watched the *Ocean Constellation* slip away from the pier, feeling like she was watching her case sail away with it.

"We should have stopped that ship," she told Stevens and LePlavy. "That little guy knew something. I know he did."

"Maybe," Stevens said. "Or maybe he was just scared."

"Maybe he had something else to hide," LePlavy said. "Maybe he's smuggling drugs in his knapsack. Lot of narcotics coming into the country on those ships."

"Exactly," Stevens said. "Would be hard to convince a judge we have to tie up a sixty-thousand-ton ship just because one of the crew is giving us the side eye."

Windermere said nothing. Just watched from the pier as the *Ocean Constellation* slowly turned in the harbor until its bow pointed toward open ocean.

Soon as that ship hits international waters, we're screwed, she thought. *That shady crew member will jump off the boat the next stop away maybe, and he'll disappear forever. We've lost him.*

"Maybe we can get a helicopter," she said.

Stevens looked at her. "What?"

She gestured out over the water. "Fly out to the boat, keep interviewing the crew. One by one, this time. Maybe that guy opens up when his friends aren't around."

"A helicopter." LePlavy laughed, incredulous. "I, uh—Are you serious?"

"She's not serious," Stevens said. He turned back to her. "We need more than a hunch, Carla. We need something solid."

She was about to tell him to screw the hunch when her phone started to ring. Mathers. She answered it. "Tell me good news, Derek."

"Maybe I should call back," Mathers said.

"Uh-oh," she said. "What did you do?"

"I—" He let his breath out. "I let Irina call her parents," he said. Then, before she could say anything: "I had to do it, Carla. Legally, we can't just keep her locked up incommunicado. The translator put the screws to me. She was going to call a lawyer."

Windermere glanced at the other two agents. Stevens met her eyes, gave her a look: *What's up?* She turned away.

"Okay," she said, "so you disobeyed my instructions and gave Irina the phone. What else?"

"Well, here's the thing," Mathers said. "It sounds like whoever has the little sister, they have people in Romania. They paid the girls' parents a visit."

Windermere closed her eyes. "Jesus."

"Yeah. I guess they left a picture of Catalina and some kind of warning note. And they—well, they killed the kid's dog."

"The dog."

"Irina says Catalina loved that dog. They cut him up and told the parents if they tried to intervene with the case, they'll do the same to Catalina. She's pretty scared, Carla," he said. "She wants to get out of here."

"She wants to—Where the hell does she want to go?"

"I don't know," Mathers said. "She just wants to go. And legally, Carla, I don't think we can stop her."

Windermere opened her eyes. Out in the harbor, the *Ocean Constellation* was picking up speed now. In a few minutes, it would disappear forever.

And now Irina Milosovici wanted to walk. Windermere clenched her fists, felt her whole body tense. "Jesus Christ," she said. "Are you kidding me, Derek?"

45

"**WELL, OKAY,**" Stevens told Windermere. "Let's forget about Irina for a second."

Windermere shook her head. "We can't just—"

"Mathers and Harris can stall her until we get back," he said. "We go home to Minnesota with a break in this case and that girl won't be so eager to walk, I promise."

Windermere opened her mouth to reply. Thought better of it apparently, and sunk down in her seat and said nothing.

They were in LePlavy's car, driving away from the empty pier where the *Ocean Constellation* had docked. Stevens watched Windermere from the backseat, figured he understood his partner's frustration.

Mathers was right about Irina, of course; it was against the law to keep the poor girl from contacting her family. And of course she was scared. But she wouldn't get anywhere by running.

In the front seat, Windermere opened her eyes. "I'll tell you one thing," she said. "That girl isn't getting out of FBI custody."

"Of course not," Stevens said. "She's a witness in a major investigation. She's not going anywhere."

"Legally, you can't just keep her in a cell, though," LePlavy said. "If she doesn't want protective custody, you can't force it on her."

"So what the hell is she supposed to do?" Windermere said. "Get her own apartment somewhere? What if she wants to go home? Just pack up and head back to Romania with Mommy and Daddy?"

"I guess we petition a judge," Stevens said.

Windermere made a face. "Fucking Mathers," she said.

Stevens sat up. "Yeah," he said, "but we're not completely screwed here, Carla. We still have a case."

"That ship's the one that delivered these women," LePlavy said. "You're pretty sure of that, right?"

"We're sure," Stevens told him. "Based on the timeline and that Newark phone number—"

"Which has given us absolutely nothing," Windermere said. "Derek says there's nothing in that number's records but a bunch of anonymous calls. Started two months back and ended with this delivery. These guys were too goddamn careful."

"They gave us Newark." Stevens sat forward. "And we have the *Ocean Constellation* and Irina's description of the container. This harbor is lousy with checkpoints and security cameras. If we do some digging, we'll find that box."

LePlavy met his eyes in the rearview mirror. "Well, okay," he said. "Let's dig."

46

STEVENS AND WINDERMERE waited while LePlavy called in a warrant. Then they all drove to the Port Authority office, where the supervisor was waiting with his hands on his hips and an *I don't have time for this shit* expression on his face.

"We're on the hunt for a forty-foot red container that came off the *Ocean Constellation*," Windermere explained in the supervisor's office. "The owner is shipping women into the country through your facility, so let's just assume you're going to bust your ass to help us, okay?"

The supervisor looked at her. Looked at Stevens and LePlavy. "You know that ship dropped off a thousand boxes," he said. "You—"

"We know," Windermere told him. "Just hook us up with the tape."

> > >

THE SUPERVISOR LED THEM TO the Port Authority's security office, a large, windowless room filled with computer screens and banks of monitors. The place was *cold*, the air-conditioning on full blast, but Windermere forgot about the chill as soon as the supervisor brought up the footage from the *Ocean Constellation*'s arrival.

The Port Authority had cameras everywhere. On the pier and in the parking lots, in the vast marshaling yards amid stacks of containers, at the customs checkpoints and the entry and exit gates to the facility. They had manifests, too, and electronic scanners to track each container as the cranes lifted them from the ships, placed them on the backs of trucks or on train cars that shunted them away from the pier.

"Amazing," Windermere told Stevens and LePlavy. "If we can pin down which box is ours, we can trace the manifest to the shipper, easy."

"Sounds good to me," Stevens said. "Let's get to work."

> > >

THEY STUDIED THE MONITORS FOR hours, an endless procession of containers of all sizes and colors.

How many of these boxes hold women? Windermere thought.

Most of the boxes had logos on their sides, the names of shipping companies or railroads, or big-box discount stores. Windermere watched them move from ship to shore and out through the exit gates, felt her senses dull with the monotony, the chill in the room the only thing keeping her awake.

She realized she was shivering, was about to ask for a sweater or a blanket—hell, a parka—when she caught the flash of red. "There," she told Stevens and LePlavy, pointing at the screen. "Check it out."

The two men squinted at the screen. Watched as a giant gantry crane lifted a plain red container from the *Ocean Constellation*'s hold and deposited it on the back of a flatbed truck.

"That's a red tractor," Stevens said, and she could tell from his voice that he was starting to feel it. "Just like the one Irina described."

LePlavy copied something into a notebook. "I'll run the owner data," he said, standing. "You guys keep watching, make sure this is the one."

"It's the one," Windermere said. She could feel it, plain and clear as she felt the sailor on the *Ocean Constellation* was hiding something. "Hurry up and tell us who owns this thing."

LePlavy hurried off. Stevens hit play on the monitor again, and they watched as the driver of the truck slowly pulled out from under the crane, the container secured on the back of his flatbed. Windermere imagined the women inside, their fear, their disorientation. She closed her eyes and tried to chase the thought from her mind.

We'll find who owns this box, she thought. *We'll track them down. We'll find Catalina Milosovici and the rest of the women.*

We'll make these bastards pay.

47

THE TRUCK IDLED away from the pier, the giant cranes, the *Ocean Constellation*. Navigated the massive stacks of waiting boxes and lined up at the customs checkpoint that guarded the facility. Stevens and Windermere watched as the truck waited. The line was long. Windermere wrapped her arms around herself and exhaled, half expected to see her breath in the air.

Beside her, Stevens tapped his fingers on his knee. "I keep waiting for a camera angle that's going to show us this guy's face," Stevens said.

"We already know the guy, Stevens," Windermere said. "Hell, we have sketches of both of them."

The truck inched forward. Windermere watched the screen. Ached to reach through the camera and just stop the truck, open her up, and free the damn women right there. Hated that she couldn't. Hated that she knew what happened next.

Finally, the truck made the customs checkpoint. From what Windermere could tell, some trucks were pulled aside for secondary screenings. A small fraction were directed through an X-ray scanner. The *Ocean Constellation* had arrived on a busy day at the port, though. Most of the trucks drove away unchecked.

The red truck and its red box were among them. Windermere watched the truck idle through the checkpoint and out onto the surface road beyond the facility. There were no more cameras here. The truck drove offscreen and was gone.

"And off they go," Stevens said, pausing the footage. "Let's see if LePlavy could dig up any dirt."

> > >

BUT LEPLAVY DIDN'T COME BACK with much.

"The good news is it's probably your truck," he said. "The tractor's a rental, leased from a national heavy-equipment distributor. The flatbed chassis's the same, but from a different distributor. Both leased to a company called ATZ Transport, out of Elizabeth, New Jersey."

"That's just down the road," Stevens said. "Right? Let's go get them."

LePlavy shook his head. "It's a front," he said. "It's a P.O. Box. ATZ Transport is owned by a numbered company based on the Isle of Man. There's no cracking who owns *that* company, not without some serious help from Interpol."

"And the box?" Windermere asked.

LePlavy sighed. "The box is the same story, only it's owned by a *different* shell company, which is owned by a different numbered company in a different overseas tax haven." He looked at them both. "Basically, what I'm saying is, these guys are pros. They know to hide their assets. And it's going to take a hell of a lot of sifting through ownership statements to find them."

Windermere felt the electricity in the air evaporate. Felt, honestly, like she'd been punched in the stomach. "But you have the box coming into Trieste, right?" she asked. "So we just trace it back from there. Don't they have a record of where it came from?"

"You'd think so," LePlavy said, "but the EU customs officers only have what's on the manifest: one forty-foot container, owned by the aforementioned shell company, carrying . . ." He checked his notebook. "DVD players from the Czech Republic. Which we know is a lie, since your victim entered the box in Bucharest. Basically, this whole operation is a ghost before the box shows up in Trieste."

He gestured to the monitors. "What about the security footage?" he asked. "You guys find anything useful?"

"Nothing," Windermere said. "The box landed on a flatbed and drove off the lot. Disappeared into oblivion."

"We were hoping you'd get us our lead," Stevens said.

"I can get in touch with Interpol," LePlavy said. "Try and convince them to help me track down this chain of ownership. FinCEN, too, the Financial Crimes Enforcement Network, down in Virginia. Maybe they can open up some doors."

"These guys are human traffickers," Windermere said, her

frustration mounting. "Scum of the earth. Let's just go Patriot Act on their asses."

"We'll try," LePlavy told her. "Two numbered companies in two different offshore havens, though; it's going to take time."

Stevens met her eyes, and Windermere could tell he was thinking the same thing she was. *We have a whole box of women in danger, and probably more. Time is the last thing we can spare.*

48

BOGDAN URZICA FELT the truck slowing. He sat up, blinking, rubbing his eyes. "Where are we?" he asked Nikolai, peering out at the gloom.

Beside him, Nikolai steered the truck to a stop at the side of the road. They were off the highway, Bogdan realized. There was no light anywhere except for the headlights of the truck, piercing the darkness for thirty feet, illuminating a teeming swarm of bugs and nothing but a flat, single-lane blacktop beyond.

Nikolai shifted the truck out of gear, turned off the engine. "Quick stop," he told Bogdan. "I'm going to feed the bitch. You go back to sleep."

He opened the door and climbed down from the cab, and Bogdan closed his eyes again, basking in the warm air from Nikolai's open door. The night smelled like a farm, and Bogdan imagined he was back in the home country, a child, visiting his grandparents outside of the city. He'd imagined, once, that he'd like to work on a farm; it was a simple, honest life, anyway, and his grandparents seemed happy enough. Maybe he would purchase a farm someday, when he was finished running girls for Andrei Volovoi. After this trip, he could use a taste of something simpler.

> > >

WHEN HE OPENED HIS EYES again, fifteen minutes had passed. Nikolai was not in the truck; his door hung half open, and there were flies swarming into the cab. Bogdan sat up. "Shit."

He reached across the cab for Nikolai's door, couldn't reach it. He was about to slide across and slam the thing closed when an ugly thought crossed his mind.

What if the girl had escaped?

Her sister had done it. The girl had been right behind her. She could have felt the truck slowing and waited for Nikolai to open the door. Struck him on the head and run off into the night.

Shit, but the Dragon would kill them both.

Quickly, Bogdan opened his own door and climbed out of the truck and down to the road. Walked back along the shoulder to the end of the box. The door hung open. There was nobody there.

Drawing his weapon, he climbed into the back of the box. Stepped around the cardboard boxes to the little door to the false compartment. "Nikolai?"

Silence. Then, a girl's sobs.

Bogdan drew a flashlight from his belt and shined it into the dark compartment. The beam was weak and he couldn't see anything. He ducked through the little doorway and swung the flashlight again.

There, in the corner, a jumble of limbs and shadows. Nikolai on top of the girl, his tongue at her ear, his hand fumbling with the zipper of his jeans. He was laughing, muttering something, and the girl was crying and struggling beneath him. He'd torn her shirt, Bogdan saw. Forced her pants to her ankles. He intended to rape her.

Bogdan felt his anger rise. Nikolai, the fucking animal.

Bogdan slid his pistol back into his waistband. Then, his heart pounding in his temples, he crossed the compartment toward Nikolai and the girl.

49

NIKOLAI STRUGGLED WITH the girl. He hadn't noticed Bogdan yet, was fighting to keep the girl pinned while he fumbled with his jeans. Bogdan grabbed him by the shoulder. "Nikolai."

Nikolai snarled at him, shoved him aside. "Fuck off, Bogdan," he said. "I'm getting a taste of this little bitch."

"You're an idiot." Bogdan grabbed Nikolai again, harder this time, as the girl scuttled away into the corner. "The Dragon will kill us if he finds out."

"So he won't find out," Nikolai said. "Now fuck off and leave me to her."

Nikolai shoved him aside, staggered after the girl. Bogdan stood in his way. "*You* fuck off," he said. "Forget the girl."

Nikolai's eyes were wild, his mouth open, a rabid dog. "Get out of my way, Bogdan," he said. "Or I'll move you."

Bogdan stood fast. Stared him down.

Then Nikolai threw the punch. A roundhouse haymaker. It caught Bogdan off guard, though he knew he should have anticipated it. Knocked him staggering backward, across the compartment, knocked the flashlight away. With a snarl, Nikolai leapt for the little girl again.

Bogdan landed on his back, his head in a daze. Stood just as Nikolai reached the girl. Just as he pulled open his jeans. The girl screamed and crawled backward, but there was nowhere to go.

Bogdan drew his pistol. Crossed the compartment and pressed the weapon to the back of Nikolai's neck. "Enough," he said. "Now."

Nikolai stopped moving. Bogdan could feel the girl's eyes on him as the compartment went silent. "I hope you don't draw your weapon without intending to use it, Bogdan," Nikolai said slowly.

Bogdan held the gun steady. "Would you like to find out?"

Nikolai didn't respond for a moment. Then he pushed himself from the girl. "You wouldn't shoot me," he told Bogdan. "The Dragon would kill you."

"The Dragon would understand," Bogdan replied.

Nikolai studied him, panting heavily. The girl watched them both. Bogdan felt his jaw throbbing, ached to touch it. Knew as soon as he blinked, Nikolai would be on him.

An eternity passed. Finally, Nikolai shrugged. "Your turn to drive," he said, brushing past Bogdan and out of the compartment.

Bogdan waited until he heard his partner drop out of the back of the box. Then he retrieved his flashlight and hid the gun back in his waistband. The girl half sat, half lay on the floor in front of him, her clothing torn and askew. She watched him, her eyes serious.

Bogdan looked at her. "What?" he said.

She didn't say anything.

He waited, but she didn't speak. "Goddamn it," he said finally. "Fix yourself." Then he turned and walked out of the compartment.

50

CATALINA PULLED HER clothing together as best she could as the truck began to move again. The scar-faced monster had torn her shirt nearly in half, had ripped the buttons from her pants. Never mind that the clothes were dirtier than anything she'd ever seen in her life; now she had to clutch them about her like rags just to cover herself.

Still, the monster hadn't raped her. Catalina wondered if the man's friend would have shot him if he'd continued to try. If the man would kill his partner to protect her. The two men had argued in English, and she'd understood none of it. Had no idea why the other man had defended her.

He wants to keep you safe, she thought. *For wherever they're taking you.*

This was the logical answer, she knew. The thugs had kept her behind when every other woman was gone. They were saving her for something, somebody. The man without the scar knew it. The man with the scar didn't. Or he didn't care. It was that simple.

Still, she'd seen something in the other man's eyes when he looked at her. It wasn't just that he was doing his job. The man looked at her like she was human. His scar-faced friend looked at her like she was meat.

The truck rumbled on. Catalina sat in the darkness, clutching her clothes to her, wondering how long she would be left in here. Wondering what would be waiting for her when the truck finally stopped, and wondering how she could convince the man without the scar to protect her.

51

VOLOVOI STARED AT his phone. "Tried to rape her," he said. "And where the hell were you, Bogdan?"

On the other end of the phone, Bogdan Urzica didn't answer for a beat. "I was asleep," he said finally. "He said he was going to feed the girl. I had been driving all day, Andrei. I'm sorry."

Volovoi paced the sidewalk outside the restaurant. Through the windows, he could see Veronika and Adriana at a table, coloring with crayons as they ate their pizza. He'd driven out to Brighton Beach to meet them for lunch, take them off his sister's hands for a few hours. He had hoped, after another long night of spreadsheets and red ink, to escape from the headaches of his job for a while. He had hoped he could avoid thinking about business.

Only now, Nikolai Kirilenko was assaulting the merchandise.

"The Dragon wants that little girl for himself, Bogdan," Volovoi said. "He will kill us all if he doesn't get her. For Christ's sake, keep Nikolai off of her, okay?"

"I'll try," Bogdan told him, "but I have to sleep sometimes."

Volovoi closed his eyes. *Christ.*

"Where are you?" he said finally. "How long until you're here?"

"We're in Omaha," Bogdan told him. "A couple more days. We've been trying to be cautious, keep to the speed limit, keep off the main roads. After Club Heat—"

"Yes," Volovoi said. "Caution is good."

But the longer the little girl is out on the road, the greater the danger that something will happen to her, he thought. And Bogdan Urzica has already proved once that he is incapable of controlling Nikolai's urges. The dead cop in Minnesota can attest to that.

Volovoi looked in at his nieces again. Rubbed his eyes. In a day, he was to meet with the Dragon's buyer in Manhattan. Bogdan and Nikolai would still not be home. And who could predict what new stupidity Nikolai would invent in the meantime?

"Keep the little girl safe," Volovoi told Bogdan. "I will come out to meet you. I will take her off your hands, and I will deliver her myself to the Dragon. That way, we can both be assured that nothing will go wrong."

Bogdan considered this. "Okay," he said. "When will you meet?"

"Tomorrow evening," Volovoi told him. "I will drive out into Pennsylvania, Ohio. We'll meet, and I'll take the girl."

"Understood," Bogdan said. "And what about Nikolai?"

Volovoi turned from the window. Looked out across the parking lot. If the angle was right, he could just about see Manhattan in the distance. "I'll deal with Nikolai," he told Bogdan. "Just keep the girl safe."

52

ANDREI VOLOVOI KNEW he was a hypocrite.

He was a man who made his living stealing women, and selling them as though they were commodities. He'd paid for a Cadillac truck this way, a penthouse loft. He'd built a life in America—hell, he'd made the down payment on his sister's house, paid for the first year of Veronika's private school tuition. He made a good living, relatively speaking, and all of it thanks to the women in his boxes.

By rights, he should not have been able to sleep at night. By rights, he should not have been able to sit across from his young nieces in a Brighton Beach pizza parlor, watching them color their unicorn pictures and debating with them whether to have ice cream or brownies for dessert. By rights, Andrei Volovoi should have known he was a monster.

But Volovoi didn't think of himself as a monster. He was a criminal, sure, more or less amoral. He was a hard man in many ways; one had to be, to succeed in business in America. And Volovoi was a businessman. He was a man who could fill a void in the American marketplace, and anyone who could manage that deserved to get rich. The women who filled his boxes had written their own tickets. Mike hadn't kidnapped them. They'd been naive, and stupid, and they deserved their lot in life.

This is what Volovoi believed. This is how he rationalized his occupation on afternoons like this, with Adriana tugging his arm and asking for more juice, with Veronika teasing him, asking him when he was going to get a girlfriend. This is how he looked his nieces, his sister, in the eye.

This New York project, though, and this situation with Catalina Milosovici—hell, everything to do with the Dragon—it all rubbed Volovoi raw. These were girls—barely teenagers—the Dragon was selling. In a few years, Veronika could be one of these girls.

This was a different situation altogether. And now Volovoi had agreed to meet the Dragon's buyer, and in reality, there was only one answer the Dragon would accept. No matter how hard Volovoi worked to reduce his redundancies, the Dragon would always have his hand in Volovoi's wallet. And the only way to get him out was to join him in New York. To sell young girls.

"You're not terribly ugly, Uncle Andrei," Veronika was telling him. "How come you never meet any women?"

Volovoi tried to think of the last woman he'd taken to dinner. Couldn't. Saw Catalina Milosovici instead, pale and grimy in her photograph. Saw Veronika, instead, in her place. Adriana.

The best way to keep your nieces safe is to keep the Dragon happy, Volovoi thought. *And the best way to keep the Dragon happy is to join him in New York.*

Veronika cocked her head. "Uncle Andrei?"

So he would be a hypocrite. He would sell his soul. So be it. Volovoi turned away from Veronika, pretended to look out the window. "I am too busy at work," he said, hiding his eyes. "No time for a woman."

53

STEVENS AND WINDERMERE spent the night in Newark and flew home to the Twin Cities the next morning. Mathers was waiting for them in CID when they arrived. He had rings under his eyes; his clothes were rumpled, and he hadn't shaved. Windermere wondered if he'd spent the night at his desk.

Serves him right, she thought. *That'll teach him to ignore my instructions.*

"Carla." Mathers stood as they approached. "Kirk. Jesus Christ, I'm sorry. I—"

"Can it." Windermere breezed past him. "My office, Derek. Give us a status report."

Mathers hesitated, and Windermere forced herself not to turn back to him. She knew Mathers felt shitty. Hell, she felt sorry for him, knew he was hurt, knew she'd done it to him. She wanted to forgive the big lug, but she'd do it later. There were bigger issues right now.

Mathers followed her and Stevens into her office. Just as he closed the door, the phone rang. Agent Harris. "I need a progress report within the hour," he told her. "Get your shit in order."

"Yes, sir." She hung up the phone and turned back to Mathers. "Go."

"Okay." Mathers drew himself up. "I spent the night on the phone with a friend of yours from New Jersey, an Agent Zach LePlavy, who put me in touch with some people at Interpol. Apparently they know this Mike character Irina was talking about, the American guy who put her and Catalina in the box. They've been chasing him for years, but they've never been able to catch him."

"That's supposed to make me feel better, Derek?" Windermere said. "There's a girl's life at stake here."

"I'm working on it," Mathers said. "Interpol says this guy Mike deals with an importer they call the Dragon. Some shadowy underboss type, real bad reputation. They believe his name is Demetriou, Pavel Demetriou, but nobody has actually seen him for years. If Mike's the one selling women, though, they're going to this guy."

"The Dragon," Stevens said. "Can we get that back to LePlavy and his Organized Crime people? Maybe they know something."

"Already done. So far, no hits. Sounds like this guy's a bigger deal in Europe than he is over here."

"So basically, we have nothing," Windermere said. "That's what you're saying."

"We have the big boss man," Mathers said. "And maybe Interpol can—"

"We have a guy named 'the Dragon,'" Windermere said, "who nobody's ever seen. Big goddamn deal."

"We're working on it," Mathers said. "I lit some fires. Short of going over to Romania myself, I think I did all I could."

Maybe you should *go,* Windermere thought, but she held her tongue.

"Oh," Mathers said, reaching for a sheet of paper. "Interpol faxed over this." He handed the paper to Windermere. On it was the picture of Catalina Milosovici and the note that Mike had left for her parents. The girl was a smaller, dirtier copy of her sister, her eyes sunken, her skin pale. Windermere passed the picture to Stevens, who stared at it a long time without saying anything.

"What about Irina?" he asked finally. "Where do we stand with her?"

"She still wants to go," Mathers said. "She's terrified here, and that translator's telling her she doesn't have to stay. Which she doesn't, but why the hell would she want to leave?"

"Because you gave her that phone call," Windermere said. "And you scared the shit out of her."

Mathers winced. "Come on, Carla. I'm doing all I can here."

He looked across the room at her, and she quickly turned away. Couldn't stand to see him. *Anyone else,* she thought. *Anyone else makes this mistake and I tear them a new asshole and walk away satisfied. It* had *to be fucking Mathers.*

For a moment, nobody said anything. Then Stevens cleared his throat. "Let's see if we can't convince Irina to stick around at least," he said, glancing at the picture of Catalina again. "Try and keep this situation from getting any worse."

54

"SO HERE'S THE thing," Stevens told his wife. "Irina Milosovici called home, as was her legal right. Got ahold of her parents, who told her that some gangsters had come by with a picture of her sister, and had cut up her dog as a warning."

He'd dropped in on Nancy at work, figured maybe his wife could help him navigate the legal issues around Irina's sudden desire for freedom.

"My God," Nancy said. "But that means Catalina's alive at least, right?"

"We think so," Stevens said. "I mean, the implication of the warning was that if Irina continued to cooperate with us, the traffickers—we think the boss is this guy called the Dragon—would hurt her sister."

"The Dragon, huh?" Nancy said. "He sounds cuddly."

"I guess it doesn't change much," Stevens said. "We're still looking for a way to find Catalina. But in the meantime, the parents want Irina home. We, obviously, don't want her to leave. But legally, we're not sure we can keep her."

Nancy thought it over. "I think, legally, she can walk if she wants," she said. "If I were her lawyer, I'd certainly advise her to stay put, but if she wants to pack it in, the government isn't going to want to detain her, no matter how many murders she's witnessed. She calls the consulate, it's an international incident."

"Yeah," Stevens said. "That's what we're afraid of."

"You want her to stay. Her parents want her to go." Nancy looked at him. "What does she want?"

"She wants to get out of FBI custody. Wants to get out there and find Catalina."

"What, just set off on her own?" Nancy grimaced. "Well, she obviously can't do that, Kirk. Let me talk to her."

> > >

IRINA MILOSOVICI SAT IN A holding cell, staring at the walls and trying not to think about Catalina. It wasn't working.

You did this, she thought. *You doomed your own sister. You need to get out of here and go and save her yourself.*

Footsteps down the hall. Irina stiffened. There were guards outside, more big American policemen with bulletproof vests and guns. More potential threats, more risks. More men she would never be able to trust.

But when the door swung open, it wasn't the devil-faced man or a terrifying policeman, but Kirk Stevens and his beautiful wife. Maria followed them in, stood between Irina and the Stevenses like a protective parent.

Nancy Stevens said something to Maria. "They want to talk to you," Maria told Irina. "The woman says you don't have to talk if you don't want to."

Irina looked at Nancy Stevens and her husband. The police agent looked tired. He looked anxious. Irina felt sorry for him. He was only now realizing how outmatched he was.

"Will they let me out of here?" Irina asked.

Maria relayed the question. Nancy glanced at Stevens. Pulled up a chair and sat beside Irina, her elbows on her knees. "Here's what we know," she said, as Maria translated. "The man who has Catalina is a gangster named . . ." She turned to her husband again.

"Pavel Demetriou," Stevens said. "Also known as 'The Dragon.'"

"The Dragon," Nancy said.

Irina frowned. "Why are you telling me this?"

"We're telling you because we want you to know what we're dealing with, Irina," Nancy said. "We believe this Dragon man used his contact in Romania to give your parents the warning."

"Mike." Irina felt her breath catch. "My parents said his letter swore they wouldn't hurt Catalina if I just kept my mouth shut and went home."

"They were lying," Nancy said. "You think they're just going to forget about you? You know too much, Irina."

Nancy reached out, touched her arm. "You don't have to talk to us," she said. "You don't have to say anything if you think it will risk Catalina's life. But if you leave, Irina, we can't protect you, and chances are you'll die. And if you die, they'll probably kill Catalina, too."

Nancy's eyes were kind, her expression sympathetic. She was right, Irina knew, and she hung her head and said nothing.

"I can get you out of this cell," Nancy said. "Into a halfway house, with plenty of protection. You can talk to your family and go outside if you want to, and in the meantime, my husband and his partners will bust their humps searching for Catalina. Just promise me you won't run away."

Irina looked around the holding cell. Imagined a warm bed, a shower. Knew the traffickers would have her killed as soon as she returned to Berceni. Her parents, too, probably. Knew she'd never get far in America on her own.

Irina looked up at Nancy, at Agent Stevens, at Maria. "No men," she said. "Please. Not even policemen."

"No men," Nancy said. "I promise."

55

"I DON'T GET IT." Windermere said. "So the girl's still not talking? What did we accomplish here, Stevens?"

Stevens watched the electronic floor numbers flash by above him as the elevator climbed. "She's staying put," he said. "Nancy's moving her to a halfway house under U.S. Marshal supervision, and in return, she promised not to flee the country or go underground."

"Yeah, but she's not talking," Windermere said. "So what?"

"So she's still here, I guess," Stevens said. "We can keep working on Irina while we search for Catalina. And in the meantime, the Dragon doesn't kill her."

"Great." Windermere rolled her eyes. "This sounds like a really good deal for Irina Milosovici, Stevens. But it doesn't do jack shit for us. How are we going to save this girl's sister if she won't help us?"

Stevens leaned against the wall. "Yeah," he said. "When you put it that way."

"It sounds pretty damn slim, doesn't it?" she said. "We need something better."

The elevator doors slid open. Stevens and Windermere walked out into the FBI's Criminal Investigative bullpen and across to Mathers's cubicle, where the junior agent was just hanging up his phone.

"Where do we stand with Interpol?" Windermere asked him.

"Stevens here just undid the damage you caused with Irina and bought us a little time, Derek, but we need leads to work with. So I hope that was a long-distance call."

Mathers scribbled something on a notepad. "It *was* a long-distance call," he said. "But not to where you're thinking. Agent LePlavy and I are still tag-teaming with Interpol and the Financial Crimes guys. In the meantime, maybe you can do something with this."

He handed her the notepad. Windermere took it. "What is it?"

"Anonymous tip made to the field office in Billings, Montana," Mathers said. "Guess someone called in, said they saw those sketches we sent out of Irina's bad guys."

Stevens felt his heart syncopate. "They made the drivers."

"That's right," Mathers said. "The scar-faced thug and his buddy both. The tipster said both guys came into his restaurant, parked their big truck in his lot. Said they had heavy accents and they didn't talk much, but they ate sandwiches and kept checking their watches." Mathers paused, his smile growing. "Said he overheard something they said just before they paid the bill. Something about needing to go meet the buyer."

"Billings, Montana," Windermere said. "That must be where they were headed after Duluth."

"It's a straight shot down I-90," Stevens said. "It makes sense."

"I'll say it does." Windermere grinned at Stevens. "I'll book us a flight, partner. You go pack another suitcase. We'll hit Billings tomorrow."

56

THERE WAS A teenage boy sitting in Stevens's living room when he returned from Brooklyn Center. The kid was sprawled out on the couch, watching some kind of gross-out teen comedy, soda cans and empty potato chip bags everywhere. He sat up quickly when Stevens walked in.

"Oh, hi," he said. "You're Mr. Stevens."

The boy was Andrea's age, tall and skinny, his hair sandy blond. He wore flower-print shorts and a faux-vintage tee, a typical teenager, and he blushed and shifted his weight and looked away quickly when he caught Stevens's eye.

"Dad?" Andrea Stevens poked her head in from the kitchen. "Hey," she said, hurrying into the living room and picking up the garbage from the couch. "Hi. You're home early. We're just watching a movie. I'm making some lunch. Are you hungry?"

Stevens regarded his daughter, then her companion. "Am I to assume this is Calvin?"

Andrea blushed bright red. *"Dad."*

"Calvin Tanner," the kid said, holding out his hand. "It's good to finally meet you, Mr. Stevens. Andrea said you were away on business?"

"I was." Stevens shook the kid's hand. "I will be again shortly."

"You're a cop, Andrea said?"

Andrea was still blushing. "A BCA agent, I said."

"So what are you working on?" Calvin asked. "Anything crazy? Andrea said you hunt down crazy bad guys, like that guy from our school, Tomlin. That was you, right? What are you working on now?"

"Nothing so crazy," Stevens said. "Where's your brother?" he asked Andrea.

"At Greg's house," she said. "I think they went swimming or something. Are you going away again?"

He nodded. "Tomorrow probably. Billings, Montana."

"It has to do with that woman? From up north?"

"It does," he said.

"Cool." She shifted her weight. "Okay, so you met him, Dad. Can I have some privacy now?"

Stevens looked at her. At Calvin. At the TV, where a man in a diaper was running through a shopping mall. Calvin glanced at the TV and then grinned up at him, sheepish. "It was sure nice to meet you, Mr. S."

Mr. S., Stevens thought, as he went upstairs to pack. *Can I have some privacy, Dad?*

Maybe he was romanticizing things a little, but Stevens figured it wasn't so long ago that his daughter would have run to the door to greet him, would have begged him to tell her all about his new case. Hell, she'd even started talking about becoming a cop herself. Now, his biggest case yet, and all she cared about was a little privacy with Calvin.

Kids these days, Stevens thought. *No wonder Nancy's frustrated.*

57

ACROSS TOWN, Carla Windermere stared at Derek Mathers across her living room and wondered how she was supposed to feel.

On the one hand, the guy had screwed up her investigation, the biggest damn case she'd ever worked. He'd made a dumb mistake and nearly scared Irina Milosovici back to Romania, and even now Windermere figured the odds the girl would do any more serious cooperating were long, long, *long*.

But he'd apologized for it. He'd spent the night at his desk, busted his ass with Interpol, and managed to dig up a damn solid lead. To-morrow, if there was any justice in the world, she and Stevens would track down another buyer in Billings, while Mathers and LePlavy pinpointed the identity of the shipper who'd imported the Milosovi-cis' container. Her colleague had done good.

Even so, Windermere kind of hated him.

"I said I'm sorry, Carla," he told her from the window. "I said it a hundred times, it was an honest mistake. What am I supposed to do about it?"

"You should have known better," she said. "I told you to wait until Stevens and I got back, and you didn't listen. You just have to be smarter."

Mathers flinched, and she knew she'd touched a nerve. "I guess I'm just a big dumbass, huh?"

She closed her eyes. "Come on, Derek."

"Just a big dumb lug. That's what you call me, right?" He glared at her. "Guess I finally proved you right."

"Derek—" She approached him, but he turned away.

"This is stupid," he said. "It was a bad idea to begin with, us hooking up. We work together. Something like this happens and it all goes to shit."

"It wouldn't have happened if—" She caught herself too late.

"If I hadn't fucked up, Carla, yeah, I know. If I wasn't the department meathead." He sighed. "Look, the point is, I don't even know what we're doing anymore. Even before I fucked up your case."

"*Our* case," she said.

"Whatever. It's *your* case, Carla. You and Stevens."

"*Please* don't bring Stevens into this."

"Well?" he said. "You've always been hung up on him, Carla, even while you're hooking up with me. I don't even know why I bother." He turned to leave, brushed past her. "I should go."

Windermere followed him to the door. "Don't go," she said, and knew she meant it. "Just forget it, Derek. I'm sorry. I'm an asshole."

"Don't be sorry," he told her, one hand on the doorknob, his blue eyes dark. "It makes you a hell of an agent anyway."

Then he walked out, and the door slammed closed, leaving Windermere standing alone in her little entryway, feeling like, however she was supposed to be feeling about the situation, this wasn't it.

58

BOGDAN URZICA RUBBED his jaw as he piloted the big Peterbilt into the outskirts of Chicago. Beside him, Nikolai chuckled in the passenger seat.

"That will teach you to get in between a man and his woman, Bogdan," he said, smirking across the cab at his partner.

In the driver's seat, Bogdan said nothing. He still hurt from the haymaker Nikolai had thrown at him, and he'd driven all night on minimal sleep, replaying his conversation with Andrei Volovoi in his head.

"I mean, seriously," Nikolai continued. "I was only trying to get to know her better. Test her out for the Dragon. Quality control, do you know what I mean?"

Bogdan ignored his partner. Kept his eyes on the road as the highway widened, a collection of warehouses and train tracks and truck-stop motels peeking through the trees. He watched a highway patrol cruiser approach in an oncoming lane, held his breath until it had passed. There were sketches on the news now, Bogdan knew. His face and Nikolai's, too. The truck was a liability. The police would be hunting for it.

I'll deal with Nikolai, Andrei had promised.

Nikolai leaned over and spat brown tobacco juice into his ubiquitous Big Gulp cup. "You are such a princess, Bogdan," he said. "Do you really think the Dragon is going to give you a gold star for bringing him his little bitch?"

Bogdan wondered if Nikolai could sense his apprehension. "We will not be delivering the little girl to the Dragon," he said. "Andrei is coming. He will take her off our hands tonight."

"He's coming out *here*?"

"To meet us," Bogdan told him. "He will take the girl himself. It's too risky to leave her with us."

Nikolai said nothing for a moment. Studied the road. Then he laughed. "You pussies," he said. "You're all so afraid of that fucking Dragon."

"And you're not?" Bogdan said.

"No, Bogdan," Nikolai said, "I'm not. He's an ugly punk with a terrible beard. Let him come for me. I will shave that beard off of him."

Nikolai laughed, that ugly, terrible laugh. Bogdan said nothing. Just drove.

"Let Andrei Volovoi come for the girl," Nikolai said finally. "The little bitch stinks anyway; he can have her."

"I'm sure he will be happy to have your permission," Bogdan said.

"We'll hand the girl over tonight," Nikolai said. "Andrei will pay us. Then we'll find a steak and somebody to fuck us, Bogdan, what do you say?"

Bogdan said nothing. Kept driving. *You're already fucked, Nikolai,* he thought. *It's only a matter of time.*

59

NANCY STEVENS GESTURED into the sunny little room and smiled and said something in English. Behind Irina, Maria began to translate, but Irina waved her off. She understood the American well enough.

It was a nice little bedroom, with a twin bed and a writing desk and a closet with a handful of droopy wire hangers. The curtains were dusty, and the walls were bare, but it was better than a prison cell—or that fetid box. It was, Irina understood, her new home.

"It's a house for battered women," Nancy Stevens had explained, through Maria, on the drive over. "Many of them are new to America, like you. It's very safe. It's communal. A way to help you feel like a human being again."

A human being. Irina had wondered how she could feel anything close to normal ever again with Catalina still missing. She couldn't imagine ever feeling safe on the streets, couldn't picture a night without terror and that paralyzing guilt. But she'd followed Nancy anyway, up the front steps of the facility—a shabby old house in a quiet neighborhood—and into the lobby, where a friendly, middle-aged woman had written Irina's name on a clipboard, and a handful of other hollow-eyed women had lingered like wraiths, watching her.

Her English was still rotten. Maria wouldn't be around, not all the time, but Nancy Stevens wasn't dissuaded. "You'll pick it up quickly," she said. "The staff here can help you, and if you ever do need her, Maria's just a phone call away. So am I, for that matter."

"My sister," Irina said.

Nancy's smile didn't waver. "My husband's making progress," she said. "Believe me, if anyone can find her, it's Kirk. In the meantime, you just take it easy and try to relax, okay?"

Irina wondered how the woman could be so optimistic. If it was an American thing, this relentless positivity. *Your lives are so easy,* she thought. *Big-screen TVs, movie stars, McDonald's hamburgers. Of course you're happy; you've never seen hardship.*

But that was mean. Nancy Stevens was trying to help her, and if Irina had to be anywhere while she waited to find out Catalina's fate, it might as well be here. She sat on the bed, tested the mattress. Met Nancy's eye and nodded. "I can stay here."

"Sure you can." Nancy pulled back the curtains and gestured out the window. "Come see."

Maria translated, and Irina joined Nancy at the window. Followed her gaze to the dark American sedan parked across the street, the two men inside.

"The marshals are staying," Nancy said. "They'll be watching the house day and night, to protect you."

Irina pictured the men inside the dark sedan. They'd been kind enough on the drive to the house, quiet and deferential. But she had been terrified of them nonetheless.

"And if you ever feel worried, or anxious, or anything . . ." Nancy took a business card from her pocket. "Day or night, okay?"

She winked at Irina. "I'll work on my Romanian." She hugged Irina quickly, shocking the hell out of her, and then waved good-bye from the door. Irina waved back, forced a smile, waited as Nancy and Maria closed the door behind them. Then she walked to the bed, lay down and stared up at the ceiling, and thought about Catalina and Nancy Stevens, and hoped the pretty American's faith in her husband was well placed.

60

THE CLIENT WAS a short man, narrow and nearly bald. He was among the richest men in Manhattan. He was also a pervert, and knew plenty more of the same.

"Blondes," he told Volovoi, leaning across the table. "That's my taste, personally. There's something about a pretty young blonde that just—" He laughed and cut a piece of his steak. "Well, you know what I mean."

Volovoi looked around the restaurant, at the skyscrapers outside the windows, and struggled to calm his queasy stomach. Beside him, the Dragon appeared far more at peace. *This is the man who will make us both rich,* his expression seemed to read. *This is the only way you'll survive.*

"We can supply blondes," the Dragon said. "Can't we, Andrei?"

Volovoi glanced at the Dragon. Then at the client. "We have plenty of blondes," he said slowly.

"Plenty of blondes," the Dragon repeated. "What did I tell you, Lloyd? Do your friends share your tastes?"

Lloyd shrugged. "Hell, they like all kinds," he said, chewing. "I don't exactly keep a database." He grinned back at the Dragon. "But I know they like them young. The younger the better."

The Dragon laughed. "But of course."

"There are thousands of beautiful women in this city, and all of them can be bought," Lloyd said. "Not so much if your tastes skew below the age of the average college freshman."

"Young is no problem," the Dragon told him. "Young is our specialty. We can supply women as young as you and your friends desire, can't we, Andrei?"

Volovoi thought about his family. Thought about the lines of red numbers in his accounting spreadsheets. Thought about the Dragon's wolfish smile, his outstretched hand. The thousands of dollars that bled from the operation directly into the Dragon's accounts every month.

You were stupid, he told himself. *You were played. This is what the Dragon wanted from you all along. Your name on the lease. Your face on the franchise. Your neck in the noose if anything goes wrong.*

And his hand in the cash register as the money piles up. As the girls arrive for sick bastards like this.

You were played, Andrei Volovoi. Like a mouse in a trap. And there isn't a damn thing you can do about it now.

The client was studying him. So was the Dragon. "We can do young," Volovoi said, forcing the reluctance from his voice. "So long as the price is agreeable."

Lloyd took another bite of his steak. "Of course," he said. "Let's talk numbers."

Volovoi looked out the window again. The restaurant sat high atop a midtown skyscraper; far below, the city bustled and blared with midday traffic. Up here, though, the air was calm, the restaurant soothing and airy and quiet. This was privilege. This was wealth. Volovoi felt as comfortable here as he would at the bottom of the ocean. He did not belong. He would never belong. And he was sure that everyone in the restaurant could see it.

"Two hundred thousand," the Dragon told Lloyd. "Minimum opening bid. We will negotiate on a per-case basis from there."

Lloyd pursed his lips. The Dragon waited. Even Volovoi held his breath. Two hundred thousand per girl was a significant upgrade. Even if the Dragon continued to demand his percentages, there was no way that Volovoi wouldn't get rich.

Forty girls in a box at two hundred thousand a girl meant eight million dollars a shipment. Surely, the Dragon had been greedy. There was no way that Lloyd would agree.

But then the client nodded. "Two hundred sounds reasonable," he said. "My contacts shouldn't have a problem with that kind of ballpark."

"Perfect." The Dragon turned to Volovoi. "Then I'd say we're in business. All right, Andrei?"

Volovoi pretended to stall, though he already knew his answer. At this price point, there was no way he could decline. Not with the Dragon's claws so tight around his neck. Not with his operation at the brink of failure.

"Cash up front," he said finally. "Wired overseas."

The Dragon laughed. Lloyd smiled. Even Volovoi let himself exhale.

"There is a shipment arriving in two days," the Dragon told Lloyd. "I will make sure Andrei has the merchandise ready for you as soon as possible."

"Perfect," Lloyd said. "And no pressure from the authorities, I assume? You run a clean operation?"

"Perfectly clean," the Dragon said. "We take care of any issues quickly and with finality. Right, Andrei?"

Volovoi thought about the FBI insects. About Bogdan's and Nikolai's faces on the news. He would have to kill them both, he realized. The Manhattan expansion was the big leagues. Both men were now liabilities.

"I run an airtight operation," he told Lloyd. "Your contacts are safe."

"A couple of days, then." Lloyd reached for a bottle from the bucket that waited tableside. Then he winked at Volovoi. "Champagne?"

61

BILLINGS, MONTANA.

Stevens and Windermere sat in an unmarked FBI Tahoe, staring out at a grungy brick building a block from the railroad yards as their driver, a local field agent named Fast, worked the Billings PD for backup.

The building was unremarkable, a little box with no ornamentation, blacked-out windows, and a solid-steel door. There was a black E-series cargo van parked in the alley alongside the place, a black hole in the shadows as the last light of day slipped away. The Blue Room, the place was called, and if their information was correct, this was where Irina Milosovici's traffickers had sold their last group of women.

Windermere shivered. "Men," she said. "Bring a girl to a place like this and the last thing she's thinking about is getting her rocks off. But a guy will chase tail anywhere, I guess."

"Hey now," Stevens said.

She snorted. "Sorry," she said. "You're a paragon of virtue, Stevens. The last decent man."

Stevens looked out at the building again. "Tell that to my daughter," he said.

> > >

THEY'D ARRIVED IN BILLINGS THAT morning. Met Agent Fast in the airport parking lot, spent the first half of the day visiting strip clubs and massage parlors and combing for leads. It wasn't until Fast suggested lunch, though, that they'd caught their break—a pretty young waitress who overheard the conversation, caught Windermere telling Fast she wasn't really interested in visiting any more strip clubs.

"I mean, naked girls are nice and all," Windermere was saying, "but we're not looking for lap dances right now. This is sex trafficking. We want girls who aren't exactly happy to find themselves in Billings, scenic though it may be."

"You want the Blue Room," the waitress said. She was a younger woman, pretty, a shy smile on her face. Amy, her name tag said. "At least that's what I hear."

Windermere slid a chair out beside Fast. "Set those plates down a minute, Amy," she said. "Why don't you have a seat."

Amy hesitated. Then she sat. Then, blushing bright red, she told them what she knew.

"I only heard about this from my boyfriend." The waitress looked around at Stevens and Windermere and Fast. "And it's not like he, you know, goes there. He just knows about it from some guys at work."

"No problem," Windermere said. "Just tell us what you know about this place. The Blue Room, you said. It's a bar?"

Amy shook her head. "It's not, like, anything, I don't think. That's not even its real name. They just call it the Blue Room because it's a blue room where they keep the girls."

"The girls," Stevens said. "Dancers?"

"Hookers," Amy said. "At least that's what Erik—my boyfriend—heard from his buddy. I guess it's like a brothel or something, five or six girls in a house somewhere, and none of them speak any English."

"Sounds like our spot," said Windermere. "So where is this place?"

Amy shrugged. "It's not like Erik told me everything. Anyway, he never went there."

"But his buddy did," Windermere said. "What did you say his name was?"

Amy went red. Looked around the diner. "Oh, darn it."

62

AMY'S BOYFRIEND'S BUDDY was a guy named Collins, a new father with an old pickup truck. Stevens and Windermere met him on his front stoop, convinced him he'd be better off talking right now, informal, rather than causing a scene in front of his young wife.

"It was just the one time," he said after bumming a smoke from Fast. "I mean, I knew it was stupid, but a couple guys said the place was cool. Said, like, you could get whatever you wanted there. *Whatever* you wanted, and the price was all right. I mean, I dunno, I got curious."

"With your wife being tied up with the baby and all," Windermere said. "I bet she didn't have much time left over to pay attention to you, huh?"

Collins winced. "I knew it was stupid," he said. "Look, what's the big deal, anyway? They bring in the FBI to investigate prostitution now?"

"Prostitution? No. Sex trafficking? You bet."

"Oh, shit." Collins looked back at the door. "Nobody told me those girls were—you're saying—"

"Reason why the price was all right," Windermere said. "Those girls weren't seeing a dime. So why don't you tell us all you can about the Blue Room?" She looked him in the eye. "Start with where we can find it."

63

NOW STEVENS AND Windermere waited outside the Blue Room. Fifteen minutes passed. The backup arrived, two squad cars with Billings PD markings.

"Tell them to wait somewhere inconspicuous," Stevens told Fast. "Out of sight. And make sure they're ready to move when we need them."

Fast relayed the message. "Let's wait this thing out a little longer," Windermere said. "See if anybody wants action tonight."

They waited. The cruisers drifted away, and darkness settled around them. A long freight train rumbled out of town. Windermere stared out the window, her breathing so slow and steady she almost sounded asleep. Then she straightened. "First contestant."

A pair of headlights up the block, idling toward the railroad yard and the parked Tahoe. The headlights ran a stop sign a street away, slowed outside the brick building and stayed there, in the middle of the road, an old Pontiac Bonneville, a boat of a car. The driver didn't move behind the wheel, just sat in place for a minute or two.

"*Go on,*" Windermere whispered. "*Get in there and get you a girl, cowboy.*"

The driver let off the brake and the Bonneville idled to the curb and parked. The driver was a man, medium height, his face hidden by darkness. He walked around the car and up the sidewalk to the brick building and the plain steel door. Glanced back at the Bonneville once and then knocked.

The door swung open. There was nothing behind it but shadows. No bad guys. No girls. Just darkness, tinged a faint hint of blue.

"Looks like a blue room to me," Windermere said, reaching for the door handle. "Let's check it out."

> > >

THEY CROSSED THE STREET TO the grungy brick building and the featureless steel door. Beside the door were two blacked-out windows. On the second floor, three more.

Windermere rapped on the door and listened to the sound reverberate. She'd worked a murder at an underground poker game a couple years back. It went down in a warehouse complex, a nondescript little building with a roll-up door and a steel door like this. There was a security camera up top, to keep out the riffraff, though it hadn't done its job that night. This place didn't have a security camera. But nobody was coming to answer the door.

She knocked again. Waited. No answer. "You want to watch the door while I check around back?" she asked Stevens.

Stevens looked across the front of the building, then back at Fast. Windermere snorted. "You afraid a girl can't go into the shadows by herself?" she said. "You check the back, then. Assuming you're not afraid of the dark."

"Terrified." Stevens walked down to the sidewalk and started toward the alley. Then he stopped. "Carla," he said, staring up at the building. "Come here."

Something in his voice made Windermere tense. She followed

him to the sidewalk, followed his gaze to the three windows on the building's second floor. Sucked in her breath when she saw it.

Two of the windows were completely blacked out. The third showed a slim triangle of light in the bottom corner, a sheet turned back. From inside the triangle, a woman's face peered out. A girl, more like it. Her face was mostly shadow, but where the light hit, she looked gaunt. Bruised. Hollow-eyed.

The girl met Windermere's eye, and Windermere felt a sudden anger well up in her chest. "Come on," she told Stevens, reaching for her Glock. "Let's go see who's running this shithole."

64

WINDERMERE HURRIED BACK up to the Blue Room's door as Stevens ran for the Tahoe to rouse Fast. She drew her Glock, her heart already racing, and pounded on the steel door. *"FBI. Open this door."*

She wondered what she would do if the bastards didn't want to come out. Wondered if she could restrain herself. A girl's face in a window was hardly probable cause, and the waitress's boyfriend's buddy's testimony wasn't enough for a search warrant. But she couldn't walk away now, not after seeing that girl's face.

She beat on the door again, still mulling her options, when someone inside rendered the whole debate moot. With a shotgun. There was a *BOOM* like thunder and a front window exploded.

Windermere dove to the ground, looked back and saw Stevens stagger backward, and for a brief, horrible moment, she thought he'd been hit. Then he pulled himself upright, yelled something to Fast, and bolted for the building.

Somewhere nearby, sirens spooled up. Engines roared. The cruisers flew down the block and screamed to a stop in front of the building. The shotgun boomed again, blowing out the other window. Inside, women screamed. More glass shattered. Stevens was crouched beside the first window, his gun drawn. The windows yawned open, their light alien blue. This was the Blue Room, all right. This was someone's last stand.

Windermere shouted back to the Billings PD uniforms, told them to contain the building from the back. Was about to call out to Stevens when the steel door flew open. Windermere swung at it with her Glock, nearly blew a hole through a terrified blond girl in a cheap negligee as she came booking out the doorway for the sidewalk. Windermere lowered her gun, caught the girl. Ducked her head and dragged her, screaming, to Fast.

"Watch her, goddamn it," she told the Billings agent. "And call for more backup."

The doorway loomed now, wide open. More women's screams from inside. There was no time to wait. Windermere ran for the doorway, heard Stevens fall in step behind.

> > >

STEVENS FOLLOWED WINDERMERE into the building, his heart pounding. Inside, the Blue Room was chaos: overturned threadbare furniture, dim blue light and gun smoke, panic and pornographic posters and a maddening soundtrack of heavy rock music. Nobody in sight.

Ahead of Stevens, Windermere took up a Weaver stance and crept into the room, her back to the wall, her Glock aimed at a doorway marked by gauzy curtains, and the stairway that led to the upper floor of the brothel. The screaming was coming from upstairs.

Windermere motioned at the row of curtains. Covered the doorway as Stevens circled around. At her signal, he pulled the curtain aside and ducked back, ready for the shotgun.

Nothing.

The curtain opened onto a slim corridor. A couple doorways facing toward the street, another blacked-out window at the end, this one intact. Both doors opened inward; both were open. Stevens checked the first room, found a tiny bedroom just large enough for a single bed and a makeup table. A rack of skimpy costumes in a tiny closet. The window was blown out, revealing the street and the cruisers beyond. There was nobody inside.

Stevens covered Windermere as she checked the second room. Identical, and just as empty. The rock music throbbed somewhere overhead. They crept back out to the Blue Room's antechamber.

Footsteps on the staircase, fast and urgent. Stevens swung around with his sidearm, found another terrified woman running for the exit. The shotgun boomed down from behind her, obliterating a lamp and a poster of the '98 Playmate of the Year. More footsteps now, heavier—work boots on wooden stairs. The guy made it halfway down before he noticed Stevens and Windermere. He was a big guy, middle-aged, a red beard. He swore and swung the shotgun around, and Stevens shot him without thinking, reflexive. The guy gasped, dropped the shotgun. Tumbled down the stairs and landed in a heap at the bottom.

The whole room seemed to pause. The shooter didn't move. Stevens trained his Glock on him as Windermere crossed to the guy, kicked the shotgun away. Looked up the stairwell and then back at Stevens. "Nice shooting, partner," she said. "That guy would have splattered us."

Stevens leaned against the wall. Tried to catch his breath. "Gotta be more of them."

"You wanna check the second floor?"

"Sure," he said.

She looked him over. "You okay?"

Before he could answer, another scream from upstairs. This one more urgent, a desperate plea. Stevens started up the stairs. "Let's go."

They hurried up the staircase, as stealthily as they could. Stevens led this time, made the top of the stairs and swung around, getting his bearings.

Another long corridor. More doorways. Red light up here, and more awful rock music, more X-rated posters on the walls. The lingering scent of sex and sweat and marijuana smoke. The first door was open. The screams came from inside.

Stevens crept across the hall to the doorway. There was a girl in the room, he saw, the same one they'd seen from the street. She was young, sixteen or seventeen, no more than a child, her face bruised and tearstained, her skin pale. She wore pigtails and heavy makeup and a child's white underwear. There was a man with her, his back to Stevens. He struggled with her, swearing, fighting to hold on to her.

The girl screamed again. Tore away. The man slapped her and

something triggered in Stevens, and he was inside the room before he realized it had happened, crossing the floor toward the man and the girl, his blood like a bass beat in his ears. The girl saw him coming, betrayed him with wide eyes, and the man spun around, raising a pistol.

It happened in milliseconds. The man reached for the girl with his free hand, wrapped his meaty forearm around her neck, and pulled her closer. Brought his pistol to aim with the other hand. Stevens locked eyes with the girl, froze for just a moment. Just long enough for the bastard to get a shot off.

Then Stevens shot back. Windermere, too. The guy dropped the girl and went staggering backward. Hit the wall and slumped down to the floor as the girl crawled away, sobbing. Windermere rushed the shooter, kicked his pistol away, as Stevens reached for the girl.

He wanted to comfort her, tell her she was safe now. Knew he should get her out of the building to safety, knew there might be more gunmen. He couldn't move, though. Couldn't breathe. Felt like he'd been kicked square in the chest. He brought his hand to his shirt, felt the torn fabric. Tried to exhale and coughed instead, violent. Windermere looked back at him. "Oh," she said. "Oh, shit."

Stevens made a face. "Goddamn it, Carla," he said. "I think the bastard shot me."

65

VOLOVOI DROVE WEST in the morning, aimed his Escalade out of Manhattan and along I-80 across New Jersey. Called Bogdan Urzica on his cell phone when he crossed the Pennsylvania line.

"It's me," he told the driver. "Where are you?"

Bogdan's voice was fuzzy with fatigue. "Just outside Toledo," he said. "We hit traffic through Chicago."

"The girl is okay?" Volovoi asked him.

"She's fine," Bogdan said. "I fed her a couple hours ago. She's still breathing. No further problems."

"Excellent," Volovoi said. He glanced across the Escalade at the AAA road atlas he'd picked up when he'd stopped to fill the Cadillac's tank. "I am coming to get her," he said. "We will meet in Hermitage, on the Ohio-Pennsylvania state line. Call me when you're close and I'll give you your instructions."

"Hermitage," Bogdan said. "The state line. We'll be there."

"Excellent," Volovoi said again. He shifted the road map in the passenger seat. Underneath was his pistol, a .45 caliber Beretta, sleek and black and deadly. "I'll be waiting."

❯ ❯ ❯

VOLOVOI DROVE ACROSS PENNSYLVANIA through the morning, sharing the interstate with long-distance truckers and tour buses, the odd state patrol cruiser lurking on the shoulder. He drank coffee and loaded and reloaded the pistol on the passenger seat, and he thought about Bogdan Urzica and Nikolai Kirilenko, and about his meeting with the Dragon.

So he would expand into New York after all. He would sell girls to rich perverts, instead of women to country bumpkins. What, in the end, was the difference? Volovoi knew he should be happy. No longer would he be enslaved to the Dragon. No longer would he stock his shitty New Jersey loft with a collection of drug-abusing idiots. He would move up in the world. He would be rich, soon enough.

Still, though. To this point in his career, Volovoi had succeeded in convincing himself that the young women he imported to America deserved what fates befell them. They were stupid, greedy bitches, too naive to recognize the hustle. They were adults; they'd made adult decisions. It was their own fault if they fell into Mike's trap.

Children, though? Volovoi knew that the American wouldn't gather up the girls for the New York buyers the same way he tricked Andrei Volovoi's women. No thirteen-year-old schoolgirl would fall for Mike's tricks, his promises about movie stars and magazine shoots and expensive, fancy cars. Mike would have to find the children some other way. He wouldn't leave them a choice.

Volovoi knew he was splitting hairs. He knew he was a hypocrite, and that all of the self-justification in the world couldn't rationalize how he paid for his Cadillac. The Dragon wanted children, and children would make Andrei Volovoi very rich.

Still, though, it gnawed at him.

He drove until he reached the interchange at Hermitage in the midafternoon, just miles from the Ohio border. Pulled off the interstate and drove south, away from the town, down a lonely, two-lane country road, until he came across an abandoned gas station.

It was an unremarkable little spot. A couple broken pumps and the cinder-block building, the windows boarded up or smashed in, nothing but shadows inside. There was a small garage tacked on to the building, one work bay and a broken door, the ground within littered with garbage and detritus.

Volovoi backed the Escalade into the garage, as far back as he could go. The Cadillac was sleek and black; it disappeared in the shadows. He took the pistol from the passenger seat and tucked it in his waistband. Pulled out his cell phone again and called Bogdan Urzica.

"Are you close, Bogdan?" he said when the driver picked up. "Here is where you will meet me."

66

BOGDAN URZICA'S HEART pounded as he slowed the Peterbilt at the interstate off-ramp. Outside, the afternoon was fading to evening; in his mirrors, the sunset was blinding, and to the south, where Volovoi waited, the shadows grew longer.

In the passenger seat, Nikolai tapped his feet and drummed on the dash, all energy and nervous anticipation.

"Shit, I can't wait to be rid of this little tramp," he said. "Hurry up, Bogdan. It's Andrei's turn to worry about her for a while."

Bogdan searched for road signs through the bug-spattered windshield. "Soon enough, Nikolai," he said. "Soon enough."

He was sweating, he realized. It was a hot day, and the Peterbilt's air-conditioning system was wonky, but it wasn't the heat that was causing Bogdan to perspire.

In a few minutes, Nikolai Kirilenko would be dead. Bogdan watched his partner fiddle with his ubiquitous Big Gulp cup, utterly oblivious. He wondered if Andrei Volovoi would make the kill painless. If Nikolai would scream when the end came, if he would beg for mercy.

Bogdan wondered if he would miss Nikolai. He slowed the truck at an intersection. In the distance, he could see the old gas station Andrei had described. The place appeared deserted. There was no sign of Volovoi anywhere.

"There's the spot," Bogdan said, releasing the brakes and idling the truck into the gas station's little lot. "Maybe we're early."

Nikolai reached for the door. "Small mercies," he told Bogdan. "I'm desperate for a shit."

Bogdan parked the rig. Watched his partner drop from the cab and hurry across the parking lot to the gas station buildings. Watched him circle behind them, his face a mask of urgency and pain.

There was movement from the little garage at the front of the gas station. As Bogdan watched, Andrei Volovoi emerged from the shadows. He regarded the Peterbilt, then the gas station, where Nikolai had disappeared. After a moment, he walked, slow as death, around to the rear of the building.

He'll die with his pants down, Bogdan thought. *Kind of suits the bastard.*

Volovoi disappeared around the side of the building. Bogdan watched the shadows for a moment, waiting, tensed for the shot that would end his partner's life. Nothing happened. The evening air was still. Bogdan hesitated, then reached for the door handle.

No sense just sitting here, he decided, sliding his pistol into his waistband. *I'll get the little tramp ready for Andrei.*

67

VOLOVOI WATCHED THE idiot Nikolai run to the gas station as Bogdan Urzica waited inside the truck.

Perfect, he thought, creeping out from the little garage. *Stay where you are, Bogdan. I'll deal with you in a minute.*

Nikolai was making foul noises behind the little building. Volovoi could hear them as he approached the rear wall. The bastard was disgusting, a pig, a waste of space and air, and momentarily, Volovoi wondered how Bogdan Urzica had tolerated the man for so long.

Patience, he decided. *Or desperation.* Bogdan Urzica had debts with unsavory people, an addiction to underground poker games. He needed the money. The steady work. Driving women for Volovoi was the closest Bogdan Urzica could get to a reputable job.

Still, Volovoi thought, listening to Nikolai cackle as he unleashed another hellacious fart, *what a hardship.*

Volovoi pulled out his pistol, and circled around the rear of the gas station just as Nikolai hitched his pants up, catching him fumbling with his belt, a stench in the air. Nikolai saw him, grinned wide.

"Andrei," he said. "How fortunate for us both you didn't arrive a minute earlier. You may have been scarred for—"

Then he saw the gun.

Volovoi didn't hesitate. He raised the gun and pulled the trigger, watched the smile fade away from Nikolai's face.

"Andrei," Nikolai said, grabbing at his wound. "What are you—" He collapsed to the ground before he could finish the sentence. Volovoi shot him again anyway.

One idiot down, he thought, watching Nikolai gasp and bleed and die in the dirt. *One to go.*

> > >

BOGDAN HEARD THE FIRST SHOT as he unlocked the false compartment in the back of the box. Heard the second shot a moment later. Felt a sudden relief as the shots echoed briefly, as the silence descended again.

So long, Nikolai Kirilenko, he thought. *It wasn't nice to know you.*

The girl's eyes were wide in the back of the box. "Not to worry," Bogdan told her. "That was only my partner. He will not bother you anymore."

The girl didn't answer. Didn't move. Bogdan held out his hands. "Come on," he told her. "Change of scenery. You'll be going the rest of the way with my friend."

The girl still didn't move. She stared at him, a pitiful little wench. Bogdan studied her, the grime on her skin, her filthy, ragged clothing. Really didn't want to have to carry her.

"Come on," he said. "Are you going to make me drag you out of there?"

The girl walked slowly to the false door. Bogdan watched her approach. Moved back from the doorway to give her space to walk out.

"Nothing funny," he told her. "I don't want to have to hurt you."

The girl said nothing. Stepped out of the compartment and into the back of the box. Bogdan turned to the back doors. Then he stopped.

"Andrei," he said, his breath catching. "Jesus. You scared me."

Andrei Volovoi stood at the rear of the box. He was a good sized man, dark, his eyes devoid of humor. In his right hand, he held a pistol. A big one, a .45, from the look of it.

Volovoi said nothing. He looked at the little urchin, then at Bogdan. "This is the girl?" he asked.

"This is the girl," Bogdan said. "I don't know what the Dragon wants with her, though. He could get a hundred better-looking girls just by snapping his fingers. Why is this one so special?"

"She's special, Bogdan, because her sister is in FBI custody," Volovoi said, watching the girl step down from the box. "She's special because you let her sister get away."

Bogdan stepped out of the box and landed beside Volovoi and the girl. His heart was pounding again. His nerves tense. He felt his pistol in his waistband, the worst-case scenario. Beside him, the little girl's eyes were wide. She could feel the tension, too.

Bogdan forced a smile. "Anyway," he said. "Here she is, for the Dragon's approval. Unharmed, more or less."

"More or less," Volovoi repeated. Then he turned toward the gas station, the Escalade parked inside the garage. "Come on."

Bogdan led the girl across the gravel lot. The girl stumbled; the ground was uneven and rough, no doubt, on her bare feet. Bogdan dragged her, ignored her protests.

Just get me the hell out of here, he thought. *Just end this fucking situation and let me go home.*

The garage seemed impossibly dark, the light of day making its last stand outside. The Escalade was a void in the middle, a black hole. Volovoi climbed in the driver's seat, turned the engine over. Idled the big truck halfway out of the garage. Then he stepped out again, the engine still running. Circled back to Bogdan and the girl.

"The passenger seat," he told Bogdan. "Strap her in good."

Bogdan pulled the girl forward. The girl whimpered, but she didn't struggle. She let Bogdan open the door for her, climbed up into the truck. Sat, stone-faced, as Bogdan fumbled with her seat belt, as he tightened it around her.

"There," he said. "Good enough."

He straightened, ready to tell Andrei good night and good riddance, tell him he'd dispose of the truck and the box and see him back in New Jersey, maybe ask for some time off before the next shipment arrived. He was already imagining a hot shower, a bed, maybe a girl of his own, hell, maybe a fucking vacation, some beach somewhere. He was ready to forget about the little tramp and about Andrei Volovoi, about the Dragon. Maybe he was even ready to buy a farm somewhere, go back to the simpler life. Who knows? He was free. He could do anything. He—

Then Bogdan heard the click as Volovoi cocked back his hammer.

68

BOGDAN DIDN'T TURN around, didn't look at Andrei Volovoi. Kept his eyes on the girl in the passenger seat.

"Andrei," he said. "What the hell are you doing?"

"Step away from the car, Bogdan," Volovoi said. "Nice and slow, if you please."

Bogdan's mind raced through about a million thoughts at once. He had suspected this would happen, had hoped that Volovoi would be reasonable, but knew the Dragon, especially, may have demanded blood. And Andrei Volovoi wasn't in the business of saying no to the Dragon.

This ambush, then, wasn't entirely a surprise. Hell, Volovoi had killed Nikolai. Of course he'd be tempted to clean up all of his loose ends.

"Back," Volovoi said. "Back away now, Bogdan."

Bogdan steadied his breathing. Tried to calm his heart, keep his voice flat. "Okay, Andrei," he said. "Whatever you say."

He made to back away from the truck's door. Heard Andrei step back along with him, create a little distance. He inched down with his right hand until he felt the pistol at his waistband. Volovoi was still backing up. He hadn't noticed.

Quickly, Bogdan drew his pistol. Lunged forward and down, out of Volovoi's firing range, heard the blast as Volovoi pulled the trigger. Felt the bullet fly past his ear, heard it ricochet off the Escalade's sheet metal, the girl screaming. Bogdan rolled forward, reached for the girl. Held his pistol to her ear as she squirmed in her seat, and spun around to face Volovoi.

"Don't you fucking do it," he told Volovoi. "I'll put a bullet through this girl's brain, and where the fuck will that leave you, Andrei?"

Volovoi's breathing was ragged. His nostrils flared. His eyes were narrow and his lips a thin line. He held the gun level with Bogdan's forehead, his expression leaving no doubt that he itched to pull the trigger. But he wouldn't, Bogdan knew. Not while the girl was in danger.

"I'll kill her," Bogdan told him. "I'll kill her right now, and no matter what you do to me, you'll still have to go back to the Dragon and tell him you lost his prize. And what do you think he'll do then, Andrei?"

Volovoi said nothing. He looked from Bogdan to the girl and back again. Slowly, his breathing calmed.

"He'll kill you," Bogdan said. "He'll kill your family, too, Andrei, those precious nieces of yours. So unless you want them dead, you'll drop that fucking gun and take another big step backward, understand?"

Volovoi still said nothing. Bogdan could practically read the man's thoughts, the calculations running through his mind. He pulled the girl closer to him, stretching the seat belt tight across her thin frame, and screwed the barrel of his pistol into her cheek. The girl squirmed and whimpered. Bogdan held her tight.

Bogdan watched Volovoi run through the variables. Watched as the trafficker, seething, finally lowered his pistol.

Bogdan exhaled. "Good man," he said. He took the gun off the girl. Aimed it at Volovoi. Held it on the trafficker as he circled around the Escalade. As he reached for the driver's-side door and pulled it open.

He aimed the pistol across the Cadillac's hood. "You should never have tried to fuck with me, Andrei," he told Volovoi. Then he pulled the trigger and Volovoi went down.

The girl screamed again. Bogdan climbed behind the wheel of Volovoi's truck, the engine still running. Slipped the pistol down between the seat and the door, shifted into gear, and drove past the Peterbilt tractor and the empty box and out of the lot.

69

"LIKE HELL YOU'RE telling Nancy."

Windermere looked at Stevens, rolled her eyes, and reached for her cell phone. From the ambulance, Stevens tried to stand, swayed, gave it up and sat down again.

"Your wife will kill me if I don't tell her you got shot, partner," Windermere said. "And unlike your friend upstairs, I don't think she'd aim for the chest."

Stevens leaned his back against the door of the ambulance. Windermere watched him, thanked God for about the eightieth time they'd swiped Kevlar vests from Fast's truck before entering the Blue Room. Thanked God that piece of redneck trash hadn't had time to try for a headshot, and that the blunt force trauma Stevens had absorbed was enough to take the wind out of him and leave a hell of a bruise, but nothing more.

"I'm fine, Carla," Stevens said. "You know how much Nancy hates this cowboy stuff."

"She barely trusts me as is," Windermere said. "I swear to God, she'll kill me."

"So I'll tell her," Stevens said. "Scout's honor. Soon as this case is closed."

The case. The Blue Room was now swarming with Billings PD and whatever Montana G-men Agent Fast had been able to dredge up. The shotgun shooter and his buddy had been the only men armed in the brothel; there were three other sad-sack losers huddled in the girls' little bedrooms with their dates pressed in front of them. The Billings PD had booked the lot of them, taken them down to a holding cell for whenever Windermere got around to questioning their degenerate asses.

There were girls, too, of course—the first two escapees, the young one Stevens had almost got his ass blown off trying to save, and four more in the back rooms. None of them had much in the way of clothing, and Windermere had detailed a Billings uniform to find coats, shirts, and sweatpants before she piled the lot of them into a police van to await questioning themselves.

Not that any of them spoke much English. The johns were terrified and would probably spill everything they knew, which would damn the two men upstairs but mean jack shit to the Dragon.

"I wish those two dirty bastards didn't have to die," Windermere said.

Stevens met her eyes. "You're thinking we just dried up our own trail."

"I mean, they were filthy. I don't mind that they're dead, but . . ."

"We saved seven victims, though," Stevens said. "That little girl—"

"Is safe," Windermere agreed. "But there's another truckload just like her coming down the pike, unless we can trace this back to the Dragon."

"I know," Stevens said. "So?"

"So we have a mountain of paperwork to do as far as this fiasco is concerned," Windermere said. "We have three johns to interview, and the girls, too, if we can find translators. Not that the Heat girls in Duluth gave us much more than Irina did, but maybe we get lucky this time. Maybe *these* girls recognize the Dragon."

"Right," Stevens said, and Windermere could see for the first time how tired he appeared, how utterly depleted.

"We'll finish this," she said. She sat down beside him, put her arm around him, pulled him to her. "I'll work these johns," she said. "Start on the paperwork. You go somewhere and rest. You get shot, I figure that earns you the night off."

Stevens nodded. "And Nancy?"

"You tell her later," Windermere said. "But Stevens, I swear, if this comes back on me, I'll shoot you my damn self."

70

CATALINA SAT IN THE passenger seat and watched the thug drive. The big man said nothing, his brow furrowed in concentration and worry, his nervous eyes jumping between the rearview mirror and the road.

She wondered what had happened. Where the thug's partner was, the scary scar-faced man who'd tried to force himself on her. She wondered who the other man was, the man whose truck they'd stolen. Mostly, she wondered what had happened to the humanity she'd seen in this thug's eyes.

Outside, night was falling. The SUV's engine howled. The thug drove with one hand. With the other, he pulled out an iPhone. His eyes flicked from the screen to the road, his lips moving, but not saying anything.

Catalina shifted. "Where are we going?" she asked him.

The thug didn't answer. He muttered a swearword. Struck the steering wheel, and she recoiled from the sudden violence. She could still feel the imprint in her skin where the thug had pressed his gun. He'd been ready to kill her. He would have put a bullet inside her to protect himself from the other man.

She had been wrong to imagine this thug was her friend. He was just as evil as his missing partner. He just wanted her for something different.

She had to get out of this truck.

The thug sped down the highway. The gas station disappeared behind them. The man kept playing with his phone, barely paying attention. He was distracted. He was vulnerable. She had to do something.

Catalina felt for the seat belt across her lap. Pressed the release button quickly, before she could stop herself. Then, as the thug glanced at her, she lunged for the wheel.

The thug tried to block her, but he was too slow, too late. Catalina grabbed the steering wheel with both hands and turned it hard over. The big truck lurched onto the shoulder, tires squealing, kicking up dirt. The thug forgot about her. Fought to regain control of the vehicle. The truck bounced and bumped over grass and gravel. It was speeding too fast. The thug couldn't control it.

Catalina fumbled with her seat belt. Caught the end and struggled with it, dragged it across her lap. Slipped it back into the release just as the SUV collided with something hard and unyielding, launching the thug through the windshield and out over the hood, jerking Catalina forward until her head struck the dash. She was strapped in, though; she didn't fly through the windshield. The thug did. He left a hole, jagged, through the glass.

It was the last thing Catalina saw before she passed out.

71

KIRK STEVENS WAS never any good at keeping secrets.

"*What?*" Nancy's voice went up about three octaves. "My God, Kirk, and you didn't tell me?"

Stevens caught Windermere's eye across the modest FBI office, got a sympathetic look in return. "It wasn't that serious, Nance," he said. "I had a vest on. Barely knocked me down."

"Bullshit, Kirk. Don't pull that with me. You got *shot*."

Stevens said nothing. Knew he wasn't going to win the fight. Nancy had never been comfortable with the gunplay part of her husband's job, though lately she'd at least seemed to accept it. Still, Stevens had been dreading this conversation.

"This was, what, last night, Kirk?"

"That's right," Stevens said. "I didn't want you to get worried."

Nancy Stevens exhaled. "Well, I *am* worried, Kirk. Of course I'm worried. I haven't seen much of you in weeks, because you're out there getting shot at and God knows what else. Why shouldn't I be scared?"

"There was this girl," Stevens told her. "Probably Andrea's age, in a shitty little brothel. Too much makeup and not enough clothes, and some asshole smacking her around. I couldn't—I had to stop the guy, Nance."

Nancy didn't say anything.

"I'm sorry I didn't tell you," Stevens said. "I just don't think I can give this one up. Not until we catch these guys."

"I know," Nancy said. "I'm not going to ask you to come home, Kirk. I just want you to be careful."

"I'll be careful, Nance."

"*Really* careful, Kirk. Because I need you to come back here and be a father again sometime, after you rescue these women."

Stevens felt suddenly weary. "Andrea again?"

"*Always*, Kirk. She's sneaking out to see Calvin at all hours; she's rude when I confront her about it, won't do her chores or talk to me, even. All she wants to do is play on that stupid phone of hers."

"Shit." Stevens felt his nerves tighten. "She's still with Calvin, huh?"

"I could just use your help," Nancy said. "So don't get yourself shot again, okay?"

"Yeah," Stevens said. "Roger that."

"How's the case going, anyway? Apart from the whole you-getting-shot thing."

"The case?" Stevens surveyed the little office, the piles of paperwork. They'd filled out forms through the night and into the morning, given statements to a couple of Salt Lake City agents about the Blue Room raid, and interviewed the three unlucky johns, none of whom had any decent information to give.

Windermere was working on the girls now, but judging from her expression as she shuttled back and forth from the interview room to the coffee machine, she wasn't making much headway. Half of the girls were Bulgarian, and good luck finding a Bulgarian translator in Montana. The others came from all over—Romania, Poland, the Ukraine—and even those who could speak English knew next to nothing.

"Well, crap," Nancy said. "Something's gotta give though, right?"

"I hope so." Stevens looked across the office to where Fast had planted himself at his old desktop computer, happily sedentary again. "At least when I'm doing paperwork, I can't get shot. How's Irina doing?"

"Irina?" Nancy's tone brightened, and he could tell she was glad he'd asked. "She's fine, Kirk. I've been by to visit her in the safe house a couple of times, and she seems to be doing better. They tell me she's eating, and the staff says she's starting to interact with the other women. So, you know, she's okay."

"Hasn't remembered anything else about the Dragon, has she?"

Nancy sighed. "Afraid not, Agent Stevens. You're going to have to do the heavy lifting yourself."

"What else is new?"

"You'll get there," she said. "Hurry up and solve the case, cowboy. I miss you."

"Miss you, too." He ended the call, stood and wandered over to the coffee machine and poured himself a fresh cup, then nearly spilled it all over himself colliding with Windermere coming out of the interview room.

"There you are," she said. "Come on in here. We just caught a break."

72

SHE'D LEARNED HER English watching American TV shows in Sarajevo, she said. She apologized if it wasn't any good.

Windermere snorted. "You speak better English than half the people in this country," she told the girl. "Nothing to worry about there."

Sanja was her name. She was twenty, her features smooth and delicate. She had the hardened eyes of a soldier, though, and her skin was marked by fading bruises. She shivered. "I'm afraid," she said.

Windermere reached across the table. "You're safe, Sanja. The men who did this to you are dead."

Sanja bit her lip. "They were terrible men," she said, her eyes downcast. "Worse than the customers. They beat us until we screamed. Forced us to do things with them. They told us they would kill our families if we didn't obey."

"How long were you with them?" Stevens asked. "When did you come to America?"

Sanja thought about it. "It's hard to tell time," she said. "Maybe a year and a half, maybe two years? The days blur together."

"Sure." Stevens caught Windermere's eye. *Jesus Christ*, his expression said, and she knew he was thinking about his daughter.

"You were telling me about your friend," she told Sanja. "Her name was, what, Amira?"

"Amira, yes," Sanja said. "We came over together, in the box. We lived next door to each other in the brothel, neighbors. Never allowed to talk to each other, but we—There was a vent we could speak through, if we whispered. We talked sometimes, when there were no customers."

"What did you talk about?"

"Life. Before the box. Our families. Sarajevo." Sanja smiled. "She told me I would be perfect for her older brother, when we got out of there."

"And then?"

"And then, they found out about us. About the vent." Sanja lowered her eyes. "One of the men heard us talking. He . . ." She paused. "He beat us. Did horrible things."

She stood and turned around, lifted her shirt, exposing long faded scars across her back.

Stevens exhaled. "Piece of shit." He had an expression on his face like Windermere had never seen, every muscle tense, his mouth tight. Like he was fighting something. Like he could barely restrain himself.

Windermere reached out, touched his arm. Stevens blinked. Relaxed a little. But his jaw remained clenched. "When did this happen?" she asked Sanja.

Sanja sat down again. "Weeks ago. Maybe two weeks? Not long. And then Amira was gone."

"Gone." Stevens's voice was choked. "As in dead?"

"No, no," Sanja said quickly. "There was another delivery. They took Amira away with them and blocked up the vent so I couldn't talk to the new girl." She shrugged. "She was Romanian, anyway, I think. We wouldn't have had much to say."

"So they took Amira away," Windermere said. "Any idea where they took her?"

Sanja nodded. "She had a regular customer, a large man, very fat. After Amira left, they gave him me to play with, instead. Because we're both from Sarajevo, or because we were neighbors. I heard him ask about Amira, this customer. I didn't let on that I understood." She looked up. "I never told them I could speak English. Not the men in charge."

"So you overheard their conversation."

"The customer asked about Amira. He didn't like me the same. Amira had bigger boobs, he said. The man laughed at him. Told him Amira was gone. He could follow her to . . ." She faltered. "I'm sorry, I don't know this country well."

"It's okay," Windermere said. "Did it sound like he was talking about a city?"

"I don't know," Sanja said. "The fat man, he said it was too far, even for a pair of boobs like Amira's. 'Navada,' he said. This is a place?"

"Nevada," Windermere said. "It's a state. Where in Nevada did they send Amira? Las Vegas?"

Sanja shook her head. "I know Las Vegas. Everyone knows. I would have remembered this."

"Reno?" Stevens said. "Reno, Nevada?"

"*Reno.*" Sanja sat up. "This is the place. He said Amira went to Reno, Nevada."

"Well, hot damn." Windermere looked at Stevens again. "Reno, Nevada, partner. No rest for the wicked."

73

VOLOVOI PUSHED HIMSELF to his feet. Surveyed the empty lot. His shoulder hurt like hell where the idiot Bogdan Urzica had shot him, but he supposed he should be thankful. He was alive, wasn't he?

Volovoi didn't feel thankful. He felt angry. Disgusted.

He'd let Bogdan escape. Worse, he'd let him take the girl. Worst, he'd taken the Escalade, too, leaving Volovoi marooned at this gas station in the middle of nowhere, with no ride and no girl, and Nikolai Kirilenko's body rotting in a pile of his own shit.

Volovoi had been stupid. He'd been careless. He was exhausted, he realized, had been awake for days, couldn't sleep for the stress over the Dragon and the New York expansion, over Bogdan and Nikolai and the girl. He'd put Nikolai down easily. He'd expected Bogdan would be the same. He'd grown complacent, and lazy, and Bogdan had figured him out.

Shit.

Volovoi tore a strip off his jacket. Tied it around the bullet wound in his shoulder, fumbled in the gravel until he found his gun. It was dark out, barely a sliver of light left on the western horizon. Volovoi could just make out the low gas station building, the dim hulk of the Peterbilt and its trailer. Slowly, he made his way to the truck. Opened the driver's-side door and searched inside.

No keys anywhere. *Damn it.*

Someone would drive past soon enough. Someone would happen along this road and see the truck. Maybe they would get curious. Maybe they would want a closer look.

Maybe they would find Nikolai Kirilenko's body.

He had to get out of there.

Volovoi wiped his fingerprints from the Peterbilt's door. Scanned the parking lot one more time, saw absolutely nothing that could help him. He pressed the strip of torn cloth tighter against his bloody shoulder. Then, wincing from the pain, he walked to the road.

It was a two-lane country highway. If Volovoi thought hard, he could remember Bogdan Urzica driving the Cadillac out of the lot. He'd turned left, not that it meant anything. Given their head start, Bogdan and the girl could be anywhere by now.

Volovoi went left anyway. Hobbled along the shoulder in darkness and silence. Tried Bogdan's number on his cell phone and got nothing—no surprise. He wondered what the dumb asshole would do to the girl.

A noise behind him. Volovoi turned, saw headlights in the distance, getting closer. He hid the pistol in his waistband. Stepped out onto the road. Let the headlights find him, let the driver get a good look. The car slowed to the shoulder. A door opened. A woman's voice.

"Are you okay? What happened?"

Volovoi hobbled around to the driver's side. The driver was a young woman, her eyes wide. Her car was a Subaru, a station wagon.

"Do you need help?" the woman asked.

Volovoi took out his pistol and shot her. The woman stared at him as she fell out of the car and to the ground. Volovoi kicked her body out of the way and slid into the driver's seat. Pulled the door closed and drove.

74

HE'D BARELY GONE a mile when he saw it. The Escalade, wrecked, on the side of the road. The idiot Bogdan had driven it into a tree.

Volovoi slowed the station wagon to a stop behind the Cadillac. The truck's brake lights still blazed; they lit up the night. He turned off the engine and searched the scene for any sign of the thug or the girl. He saw nothing, just the truck, ruined, half in a ditch.

Volovoi reached for his pistol again. Checked the chamber. Pulled the driver's door open and stepped out of the Subaru, holding his gun steady as he approached the wreck.

75

CATALINA WOKE TO movement outside the wrecked truck. Somebody's footsteps, whispering through the grass. She raised her head and saw starbursts, felt pain behind her eyes. Something warm dripped down her forehead. She was bleeding.

The thug was still gone. He'd disappeared through the hole in the windshield and he hadn't come back. She wondered if he was dead. She hoped so.

She tried moving again. Felt the pain like an ax to her brain and groaned and lay her head back. She could see shattered glass, the thug's iPhone on the floor, the tree through the windshield, the truck crumpled around it, the headlights still burning. The truck had hit the tree hard. Catalina supposed it was a miracle she was alive.

Whatever had been moving outside was still moving. Catalina twisted her head around, saw nothing but pain bursts. Closed her eyes and left them closed. Whatever was out there would find her soon enough.

When she opened her eyes again, there was a man by the tree. Catalina recognized him. He was the man from the gas station, the man with the gun. The man whose truck the thug had stolen. Somehow he'd caught up to them. And he still had his gun.

He was standing in the beam of the headlights, just past the tree. Catalina shifted in her seat, craned her neck. Could just barely see the body splayed out on the grass beneath him. The blood. The man studied the body for a minute or two. Then he looked back at the truck, squinted at her through the headlights. Catalina held her breath. Pretended he couldn't see her. It was too late. He was coming her way.

Before he could reach her, Catalina leaned down, stretched out her fingers and felt for the thug's iPhone. Snatched it, quickly, from the floor, and stuffed it in the waistband of her underwear. Then she felt around for the seat belt release. Couldn't unclip the belt before the man wrenched open the door.

He was an average-looking man. He was tall, and his face was kind of flat, as though he'd been struck dead-on with a shovel. He was not as big as either one of the thugs, but that didn't make him any less scary. He held a bloody strip of cloth to his wounded shoulder, but that didn't make him any less menacing. He wore the hint of a smile on his face. It was not a mean smile, necessarily. It wasn't a victor's smile, either.

It was relief, Catalina decided. The man was relieved to see her.

The man reached in and unbuckled her. Lifted her from her seat. Catalina didn't struggle. She didn't have the energy. She let the man carry her away from the wrecked SUV to a waiting station wagon, let him buckle her into the passenger seat, let him drive her away from the truck and the body of the thug. She didn't say anything, and the man didn't either, and after the man had driven a ways, Catalina closed her eyes and passed out again.

76

It was midafternoon by the time Kirk Stevens and Carla Windermere finally said good-bye to Agent Fast and Billings, Montana, for good. They left the Blue Room's hapless johns in the custody of the local PD , while the FBI's Salt Lake City division took custody of the trafficked women. None of the women shared Irina Milosovici's desire to escape. They were terrified, all of them, thankful to be in government protection—unaware, maybe, of the lengths the Dragon would go to keep them quiet.

"Please," Sanja told Windermere as she boarded the FBI's transport van for Utah. "Find Amira. If you can."

"We'll try." Windermere watched the women climb, wide-eyed, into the van. *Probably their first real view of America,* she realized. *They've spent the rest of their time here in shipping containers and shitty bedrooms.*

Sanja took a window seat. She waved as the van pulled away, and Windermere watched until she'd disappeared. Then she turned away to find Stevens.

He was watching, too, a few feet away, lost in his own thoughts. She punched him on the shoulder. "This story ain't over yet," she said. "Wake up."

Stevens forced a smile. "Just waiting on you, partner."

They caught the afternoon flight to Denver, drank beer and watched baseball in the airport bar, and jumped on the connector to Reno. No FBI agent waited to greet them this time, so they caught a taxi down the highway to the Bureau's local detachment, where Windermere wrangled them an unmarked Ford Taurus and a head start on some leads.

"Got us a list of brothels, strip clubs, and escort services from the local vice squad," she told Stevens as she slid into the driver's seat, "but most of it looks pretty clean."

"I thought brothels were legal in Nevada," Stevens said.

"They are," Windermere said, "except for Las Vegas, Reno, and a couple other spots. So you have to leave city limits to find the legit stuff. Makes it kind of a pain for the casino guests, I guess."

"Sure," Stevens said. "Who wants to drive all the way out to the desert for some action?"

"Exactly. So there are some escort agencies and the like, but I'm not sure our guys want their girls doing out-calls."

"Out-calls?"

"Like, the girl comes to you," Windermere said. "As opposed to in-calls, where you go to the girl."

"Like the Blue Room."

"Pretty much. Mostly, an in-call is a private condo or a hotel room. Not so much a shitty warehouse blasting Nickelback over the loudspeakers."

"Roger." Stevens cocked his head. "How do you know this stuff, anyway?"

"Research." Windermere winked at him. "Unlike someone I could mention, I didn't sleep on the flight. Spent most of my time Googling Nevada hookers. God help me if Harris's IT people get ahold of my browser history."

Stevens laughed. "Okay," he said. "Anything else?"

"Let's see." Windermere drummed on the steering wheel. "I checked in with Mathers, got the latest from him, which is to say, not much. And I got pictures of the Dragon's two thugs out to Reno PD and all of the hotels and casinos in town. Figured maybe the delivery boys stopped in for a little gambling on their way out of town."

"Good thinking," Stevens said. "Lots of lines in the water. So what are we doing while we wait for a bite?"

Windermere turned the Ford onto a highway on-ramp. Gunned the engine. "What we do best, Stevens," she said. "We're going to talk to more strippers."

77

VOLOVOI DROVE THE speed limit away from the wreck. Beside him, the girl slept in the passenger seat. Slept or was unconscious, he wasn't sure, though judging by the gash on her head, she'd been lucky to survive when the Escalade crashed.

Bogdan had flown through the windshield. Volovoi had discovered him on the grass in front of the Escalade, his head nearly torn off, his face smashed and bloody. He'd lost control of the truck somehow. He'd driven straight into that tree.

Volovoi muttered a silent prayer. Somebody was looking out for him. It was about time he experienced a little good luck for a change.

He'd stripped the plates from the Cadillac. Removed the registration, wiped it clean of fingerprints. Hunted around for something flammable to set the truck on fire but found nothing. He had to leave the truck as it stood, but no matter. The thing was registered to a shell company, anyway.

The girl had stayed unconscious while Volovoi tidied the scene. While he had fussed over the truck, and over Bogdan Urzica. He'd taken Bogdan's identification. Put a bullet through his face so the first responders wouldn't recognize him from the police sketches on the news. They would trace his identity soon enough— Volovoi didn't have a hacksaw to remove the man's fingers to avoid fingerprinting—but they would not follow him back to the trafficking operation, not at first.

The girl hadn't moved when Volovoi climbed back in the dead woman's Subaru. She was very young, he noticed, filthy and bruised, her clothes no more than rags. He'd dug around in the rear of the station wagon, found a T-shirt and shorts in the dead woman's suitcase. The girl would be swimming in them, but she would be covered.

Volovoi drove east into darkness. Ditched the Subaru outside Brooklville, hot-wired a beat-up old Honda Accord and carried the little girl to the passenger seat, his wounded shoulder stinging from the exertion. It was barely a flesh wound, though. Volovoi decided he would survive.

Just get the girl to the Dragon. Then deal with your problems.

The girl looked around sleepily as he lifted her from the car, whimpered when she saw his face.

"Hush," he told her. "Go back to sleep."

Her eyes flashed defiant for a moment, her muscles tense, but Volovoi held her tight and the moment passed quickly. He deposited her in her seat and slipped behind the wheel, drove a couple miles in the Accord and swapped the plates with a rusty old Ford F-150 parked in an empty warehouse lot. Then he drove back to the interstate and pointed the Accord toward Manhattan.

The car smelled like mildew and rotten eggs, and the radio buzzed, but it drove okay, and there was plenty of gas in the tank, and as the miles passed beneath him, Volovoi relaxed a bit, even smiled a little. Whatever else had gone wrong, he'd recovered Catalina Milosovici. The Dragon would get his prize after all.

78

CARLA WINDERMERE HAD never seen so many fake breasts in her life.

She'd spent all night combing strip clubs with Stevens, searching for any hint of a lead, any industry gossip about unwilling sex workers, trafficking, illegal brothels, anything. By and large, the club managers weren't willing to talk. The dancers, though, seemed to relish the opportunity.

"European girls?" A dancer named Amethyst scrunched up her face. "I heard something about that, some underground club. Really top secret, though."

"Some asshole complained because I wouldn't blow him in the VIP room," another dancer told them. "Swore he knew a couple new girls would do it for half the price of a lap dance."

"You know where?" Windermere asked them.

Both women shook their heads. "Hush-hush, like I said," Amethyst told her. "They're here, though. Pushing the legit girls out of business."

Windermere thanked them for their time. Thanked their friends, too, and their colleagues, and the competition next door. Every woman wanted to be helpful. They all gave up information. It just wasn't enough to point to anything real.

"Maybe we need to start talking to the escort agencies," Stevens said, blinking in a sea of neon outside another strip club. "The agency women might have a better idea who their competition is."

"Probably be happy to point them out, too," Windermere said. "Seeing as how they're undercutting the prices."

"Just have to convince them to talk to us," Stevens said. "Might be easier said than done."

They walked back to the Taurus, but before they could climb inside, Windermere's phone rang. She checked it, answered it. "Windermere."

"Agent Windermere, it's Andy Tate with the Reno office. How are things?"

"Things? Things are slow, Agent Tate. Slogging through a pile of strippers, trying to get a clue. What's up?"

Tate laughed. Windermere had met the guy earlier, when they'd dropped by the office to pick up the Taurus. Tate had been the only one in the office, a slight, wry-looking man with an easy smile. She'd liked him immediately.

"Got a hit for you," Tate told her, and she liked him even more. "Cocktail waitress at the Peppermill says she might recognize your guys. I told her you'd drop by to talk to her."

"The Peppermill. All right." Windermere caught Stevens's eye. "I'm sick of strip clubs, anyway."

79

THE MAN DROVE for hours. He didn't say a word.

Catalina woke up to darkness. Her head hurt, and the new car smelled funny. She groaned and sat up and saw a vast highway outside the window, a few cars. She watched the cars as they passed her, wanted desperately to signal somebody for help. Knew the silent man would kill her the moment she tried.

He'd given her clothing at least, a T-shirt and shorts. The clothes were too big, and kind of ugly—the T-shirt had a picture of an oversized panther on it—but they were better than her rags. She'd slipped them on, taking care not to dislodge the thug's iPhone she'd hid in the waistband of her underwear. Felt a little better, now that she was covered. She was still dirty, though. She smelled bad, and her head hurt. And the silent man scared her.

The man drove at a steady speed as the darkness passed outside, and Catalina slumped down and tried to doze in the passenger seat. She could not. She was terrified. Where on earth was this man taking her?

Then the man drove his little car off the highway. Pulled into a service station. He narrowed his eyes at her. "Behave yourself."

Catalina did as she was instructed. Sat in the car as the man filled the tank. When he came back, she shifted in her seat. "I would like to go to the bathroom," she said.

The man looked at her, then at the service station. It was a vast, shiny plaza. There was a McDonald's inside, and a coffee shop, and a little store. There were other cars around, other people. "Five minutes," the man said. "Nothing stupid."

Catalina followed the man out of the car and into the plaza. There was a map on the wall in the corridor to the washrooms. CLEARFIELD, PENNSYLVANIA, the map said. Catalina didn't know what it meant, or how to pronounce it, but now she knew at least where she was.

The man walked her to the women's washroom, made her wait until there were no other women inside. Then he pushed open the door. "Five minutes," he said again.

"Five minutes." Catalina hurried into the washroom. Studied herself in the mirror and tried to wash the blood and grime from her face. The blood smeared; she was far too filthy for hand soap and paper towels. Anyway, she didn't have much time.

Catalina ducked into a stall and sat down on the toilet. Then she reached into her waistband and pulled out the thug's iPhone. Mercifully, the phone was unlocked. But she had no idea who to contact, or how.

She did not know the number for the police. Anyway, she could not speak enough English to tell them her situation. The police could not help her. But she had to do something. And time was running out.

Catalina felt her heart pounding. *Think,* she thought. *Think, you stupid little cow.*

She stared at the phone. At the menu of buttons and icons. At the bottom was an Internet icon. Catalina pressed it, and a search window came up. *Okay,* she thought. *I can use this.*

80

THE COCKTAIL WAITRESS was named Kara. She wore a tight dress and an easy smile, and she stood out like a precious stone among pebbles in the Peppermill Casino's dreary confines.

"Yeah, I remember him," she told Stevens and Windermere. "Nikolai. The dog. Looked at me like he hadn't had a woman in years."

"You met him here?" Stevens said. "At the casino?"

Kara nodded. "Craps tables. Double vodka sodas. Every time I came around, he would double his bet, showing off. Couldn't keep his hands off me."

"You talk to him?"

"A little." She shrugged. "He was betting pretty decent. They like us to flirt with the clientele, keep them happy."

"Sure," Stevens said. "Nikolai say anything about where he'd come from, what he was doing in Reno? Anything like that?"

Kara shook her head. "He was too busy trying to put his tongue in my ear. Like I said, this guy was really forward."

"Not forward enough that you'd call the manager on him, though," Windermere said.

"Are you kidding?" Kara laughed. "The pit boss saw the whole thing. It's part of the job. Make sure the customer walks away happy."

"And did he?"

She laughed again. "Nope. Wasn't like I was going to sleep with

him, anyway, but before he could try anything serious, his buddy—
the other guy from the pictures you sent out—came rumbling in like
the no-fun police, grabbed the guy and dragged him out to the parking lot. Was the last I ever saw of him."

Stevens swapped glances with Windermere. "And he didn't tell
you anything. Just that his name was Nikolai and he was looking for
a good time."

"Pretty much," she said, "except he didn't even tell me that." She
slipped a piece of paper out of her tip wallet, handed it to Stevens. It
was a slot machine ticket, a name and a number scrawled on the back
with a Keno crayon: Nikolai Kirilenko.

"Told me to call him up if I ever made it out east," Kara said. "I
admit, I maybe thought about it. He wasn't bad looking, if you forgot
about the scar."

"Maybe not," Windermere said, "but he is definitely bad. You
mind if we hold on to this number?"

"Be my guest," Kara said. "I got a whole locker full of guys' numbers in the back."

81

THERE WAS A knock at the door. Irina sat up from the window
with a start. Felt her heart pound in her chest.

The safe house was quiet. The U.S. Marshals remained outside in
their car, watching the building in shifts, as they'd done for days.

They rarely moved. They didn't come inside the house. No men came inside the house. For this, Irina was grateful.

Sometimes Maria came to visit, and sometimes Nancy Stevens. Sometimes a counselor accompanied them, a doctor, always a woman. Sometimes, when Irina didn't feel like eating in the dining room, a staff member would bring her dinner up here. For the most part, however, she was alone.

There were other women in the shelter, of course. Some were young and some were old, some were American and some were foreign, some were loud and brash and hid their wounds, and others were quiet, timid, shy, bruised inside and out. They talked to her sometimes, in the dining room, or in the computer room while they waited for their turn on the Internet, and Irina tried to answer in the bits of English she'd picked up. She didn't know much, mostly "Hi," "How are you?" and "Good-bye," and the energy required to communicate exhausted her. She retreated to her room often, paged through American gossip magazines, stared out the window at the American Marshals, and tried not to think about Catalina.

And now there was a knock at the door. Irina sat stone-still and waited, not daring to breathe. She had a sudden, terrifying premonition, saw the two ugly henchmen bursting into her room and dragging her, screaming, back to the box.

Except it wasn't the thugs who opened the door. It was a woman, another guest of the shelter. Marta, her name was. Or maybe Magda. A Hungarian woman; she knew a little Romanian. She'd come over with an abusive husband, though. She hadn't come in a box.

"I was on the computer," Magda said, her voice rushed. She was flustered about something. "Just now. After you were on."

Irina looked at her. "Yes," she said. "Okay?"

"You left your Facebook page open," Magda said. "I accidentally clicked on it."

"Okay," Irina said again. "I'm sorry. I will close it next time."

Magda waved her off. "It's not that," she said. "It's . . . There was a new message from Catalina Milosovici, but . . . didn't you say your sister was still in trouble?"

Irina blinked. "What?"

"Come see," Magda said. "Maybe I'm mistaken."

Irina followed the woman out of her little room, down the hall, and downstairs to the little cubbyhole closet that the staff had turned into a computer room. The computer was old and slow, and each woman was allowed only a half hour a day, but Irina had been using the machine more often, going on Facebook to tell her friends she was okay, going on the news websites to keep track of her sister's case, to search for information about the man Nancy Stevens called the Dragon.

Magda had left Irina's Facebook page open. Irina scanned it: her happy, cheesy profile picture, the insipid status updates from friends. She sat down in front of the computer, clicked through to Catalina's message. Stared and couldn't figure out what she was supposed to be seeing.

It was a blurry picture, taken with a camera phone. A map on a wall somewhere. CLEARFIELD, PENNSYLVANIA.

"What is it?" Magda said. "What does it mean?"

Irina opened a new window in the browser, her heart pounding. Typed *Clearfield* into the search box. The results came back entirely in English, but there was a map. Pennsylvania. Irina clicked on the map, zoomed out until she could see Minnesota.

"Yes?" Magda said. "What is it, Irina?"

Catalina had sent this picture twenty minutes ago, Irina realized. Somehow she'd gotten hold of a phone.

Irina logged out of her Facebook account. Then she dug into her pocket for Nancy Stevens's business card and walked to the phone in the hallway. She dialed Nancy's office number, but there was no answer. Of course there wasn't; it was late in the evening. The woman was probably at home with her family.

Except Nancy Stevens didn't answer her cell phone, either. The call went straight to voicemail. Irina hung up the phone. Tried Nancy's office number again.

The phone rang and rang. Finally, her answering machine picked up. Irina waited. Looked back at Magda, who watched her, her eyes wide. Then the answering machine beeped.

"Clearfield, Pennsylvania," Irina said. "My sister. She's there. I . . ." She'd nearly exhausted her supply of English. "I have to find her."

Then she hung up the phone. Magda was still watching her. "What are you going to do? Do you want me to call the police?"

"No." Irina didn't dare trust the Marshals. They were bigger than her, much stronger. What was to stop them from taking advantage?

Magda waited. Irina scanned the hallway. There was a staff member at the desk by the door, and the U.S. Marshals beyond, but she knew a back exit. Nancy Stevens was gone, and her husband couldn't help her. He'd been looking for Catalina for days without luck.

"I will do this myself," Irina told Magda. "This time, I will find her."

82

CATALINA SAT IN the passenger seat of the smelly car, feeling the weight of the phone in her pocket as the silent man drove away from the service station.

She wondered if Irina would get the message. If anyone would read it. She wondered if she should have tried another strategy. The Facebook message had been the best she could think of, under the circumstances. Her English wasn't good enough to type a text message. She didn't know any phone numbers, besides. But she didn't even know if Irina had Internet access. Her big risk was probably for nothing.

Her heart still pounded. She'd taken a huge chance. She'd known if the silent man caught her, he would probably kill her. But she had to do something, so, before she could stop herself, she'd pushed out of the washroom stall, crept to the restroom door and peered out, down the corridor, toward the big map.

The silent man stood at the end of the corridor, where it opened to the restaurants and the stores and the seating area. He was talking on his cell phone. He had his back to her.

As quick as she could, Catalina dashed out of the women's restroom. Held the camera phone aloft and aimed it at the map and pressed the button. She only had time for one picture. Then she hurried back into the washroom again.

The man must have sensed that something was the matter. He knocked on the door a moment later.

"Just a minute," she called out, locking herself in the stall. She fumbled with the phone, logged herself into Facebook, and sent Irina the picture. Then she peed, washed her hands, and adjusted her clothing. Hid the phone in her pocket again.

The man was waiting when she left the restroom. "You took too long in there," he said.

"I'm a girl," she said. "What do you expect?"

The man looked her over. "Next time you will not take so long," he said, "or we will not stop again."

He held her gaze until she nodded, and then he led her out of the service station and back to his smelly car. Catalina stumbled along beside him, dizzy with fear and relief, hoping that her gamble had worked.

83

DEREK MATHERS WAS sitting in his cubicle, trying to decide whether to call it a night or give Windermere a call, see if he could coax a smile out of her, when the phone beat him to it. Rung, loud, startling him, and he sat up quickly and grabbed for the phone, picked it up before he was fully composed. "Carla?"

"Uh, sorry." A man's voice. "This is Richardson, with the Marshals in Minneapolis. I get the wrong number?"

Mathers cleared his throat. "Shit, sorry," he said. "This is Agent Derek Mathers, FBI. What do you need?"

"I'm trying to get a hold of Kirk Stevens and Carla Windermere," Richardson said. "They around?"

"Reno," Mathers said. "Chasing leads. I'm covering this thing from home. What's up?"

The guy paused. A long pause. "Okay," he said. "I'm down at the halfway house, you know? We're supposed to be watching that Romanian girl."

Supposed to be, Mathers thought. *That doesn't sound good.*

"Yeah," he said. "Okay. And?"

"And, yeah." Another beat. "We have a bit of a problem here, Agent Mathers. According to the staff inside, that girl isn't in her bunk for lights-out. And she's nowhere else in the building, either."

Mathers sat up. "So where the hell is she?"

"That's the thing," Richardson said. "The girls inside seem to think she just took off."

"Jesus," Mathers said. "Jesus Christ."

"You said it. What do you want us to do?"

Mathers leaned back and closed his eyes, already picturing Windermere's reaction. "Find her," he said. "Find her, for God's sake."

84

"JERSEY CITY." WINDERMERE called across the office to Stevens. "That's where we'll find Kirilenko, partner."

Stevens looked up. "You think?"

"The guy gave that waitress a North Jersey cell number," Windermere said. "And it turns out there's only one Nikolai Kirilenko in North Jersey, *and* his address and lengthy rap sheet are in the NCIC database, *and* he's got a scar on his face and he's ugly as sin."

"Hot damn," Stevens said. "Send me that NCIC file. Let me get a look."

Windermere typed something into her computer. "Sent," she said. "Now I'm calling LePlavy. Any luck, he can have this guy locked up tonight. And then I'm going to call the travel agent and get us a couple tickets back to the East Coast." She grinned at him. "If we can turn this guy against his bosses, partner, this case is made."

She was feeling the rush, Stevens knew. He was feeling it, too. After all the mud they'd slogged through on this case, he'd started to wonder if he and Windermere might be snakebit. Now they'd caught a break, and Stevens could hardly wait to get back on a plane.

Windermere put down the phone and started pacing. "Newark's on it," she said. "I'll brief Agent Tate. Get him to bring up a couple agents from the Las Vegas field office, hunt around for the girls

Kirilenko delivered. We gotta figure there's one or two more stops on the supply chain if there were forty girls in that box, right?"

"Right," Stevens said. "Either before Reno, or after."

"Or both." Windermere's phone rang. "Mathers," she said, bringing it to her ear. "Hey. What's up?"

She listened. Stevens watched her, watched the smile fade from her face. Watched her skin color, her eyes darken. "Jesus Christ, Derek," she said finally. *"Are you fucking kidding me?"*

85

IRINA RAN AWAY from the safe house, through back alleys and dark side streets until she was out of breath and panting and lost, the house and the U.S. Marshals far behind her.

She walked to a busy roadway, passed hotels and restaurants and hundreds of cars, all of them filled with happy Americans with no cares, no fears, nothing at all to worry about. Nobody stopped to threaten her, but nobody offered to help, either. They kept driving along to their cheerful restaurants and their big houses, and all the while, she kept running.

She was foolish, she realized, when she stopped at a railroad crossing to catch her breath. She was alone in America, didn't speak much English. She had no money and no idea how to get to Pennsylvania, even if she could pay for a ticket. It was dangerous to be out here, in this big, foreign city, surrounded by strange men and utterly alone.

But the traffickers still had Catalina. Was she supposed to sit in that safe house and do nothing?

No.

Irina ducked down the railroad tracks, away from the main road. Took shelter in a ditch and tried to form a plan. If she could find Maria, the translator, she could at least make a start. Maybe Maria would know how to get to Clearfield, Pennsylvania.

And if she couldn't find Maria?

She would need money. She could steal a car, maybe. She was a pretty girl in a country full of lonely, hungry men. Someone would stop for her. She would outwit him. She would hijack his car and take his money and then she would drive to Pennsylvania and find Catalina. This is what she would do.

It was a dumb plan. Any man who stopped for her was a man who wanted something from her. A predator. He would expect her to do things, and he would be stronger than her.

Still, it was a better plan than sitting in that safe house, waiting for Catalina to die. She would just have to be careful. Cautious. Smart. Irina looked up and down the railroad tracks. In the distance were the skyscrapers of downtown Minneapolis. She pulled herself out of the ditch and began to walk, searching for a man and a car and an opportunity.

86

MATHERS WAS WAITING at the airport in Minneapolis. Windermere didn't say a word to him.

A major break in the case, she thought, walking to Mathers's motor pool Tahoe and climbing in the backseat. *Maybe the major break in the case. And nobody can keep their eyes on big sister long enough to see the goddamn thing through.*

She'd been steamed all the way home from Reno. Could barely get the words out to explain the thing to Stevens. "Something spooked Irina Milosovici," she told him. "According to the staff, she was playing on the computer with a friend of hers, and the next thing anyone knows, she just bolted. Told her friend she was going to search for her sister."

Stevens stared at her. "For Catalina? Jesus. Where is she now?"

"That's the fucking thing, partner. Nobody knows. The whole city's looking for her, Minneapolis PD, sheriffs, everybody. The hell if anybody can find her, though."

"She said she was searching for her sister," Stevens said. "What prompted that? Do we know what she was doing on the computer?"

"Mathers says the friend told him Irina got a message from Catalina," Windermere said. "On her Facebook account, of all things. Like a picture or something, but the friend didn't know from where."

"So Catalina got her hands on a computer somehow. Can we trace the picture? Find out the IP address and follow it back?"

"Not so far," Windermere told him. "Irina logged out of her Facebook account before she bolted from the safe house. Mathers is calling Facebook now, but he says they're holding out for a warrant, which is going to take time."

"Especially since Irina didn't technically do anything wrong by leaving the safe house, right?" Stevens said. "It's not Irina's Facebook account we need. It's Catalina's."

"Exactly. And by the time Mathers gets Facebook that warrant, who knows where Catalina will be."

"Jesus," Stevens said. "Jesus Christ."

"Yeah." Windermere ran her hands through her hair. "Fuck my life."

> > >

SHE'D CANCELED THE TICKETS TO Newark. Booked new flights to Minneapolis. Flown the whole way home stewing about Mathers, about Irina Milosovici, about the incompetence of everybody in goddamn law enforcement besides herself and, sometimes, Stevens.

Now Stevens slipped into Mathers's Tahoe beside her. "No sign of Nikolai Kirilenko yet, but LePlavy has eyes on his place in Jersey City," he told her, pocketing his phone. "They'll let us know when this guy shows up."

"*If,*" Windermere said. "*If* he shows up, Stevens."

"You guys don't have to do this." This was Mathers from the front seat, the first words he'd said since he'd seen them. "That little girl's still missing. We'll find Irina. You guys crack the case."

"Bullshit," Windermere said, and all the poison and venom spilled out. "*Bullshit* you will, Derek. I told you to keep an eye on that girl, and where the hell is she?"

Mathers set his jaw. Didn't say anything.

"Every time I leave this city, someone fucks up my case," Windermere told him. "Clearly, the only people with their heads on straight are me and Stevens. So we're going to clean up your mess here, and then we're going to resume our case, and we're going to fucking pray, for everyone's sakes, that that little girl and her friends don't get killed in the meantime. Are we clear?"

Mathers said nothing. Didn't make eye contact in the rearview mirror. Windermere sat back, watched the city through tinted windows. *Goddamn it,* she thought. *We don't have time for this shit.*

87

IRINA FOUND HER mark outside a convenience store. She watched him from the shadows.

He was about her age. Pale, his skin pockmarked with acne. He was alone, and he appeared to Irina as though he were used to it. He had sad eyes and a slight frame. He did not look threatening.

She'd been in her hiding place for ten minutes, watching customers pass in and out, trying to work up her nerve. A group of swaggering young men in baseball caps lingered by the front door, smoking cigarettes, laughing, swatting at flies. There were five of them, cocky and brash. Irina shied away from them, stuck to the darkness. Prayed they wouldn't look in her direction.

The men finished their cigarettes and disappeared inside the store. Irina let herself breathe. Inched out of the shadows a little bit. Within a minute or two, her mark showed up.

His car was old, but it was clean. It ran okay. The young man parked and fiddled with his radio, and then he climbed out of the car and started for the store. Irina pushed herself off the wall. Now or never.

"Hey," she said, stepping out of the shadows. Her voice came out harsh, too urgent. The young man flinched. Irina tried again. "Hey," she said. "You."

The young man turned around this time, his expression guarded, his body tense. He didn't look interested in her; he looked wary, as though he could read her intentions already.

"You," she said again. She put a smile on her face, approached him slowly. "Do you want to have me?"

The young man shifted his weight. "Um," he said. "I don't—"

"I want *you*." Irina tried to sound seductive. Put her hand on her hip, dared the young man to admire her legs. "Will you take me somewhere?"

"Um." The young man looked around again. "I just need some milk, lady. Whatever you're selling, I don't really—"

"Forget the milk," Irina said. "Take *me*."

The young man laughed, a childish burst, surprised. "I'm sorry," he said. "I can't—this is too weird."

He started toward the store. Irina followed him. *"Wait,"* she said. *"Please."*

The young man ignored her. Reached the front of the store just as the gang of men emerged from the front doors. The young man nearly collided with them. Ducked aside as they came out, pushing and shoving each other. Then the men saw Irina and stopped, nudged each other. Their eyes roved up her legs to her hips and the swell of her breasts. One of them, the tallest, said something to his friends. They all laughed.

"What's up, cutie?" the tallest one asked her. "What are you doing tonight?"

Irina didn't answer. Didn't move, just stood frozen in place. Felt a tightness in her chest. Behind the men, the young acne-faced man slipped into the store. Irina, desperate, watched him go. Wanted to call to him, but he was gone. She was alone out here, now, with these terrifying men.

"What's the matter?" the tallest one said. "You don't like me? Why you acting so scared?"

One of his friends called out something, and all the men laughed. The tall one spun around, faked a punch at his friend. Then he smiled at Irina, his teeth gleaming, his eyes narrowed.

"You don't want to be friendly?" he said. "You want to be mean?"

He took a step toward Irina, then another. Not cautious steps; he was coming for her. He would take her if he wanted, and he knew that she knew it. His friends followed close behind him. They spoke to Irina. She didn't know what they said, but their voices were mocking, singsong. They swaggered toward her. Irina ran before they could catch her.

She could hear the men's voices as she fled the parking lot, away from the convenience store and into the darkness, the night, through an industrial neighborhood, the men's laughter echoing off the vast warehouse walls. She ignored them, kept running until she was far away from the store and the men were gone.

She crawled into an alcove and huddled in the darkness. She didn't dare to move. Didn't dare to close her eyes, afraid she'd see the tall man leering at her. Or worse, she'd see Catalina. Instead, she huddled there, wide-awake and hungry and scared, cursing her failure, her ineptitude, her fear, waiting for the morning.

88

STEVENS HUNG AROUND the FBI office just long enough to get the full story from Mathers. Then Windermere kicked him out.

"Get some sleep," she told him. "Kiss your wife and say hi to your kids. Harris is going to want a full briefing tomorrow, so you might as well be well-rested."

"Yeah?" he said. "What about you?"

"You know me, Stevens," she replied. "I never sleep."

But there were circles under her eyes, and a flatness to her voice, and Stevens knew she was exhausted. Knew she was pissed off, too, and knew she'd sleep an hour or two in her office tonight, if at all. No way she was leaving anyone else in charge, not now.

"*Go,*" she said, pushing him out the door. "I'll see you tomorrow."

She signed out a Crown Vic from the motor pool for him, flung him the keys, and waved good-bye. Then she climbed back on the elevator, and Stevens couldn't do anything but find the car she'd picked out for him and drive home.

He thought about Irina Milosovici as he drove. Wondered what she planned to do. It was dark up in Brooklyn Center, away from the lights of the city, and he wondered if she was safe somewhere. If she even *had* a plan.

He thought about Catalina Milosovici, too, and couldn't even comfort himself with hope. She was most likely still out there, still alive somewhere, but Stevens only felt an aching helplessness as he contemplated what she must be enduring. It was no wonder Irina had run away. She must have felt like she had to do *something*.

> > >

THE HOUSE WAS DARK WHEN Stevens pulled up. He parked behind Nancy's Taurus in the narrow driveway and entered through the side door, quiet as he could.

He felt his way into the kitchen in the dark, fumbled with the re-frigerator and pulled out a beer. Then he stopped. Something was moving in the living room.

His senses heightened, his nerves on edge, Stevens felt around for the light switch on the kitchen wall. Found it and flipped on blinding light. Someone gasped from the living room. Someone else swore.

Stevens looked in through the doorway. Saw his daughter on the couch, framed in the light from the kitchen and bare from the waist up aside from her bra, which she was clutching to her chest in a panic. Beneath her lay Calvin, still as a log, as if Stevens wouldn't notice him if he just didn't move.

"Oh my *God*." Andrea fumbled with her shirt. "Get *out* of here, Dad."

Stevens ducked away, gave his daughter a little dignity, the image ingrained in his head. He saw Andrea, half-naked, still a child, on the couch, her boyfriend's hands on her. He saw the girl in the Blue Room, battered and bruised, could still feel the impact wound where her attacker had shot him. And he saw Catalina Milosovici, her flat stare in the photograph, Andrea's age herself and a prisoner, a victim. He stepped back into the room and fixed his eyes on Calvin.

"Son," he said, his anger rising, "you need to find your way home now."

89

"THIS IS *BULLSHIT*."

Andrea, now fully clothed, sat on the couch. Triceratops lay beside her, blissfully oblivious. Nancy sat in the easy chair opposite, and Stevens stood by the window, too angry to sit still.

"It's not bullshit," Stevens said. "And you'll watch your language, young lady."

"We weren't even—*Ugh*." Andrea flounced back against the couch cushions. "It's not like that. I'm practically grown up anyway."

"You are not," Stevens told her. "You are nowhere near an adult yet, and you continue to prove it."

Calvin was gone. Stevens realized he could have offered the kid a ride home, made him call his folks or something, instead of just letting him run off into the dark. At that moment, though, he'd been furious. Couldn't trust himself not to strangle the kid.

"I am *too*," Andrea said. "I'm practically seventeen, Dad. I'm allowed to have friends."

"Is that what you call tonight?" Stevens asked. "'Friends'?"

Andrea colored. "He's a good guy, Dad," she said. "He's not some criminal. Just because everybody you know is a piece of shit doesn't mean the world's full of them."

"*Andrea.*" Nancy glared at her. "Watch your mouth."

"So, what, Dad?" Andrea said. "You think Calvin's, like, some rapist?"

Stevens felt his anger mounting again. "I think tonight's behavior is entirely inappropriate, is what I think."

"So you want me to be some kind of nun?"

That doesn't sound so bad, Stevens thought. *Christ, where did my little girl go?*

"You *cannot* just let guys take what they want," Nancy was saying. "Andrea, you have to be smarter than that."

Andrea flung around to face her mother. "You think I don't know that? My God, it's like I'm out turning tricks or something."

Stevens and his wife swapped a glance. "You're not to see him, Andrea," Nancy said. "Not alone in the dark. Not like this."

Not at all, Stevens thought, but he didn't say it. "This is bullshit," Andrea said again. Then she stomped up the stairs and was gone.

For a moment, neither Stevens nor Nancy said anything. Then Nancy sat up. "We can't keep her from growing up," she said. "Not forever, Kirk."

"That's not growing up, Nancy," Stevens told her "Fooling around on the couch, letting some guy take her clothes off because he told her she's pretty, it's not—"

"It is, though," Nancy said. "We all did it."

"Irina's sister is the same age as Andrea," Stevens said. "That little girl in Billings, I can't even guess what those men did to her." He looked at his wife. "The world's a tough place for girls like Andrea. I don't want her getting hurt."

Nancy rose, crossed the room to him. Took him in her arms. "She's a smart girl, Kirk. She's not going to do anything stupid."

"She's naive," Stevens said. "She's too trusting. She thinks the whole world's as kindhearted as she is."

Nancy hugged him. Rested her head on his shoulder. "We can't keep her locked up forever."

"I know, Nance," Stevens said. "Maybe just until she's thirty."

90

CARLA WINDERMERE SPENT the night in the situation room at the FBI office in Brooklyn Center, working the phone and struggling to coordinate the efforts of the FBI, the BCA, the Minneapolis and Saint Paul police departments, and the Hennepin and Ramsey County sheriff's offices as the search for Irina Milosovici continued.

So far, she'd been shut out. A couple cranks had phoned in reports, but for the most part, the wire was silent. She'd sipped bad coffee and waited out the night, had turned down an offer from Mathers to crash at his place—"Closer than your condo," he'd said, "I'll sleep on the couch"—and tried to stay upright. Finally, around a quarter to two, she passed out on a desk somewhere, got a few fitful hours.

She woke up to her phone ringing. Reached for it, groggy, wiping the hair from her face and the sleep from her eyes. "Windermere."

"Agent Windermere, it's Andy Tate in Reno."

"Tate." Windermere blinked, tried to shake herself awake. "You guys miss us already?"

"Something like that." Tate gave a low laugh. "Could have used you tonight, anyway. Reno PD managed to track down those girls you were after. Place called the Bunny Lounge in Damonte Ranch. Guess a couple of the working girls had heard of it, been trying to get an officer out there for months."

"No shit." Windermere was wide-awake now. "So you found the place. You get a chance to look around?"

Tate chuckled. "Oh, I'd say so," he said. "Found us a tidy little ranch house with about fifteen girls inside, none of whom speak a lick of English. Couple low-life meth heads running the show; they were too damned high to care we were putting them in handcuffs."

Windermere rubbed her eyes. "Anything to point us back to Irina Milosovici's kidnappers?"

"Not from what we can tell. We're debriefing the girls, but, like I say, most of them don't speak English, and half of them are stoned, to boot. We'll be lucky if they can tell us their names."

"Right," Windermere said. "I mean, whatever you can find. Maybe we get lucky and one of them knows the score."

"Prevailing opinion around here says they don't, but I'll work on it anyway," Tate told her. "I'll call you if we make any progress."

Windermere thanked him. Remembered Sanja from the Blue

Room, and asked Tate to keep an eye out for the girl's friend Amira, among the Bunny Lounge women. Fifteen more girls rescued, she thought, as she ended the call. It was a pretty damn big achievement, all things considered; should have made her want to jump for joy.

Not now, though. Not with both sisters missing and Facebook dragging its feet on Catalina Milosovici's account. Not with the whole case stalled around her. Not now. Tonight, the news only made her more tired.

91

VOLOVOI ARRIVED IN New Jersey early in the morning. He was running on fumes, literally and figuratively.

The stolen Accord was almost out of gas when he pulled into the container lot. Catalina Milosovici was asleep in the passenger seat. Volovoi eyed her enviously, wishing he could do the same. He was exhausted. Hadn't slept in more than a day. His shoulder stung raw. The bleeding had stopped at least, but the wound needed treatment. Volovoi needed treatment. He needed a rest.

He parked the stolen Accord at the back of the container yard, hidden from the road among stacks of empty boxes. There was a building back there, too, a long, low, ramshackle thing. No windows. Locked doors. Volovoi woke the girl up in the passenger seat. Pulled her out of the car and across the lot to the building, made her wait while he unlocked a door. Then he pushed her inside.

The building's interior was dark, musty. A couple grimy windows and a bare lightbulb. Volovoi heard the girl gasp as she took in her surroundings. As her eyes adjusted, and she saw what the building contained.

Women, about twenty of them. Young girls in a large prison cell, stick thin, their eyes wide. He'd been culling them from the boxes as they arrived in America, had Bogdan and Nikolai pick out the youngest and prettiest for safekeeping, just in case. Just in case the Dragon's demand for royalties pushed him into a corner. Just in case he needed to appease his partner's appetite for young female flesh quickly. Just in case the last week or so happened.

Volovoi had heard on the news about the brothel in Reno, the Bunny Lounge. Another buyer raided. The Blue Room in Billings was out of commission, too. The FBI insects were hot on the trail; soon enough, they would follow the trail here. His entire operation would be closed up and ruined. He would have only New York.

Well, so be it. He would get richer in Manhattan than he'd even dreamed in New Jersey, and the Dragon would ensure the FBI agents wouldn't connect the two operations. Let them tear down his New Jersey enterprises. Volovoi would move to Manhattan with the Dragon and flourish again.

Just so long as he could survive the next couple of days.

Volovoi shoved Catalina Milosovici in a cell with the other women. Then he pulled out his phone and called one of his idiot foot soldiers.

"The container yard," he told him. "Bring me a new car, and a first-aid kit, immediately."

"With pleasure," the foot soldier replied.

Volovoi studied the girls in their cell. Pictured Lloyd, the New

York buyer, leering over his steak, and felt his stomach turn. "And have someone come out here with a truck," he told the foot soldier. "We need to get this product to Manhattan."

Volovoi killed the connection. Turned back to Catalina Milosovici and the rest of the girls. The Dragon's prize did not look out of place among the rest of Bogdan and Nikolai's selections. He wondered why the idiots hadn't picked her out in the first place.

Because they were idiots, he told himself. *One more reason they're dead.*

Catalina Milosovici stared at him. She didn't say anything. The other girls watched him, too, some of them wary, some resigned. Volovoi let them look at him. He double-checked the lock on Catalina's cell door. Then he walked to the back of the building, to a dusty, worn leather couch, and he lay down on it and slept for a while.

92

WINDERMERE SURFED THE Internet until dawn, hunting down leads and trying to chase the sense of foreboding from her mind. When the sun finally showed itself through the eastern windows, she forced herself to stand, washed up in the ladies' room, pulled a change of clothes out of the suitcase she hadn't had a chance to take home yet, fixed her makeup, and rode herd on the morning shift at the various law enforcement agencies around town.

Around eight, Stevens straggled in, looking like he'd taken her advice to get a little sleep and straight ignored it. He gave her a weak smile and a cup of fresh coffee. "How was your night?"

"Restless and uneventful." She told him about the news from Reno. "You?"

"Dramatic," he said. "Walked in on my daughter playing grab-ass in the living room with some punk from school. I took umbrage and World War Three erupted."

Despite her fatigue, Windermere had to smile. "You shoot the poor kid, or what?"

Stevens gave her a sheepish look. "Sent him packing, anyway. Told him to keep his hands to himself or I'd lock his ass up. Andrea didn't take it so well."

"I bet she could have just died. The living room, huh? She doesn't have a bedroom of her own?"

"Not for entertaining gentleman callers," Stevens said. "No boys on the second floor, house rules."

"Damn," Windermere said. "You know this kid?"

"Only from what Nancy tells me." Stevens sighed. "It's not even the kid himself who's the problem, I guess. I just don't like my daughter running with that kind of crowd."

Windermere laughed. "What crowd, Stevens? The hormonal teenage crowd? She's, what, sixteen? It's going to happen."

"Not yet," Stevens told her. "Not if I can damn well help it."

She was about to tell him he'd have better luck reversing the earth's rotation, but then Mathers walked in, Drew Harris right behind him.

"Good morning." Harris regarded Windermere, then Stevens. "I take it from your general state of bedragglement that we're not making much progress."

Windermere shook her head. "Every law enforcement agency in the region has Irina's picture," she said. "Her face is on the news. We have people looking, but—"

"But so far, no good." Harris walked to the front of the situation room. "Where do we figure she went?"

"Nobody's sure," Windermere said. "We know she's trying to find her sister, so we're watching the bus stations, train station, airport, major highways."

"Except she doesn't speak English and she doesn't know the country," Stevens said. "How in the hell would she know where to go?"

"And how would she find her sister when she got there?" Windermere made a face. "Hell, *we* don't know how to track down these bastards."

"So we're waiting on Facebook to point us to little sister," Harris said. "Odds are the traffickers have the girl locked up somewhere on the East Coast. And you guys have the name of the delivery driver and an address where he might be found."

"Yes, sir," Windermere said.

Harris looked at her. "But you came back here instead of going to find him."

"Yes, sir. The Newark guys have an eye on Nikolai Kirilenko's apartment. He hasn't shown up since they started watching."

"Still," Harris said, "that's your lead, isn't it? Wherever this guy is, he could crack your case open."

"Yes, sir," Windermere said.

"So why'd you come back to Minnesota?"

Windermere felt her temperature rising. "Sir, I thought we should help with the search for Irina Milosovici. She's a key witness in this whole thing, and—"

"And she doesn't speak any English, doesn't have any money, doesn't know the city," Harris said. "Moreover, she didn't do anything technically wrong by leaving the safe house. She's free to travel the country, Carla. And Agent Mathers is perfectly capable of chasing down Catalina's Facebook account."

Agent Mathers keeps screwing up my investigation, Windermere thought. Mathers met her eyes, his expression guarded, like he was just waiting for her to sell him out. Windermere looked away. "Sir, I just didn't feel comfortable leaving my witness in danger like this."

Harris leaned against a table. "Agent Windermere, this is a major investigation," he said. "The biggest of your career, so far. It's your ball to carry. If you want to worry about every little thing that goes wrong, you won't get the damn thing solved. You have a lead in New Jersey that could save a girl's life. Farting around with a missing person's case in Minneapolis isn't going to help the big picture."

Windermere could feel Stevens watching her. Mathers, too. She made herself meet Harris's eyes. "Yes, sir," she said. "You're right."

"Good." Harris looked at her, then Stevens. "Now get your butts on a plane and go solve this thing."

93

MATHERS FOLLOWED THEM out to the parking lot.

"Carla, I'm sorry," he said. "I didn't think he'd take that kind of line."

Windermere kept walking, crossed the pavement toward her Chevelle, a cherry red '69 that had belonged to her father. Beside her, Stevens typed something into his phone.

"It's fine, Derek," she said. "Don't worry about it."

"Yeah, well," Mathers said, "I am worried, okay? This is way beyond me fucking up our relationship, or whatever you want to call it. This is serious. This is one of us transferring to Anchorage if we don't work this out."

Windermere didn't reply. Glanced at Stevens, who'd had the good sense to fall back a step or two. "Look," she told Mathers, "it's not that bad."

"Bull," Mathers said. "You don't trust me. That's why you came back to Minneapolis. You figure I'll blow up your investigation again if you're not here to hold my hand."

"Derek," she said. "Not now, okay?"

"You know it's true, though," he said. "You put your whole case on hold just to come back and make sure I wasn't screwing everything up."

"I just—" She reached the Chevelle. Turned to face him. "This is a huge case, Derek. Every time I turn around, there's another fuckup at home base. You think that makes it easy to go out and solve this thing?"

"This is the FBI you're working with, Carla," Mathers said. "This is *me*. You think I'm a meathead, that's fine, but I know I'm a good cop, and you know it, too." He set his jaw. "And you know I'm good for you, too."

Windermere stared at him, a big hard-ass cop everywhere but those blue eyes. She realized she'd missed him, this whole case be damned. Realized she was sick of fighting with him, of not seeing his stupid smile in the morning.

He screwed up your case, her mind screamed. *And now this, this whole awkwardness bullshit, what did you think would happen?*

She'd known it was a bad idea to hook up with Mathers. Sooner or later, the romance would wear off, and somebody's feelings would get hurt. Damn it, though, she still missed him.

But there were two teenage girls missing. Probably a hundred more in boxes, on ships or on trucks. This was no time to get moony.

Windermere squared her shoulders. Fixed Mathers with a long, hard look. "We'll talk about this later," she told him. "Just find Irina, okay? Don't do a damn thing else until you find her."

Then she climbed into the Chevelle, slammed the door, and instantly regretted not telling him good-bye.

94

STEVENS'S PHONE RANG as Windermere parked the Chevelle in the long-term lot at Minneapolis–Saint Paul International. Nancy, at work.

"Hey," he said. "Don't tell me our little angel is up to no good again."

"Clearfield, Pennsylvania." His wife's voice was electric. "That's where Irina is trying to go."

Stevens frowned. "Pardon?"

"She left a message on my phone at work, Kirk," Nancy said. "My cell phone died last night before I went to sleep, but she must have tried it before she called the office. Anyway, she said she's going to someplace called Clearfield, Pennsylvania, to find Catalina."

"Clearfield." Stevens climbed out of the car and hurried after Windermere. "Where the heck is that?"

"According to Google, it's a little town in the north part of the state, along Interstate 80," Nancy said. "That must be where Catalina sent her message."

Interstate 80, Stevens thought. *Pennsylvania.* So the Dragon didn't have Catalina just yet. Or he didn't last night.

"Hold on one sec." Stevens caught up to Windermere, caught her arm. "Irina phoned Nancy at her office last night," he told her. "Left a message that she's headed someplace called Clearfield. It's a little town in Pennsylvania."

"So, what?" Windermere said. "Should I swap our tickets? Get us to this Clearfield place?"

Stevens thought about it. "I don't think so," he told her. "Kirilenko's in New Jersey. All of those shell companies LePlavy dug up are there, too. I don't think the Dragon's in Pennsylvania."

"So Catalina Milosovici is still in transit."

"Exactly," Stevens said, starting toward the terminal again. "Let's be there when she arrives."

95

CATALINA STOOD IN the cell with the rest of the young women and watched the silent man sleep on his couch. She could feel the iPhone in her waistband. She'd turned it off to conserve the battery. She had hoped that the silent man would stop for gas again, allow her to use the bathroom. She had hoped she would be able to send another message.

And now they had arrived, here, in this dingy, dark little building, with these other girls Catalina didn't recognize, and she had no idea where she was. Even if she could send a message, she couldn't tell Irina anything useful. Anyway, who's to say these other girls wouldn't betray her to the silent man? Catalina had never seen any of them before. They might rat her out to survive.

She stood and watched the silent man sleep. None of the other girls met her eyes. None of them spoke. Time passed slowly, maddeningly slow. Catalina felt her frustrations mounting.

You can't just stand and wait here, she thought. *You have a phone. Use it.*

She welled up her courage. Found a pretty blond girl with pigtails standing at the back of the cell. The blond girl stood alone. Catalina watched her until she looked up. Catalina smiled at her. "Hello."

The girl didn't answer. She stole a glance at the sleeping man and then looked away again.

Catalina inched closer. Whispered. "Where is this place?" she said. "What are they doing to you here?"

At first, the blond girl didn't answer. Catalina waited. The whole building seemed to go silent. Finally, the other girl replied. "You mustn't speak," she said softly. "They'll kill us if we speak."

"They won't kill me," Catalina told her. "They want me."

The blond girl said nothing.

"Anyway, I'm not afraid of them," Catalina said. "I have a way out of here. I just need to know where we are."

The blond girl shook her head. "I don't know where we are," she said. "They took me out of the box and put me here. I don't know anything. I—" She sobbed suddenly. "I miss my family. I just want to go home."

The girl continued to cry. Catalina watched her until she turned away, wiping her tears with her ragged sleeve, pressing her face against the bars of the cell. Catalina looked around at the other girls.

"I need to know where we are," she whispered to them. "I think I can get us out of here."

Nobody said anything. Most of the girls shied back, their eyes darting away to check on the sleeping man at the other end of the building. Catalina felt the phone at her side like an itch, felt suddenly angry.

"Come *on*," she said louder. "Why won't you help me? I can get us out of here. I—"

"Nobody knows." This was a beautiful raven-haired girl. She stood a few feet away from Catalina, watching her through eyes that were a shocking emerald green. "Nobody knows where we are. Nobody knows anything in this place."

Catalina pushed her way over. "My name is Catalina," she said. "I've been in a box for weeks. They killed my handlers yesterday, but I stole a phone. I can send a message for help, but I need to tell them where we are."

The dark-haired girl studied Catalina. "Dorina," she said. "That's my name. I was put in the box in Bucharest. I don't know when. I don't know how long I was inside."

"And they brought you here," Catalina said. "When the box arrived in America, they brought you straight here?"

"It wasn't far to go," Dorina replied. "This building was maybe fifteen meters from where they took me out of the box."

So I'm back where we started, Catalina thought. *The East Coast of America. All of that trouble, and they brought me back here.*

"I don't know where we are," Dorina whispered, "but I think I know where we're going. I overheard one of the thugs talking. He said we are supposed to go to New York."

New York! Catalina felt her breath catch. "Where in New York?" she said. "And for what purpose?"

"All I know is New York," Dorina said. "Apparently there is a man there who wants us. That's all."

Catalina considered this. New York was a big place, that much she knew. Still, this information would help. At least Irina could tell the police where to start their search.

She reached into her waistband. Pulled out the phone. "I will send a message to my sister," she told Dorina. "She escaped from the box. Maybe she can tell the authorities how to find us."

"Hurry," Dorina said. "Before the handler wakes up."

The phone seemed to take forever to power on. Finally, the screen lit up. Catalina tapped on the Internet icon. Loaded the Facebook page. Was about to log into her account when she heard a commotion outside.

"Crap." Dorina grabbed Catalina's arm. *"Hide the phone."*

Catalina jammed the phone into her waistband just as the building's door flew open, blinding the captive girls with sudden sunlight. Catalina hid her eyes, blinking, saw nothing but brightness. For a long moment, nobody moved. Then Catalina heard soft laughter. Boots on the concrete floor. A man stood in the doorway, staring in at her.

He was tall and lanky, with a wiry black beard and wild eyes. He wore a long black-leather jacket, and a wicked knife hung from a scabbard on his belt. He was the scariest creature Catalina had ever seen in her life, and he was looking at Catalina like he knew it.

"Hello, little one," he told her, smiling at her through the bars. "I am the Dragon. You belong to me now."

96

VOLOVOI WOKE TO the Dragon standing above him.

"Wake up, wake up, Andrei," the gangster was saying. "I'm ready to take delivery of my prize."

Instantly, Volovoi was awake. He pushed himself to his feet, blinked a couple of times, surveyed the building, the Dragon with his leather jacket and his knife, the girls in their cell, a couple of foot soldiers waiting by the door.

"I'd heard you'd returned," the Dragon said, smirking. "And clearly your mission was a success. When were you going to deliver my little beauty?"

In her cell, Catalina Milosovici stared out at the Dragon, her grimy face pale. Clearly, she knew what was coming.

Volovoi cleared his throat. "I wanted to finalize a few details, first," he told the Dragon. "A stolen car to get rid of, for one thing. And I had to secure the shipment of these other girls to your warehouse."

The Dragon gestured to the couch. "And you had to sleep, of course."

Volovoi cursed himself. "I had a long night with my idiots," he said. "They did not go quietly."

"I am glad you succeeded anyway, Andrei." The Dragon slapped him on the back, so hard that Volovoi flinched. "And this is a fine collection of girls for my buyer."

"I'm glad you approve," Volovoi said. "I'll have them in Manhattan this afternoon."

"And your next shipment?"

Volovoi checked his watch. Almost noon. The *Atlantic Prince* would arrive with another box in a few hours. With any luck, the FBI wouldn't find him before then.

"Three p.m.," he told the Dragon. "I'll process the girls here and have them shipped to the warehouse in Manhattan. They should be ready for the buyer and his friends by tomorrow, at the latest."

"Tomorrow," the Dragon said.

Volovoi shifted. "It is possible I could have them ready tonight," he said. "Though it would be a rush."

The Dragon waved him off. "Tomorrow is fine, Andrei," he said. "Take your time." Then he turned back to the cell, where Catalina Milosovici waited. "It will only give me more opportunity to enjoy my little prize."

The girl's eyes widened, and Volovoi felt his stomach turn. He knew what the Dragon did to his young playthings. He'd heard the stories, and if they were even half true, Catalina Milosovici was in for a short, unpleasant future.

The Dragon seemed to read his mind. His wolfish grin intensified. "Open the cell, Andrei," he told Volovoi. "Quit stalling, and let me take this one home."

97

CATALINA LET THE man who called himself the Dragon lead her out of the grungy building and back into the sunlight. It was hot outside, muggy and humid, a stifling day. In the container yard, a big American car waited, sleek and black. The Dragon opened the rear door.

"Please," he said, ushering her inside. "After you."

Catalina sat. The Dragon slid in beside her and sat close, one slick, sweaty hand on her leg. Catalina squirmed, tried to hide her revulsion. Gazed out at the little shack and wondered what would become of Dorina and the others.

New York.

"Park Avenue," the Dragon told his driver. "Let's take my little one home."

The driver shifted the big car into gear, and it idled away from the shack. Catalina studied the rows of containers. She couldn't see the smelly car the silent man had brought her in, but there was a big truck backing up to the little building. The silent men would take Dorina and the others to New York, Catalina knew. She had to find a way to tell Irina.

And she would have to do it quickly. The Dragon was going to take her to his lair, and then he would do things to her. And no doubt he would want her to remove her clothing when he did them. He would find the phone.

The Dragon was eyeing her, talking to her. He had hiked up her large T-shirt and was touching her knee, seemingly oblivious to the filth that coated her skin. She hadn't bathed since that awful hose on the docks. The Dragon didn't seem to care, though.

"Have you ever been to New York, little one?" he was asking her. "It is the center of the world, the heartbeat. Millions of people. So much money. So much opportunity." He smiled at her, another unpleasant smile. "Of course, you will not see very much of it, my little pet. You will have to imagine what this place is like."

He unscrewed a vial from around his neck. There was a little silver spoon inside, and the rest was white powder. He inhaled it through his nose, came up gasping and blinking.

He was distracted, had slid away from her to the opposite side of the car, focused entirely on his white powder and his vial. Now was her chance.

Catalina shifted her weight, slipped the thug's phone from her pocket. Held it tight between her leg and the door, away from the Dragon's eyes. She had no time for the Internet, for Facebook. She would have to type a text message and hope someone friendly received it.

It was excruciating work. The car sped over bumps and joints in the road, jostling her hands as she tried to type. The Dragon kept looking at her, fondling her leg as he talked to her. She had to wait until he turned back to his little vial again to even try.

Focus, she told herself. *For Dorina and the others, if not for yourself.*

The iPhone didn't have a Romanian alphabet. She couldn't spell in English. She would try the best she could.

P-a-r-c-a, she typed. *Park.* Each letter seemed to take a thousand years. The Dragon's fingers crawled up her bare thigh, each skeletal touch a new torture. Catalina tried to ignore the man. She kept typing.

S-t-r-a-d-a. Street.

B-a-l-a-u-r. Dragon.

Close enough.

She wondered who to send it to. Choose a number at random? Or one of the thug's contacts? She still didn't know how to alert the police. Catalina scrolled through his contacts as carefully as she could. Could not find a number that appealed to her. Couldn't make a decision, her heart pounding, the Dragon blathering on beside her.

Then she felt his hand on her wrist. "Why are you so distracted, little one?" he said. "What are you doing over there?"

Catalina froze. Dropped the phone to the floor of the car and kicked it under the seat. "Nothing," she said, trying to match his smile. "I am not doing anything. Please."

The Dragon studied her face. Catalina waited, didn't breathe. Finally, the Dragon unscrewed his little vial again.

"You are a defiant little bitch," he told her. "I could see it in your photograph. But we'll see how brave you are when you're alone with me."

He inhaled from the vial again. Catalina watched him. Kicked around with her feet on the floor, pushing the phone farther beneath the seat, fighting the wave of sadness and frustration that threatened to overwhelm her. She'd failed to send her message. Failed to help Dorina and the other girls. All she could do now was pray that someone else saved the day, and quickly, before this Dragon man and his friends did whatever they were planning to do.

Prayer. As far as strategies went, it wasn't a very happy one.

98

ZACH LEPLAVY HAD a car waiting for them in the short-term lot outside Newark Liberty International Airport, a mean-looking black Charger with a ferocious low stance. "Swiped it from the motor pool," he told Windermere, tossing her the keys. "Brand-new. Figured you guys might as well ride in style."

"Damn right," Windermere said, slipping behind the wheel. "Now, where are we going?"

LePlavy gave Stevens the front passenger seat. Slid in the back. "Nikolai Kirilenko lives in an apartment complex in Jersey City," he told the agents. "We've had eyes on it since you called in, but he hasn't showed up yet."

"We need a search warrant for the house," Stevens said as Windermere gunned the Charger's big engine and squealed out of the lot.

LePlavy grinned. "Already done." He produced a sheaf of paper from his suitcase. "I took the liberty of arranging a search and seizure while I waited on your flight."

"Hot damn." Windermere glanced at the warrant as she drove. "What about a map, LePlavy? You got one of those?"

> > >

NIKOLAI KIRILENKO'S APARTMENT WAS A lonely bachelor special: messy futon, dirty dishes, pile of suspect laundry on the floor. There was nobody home.

"Doesn't look like he's been around for a while," Stevens said, studying the film of dust that had settled over everything. "Maybe he's out on another delivery."

"I get the feeling these guys stay busy," Windermere said. "Who'd want to stick around this place too long, anyway?"

Stevens saw her point. It was a hot, humid day outside, and even hotter inside the apartment; suffocating. The building was old, wasn't air-conditioned, and Nikolai Kirilenko didn't even have a fan. After five minutes in the place, Stevens could already feel the sweat beading at the back of his neck.

They poked around the apartment and found nothing of merit. An old snub-nosed .38 in a kitchen drawer. A couple bricks of cash in rubber bands in the freezer. Shady stuff, but nothing to point them toward the Dragon.

Then Stevens knelt down to check under the futon, a ratty old thing with a smell like dirty sheets and unclean hair. The futon's base was uneven; Kirilenko had steadied it with a makeshift shim, a thin piece of plastic. Stevens slid it out from beneath the bed frame, let the futon sag as he studied the plastic. It was an ID, a union membership card.

"'The Port of Newark,'" Windermere read aloud, when he showed it to her. "Somehow I don't think this guy spent much time on the docks."

"Doesn't seem like he got much use out of his membership, anyway," Stevens said.

"Probably a sham," Windermere said. "Something to scare off the taxman. Dollars to donuts the guy never worked a day on the docks in his life. There's nothing here, Stevens. Not until Kirilenko comes back."

"If we're waiting, let's do it outside." Stevens wiped his brow. "We could use a little fresh air."

He turned for the door. Nearly ran into LePlavy coming in from the hall, his phone at his ear. "Got a witness for you two," he said. "Some guy figures he might be able to help out with your case."

"Well, hot damn," Stevens said. "Can we bring this guy in? Where is he now?"

LePlavy chuckled. "You can talk to him, for sure," he said. "Bringing him in might be a little difficult. Seems he's a thousand miles out at sea at the moment."

99

"I DON'T GET IT." Windermere leaned close to the computer, spoke into the microphone. "Why wait until now to phone this thing in? Why not talk to us when we saw you on the ship?"

On the computer screen, the witness's image blurred and distorted. His voice cracked, cut out; the picture froze. Windermere felt her frustration mounting. Wondered why the hell she couldn't conduct this damn interview on dry land.

The witness's name was Raipul. He was the same short, bearded man who'd given her the side eye when she'd checked out the *Ocean Constellation* with Stevens the first time. He hadn't wanted to talk then, but now, from a tenuous Skype connection somewhere in the middle of the Atlantic Ocean, he'd found his voice.

"I wanted to be safe," Raipul told them. "I needed to be absolutely certain. This ship—sometimes we don't leave precisely on schedule. Sometimes we make extra stops. If I spoke before I was sure we'd left the United States, the people who did this could . . ." He swallowed. "I was afraid they would find me."

"But not anymore."

He shrugged. "I am at sea," he said. "When the ship docks in Spain I will leave it and find another ship. Who will follow me? Not even the Federal Bureau of Investigation will know where I've gone."

"So, okay," Windermere said. "I guess that puts a time frame on our conversation. Why don't you tell us what you know before we lose our connection?"

"You were asking about a box," Raipul said. "A box filled with women."

"That's right," Stevens said. "Did you see it?"

"We all saw it," Raipul told them. "We all knew it was there. The women—we could hear them shouting for help."

"But you didn't help them."

"How could we? We all knew who owned the box. We knew what he would do if we told about him."

"But you're telling now," Windermere said. "Why?"

Raipul stared through the computer screen at Windermere and Stevens, and even across thousands of miles of shoddy satellite connection, Windermere could see the man's eyes were haunted.

"I think about them," he said. "The women. Even now, I think about them in that box. About how many more boxes there must be," he said. "I can't stop thinking about them."

"Us, either," Windermere said. "So, okay, Mr. Raipul, what do you have for us?"

"I've heard stories," Raipul said softly. "From the men in the harbors and the crew on these ships. They say a man named Dragon imports the women. That he operates with an American in Bucharest."

Windermere felt her impatience mounting. They knew all of this already.

"The American has a company," Raipul said. "I have heard that the Baltic Treasures Trading Company is the trader of these women. They are not the people who put the boxes on the boat. But they are the people who fill them."

LePlavy was hovering behind them, listening in. "Didn't come up in any of my dealings with Interpol," he told Stevens and Windermere. "I've never heard of that company."

"They must be Mike's cover in Bucharest," Stevens said. "He loads them into the Dragon's boxes, and sends them to Trieste."

"Works for me," Windermere said. "So what do we do with Mr. Raipul's information?"

"I'll get back in touch with Interpol," LePlavy said. "Look for background information on this Baltic Treasures company. Maybe it leads us to this American, Mike. We can follow him to the Dragon."

Windermere arched an eyebrow at Stevens. "You want to go to

Europe, partner?" She turned back to the screen. "Mr. Raipul," she said. "Stick around, would you? Don't fall overboard or anything."

Raipul's image bobbed and crackled. Then the picture froze, and his voice came out as static. "I'm going to take that as a yes," Windermere said, standing. "Let's get to work."

100

LEPLAVY CAME BACK an hour and a half later, rubbing his hands. "It's dinnertime in Eastern Europe," he said. "I had to drag a bunch of people from their *ciorbă*."

Windermere studied the agent. "You don't exactly look sorry about it."

"Not at all," LePlavy said. "Interpol Bucharest took a drive down to the Baltic Treasures Trading Company, had a look around the place. Apparently it's an exporter of electronic goods, headquarters in Romania, offices all around the Baltic states."

"Yeah," Windermere said. "And?"

"And our European colleagues found a gentleman hanging around the Baltic Treasures offices," LePlavy said. "Showed him that police sketch of the Dragon and the guy freaked out and started singing. Promised the Interpol guys the moon if only they'd protect his family."

"Talk about world famous," Stevens said. "What did the guy have to say?"

"He said the company put thirty boxes on the *Ocean Constellation* the day they shipped the women, is what he said."

"Thirty boxes," Stevens said. "Jesus. All of them filled with women?"

LePlavy shook his head. "Nah. They were mostly filled with DVD players and textiles. It's a volume game: send twenty-nine legit boxes and hope the last one doesn't get picked for a random inspection, and if it does, put up a false front and hope the customs guys get lazy. Play the odds, right?"

"So we can lean on this guy," Windermere said. "Maybe somewhere along the line he can lead us to Mike."

"I figure we'll let Interpol handle that," LePlavy replied. "The guy had something else to say, though. Apparently Baltic Treasures sent another twenty boxes out a couple weeks back, about the same time a ship called the *Atlantic Prince* docked in Trieste."

He grinned at them. "The *Atlantic Prince* calls in Newark this afternoon."

101

"SO WHAT DO you think?"

The Dragon gestured around the apartment. Catalina followed his gaze and wanted to be sick.

It was a beautiful apartment. The floor was rich dark wood, the kitchen marble and stainless steel, the ceilings high and the windows expansive. It was bigger than Catalina's parents' home in Romania, and the way the sunlight streamed in, it resembled a movie star's home. It was an incredible apartment, and Catalina knew it was where she was going to die.

Park Avenue. A skyscraper in the clouds. Catalina thought about Irina, about her family, about Dorina and the other girls, and tried not to throw up. Tried not to cry. Tried to keep herself together in front of this awful, devil-faced man, who was leering at her and showing her around as though she were a house guest, not a captive. As though he didn't intend to cut her, later, with that knife on his belt.

Catalina let the Dragon lead her. He showed her the living room, the kitchen, a vast, well-stocked library, a couple of guest bedrooms. He showed her the master bedroom, a massive bed and a pile of white powder on the bedside table. He led her back to the kitchen and fed her, gave her a ham sandwich, the first real food she'd consumed in weeks, and as she sat at his kitchen table and scarfed the sandwich down, he talked to her, asked her maddening questions about her childhood, about the town in which she'd grown up. What did her father do, he wondered. What kind of dog was Sasha? Did she share her sister's appetite for adventure? Stupid, useless questions. As though she were trapped inside some kind of madhouse.

Which, she supposed, she was. This man was not normal. He was drugged-up and maniacal, toying with her like she was a mouse in a trap. Catalina pushed the sandwich away. She'd lost her appetite.

"What do you want with me?" she asked the man, looking him in the eye. "Why have you brought me here?"

The Dragon chuckled. "No time for pleasantries, I suppose," he said. "Very well."

He took the sandwich away from her. Motioned her to her feet. Catalina stood. Followed him through the apartment to one of the bathrooms. The Dragon stepped back and ushered her inside.

"You'll find soap and shampoo in the shower," he told her. "Clean yourself. Make sure you're very clean. There's a makeup kit on the counter when you're finished, and I've chosen something for you to wear. When you're clean and dressed, I'll let you out again." He smiled at her. "Then we can start our games."

Catalina shuddered. Pushed past him and into the bathroom. The Dragon chuckled in the hallway. "Don't try anything silly," he told her. "I'd hate to have to hurt you before I'm ready."

Catalina slammed the door closed. Felt around for a lock and found none, so she waited. Held her breath and didn't move until she heard the man walk away from the door.

The bathroom was huge. It was bigger than her bedroom in Berceni. A huge shower and a deep, luxurious bathtub. A window with a view of the city.

Catalina hurried to the window. Peered down at the streets and across at the skyscrapers around here. Everywhere she looked, she could see normal people going about their normal lives. And here she was, trapped in this madman's apartment, destined to die.

The madman opened the door. "I don't hear water running," he said. "Come away from that window before I get angry, little one."

Catalina waited until he'd closed the door again. Then, reluctantly, she peeled off her dirty clothing. Ran the shower water until it was warm, and stepped into the spray and began to obey the man's instructions.

102

TWELVE HUNDRED MILES away from her sister, Irina Milosovici crawled out of her little alcove.

She was very hungry. She hadn't eaten since yesterday, when she'd had lunch with the other women at the safe house. It had been more than a day now, and she was weakened by thirst.

And she was hot. It had been frigid at night, but now Irina was sweltering hot. Even in the shadows of her little cubbyhole, she was sweating. Fighting the empty gnaw in her stomach, the parch in her throat. The shame.

She'd given up too easily last night. She'd let the men scare her, and she'd freaked out and run away. At the first sign of a threat, she'd abandoned Catalina. She was a coward. Catalina was still out there. This was no time to hide.

Slowly, unsteadily, Irina pulled herself to her feet. The midday sun was blazing; it stung her eyes as she searched the empty street.

There were warehouses in both directions—blank, windowless buildings. Railroad tracks and parking lots and abandoned cars. In the distance, Irina could see the busy road she'd fled from the night before. The convenience store was up there somewhere. It would have men. Those men would have cars. She would try again to lure one of the men. Then she would steal his car. She would find a way to Clearfield, Pennsylvania, and she would search for Catalina.

Her stomach growled. She pictured the long rows of American candy bars and snack foods, the coolers filled with cold drinks. She would have to get food before she found a man. She would need energy for the journey ahead.

Squinting, shielding her eyes from the sun, Irina pushed herself off the dirty wall and started unsteadily toward the road, the spasms of traffic, the city.

103

STEVENS STARED OUT the window of the Customs and Border Protection helicopter as Windermere relayed instructions to LePlavy through her headset.

"Tell Interpol to work on that witness," she told the Newark agent, yelling over the thunder of the rotors. "We need to know which of these twenty boxes is legitimate, and which aren't. If there's women on this boat, I want to find them."

They'd left LePlavy to coordinate the investigation from land. Commandeered a CBP Black Hawk and flown out to meet the *Atlantic Prince* as she steamed into the Upper Bay. Stevens watched the big ship as she passed beneath the Verrazano-Narrows Bridge between Staten Island and Brooklyn: a thousand feet long, she was the same length and general dimensions as the *Ocean Constellation*, though her hull was sleek and black and somehow more foreboding.

There was no guarantee that any of the boxes stacked on the

Atlantic Prince held women, Stevens knew. But if they did, it would break the case open.

LePlavy had a CBP tactical team en route to the *Atlantic Prince* on a borrowed Customs SAFE boat. "It's fast," he said. "Sixty miles an hour. They might beat you out there."

"Good," Windermere said. "I hope they do. Keep me and Stevens from getting shot."

"Those traffickers aren't going to want to give up their cargo," Stevens said, watching the *Atlantic Prince* grow larger outside his window. "So let's try and get the women out of the box before this ship docks."

Windermere glanced across the helicopter at him. "Yeah," she said. "Let's try and do that."

104

LEPLAVY CALLED BACK just as Stevens and Windermere reached the *Atlantic Prince*.

"Got a box for you," he told Windermere, reading a number off of a manifest. "Just like the *Ocean Constellation*, nineteen legit boxes, one bogey. Headed to a nonexistent company in Jersey City."

"Get the ship's crew that information," Windermere said. "Tell them to find the box for us. I want those women out of there immediately."

"Ship's crew has been informed of your arrival," LePlavy told her.

"That CBP tactical squad's nearly on-scene, as well. You probably want to wait for them, in case things get hairy."

"Fine," Windermere said. "But tell them to hurry."

The CBP Black Hawk swooped over the bow of the *Atlantic Prince*, descended into a controlled hover twenty feet above the deck. Windermere could see five or six members of the ship's crew clustered below, ready to help bring her and Stevens aboard. The customs airman slid open the helicopter's rear door. Gestured to Windermere, *Now or never*. Windermere looked at Stevens, who gave her a weak smile.

"We do too much of this cowboy shit," she told him, yelling over the wind and the howl of the engines. *"See you on deck."*

> > >

STEVENS FELT HIS STOMACH DROP out as he descended from the Black Hawk onto the *Atlantic Prince*'s bow. Wondered how a Minnesota state cop found himself in this kind of predicament all the time. Before he could come up with an answer, he was touching down on hard steel, and the crew of the *Atlantic Prince* was surrounding him, unclipping his safety harness, bringing him and Windermere on board the ship.

As on the *Ocean Constellation*, most of the crew didn't speak any English. The first officer did, though, and he met Stevens and Windermere inside the ship's accommodations tower.

"Your colleague onshore relayed your request," he told Stevens and Windermere. "In general, it's not possible to access the cargo during a voyage. But this box, luckily, is at the top of a stack. If you're careful, you should be able to get up there."

"Perfect," Windermere said. "So let's do it."

They hurried out of the tower and back out to the cargo deck. Met the customs tactical team, four hard-looking men with assault rifles and combat-zone body armor. Windermere explained the situation.

"We have a box we suspect is full of women at the top of that stack," she said, pointing skyward. "We need to get up there and get inside."

The leader followed her gaze. The box was five containers up, fifty feet above deck, a hundred-odd feet above sea level. Stevens felt his stomach churn, felt suddenly aware of the motion of the waves against the ship's hull. The swell was a light one, but there were no handrails up there. Any slip could be fatal.

"Maybe we should wait," he told Windermere. "It's a hell of a risk letting forty disoriented women loose up there."

Windermere shook her head. "The longer we wait, the better the chances that the Dragon figures out what we're up to," she said. "We want to catch this guy, Stevens. We'll just have to be really freaking careful."

Stevens considered the stacks again. Weighed the odds. Figured he'd rather try and corral all those women than see the Dragon get away clean.

"Okay," he said. "Let's do it."

105

THE TACTICAL TEAM scaled the containers one at a time, beginning with the lowest stack at the bow of the ship. They climbed atop the first ten-foot box with rope and brute strength, dropped a rope ladder behind so that Stevens and Windermere could follow. The ship swayed as they climbed. The breeze picked up. In the distance, Stevens could see thunderheads. There was a storm coming.

The ship steamed beneath the Bayonne Bridge as the team worked their way to the box. She made her way slowly into the Newark Bay, met a flotilla of tugboats as she approached the massive gantry cranes on the New Jersey shore.

Windermere picked up her radio, called LePlavy. "Don't let them dock this ship before we find those women," she said. "Stall until I give the go-ahead, okay?"

LePlavy said something that Stevens couldn't make out, and then Windermere stowed her radio again. Ahead of them, the tactical team clustered around a nondescript brown container, similar to every other box on board.

"This is the one," the tactical leader told them. "You want we should just cut it open?"

"Yeah, but be careful," Windermere told him. "I wouldn't put it past these bastards to leave a booby trap."

The leader flashed her a thumbs-up, and Stevens and Windermere hung back as one of the tactical guys produced a pair of heavy-duty bolt cutters from his belt. Stevens watched the man approach the box, watched him cut the lock. Watched the man's colleagues cover him with their weapons.

Stevens drew his pistol, too. Windermere did the same.

Slowly, the tactical team slid the container door open. The men drew back instantly, one of them gagging. A moment later, Stevens caught the smell, a noxious, too-sweet blend of human waste and vomit. He held his breath and inched closer, his pistol still drawn.

Inside the box was a false compartment, as Irina had described. Stacks of cardboard boxes holding cheap DVD players. The tactical team moved the boxes away, slowly, methodically, revealing the hidden compartment behind.

Sounds now. A pounding from within, weak but audible.

The tactical leader shined a light at the door. His man fiddled with his bolt cutters. Stevens felt his heart pounding. *Come on,* he thought. *Come on, get them out.*

The tactical man cut the lock. Pulled the ruined shards clear and pulled open the door. The smell was even worse now. Inside was darkness. Stevens searched the dark for survivors, praying it was survivors and not bodies they'd find.

Then the first girl appeared. Cautious, her eyes wide, her pale skin stretched drum-tight over her cheekbones. Another emerged from the gloom, leaning against the dirty walls of the box for support, then another, none of them older than sixteen or seventeen. Windermere rushed forward to help, glanced back at Stevens, paused when she saw the look in his eyes, his clenched fists, his whole body paralyzed.

"Shit," she said. "You okay, partner?"

"We have to get these bastards, Carla," Stevens said, and knew when he said it that he meant to kill them, every piece-of-shit trafficker with a hand in this mess, evidence or no evidence, justifiable or not.

Windermere met his gaze. "We do," she told him, "and we will."

106

"I NEED MEDICAL staff for these girls," Windermere told LePlavy. "I need someplace to house them, and enough agents to guard them. And I need to keep this a secret until we follow that box to the Dragon, or whoever's in charge of this mess."

LePlavy had met them on the pier, after the *Atlantic Prince* docked. They'd left the trafficked girls in the crew's mess on board the ship, found them food and fresh water and supplies from the infirmary, left them with the tactical squad and more customs agents from the port. Now they watched the *Atlantic Prince* from inside the Charger, waiting as the ship was unloaded.

"Someone's going to come for that box," Windermere said. "Wherever they take it, we're going to follow them. With any luck, they'll take us right to headquarters."

"Irina said she wound up in a container yard," Stevens said. "The thugs hosed her down and put her and Catalina back inside the box and drove away. Probably these guys will do the same thing. What if all we're getting are a couple more thugs?"

"We arrest them for being ugly and lean on them," Windermere replied. "Hope they're smart and selfish enough to turn on their bosses."

"Smart doesn't seem to be their MO. And if their employer is the Dragon, these guys might be too scared to talk."

"They'll talk," Windermere said. "I'll make sure of it."

"Anyway, we got the girls out, right?" LePlavy said. "Forty lives saved. That's a pretty damn good day, I'd say."

"Sure," Stevens said. "But Catalina Milosovici is still out there."

"And so are the guys who did this," Windermere said. "We're going to put a stop to them." She glanced at her watch. "Just as soon as that damn box appears."

Stevens opened his mouth to reply, but LePlavy beat him to it. "Guess you called it," he said, pointing out the windshield. "That's our bogey, right?"

Alongside the *Atlantic Prince*, a tractor and an empty flatbed waited for cargo, while above it a crane lifted a box from the ship. The box was dull brown, and just looking at it, Windermere could smell the sickening stench from inside. As she watched, the crane carried the box across the ship to the shore and lowered it carefully to the back of the flatbed.

"Get on your radio, LePlavy," Windermere said, shifting the Charger into gear. "I want eyes on this truck from as many angles as possible. No way we let the bastards get away."

107

VOLOVOI STOOD IN the container yard and watched the sunny summer day turn gloomy. In the distance, a thunderstorm was brewing; already, the wind was whipping up a brisk breeze through the stacks of containers, and purple thunderheads loomed to the south. The air was humid, muggy, stiflingly hot, tense with implied violence.

A helicopter droned by in the distance. Volovoi checked his watch. The ship would have arrived by now. With any luck, the longshoremen on the pier would off-load the box quickly. Volovoi's nerves were on edge; he was reluctant to be here. Every minute spent waiting was another minute the FBI could catch up to him.

He'd napped for an hour or two, maximum, before the Dragon arrived. Woke up groggy, his shoulder aching, had handed little Catalina Milosovici over to his partner and supervised as his soldiers loaded the rest of the girls into the truck to Manhattan.

He'd kept a couple of his soldiers behind, a giant lug wrench named Marek, who'd driven off to the pier with a truck and a flatbed chassis to await the new box, and a skinhead named Sladjan Dodrescu, who presently lounged in the shade in his purple Dodge Durango, smoking marijuana and enjoying the air-conditioning, waiting for Marek to return. They would unload the new girls here, hose them down, feed them, weed out any who were sick or dead or undesirable to the buyers. Then they would pack them into a new box and take them to Manhattan.

It would be the last shipment they would process in this lot, Volovoi knew. He would have to retool his entire operation for the New York expansion, wipe clean any trace of his New Jersey operation. Even soldiers like Marek and Sladjan Dodrescu would have to be disposed of.

Volovoi walked away from the Durango and the little store building and wandered out through the stacks to the service road. Smoked a cigarette at the gate and studied his surroundings. He'd chosen a good location for his yard, an unremarkable and anonymous flat of industrial land close enough to the container harbor and the New Jersey Turnpike, and isolated enough to prevent any neighbors from getting nosy. What neighbors there were were mostly trucking firms, warehouses, and interchange points; a railroad yard lay about a half mile inland, and the service road was bisected with sidings and access tracks.

The helicopter flew by again overhead, and Volovoi shielded his eyes and searched for it in the sky. Tried to gauge how far away it could be. He couldn't find it, gave up, snuffed out his cigarette. Was about to turn back to the Durango and its blessed air-conditioning when he saw movement down the head end of the service road. A container rig turned the corner, drove up toward the yard. It was Marek's rig. The shipment was here.

Volovoi walked to the chain-link gate, slid it all the way open. Then he made his way across the gravel lot to where Sladjan Dodrescu waited in the Durango, surrounded by containers. Overhead, the helicopter circled again. Volovoi thought of the FBI investigators and felt his senses tingling. Motioned to Dodrescu to roll down his window.

"Keep the engine running," Volovoi told him, scanning the sky. "And make sure your gun is loaded."

108

WINDERMERE DROVE THE Charger inland, hanging far enough back from the container truck so that the driver wouldn't recognize the tail. The land around the harbor was low-lying and industrial; in the distance, more spindly cranes reached toward the sky, unloading more shipping containers from more leviathan ships. The truck driver picked his way past refineries and across railroad crossings, dodging tanker trucks and flatbeds and chunky oversized lifters painted the gaudy colors of a child's sandbox toys. In the distance, a jet plane descended from the sky, on final approach to nearby Newark Liberty International.

LePlavy talked on his radio in the backseat, coordinating the support units he'd corralled to meet the container truck and its cargo wherever it stopped.

"We have air support, too," he told Stevens and Windermere. "That customs helicopter is trailing us overhead. Make sure we keep a good eye on these guys."

"Tell them not to get too close," Windermere said. "We don't want to spook them."

LePlavy gestured through the windshield as the truck turned a corner. "Even if we did spook them, where the hell would they go?" he said. "As long as that chopper has eyes on them, they won't get away."

Just being careful, Windermere thought. *We don't want to mess this up again.*

She slowed the Charger and followed the truck through the intersection and down a long, ruler-straight road. On either side were more empty lots, a few warehouses. LePlavy leaned forward and pointed at a white cube van approaching from the opposite direction.

"Our guys," he said. "Got a whole tactical team loaded in the back of that rig."

"What else do we have for support?" Stevens asked.

"As many field agents as I could muster," LePlavy said. "Plus backup from Elizabeth and Newark PDs. They're in position behind us, and they move at my signal."

Windermere thought about the shootout in the Blue Room. About how a man earned himself a nickname like "The Dragon." "Your backup," she said. "Are they armed?"

"They're armed," LePlavy said. He pointed out the window as the container truck turned off the road and into a gravel yard full of boxes. "This must be the spot," he said, reaching for his radio. "Let's go get them."

> > >

VOLOVOI HEARD THE RUMBLE AS the container truck turned in from the service road and onto the gravel lot. Heard the throb of the helicopter, high overhead, and the ominous, low growl of thunder in the distance.

Sladjan Dodrescu waited in the Durango, his pistol on the dash. Volovoi paced, nervous, listening to the crunch of heavy tires on loose stone as the truck idled through the stacks of containers to the clearing.

The helicopter buzzed overhead like a bee in his ear. Marek slowed the big truck to a halt. Cut the engine. Volovoi waited.

The air was still. Sticky. He was sweating through his shirt. Today's box was shit brown, bruised and dented. It sat on the back of the flatbed like a bomb.

Marek climbed from the cab. Circled around toward Volovoi. "You want me to open the box?"

Volovoi didn't answer. Was that a car's engine he could hear, somewhere beyond the containers? A truck? A plane?

He looked at the box, and at Marek again. Nodded.

Soon enough, he thought. *Soon enough, we'll know.*

Marek took a pair of bolt cutters from the truck and walked to the rear of the box. Paused at the doors a moment. Volovoi watched him. "What's the problem?"

"The lock," Marek said.

"You can't cut it?"

"No," Marek said. "It's not there to cut."

Volovoi started toward the box. Then he stopped. He saw the helicopter now, high in the sky. It was closer than he expected, an angry black insect. Volovoi was sure he could hear engines, too, out on the service road, through the stacks of containers. And the lock was gone.

Too much coincidence.

Volovoi started running for the Durango just as the first police cruiser appeared through the stacks, lights up, tires skidding on the gravel. There were more cars behind it, unmarked sedans and a white cube van, all of them screaming in like an invading army.

"Police," Volovoi screamed to Marek. He pulled out his pistol, took

aim at the first police car. Fired two shots at the windshield and then hurried around the Durango, pulling himself into the passenger side.

"Go," he told Dodrescu. *"Get us out of here."*

Dodrescu gunned the engine in reverse as the police returned fire. Volovoi heard glass break, heard the thud as police bullets perforated the Dodge's sheet metal. Dodrescu slammed his foot down and the truck launched backward, away from the police, deeper into the stacks.

Outside, Marek had his gun drawn, a MAC-10 automatic, and was crouched behind the box, trying to fend off the cops. As the Durango screamed past him, Volovoi saw the big soldier stumble back, herky-jerky, as the police bullets hit him.

Dodrescu spun the wheel. The Durango slid on the gravel, careened around sideways. The driver punched the gear shift into drive and was on the gas again, aiming the Dodge through a break in the stacks of containers, away from the police cars and away from the road, a respite, but brief. The whole lot was ringed by heavy-duty fencing, Volovoi knew. Concrete barriers and barbed wire. Even the big Dodge would never make it through.

"We have to get back to the gate," he told the driver. "Make it out before they block us in."

Dodrescu set his jaw. Turned the Durango down a long corridor of boxes. Volovoi shifted in his seat, looked out the rear window. Could see the first pursuing police car make the same turn.

"Hurry," he said. "Drive for your life."

The Durango surged forward, the engine roaring. The SUV reached the end of the long corridor, and Dodrescu turned again, back toward the main road. Through gaps in the boxes, Volovoi could see the brown container, the tractor, Marek's body. A light show of police cars and tactical units.

Dodrescu sped the Durango through the boxes, slalomed around a patrol car, and kept going. In the background, Volovoi could hear shooting. Saw sparks explode off the boxes as bullets struck them.

They were at the front of the lot now. The boxes fell back. Twenty yards ahead was the gate, a couple more cruisers waiting. And the cube van from down the street. The police were backing it into position, blocking the gate. In thirty seconds there'd be no way out.

"You see that?" Volovoi asked.

Dodrescu kept his foot planted. "I see it," he said.

Volovoi rolled down his window. Leaned out with his pistol and fired at the van, at the cruisers beside it, at the low-slung Dodge Charger lingering in the background. The police returned fire. The Durango didn't quit. Dodrescu drove with steel nerves, aiming for the rapidly dwindling hole between the white van and the fence.

Volovoi emptied his magazine. Then he ducked for cover. Watched the white van approach, watched the gap narrow. Dodrescu didn't slow down. Didn't waver. The fence got closer. The hole got smaller. Volovoi gripped his armrest and braced for impact.

Crash. Sparks. The Durango jolted like it had taken a punch. Metal squealed against metal. The police were still firing. The Durango's engine revved higher as Dodrescu kept his foot down. The SUV shimmied, struggled, shouldered its way through. Wheels spun. Gravel spat. More bullets, everywhere.

This is it, Volovoi thought. *This is how you die.*

Then the Durango surged forward. Cleared the white van and bounced off a Newark patrol car, sending it spinning backward. Dodrescu fought the wheel, struggled to keep the Durango under control. Aimed the SUV down the service road and kept going.

> > >

STEVENS AND WINDERMERE WATCHED THE Durango muscle through the gate. Watched the driver wrestle it through a couple patrol cars, point it inland, down the empty service road. The big SUV was riddled with bullet holes, its windows shattered. Windermere couldn't see how either occupant had survived without injury.

LePlavy was outside the Charger, hollering on his radio. "One man on the lot," he told Stevens and Windermere, through the window. "The delivery driver. Dead."

One man. *Not the Dragon,* Windermere thought. *No use to us now.* "We have to follow that SUV" she said.

"I have air support on him," LePlavy said. "No way he gets far."

Windermere shook her head. "Not going to risk it, LePlavy," she said. She glanced at Stevens. "You ready?"

"You know it," Stevens said.

"Good," she said. "Hang on. It's going to be some cowboy shit up in here."

She stood on the gas pedal. Pulled off the kind of tire-screaming launch she used to dream about trying in her daddy's Chevelle—the kind she wouldn't dare to pull now, not with her dad dead and buried—all burning rubber and that howling engine, Stevens pinned back to the passenger seat.

The tires found traction. The Charger leapt forward, sped down the service road toward the intersection, the shot-up Durango in the distance.

Beside her, Stevens clung to the armrests. "Jesus, Carla."

"Better than sex, Stevens," she said, her foot to the floor. "Draw your weapon."

109

VOLOVOI SAW THE helicopter overhead and knew he was fucked. He'd known the police would chase him; he could see the black Charger turning off the service road behind them, barreling down the long straightaway. The Charger didn't worry Volovoi. Dodrescu was a good driver. He could evade a police car.

A helicopter, though, was another matter.

"We need to do something," Volovoi told the driver. "Find a hiding place."

To the left was the train yard, flat land, mostly empty. A switch engine shunting cars a few hundred yards down. On the right were more warehouses, vacant lots, a long finger of ocean, and a couple of piers. Ahead was an overpass, an on-ramp to the New Jersey Turnpike.

"We could hide beneath the overpass," Dodrescu said. "Change cars."

Volovoi couldn't see another car for miles. Unless they killed the police officers in the Charger, they would have no vehicle to take.

We could run for it on foot, Volovoi thought. *Every man for himself.*

It was not a good idea, either. The police had a whole squad of officers raiding the container lot. They would canvas the area. Nobody could hide for long.

Then the Durango slowed. Volovoi looked at Dodrescu. "What the hell are you doing?"

Dodrescu had his hand to his stomach. His fingers were red. He'd been shot, Volovoi realized. Somehow, in the confusion, he'd been shot in the stomach. He'd driven them away from the container yard, but he wouldn't drive them much farther.

"Keep going," Volovoi told him. "I'll find you help. Just keep driving, damn it, if you want to live."

> > >

STEVENS REGAINED HIS BEARINGS IN the passenger seat as Windermere kept the Charger red-lining. Called LePlavy on his cell phone, gripping his pistol in his free hand.

"Tell that helicopter to keep on this guy's tail," he told the Newark agent. "We can't lose him."

"Helicopter's got him," LePlavy said. "I'll keep you updated."

In the distance, the Durango turned toward an on-ramp and the interstate beyond. Stevens pointed through the windshield. "See it?" he asked Windermere.

In the driver's seat, Windermere's brow furrowed. "I see it, Stevens," she said. "Just wish this damn car would haul a little more ass."

> > >

DODRESCU WAS GETTING PALER. SOON he would go into shock, Volovoi knew. He would stop driving, and then they would need a new plan.

"Keep going," Volovoi told him. "We will find someone to help you. Just get us away from here."

Dodrescu put his foot to the gas and drove on. Behind the

Durango, the Charger was gaining ground. The helicopter still shadowed them, high in the air. The net would close in again. Soon, there would be no escape.

What now? Volovoi thought. *What do we do?*

He studied the overpass ahead, the highway on-ramp, the tops of cars and trucks just visible above. Searched his brain for an answer. Then he saw it.

A big Boeing airliner roared by overhead, minutes from touchdown at the Newark Liberty Airport. The Durango was pointed directly into the flight path. The helicopter wouldn't be able to follow.

"The airport," Volovoi said, pressing a fresh magazine into his pistol. "Take us to the airport. And hurry."

110

LEPLAVY CALLED Stevens back.

"The helicopter lost him," he said. "He's in Newark Liberty airspace. No way they can get a chopper in there without crashing like eight planes."

"Shit." Stevens looked out the window. Saw the lights of an approaching jetliner against the thunderclouds in the distance. "I guess there's no rerouting the planes, either."

"Not on your life," LePlavy told him. "Can't even change runways, not with the storm coming. I'll notify the airport police, though, get their ground units involved."

"Do it," Stevens said. "We'll try and keep up until they arrive."

He ended the call. Watched the speeding Durango race across an interstate overpass toward the Newark Liberty terminals. To the left was the airfield. Planes landed. The thunderstorm approached. Stevens could see lightning in the distance. Meanwhile, the Durango didn't show any sign of slowing down.

"That didn't sound good," Windermere said.

"It's not," Stevens said. "Airport airspace. No helicopter. Unless airport police can scramble some units, we're on our own, Carla."

"'On our own.'" Windermere narrowed her eyes. "What else is new?"

> > >

DODRESCU HELD OUT ACROSS THE New Jersey Turnpike. Kept driving as the road skirted around the Newark Liberty airfield. To the left now were employee Park and Ride lots, aviation supply warehouses. To the right was the Lincoln Highway, speeding traffic. Soon, Volovoi knew, they'd arrive at the terminal buildings. There would be public parking lots. Chaos. If their luck held, they could ditch the Durango and shake free of the FBI agents in the Charger behind them.

Just a few minutes longer, Volovoi thought. *Hold it together just a few minutes more.*

But Dodrescu didn't have a few minutes. As the Durango raced through an intersection, he slumped and went unconscious, let his foot slip from the gas pedal. The Durango veered left, toward the oncoming lane. Volovoi glanced over, saw the kid, swore. *"Shit."*

He reached across for the steering wheel. Guided the truck into the correct lane. Felt the truck slowing. Knew the Charger was gaining. Didn't want to let the cops close any more ground.

There was a grassy median on both sides of the road. To the right was the Lincoln Highway. To the left was a low office complex, protected by a concrete barrier. Volovoi turned the wheel left. Aimed the truck at the barrier. Held the wheel steady and braced himself for the crash.

The truck slammed into the barrier. Collided on its front quarter and bounced off. The bumper disintegrated. Concrete crushed metal. Volovoi fought to keep the wheel steady, rode the big Dodge along the barrier as sparks flew, as the concrete slowed the truck. As soon as the truck stopped, he leapt out from his seat. Leaned back in toward Dodrescu, slumped over the wheel, and took aim with his pistol. Shot him twice in the head. Then he ran.

The Charger was closing distance. It sped toward Volovoi, three hundred yards away. No time to spare. Volovoi ran back to the road. Met a gray Acura coming head-on and stepped out in front of it, waving his gun so the driver could see. The driver slammed on his brakes. The Acura screamed to a stop.

Volovoi circled to the driver's side of the car. Pulled the driver from his seat. Barely heard the man's screaming. Shot him once in the head and climbed behind the wheel. Left the man's body on the road and drove off.

> > >

WHATEVER RELIEF WINDERMERE THOUGHT SHE'D felt when she saw the Durango slow was gone as soon as she saw the big thug wave his pistol.

"Oh, no," she said, watching him flag down a little gray Acura. "Oh, *shit*."

Beside her, Stevens rolled down his window. Took aim with his pistol, but couldn't get a clear shot. The thug was dragging the driver from the car. Windermere urged the Charger forward. Swore at it. Cajoled it. Couldn't close the distance in time.

The thug shot the driver. Dropped him to the pavement like trash. Climbed inside the Acura and sped away from the body.

Fuck," Windermere said. "God damn it, Stevens."

Beside her, Stevens still had his pistol raised. Wasn't shooting. Couldn't shoot. Too many bystanders. Too many civilians. She was driving the Charger too fast for a clean shot.

Windermere watched the Acura speed away. Wanted to follow, knew she couldn't. Not with a gunshot victim dying on the pavement in front of her.

She took her foot from the gas. Slammed on the brakes. The Charger slid a little, jolted as the ABS kicked in. Came to a stop fifteen feet from the Acura driver.

Stevens was out of the car before she'd shifted out of gear. Ran to the man as fast as she'd ever seen him run. By the time she'd climbed from behind the wheel, though, Stevens had slowed. Was looking back at her, shaking his head. Windermere took a few steps, saw what Stevens had seen. The driver had been shot in the head, point-blank. He was dead.

And she couldn't see the little gray Acura anywhere.

111

VOLOVOI DROVE THE Acura away from the airport. Took surface roads into Newark, hearing sirens everywhere. The police would be looking for the car, he knew. They'd know the plates as soon as they identified the driver.

This was as bad as he'd expected. The FBI had traced him to the New Jersey yard. If appearances were correct, they had followed the box. They had helicopter support, multiple police agencies. They had planned a sting. They knew a lot.

They had the box. They had the container yard. They had his latest supply of women, the Dragon's women. The New York women. And now they had Sladjan Dodrescu and his Durango, too.

Volovoi parked the Acura behind a liquor store, hiding it behind a dumpster and an old Chevy stripped bare. Made a call on his cell phone to one of his soldiers. The soldier answered, laughing. It sounded like he was having a party.

"Meet me on Adams Street," he told the soldier. "Right now."

The soldier agreed. He wasn't laughing anymore. Volovoi ended the call and settled into the shadows to wait.

The wind picked up while he waited. Rain began to fall, little drops here and there that foreshadowed the chaos to come. Volovoi took shelter under an awning and stared out at the street, watched the daylight disappear as though someone had switched off the lights.

Thunder rumbled in the distance. Lightning flashed. Volovoi ducked away and waited for the soldier.

The soldier arrived in a black BMW. Flashed his lights at Volovoi and pulled over. Volovoi crossed to the driver's side, opened the door.

"There is an Acura in the alley," he said. "Keys in the ignition. Dispose of it for me."

The soldier was a young man. There was a tattoo of a tiger on his neck. He looked at Volovoi, then back at his car, ready to complain. Volovoi fixed his eyes on him.

"Dispose of it now," he told the soldier. "Dispose of it properly. I will take care of your car."

The soldier scowled, but he vacated the driver's seat. Volovoi climbed inside. Closed the door. Turned off the shitty rap music the soldier had blaring, and pulled out his cell phone again and called the Dragon.

"My last shipment is compromised," he said when the Dragon answered. "I am compromised. If we want to sell our women, we need to move quickly. Tell your buyer to meet me tonight."

112

IRINA WATCHED THE convenience store for fifteen minutes before she crossed the street. Cars came and went from the tiny parking lot. Pedestrians wandered by, men and women, mostly black. Irina watched them, weighing her dwindling courage. Finally, she crossed the road.

The parking lot was empty when she reached it. A woman and a little girl walked out of the store. The woman carried a shopping bag. The girl held a slushy drink. She held the door for Irina, who ducked her head and hurried inside. She would steal food and water. Then she would find a car.

The man behind the counter had brown skin and a turban. He was watching a soccer game on a crummy little TV. His counter was protected by a box of thick plexiglass, most of it smeared, smudged, or scratched. Irina avoided the man's eyes, walked quickly to the back of the store and the long line of drink coolers. Found a cooler with eight different brands of water, slid open the door and let the cool air waft over her until goose pimples appeared on her forearms. She chose a large bottle of water, fought the urge to drink it then and there. Slid the cooler door closed and walked to the candy bar aisle, feeling the clerk's eyes follow her.

She would have to run, she knew. He would not take kindly to her thievery. There was no telling what he would do to her if he caught her.

The store's aisles were filled with food: candy, potato chips, crackers, and canned goods. Irina grabbed at random, took a couple of chocolate bars and a package of beef jerky. Hesitated in the aisle, hoping another customer would appear, someone to take the man's attention away from her.

No customers came in. She was alone in the store. The man watched her like he could read her mind.

There was a row of newspapers on a rack by the door. As casually as she could, Irina walked over. Examined the headlines, though she couldn't read a word of them. Flipped the paper over and was startled to see her own face. It was a picture the police had taken, shortly after she'd been captured in that muddy parking lot in the woods. She was surprised at how gaunt she appeared, how afraid. Hardly a woman anymore, and certainly not sexy. She wondered what man would have paid for her in that condition. What man would let her lure him away from his car.

The clerk was still staring at her. She could feel his eyes boring into her back like laser beams. Slowly, she turned the newspaper back over, hiding her face. Then, her heart thudding in her chest, she stepped toward the door.

"Hey." The clerk started out from behind the counter. He came quickly toward her. Irina pushed the door open and ran.

She stumbled out into the parking lot, her arms full of stolen food, her balance unsteady. The clerk was faster than he looked; he was right behind her and gaining. She ran into the lot, skidded on the pavement, kept running. Heard the clerk behind her and dodged away as he reached for her.

She ran around the side of the store, skidded again, lost her balance and tripped, careening forward until she collided with someone. Another man. She tumbled to the pavement, her food flying everywhere. Scraped her knee, tore her jeans, slid to a sudden stop. The clerk rounded the corner and came for her.

Irina fumbled for her food. Heard the man laughing above her and looked up and froze. It was one of the men from the previous night, from the gang who'd confronted her in this very parking lot. He was barely more than a teenager, regarded her like a cat looks at a mouse. He was laughing at her.

Irina scanned her surroundings from her knees. Saw her candy bars, her beef jerky, her water. No way to protect herself. A few feet away, though, a broken beer bottle. She scrabbled for it, closed her hand around its neck as someone approached her from behind, the clerk or the man. Pushing herself to her feet, she spun around, swinging.

113

THE DRAGON HAD brought her a cocktail dress.

It was a pretty little number, short and flirty. Catalina studied herself in the mirror and wondered how the Dragon had guessed her size. It fit perfectly, clung to her waist and her hips before falling loosely to mid-thigh. Only in the bust was there room for improvement, and there wasn't much she could do about that.

She fixed her makeup in the bathroom mirror, feeling increasingly absurd. He'd brought her heels, too; she resembled an actress, or maybe just an expensive prostitute. She'd never worn makeup before, struggled to apply her mascara. The Dragon knocked on the door. "Hurry up, little one," he said. "You've taken long enough in there."

She applied some lipstick. Good enough. She wasn't going to slave away to make herself look pretty just so he could—

Just so he could what?

She forced the thought from her mind. She knew what the Dragon wanted from her. She knew he would probably get it. She could only hope that he would decide not to bother Irina any longer, or her parents, if she gave it to him willingly.

A storm was descending on the city when she tottered out of the bathroom, unsteady on her brand-new high heels. She struggled to maintain her balance as she walked out to the living area. The

Dragon had dimmed the lights in the dining room, lit candles and set them on his ugly dining room table. There was a meal waiting for her. A bottle of wine. The Dragon stood at the head of the table. He wore a dinner jacket. He looked as absurd as she felt, with his big beard and unkempt hair, his toothy, wicked smile. Behind him, sheets of rain pelted the window.

The Dragon licked his lips when he saw her. "You're the perfect prize, little one," he told her, eyeing her up and down. "Come sit down."

Catalina froze. Every instinct she had told her to run, run as fast as she could, kick off those heels and bolt for the door. She didn't, though. She knew the Dragon would catch her. She swallowed her fear and walked to her chair.

The Dragon waited until she'd sat at the table. He filled her glass with wine, loaded her plate. "I ordered in," he told her. "Duck. Have you ever tried duck before, girl?"

Catalina shook her head no. The man was jumpy, she noticed. Erratic. His eyes were alight, his wicked smile wide. Catalina watched him, unnerved by his agitation. Wondered how long he would keep up this stupid game.

"Drink up," he told her, motioning to her wineglass. "We have a long night ahead of us."

She picked up the glass, hesitant. Sipped the wine. The Dragon smiled at her again. Sat back and admired her as the storm began in earnest outside.

114

LEPLAVY BROUGHT THE rain with him. It started slow enough, a few scattered drops here and there, but when the storm arrived, it arrived in earnest, sending lashing sheets of water down on the crashed Durango and the body of the Acura driver, on Stevens and Windermere, and the rest of the FBI agents, medical personnel, and local police who stood guarding the scene.

They'd found another body in the Durango. The driver, a young guy with a bullet in his head. He'd been shot in the stomach, too.

"The guy drove until he couldn't drive anymore," Windermere said, ducking into the Charger with Stevens to wait out the storm. "As soon as he crashed, our passenger killed him. Then he ducked out and killed our man here for his car."

"Didn't want to leave a witness," Stevens said. "Even if they played on the same team."

Windermere looked across the service road at the Durango, where Agent LePlavy was pacing, talking on his cell phone. "So who was he?" she said. "Is this the guy we're looking for, Stevens? Is this guy the Dragon?"

Stevens thought about it. "With the thug at the lot and this guy in the truck, that makes three men at the scene," he said. "Irina only saw two. This guy's probably management, whoever he is."

"And we lost him." Windermere ran her hands through her hair. "I cannot believe we let that asshole get away."

"We have him scared now," Stevens said. "Scared people make mistakes. Sooner or later, we'll smoke him out of hiding."

"You believe that?"

"I do," he said.

Windermere said nothing. Pursed her lips. Stevens cocked his head. "What?"

"I was just thinking," she said, "if you're right and we are scaring these guys. You remember what they did when they couldn't get to Irina?"

"They went after her sister," Stevens said. "They doubled down on Catalina."

"So maybe call your family," Windermere said. "Tell them to hole up somewhere, just in case. Better safe than sorry, if these bastards get desperate."

Stevens didn't say anything. Was still saying nothing when LePlavy came over, slid into the backseat, soaking wet from the rain.

"We ID'd the bodies," he told them as lightning flashed above. "Marek Costel, back at the container yard. This guy in the truck is named Sladjan Dodrescu."

"Sladjan Dodrescu," Windermere repeated. "I won't ask you to spell it. Either of these guys into anything major?"

"Couple bids for assault, B and E, stuff like that. Probably they're just thugs, pawns in the game."

"We need the king, LePlavy," Windermere said. "How do we get him?"

"Container yard's registered to a numbered company out of Malta. I forwarded the details to Interpol, waiting to hear back, probably not going to get much out of them."

He looked at them. "There was a little house on that property, too," he said. "A jail cell inside, iron bars and everything. Nobody there, though. They're all gone."

"Jesus," Windermere said. "We need something here, Zach. Anything. What do you have?"

LePlavy paged through his notebook. "I have an address on Sladjan Dodrescu," he said. "You want to take a look?"

"Probably not going to get much," Windermere said. "But we'll check it out anyway. Meanwhile, you find us something better."

"I'll try," LePlavy said.

"Do, or do not," Windermere said. "There is no try."

115

TWELVE HUNDRED MILES from New Jersey, Derek Mathers sat at his desk in the FBI's Brooklyn Center fortress, listening in on the Minneapolis PD scanner and wondering how the hell he'd get Windermere back if he let Irina Milosovici slip through his fingers.

He'd been sitting at his desk for hours, watching the time tick away on his computer clock, cold-calling every police agency in the region and hoping somebody would come up with a lead on the missing woman. The scanners had been silent, and the phone calls yielded nothing. Irina Milosovici was a full-on ghost.

Mathers's stomach rumbled, and he tried to remember the last time he'd eaten anything. Couldn't. He pushed back from his computer, figured maybe he'd raid the vending machines down the hall.

Then the scanner lit up through his headphones and he wasn't thinking about food anymore.

Some kind of stabbing, the 4th Precinct. A girl outside a convenience store, one man injured. "Girl tried to steal some food from the store and bolted," the dispatcher said. "The clerk followed her outside, and she attacked a bystander with a piece of broken glass."

Mathers pulled back up to his computer. Fiddled with the volume and listened some more. Got nearly nothing. A patrol car nearby had taken the call, and that was pretty much that.

So he picked up his phone. Called Minneapolis PD, introduced himself, and asked for more information. Got—predictably—not much, but they patched him through to the dispatcher.

"White girl, dark hair, wearing jeans and a T-shirt," the dispatcher said. "Maybe twenty or so. Store owner didn't have much of a description. Guess he wasn't really speaking good English."

"Yeah," Mathers said. "Thanks anyway."

White girl, dark hair. Jeans and a T-shirt. Could be anybody. Still, Mathers was curious. And he was hungry, and he knew a decent burger joint in the 4th, not too far away from the scene of the stabbing.

He poked his head into Drew Harris's office. "Headed out, boss," he said. "Might have something on big sister."

Harris looked up from a tuna sandwich. "Yeah?" he said, chewing.

"Some white girl just stabbed a dude with a piece of broken glass in the 4th. Kind of matches Irina's description. I figure it's worth a look, anyway."

"No doubt." Harris regarded his sandwich with distaste. "You pass by the Burger Barn, pick me up a bacon double."

> > >

MATHERS DROVE SOUTH FROM BROOKLYN Center in a motor pool Impala. Followed the highway into the 4th Precinct: heavy industry, rail yards, low-income housing facing the tracks. Found the convenience store without much of a problem.

His stomach growling, he parked the Impala beside a Minneapolis PD cruiser and climbed out of the car. Found the uniform administering first aid to a young black kid in a baggy Tupac T-shirt. The kid was bleeding from his arm, but it wasn't bad. He seemed more embarrassed than injured.

Mathers flipped his badge open, showed it to the kid. "You're the guy she stabbed, I guess."

The kid spat. "Fucking bitch."

"How'd it happen?"

"I was just standing here, man." The kid scowled. "Yo, I already said this. Why I gotta do it again?"

"Just talk," Mathers told him. "Sooner you talk, sooner you're out of here."

The kid glared at him. "Look, man, I was just minding my own business. The bitch come running out, trips and falls. I walk over like, you know, need some help or whatever, she spins around and sliced me open."

"She say anything to you?"

The kid squinted. "What?"

"The girl. Did she say anything to you? Anything at all."

"Nah, man." The kid shook his head. "I was speaking to her, but it wasn't like she knew what I was saying. She looked *scared*, though."

Probably terrified out of her mind, Mathers thought. "What'd she look like?"

The kid sighed and scuffed his shoes. Then he told Mathers what he already figured. The girl who'd robbed the store was Irina Milosovici. Pale skin. Dark hair. Pretty face. Same clothes she'd been wearing when she bolted from the safe house.

"Call this in to your dispatch," Mathers told the uniform. "I need all available units looking for this girl at the FBI's request, got it?" He paused. "And see if you can get me a translator."

116

LLOYD WAS WAITING when Volovoi arrived at the Dragon's warehouse.

It was a little brick building in downtown Manhattan, Alphabet City, plain and nondescript. Graffiti-covered walls, few windows. Volovoi parked his soldier's BMW in the little loading area behind the warehouse, pulled in close behind Lloyd's car, a fancy gray Bentley. He climbed from the BMW and hurried through the rain to the building's back door, unlocked it, and stepped inside, dripping wet. There was a soldier waiting inside, Tomas. Another idiot.

"Get the girls," Volovoi told him. "Line them up for the buyer. And make sure the blondes are in front."

He watched Lloyd hurry across the parking lot, struggling with his umbrella as forked lightning licked at the skyline beyond.

This was it, Volovoi knew. This was the do-or-die moment. The FBI was no doubt investigating Marek Costel and Sladjan Dodrescu. Even if both men were dead, their families would talk. Their friends. Sooner or later, the FBI would trace the goons back to Andrei Volovoi. Soon enough, Volovoi figured, he'd see his own face on the news.

He would have to sell the girls quickly, as many as possible. Unload them before Lloyd and his friends found out about the FBI investigation. They would cancel their connection the moment they felt the heat. Their interest in the Dragon's women would evaporate. And then what?

The Dragon would be unhappy. He would kill Volovoi. And if he couldn't get to Volovoi, he would kill Veronika and Adriana, his little nieces, instead. The Dragon would not rest until he'd exacted his due.

Volovoi chased the thought away. Never mind that. He would sell the girls to Lloyd and his friends. He would deal with the Dragon when he needed to.

Footsteps from the hallway. The girls, tottering up from the basement in short dresses and heels, made up like movie stars, prom queens. Volovoi followed them into the main room, looked them over. They shied away, wide-eyed and nervous.

"Behave yourselves," he told them. "This is your chance to make an impression. Believe me, what this man and his friends have in mind for you is nothing compared to what will happen if you disappoint me."

The girls said nothing. They were young, very young, but they had cleaned up nicely. Lloyd would be pleased.

Speaking of Lloyd—

Volovoi turned back to the door, just as Lloyd arrived. "Mr. Lloyd," he said, ushering the man in. "Welcome. I hope you are ready to buy."

117

THERE WAS A girl in Sladjan Dodrescu's house. Her name was Lola Rosario.

"Yeah, I been seeing Sladjan," she told Stevens and Windermere, once she'd let them into the filthy living room and out of the rain. After they'd explained the situation, the dead man in the Durango. "I guess you could say he was my boyfriend."

"I'm sorry for your loss," Windermere said. "Any idea what your boyfriend was doing at the harbor today?"

Rosario shifted on the couch. Brushed aside a stale corn chip. Dabbed at her eyes. "I don't know," she said. "He wasn't here, was he? Dude worked all the time. How should I know?"

"What kind of work was he into?" Stevens asked her.

"What's this about, anyway?" Rosario said. "You said he was shot, right? So why the hell are you coming at me for?"

"It's FBI shit," Windermere said. "Let's cut to it. What was your boy doing today?"

"Driving in his Durango." Rosario shrugged. "It's not like I was dating Sladjan for so long, you know?"

"Still, you've got to know something," Windermere said. "I know he had to come home some nights, complain about his job, right?"

"Everyone complains about their job," Stevens said.

"Sure he did, he was always bitching," Rosario said. Then she brightened. "Oh, shit, I remember. He was real proud of himself, too." She looked around. "I guess, like, a couple of his coworkers got fired or something, so he was thinking he was going to get promoted. Like, most of the time he just sits around and doesn't do much, I guess, but these other guys, they did a lot of travel for work and stuff, a lot of really interesting shit. So he was excited."

Stevens and Windermere swapped glances. "The drivers," Windermere said. "You know where he did all this sitting around, Lola?"

"I mean, I don't know, like, what he did for a living, but I kind of know *where*," Rosario said. "This dude's loft in Newark. I think it was his boss's place."

"Sure," Stevens said. "You think you could find this loft for us?"

Rosario nodded. "I've been there a couple times, for parties and stuff," she said. She paused. "You're going to get the guy who did Sladjan, right?"

Windermere looked at Stevens again. "Yeah," she said. "We're going to get him."

118

THERE WERE POLICE cars everywhere.

Irina hid in an alley a few blocks from the convenience store. Around her were small one-story homes, unkempt lawns, rusted cars. Dogs barked as she passed their yards, growled at her when she hid. She'd dropped her stolen food in the parking lot and she was still hungry, and very thirsty. She couldn't find a car to steal.

And the police cars were everywhere.

She'd fled from the sirens at first. There hadn't been many. She'd seen one police car speed past, and ducked behind a parked car to hide until it was gone. She kept moving. Time passed, an hour or so. Then, suddenly, more police cars appeared.

They knew.

Irina huddled in the alley and debated her options. The police would take her in. They would arrest her for attacking the black man, for defending herself, or they would bring her to the FBI. They wouldn't let her go to Clearfield, Pennsylvania, to find Catalina.

Never mind. Irina knew there was no way she would get to Pennsylvania anyway, no matter the situation. She did not know how to drive on American roads. She didn't know how to read American maps. She was a skinny, pitiful little wretch and no man would let her into his car. Her whole plan was silly, and she would be better off at the safe house instead of risking her life on these streets. She should go back to safety. She knew this.

Still, she was afraid. The police officers were men. Maybe they were corrupt. Maybe they would take her for themselves, the same way the man at the convenience store had wanted to do. She crouched in the alley, paralyzed by indecision. She didn't hear the police cruiser roll up.

A door slammed. A man's voice, harsh. Irina looked up to find a young policeman approaching, his hand on his holster. He'd taken the black man's side, she realized. He would not be her ally. He would throw her in jail.

Irina stumbled to her feet. She tried to run, her legs unsteady. The cop was on her immediately. He grabbed her shoulder, rough. Spun her around. She swung at him. Kicked. Twisted away and kept running.

The cop chased her. She could hear him behind her, yelling at her. Yelling into his radio. More sirens. More police cars. His footsteps. She ran.

At the end of the alley, another police car appeared. Squealed to a stop and two more cops piled out, two more men. She was trapped.

They came at her rough, like she was the bad guy. Like she was the threat. They swarmed her, and she fought them, fists and feet. They caught her arms, held her back, and still she fought, swearing and spitting, struggling as they dragged her out of the alley and toward the patrol car.

Then someone called out, and they slowed. Their grips on her arms loosened. Irina followed their eyes to a flat gray sedan parked haphazardly in the middle of the road. A man, blond and muscular and good-looking in a black suit, approached them. She recognized him. Agent Mathers.

Mathers gestured to the cops, and they released her. She was tempted to run. Tempted to fight. The FBI agent held his hands out, palms up. Smiled at her. A friendly smile.

Still, she was tense as he came near her. She was ready to run. Then he leaned in, looked in her eyes, and told her, in awful Romanian, *"I'm your friend. There's nothing to be afraid of."*

She looked at him. He repeated himself, his accent atrocious, his pronunciation almost indecipherable. He smiled at her sheepishly, like he knew how bad he sounded, and Irina felt herself tense again as her body was racked with sudden, uncontrollable laughter.

119

LOLA ROSARIO GAVE them an address, an old brick warehouse in downtown Newark, recently converted to lofts. The penthouse belonged to somebody named Andrei Volovoi.

"LePlavy says he's Romanian," Stevens told Windermere. "Immigrated to America about five years ago, no criminal record. No record of employment, either. LePlavy says from his picture he's a ringer for the third guy at the container lot, earlier."

"So he's the guy who did Sladjan Dodrescu," Windermere said. "Andrei Volovoi. How does he tie into the Dragon?"

Stevens stared up at the apartment building, at the tactical team piling out of an FBI bread van down the block. "I don't know, Carla," he said. "Let's get up there and find out."

> > >

ANDREI VOLOVOI'S HOME WAS ONE big room, granite and marble and exposed brick and beam, a large balcony with a view of the Manhattan skyline in the distance, a messy kitchen and an unmade king-size bed behind gauzy curtains. Empty food cartons everywhere, drug paraphernalia. Two girls on the couch, smoking a joint.

They spooked when the tactical guys burst through the door,

huddled together and screamed and wouldn't stop. Stevens braced himself, figured the women were some of the Dragon's human cargo, felt a sudden excitement when he realized these girls forged a solid link between Volovoi and the skin trade.

Then one girl, a bottle blonde, looked him dead in the eye. "Please don't hurt us," she said with a Jersey Shore accent. "The drugs aren't ours, I swear."

Americans. Shit.

Turned out the women were Volovoi's paid companions. Party girls. "He pays us to hang out," the Jersey blonde—Carrie—told Stevens and Windermere. "Come around for the parties, flirt with his friends, you know, dance and stuff."

"Sure," Stevens said. "You know where he is now?"

"Andrei?" Carrie glanced at her friend, who'd so far stayed silent. "We don't really ask questions. He's not really the talkative type."

"When'd you see him last?"

"God, like, a couple days ago, maybe?"

"But you're still here," Windermere said.

Carrie shrugged. "There was a guy here, earlier. Andrei's friend, or whatever, just hanging around. You never know when the party's gonna start, you know?"

"I guess so." Windermere walked to the window. "We're looking for a guy named Pavel Demetriou, calls himself 'the Dragon.' I don't suppose you've heard that name before, have you?"

"The Dragon?" Carrie made a face. "Yeah, I heard it. He's some big-time guy—like, *really* big. I think he was Andrei's partner."

Carrie's friend spoke up for the first time. "I heard he's the guy who made Andrei kill Bogdan and Nikolai."

"Nikolai, like Kirilenko?" Stevens said. "Andrei Volovoi killed them?"

"That's what everyone's saying," Carrie said. "They say Andrei killed them on account of they screwed something up on the job."

"It's shitty," Carrie's friend said. "I liked Bogdan. He was cool."

"Bogdan," Windermere said. "Bogdan who?"

120

"BOGDAN URZICA," LePlavy told Windermere over the phone. "Another Romanian national, but this guy's not as good as Andrei Volovoi at keeping himself hidden. He's in the NCIC database with a pretty picture and a decent record, mostly grand theft auto and the odd assault charge."

"Sounds like a real peach," Windermere said. "Does this guy have an address?"

"Hoboken," LePlavy said, "but Bogdan ain't ever coming home. State police in Pennsylvania found his body outside a little town called Hermitage early this morning. Guess he'd crashed his Cadillac Escalade. Wasn't wearing a seat belt, flew right through the windshield. Managed to get shot in the face after he landed. They used his fingerprints to identify him."

Windermere pursed her lips. "Volovoi did him," she said. "Just like the girls said. How far is Hermitage from the rest stop where Catalina sent her message?"

"About a hundred and twenty miles west, give or take," LePlavy told her. "According to the state troopers, the Cadillac was stripped clean. No registration, no license plates."

"What about the VIN number?" Windermere said. "Surely they can trace it."

"They can," LePlavy said. "It's registered to ATZ Transport. Same shell company that leased the truck that was hauling Irina and her sister."

"So we can tie this thing to the traffickers," Windermere said. "That's a start. Where do we go from here?"

"I'm glad you asked," LePlavy said, "because here's the punch line: Facebook finally came through on that message Catalina Milosovici sent to her sister last night, and apparently, she sent it from a cell phone." He paused. "Bogdan Urzica's cell phone."

121

LLOYD HADN'T LIED about his preference for blondes.

The little man surveyed the girls with satisfaction, muttering his approval. "Yes," he told Volovoi. "These are perfect for our needs. My contacts will be thrilled with this kind of quality."

"You will buy them, then," Volovoi said. "Two hundred thousand dollars apiece."

Lloyd laughed at him. "Come now, Mr. Volovoi," he said, pulling the girls closer to him. "Where's your sense of salesmanship? Don't I at least get to sample the wares?"

There's no time, Volovoi thought. *Purchase these women. Call your friends, and invite them here, too. One night only. Big sale.*

Buy, before the FBI comes knocking.

But Lloyd wasn't ready to buy. He'd pulled two blond girls from Volovoi's lineup, a comely sixteen-year-old in a red dress, and a younger girl, her hair styled in pigtails.

"Yes," he told Volovoi. "All in good time. These are exquisite specimens, and they deserve to be appreciated."

The girls struggled in his grasp. The younger girl began to cry. *Four hundred thousand dollars,* Volovoi thought, gritting his teeth. *I could get Veronika and Adriana out of the country with that money. Fly them somewhere safe, away from the Dragon.*

"I believe there is a private room in the back," he said finally. "Take all the time you need."

Lloyd chuckled. "I certainly intend to, Mr. Volovoi," he said. He led the girls down the hallway, toward the Dragon's private room. Volovoi watched him go, realized once he was gone that his fists were clenched, his whole body tense. He exhaled. Forced himself to try and relax. Turned away from Tomas and the girls and thought of his nieces again, of a life without worry, a life without the Dragon.

Fat chance, unless he could sell these women fast.

"Fuck," he said, reaching for a cigarette. *"Fuck me."*

122

WINDERMERE DROVE THE Charger back to the FBI's Newark office. If the rain had let up, it was only slightly; lights blurred through the windshield now that darkness had fallen, the wipers unable to keep up with the downpour.

"So, okay," she said. "What the hell happened in Pennsylvania?"

In the passenger seat, Stevens turned away from the window. "The girls in the apartment said Volovoi killed Bogdan Urzica and Nikolai Kirilenko because they screwed up on the job. Bogdan's dead. So we know Volovoi got to him."

"And we know Volovoi made it home, because we chased him around Newark airport this afternoon," Windermere said. "So chances are Nikolai Kirilenko is dead, too. But where does the Escalade come in? How come Bogdan wasn't driving the container rig?"

"Who knows?" Stevens said. "Maybe something went wrong. Bogdan caught up to Volovoi's plan and tried to escape. Then Volovoi caught up to him and finished him off."

"And drove back to New Jersey," Windermere said. "With Catalina, hopefully."

"Catalina sent her message a hundred and twenty miles east of where Bogdan died," Stevens said. "With Bogdan Urzica's phone. I'm thinking there's no way she gets her hands on it before this whole fiasco goes down with Volovoi, which means she sent the message after Bogdan Urzica died."

"It makes sense to me, I guess," Windermere said. "But this is all ancient history, Stevens. How do we get our heads into the future?"

Stevens found his reflection in the window glass. "I just bought my daughter an iPhone," he said. "We put one of those 'Find My iPhone' thingies on it—"

"Apps," Windermere told him. "They're called apps. All these smartphones are GPS-enabled."

"That's what I thought," Stevens said. "So there should be a way to triangulate the location, right? If Catalina somehow still has the phone—"

"We can find her," Windermere finished. "Good thinking, Stevens. Let's hope she kept her little hands on it."

123

"I GREW UP in the home country a piece-of-shit nobody," the Dragon said, his speech slurred from the wine and whatever else. "I made myself into a boss, do you understand? I killed and pillaged until I was a Dragon."

Outside the apartment, the sky was nearly black, the rain and wind billowing against the apartment windows, so hard that Catalina wondered if the skyscraper would topple.

"New York," the Dragon was saying. "This is where the money is.

The power. If you become boss of New York, you are boss of the whole country. The whole world, even. Who can stop you?"

Catalina forced herself to look at him. Her head was foggy; she was light-headed from the wine he'd forced on her. But she had to think clearly. "The other girls," she said. "What will you do with them?"

The Dragon stopped talking about New York. A smile slowly spread across his face. "Why do you care about the other girls?" he said. "Did you make friends, little one?"

Catalina didn't answer. "I will sell them," the Dragon said finally. "My friend, Andrei Volovoi, perhaps you might have met him. At this very moment, he is finding new homes for them."

"What kind of homes?" Catalina asked.

"Good homes," the Dragon said. "Rich homes. Your friends will be pets for wealthy men. Pretty toys. They will amuse their owners until they become boring, and then . . ." He snapped his fingers. *"Poof."*

Catalina didn't say anything. She thought of Dorina and the others, all of them locked in apartments like this one, forced to entertain psychopaths like this one. She felt her stomach turn, felt faint.

"They will kill them," she said. "That's what you mean."

The Dragon smiled wider. "Their owners will throw them away like old, useless toys," he said. "The men will buy new toys to replace them. I will sell them those toys. And I will become very rich."

Catalina blinked her eyes, tried to force the fuzziness from her brain. There was no time for distraction. She had to stop this madman.

But what could she do? The Dragon would gut her the moment she made a move for the door. He was too strong for her. He had his long knife. There was no escaping this apartment, not while the Dragon watched her.

The storm crashed outside, lightning and thunder. The Dragon pushed himself from his chair.

"Enough talk," he said, circling the table to where she sat. "It's time to play now. Stand up."

He held out his hand, waited for her to take it. She could see the knife at his belt, and wondered if she could take it from him before he reacted.

"Stand up, little one," the man said, an edge to his voice and in his bleary, unfocused eyes. "Don't make me wait."

Catalina looked at the knife again. Knew she'd never reach it in time. Slowly, heart pounding, she took the Dragon's hand. Let him pull her up and lead her out of the kitchen and down the long hallway, toward his bedroom.

124

LLOYD CAME BACK quicker than Volovoi had expected. He'd left the girls behind.

Volovoi stubbed out his cigarette. "Well, Mr. Lloyd?" he said. "Which girl would you like? Or perhaps you want both. We could work out a package deal. Three hundred thousand for the pair."

Lloyd didn't answer, avoided Volovoi's eyes. Brushed past him, walked across the selling floor toward the back of the warehouse, the exit. Volovoi followed him. "Where are you going?" he said. "Is something wrong?"

Lloyd stopped and turned back, held out his smartphone. "Are you aware," he said slowly, "that your face is on every major news network in the country?"

Volovoi forced a smile, a calm voice. "Mr. Lloyd," he said, "I assure you—"

"Go ahead." Lloyd thrust the phone at him. "See for yourself."

Reluctantly, Volovoi took the phone and scanned the screen: CNN, a lead story. His picture. His name. RUTHLESS HUMAN TRAFFICKER.

Volovoi handed the phone back to Lloyd. Kept his voice calm. "These people know nothing about my current affairs," he said. "They have discovered my New Jersey operations, which I have long ago closed down. I assure you, Mr. Lloyd, you are perfectly safe here."

Lloyd shook his head. "You promised discretion," he said. "Secrecy. How am I supposed to feel safe when Wolf Blitzer is showing my broker's face to everyone in the country?"

"I assure you," Volovoi said again, "you are safe. Please, Mr. Lloyd—"

"Be that as it may," Lloyd said. "My friends and I can't do business with you. It's too risky." He punched a number into his phone. "Best of luck, Mr. Volovoi," he said. "I wish I could have spent more time with your girls. They were lovely."

He held the phone to his ear as he walked to the door. Volovoi followed him, felt his frustration mounting, his anger. "Who are you calling?"

"Your partner, of course." Lloyd didn't even bother to turn around. "I imagine he'll want an explanation as to why I'm severing our relationship. I hope he understands it's nothing personal."

The Dragon. Nothing personal. Volovoi watched Lloyd reach the door. Heard the tinny buzz of the speaker as Lloyd placed the call. The Dragon would be furious. He would kill Volovoi, and he would kill his family. His nieces, to be sure.

Volovoi took his pistol from his waistband. Walked quickly behind Lloyd, aimed the gun, and fired. Lloyd pitched forward, hit the door and toppled over, left a bloody trail in his wake. Volovoi put another round into the mess in the back of his head. Then he picked up Lloyd's phone and killed the connection.

125

THE DRAGON LED Catalina to his bedroom. Pushed open the door and stepped aside for her, his eyes watery and unfocused as they watched her. Catalina walked into the room, swaying slightly on her heels.

The room hadn't changed since she'd first seen it that afternoon. It seemed different now, though, dangerous. She felt a cold emptiness in her stomach as she stood on the threshold.

Maybe it was the storm raging outside. More likely, it was the man standing close behind her, his hunger for her palpable. There was a platter on the bedside table, a pile of white powder. "Cocaine, little one," the Dragon said. "Have you ever tried it?"

She shook her head no, and he chuckled. "You will, tonight," he said.

She felt his hands on her back, caressing her shoulders. Fought the urge to throw up when his fingers trailed down to the zipper on the back of her dress, when he slipped the zipper downward. She stared straight ahead, numbed herself to his touch, caught her reflection in the dark windows and looked away as he slipped the dress from her shoulders.

He circled her, admiring her. She stood before him now in only her underwear, felt a sudden hot flush of shame as his eyes tracked across her body. She could feel his gaze like it was his hands on her, though she knew she would feel his actual hands soon enough, and that they would be worse.

She tried to think about her family. Her sister. Her dog. Instead, she thought only about Dorina and the others, sold to similar psychopaths, to suffer and die the way she would. She felt suddenly responsible, suddenly helpless, and she wanted to cry. She would never leave this room, she realized, not alive.

The Dragon rubbed the front of his slacks lewdly as he pulled her to the bed, to the nightstand and the pile of cocaine. "Go ahead," he told her. "You'll love it. I promise."

She looked at him, then the pile of white powder. Wondered what she was supposed to do with it. The Dragon gestured to the pile, waiting, his hand insinuating circles at the small of her back.

She approached the cocaine cautiously. A few lines had been drawn, and a straw lay beside them. She gathered she was supposed to ingest them through her nose.

She didn't get the chance, though. The man stiffened beside her. Searched his pockets and came out with a vibrating phone. He looked at the number. "Shit," he said. "My apologies, little one." He smiled again. "We'll continue our fun in a minute."

126

LLOYD'S PHONE BEGAN to ring. Volovoi stared at it. The number was blocked, but he knew who was calling. Knew it was the Dragon.

He turned to the thug who stood guarding the girls. "Get them back downstairs," he said. "Hide them."

The thug obeyed. Corralled the girls and marched them out of sight, downstairs to a storage area where they'd be secure. Meanwhile, the phone was still ringing. Volovoi dropped it to the floor and stepped on it, ground it beneath his feet until the ringing stopped, and the phone was nothing but shards of plastic and glass.

It wouldn't matter, he knew. It was a temporary fix. The Dragon would figure out what had happened soon enough.

Volovoi glanced down at Lloyd's body. The client was still dead. He put his pistol away and pulled out his own cell phone, dialed a number as he walked to the front of the warehouse.

"It's Andrei," he said when his sister picked up. "Take the girls and get out of the city. Leave now, and tell no one that you're going. I'll contact you when it's safe to return."

His sister made to argue. Volovoi cut her off. "*Leave*, Ileana, for the sake of the children. Leave tonight."

Ileana didn't answer for a beat. Volovoi opened his mouth again, ready to plead with her. His sister cut him off. "We'll go," she said, her voice flat. "Whatever problems you have caused for yourself, Andrei, solve them."

"I *am* solving them," he told her, and ended the call. Looked around the empty warehouse, the buyer's body by the door. Before he could do anything else, his phone began to buzz again. It was not Ileana. It was the Dragon.

Volovoi answered the call as calm as he could. "This is Andrei."

"What are you doing?" The Dragon's voice was slurred, like his thoughts were too fast for his tongue. "Is everything okay?"

"Everything is okay," Volovoi told him. "Everything is fine."

"I just had a phone call from Lloyd," the Dragon said. "He hung up before I could answer. And he's not answering his phone anymore. What is happening over there, Andrei? Is everything okay? What are you doing?"

He's high, Volovoi realized. *He's drunk or he's high and he's playing with that little girl of his.*

"Everything is fine," Volovoi said again. "Mr. Lloyd is just testing out a couple of our products. No doubt he simply called you by mistake."

The Dragon said nothing. Volovoi could hear him breathing.

"The sale is proceeding smoothly," Volovoi continued, after a beat. "I am quite sure Mr. Lloyd appreciates the quality of our product. He is ready and willing to buy."

Another long silence. "Good," the Dragon said finally. "Very good, Andrei. I told you, these men will make us rich."

Volovoi looked again at Lloyd's body. "You told me," he said. "You did."

"Call me when you are finished," the Dragon said. "We'll celebrate together, Andrei. Maybe I'll save you a piece of my little toy."

Volovoi felt his stomach turn. "I will call you as soon as I'm finished," he said.

He killed the connection. Looked around the empty warehouse again, at Lloyd's body in a pool of blood by the door. He thought about his sister and his nieces. About how angry the Dragon would be when he found out the buyer was dead.

He can't find out, Volovoi decided. *He must never know.*

Volovoi pocketed his cell phone. Pulled out his pistol and loaded a fresh magazine. Then he walked to the door, stepped over Lloyd's body, and hurried out into the driving rain and the darkness.

127

NOBODY AT T-MOBILE was willing to play ball at first. But they hadn't met Carla Windermere.

"Takes a couple of days, usually," the guy told Windermere. She'd mowed through a succession of customer service reps to get to him, and she was about ready to call up the company president himself. "Best we could do is, I dunno, say tomorrow by noonish?"

"You have an hour," she told him. "Then I call my friends at Homeland Security and put your name on a no-fly list, understand? Get to work."

"Jesus," the guy said. "I think I'm supposed to ask for a warrant for this."

"Go ahead," she told him. "You want to ride Amtrak for the rest of your days? Get it done."

She ended the call. Met Stevens's eyes, gave him the hint of a smile. "Let's see if that works."

128

PAVEL DEMETRIOU PUT down his cell phone. Stared across the bedroom at the little girl who stood, hugging herself and shivering, by the bed. She was a delectable specimen, a perfect little plaything, but right now, the Dragon hardly noticed her. He was thinking about Andrei Volovoi. About Lloyd.

Volovoi had sounded different on the phone. He had not sounded confident, or composed. He sounded stressed, worried, urgent. He'd sounded like he was lying.

Lloyd had called. Lloyd had hung up the phone before Demetriou could answer. Demetriou had tried to call back. The phone had rung at first. Nobody had answered. Demetriou had tried again. This time, the line went straight to voicemail.

And Volovoi had sounded shaken. Maybe it was paranoia, the Dragon thought. Maybe it was the cocaine and the girl, making him crazy. Or maybe his instincts were right, and Volovoi was hiding something. Maybe the sale wasn't going as smooth as Volovoi had claimed.

The girl was watching him. The Dragon smiled at her. Gestured to the cocaine. "Help yourself, little one," he told her. "I'll be with you shortly."

Then he made another phone call. Tomas, this time, Volovoi's thug. He'd driven the girls to Manhattan. He was in the warehouse with Volovoi. He wouldn't dare lie to the Dragon.

Tomas answered on the second ring. "Hello?" he said. He sounded wary.

"What is going on?" the Dragon asked him. "Are you at the warehouse with Andrei Volovoi?"

"I am at the warehouse," he said. "Volovoi just left. Did you try his cell phone?"

"Never mind," the Dragon said. "Where did he go? Is the buyer with him?"

"He didn't say where he was going," Tomas said. "And the buyer . . ." He cleared his throat. "The buyer is, uh, dead. Volovoi shot him."

The Dragon exhaled, long and slow. "Why did Volovoi shoot the buyer, Tomas?"

"There was an argument," Tomas said. "I believe the sale fell apart. The buyer started to leave, and Volovoi shot him."

The Dragon ended the call. Stood in the middle of the bedroom and tried to focus his thoughts. Volovoi had killed the buyer. He'd disappeared somewhere. And the little tramp still hadn't touched the cocaine.

The Dragon put down the phone and crossed the bedroom to his closet, dragged out a duffel bag and unzipped it. Inside was a pile of guns. He pulled out a machine pistol, a semiautomatic TEC-9.

"Don't be alarmed, little one," he told the girl, relishing the way her eyes widened. "It's better to be safe than sorry, I find."

129

STEVENS CALLED NANCY while he and Windermere waited to hear back from T-Mobile. He'd talked to his wife earlier, asked her to take the kids to the FBI building in Brooklyn Center, and now he wanted to check in again, make sure they'd made it to safety. Couldn't explain why, really; maybe it was that he'd already been shot once on this case, or maybe he just wanted to make sure his own family was all right, one more time. This case had been a dangerous game. High stress. And Stevens was pretty sure the toughest part was yet to come.

"It's me," he said when Nancy picked up her phone.

"It's you," she said. "Where are you?"

"New Jersey. FBI office in Newark." He stared out the window at the night beyond. "Just had a big storm here."

"Oh yeah?" Nancy paused. "It's been sunny here. Hot. You know."

"Yeah," Stevens said.

Another pause. "What's up, Kirk? You calling to chat about the weather, or what?"

"Just wanted to say hi," he said. "See how you guys are doing. Check in, that kind of thing."

"Bull," Nancy said. "Why are you really calling?"

Stevens caught his reflection in the glass, had to smile. It was a foolish man who tried to put one over on his wife. "Yeah," he said. "Okay, you got me. This case is coming down to the wire, Nancy."

"You're getting close?"

"I think tonight's the night," he said. "I just wanted to hear your voice before it all goes down, in case—"

"Shut up," she said. "Don't even, Kirk. Go take these guys down and come home tomorrow. This FBI imprisonment thing is getting old."

"It's for your own good, though," he said.

"Yeah, well, it sucks," Nancy said. "You want to say hi to the kids?"

He talked to his son, asked about baseball, asked about Triceratops ("He ate nine and a half muffins from the FBI kitchen, Dad"), and then JJ put Andrea on the phone.

"Hey, Dad."

"Hey, kiddo," he said. "How're you doing?"

A beat. A sigh. "I'm good."

"How's your day?"

"It's okay," she said. "Boring. How long do we have to stay here?"

"Just until I finish this case," he said. "Another day or two, maybe. I just want to make sure the guys we're chasing don't try anything crazy, you know?"

She sighed again. "I guess."

He stared out the window and felt like he was trying to hog-tie an eel, the way the conversation was going. "How's your day?"

"I said already. Boring. Mom won't even let me—" She stopped herself. "Not like it's much different from real life, anyway. Now that you guys chased Calvin away."

Stevens let his breath out. "We'll talk about Calvin when I get home, Andrea."

"Whatever," she said. "Here's Mom."

"Wait," he said. "Andrea—"

But she was already gone. A beat of silence, muffled voices, and then Nancy came back. "Sorry about that," she said. "She's been a terror lately."

"I'll be home soon," he told her. "I'll set her straight."

"You'd better," Nancy said. "I'm about out of ideas. Solve this thing and get your ass back here, mister. I'm lonely."

"Yes, ma'am." Stevens laughed. "I'll talk to you later."

He ended the call. Saw Windermere pacing the hallway. She stopped when she noticed him. "Everything cool?"

"Mostly," he said. "They're safe, anyway. Andrea's still mad about the whole boyfriend thing. I think she hates me."

Windermere cast a wry smile at him. "Maybe," she said. "Probably she has a beef with a life sentence of parental-enforced celibacy."

"Don't you start," he said. "She's too young to date. She's sure as hell too young to be fooling around in the living room."

"Better than the backseat."

"*Carla.*" He looked at her. She nodded an apology, and he sank back in his seat. "Anyway. Sorry. You talk to Mathers lately?"

Windermere's eyes were impassive. "Nah," she said, and started pacing again. "It's not like I need to screw that situation up anymore than it already is."

130

THE T-MOBILE GUY called back exactly one hour later. "Manhattan," he told Windermere. "Upper West Side. I can narrow it to an eight-block radius, but that's the best I can do."

"Do better," Windermere told the guy. Then she turned to Stevens. "The Big Apple, partner. We have an eight-block radius to work with."

LePlavy looked up from his computer. "You guys go," he said. "I'll call the Manhattan field office, get some feet on the ground over there."

Windermere held up the phone. "Keep bugging T-Mobile while you're at it," she told LePlavy. "See if they can't narrow down the phone's location any better."

"And make sure the NYPD has a picture of Catalina," Stevens said. "Every cop in Manhattan, get them looking for her."

LePlavy straightened. "On it."

Windermere was already at the door. "Find the car, partner. We're moving."

131

IT WASN'T WORKING. Whatever the Dragon was trying to do, it wasn't working.

He'd stopped trying to force the cocaine on her after the phone calls. For a moment, Catalina dared to believe he'd forgotten about her. He'd stared at her with vacant eyes, barely saw her, put down his phone and dug out a bag from his closet. Inside the bag were guns, lots of them. He pulled out a mean-looking machine pistol and showed it to her.

"I hope you're ready for a party," he said. "I suspect we might have an uninvited guest tonight."

Who? Catalina thought. The Dragon's phone calls had been in English. She hadn't understood them. Staring at the machine pistol, though, she felt a little stirring of hope. Whoever was coming was an enemy of the Dragon. And that made him a friend of hers.

She'd hoped that this new development would make the Dragon forget about her, about the awful things he was planning to do to her. How could he want to hurt her when someone was coming for him?

But apparently the maniac was unconcerned. He put the machine pistol on a dresser, far away from the bed, a million miles from her reach. Then he crossed the room to her. He moved fast, his jaw set. He wasn't smiling anymore. Whatever he wanted to do now, he wasn't happy about it.

She watched as he dove into the cocaine on the nightstand. Watched him come up again, swearing, blinking, his wiry beard coated in the white powder. He looked around the room, licked his lips. Shoved her down onto the bed and was on top of her before she knew what he was doing.

He was heavy above her. He wasn't a big man, but he was bigger than her. He crushed her into the bedsheets, pawed at her body. She could feel the handle of the knife digging into her hip and she squirmed beneath him, wriggled away from his hot breath, his tongue.

"Come on, little one," he told her, raspy. "We might as well play together while we still have time."

She reached for the knife as he began to kiss her neck. Closed her fingers over the handle and tugged. The knife didn't move. It was stuck in its scabbard. The Dragon sat up and slapped her.

"Hands off," he said. "Don't get frisky, do you hear me? This is my show."

The slap hurt. Her face stung. Her ears rang and her thoughts swam. Catalina watched the Dragon remove the knife. He held it up so she could see it, the glint of the light on the blade. It was long and curved and awful, and she struggled and shied away. The Dragon sneered at her.

"Behave yourself," he said. "Behave yourself and this will all be easy."

He put the knife on the nightstand, beside the cocaine. Inhaled another mountain of the drug and came back to the bed, fumbling with his belt, the zipper on his pants. He was growing frustrated. He wasn't looking at her.

"Come on," he said. "Fucking bitch, come on."

Catalina eyed the knife on the nightstand. It was close. It wasn't close enough. She wouldn't reach the nightstand unless she stretched, and even then, her fingers would barely graze the cocaine. She would have to lunge for the knife, and the man was faster, and stronger. She reached anyway, scrabbled with her fingers, squirmed on the bed.

The Dragon swore again. He slapped her again. Curled his lip as she screamed. He was touching himself now, she saw. It wasn't working.

"Too much cocaine," he said. "Fucking bitch. Fucking Volovoi. *Fuck*."

Catalina felt her head swimming again. Couldn't focus. The wine probably, and the man above her. The knife lay inches from her grasp. She shifted on the bed as the man struggled and swore. Strained with her fingers and tried to will the weapon closer.

132

VOLOVOI PULLED THE BMW to a stop outside the Dragon's apartment building. Around him, traffic swarmed Park Avenue. Cars and taxis and buses. Police cars. Lots of them, but no sirens, not yet.

Volovoi pulled the BMW to the curb. Stared up at the building, the DuPont, some fancy tower. A hell of a lot nicer than his apartment in Newark, anyway, not that he would ever see the place again. Volovoi figured he would be lucky to see New York again, hell, America. His face was on every news program in the tristate area.

The smart play would be to get the hell out right now. Stay in the BMW and keep driving, get away from Manhattan and just go. Find somewhere quiet to hide until the attention died down, then get the hell out of the country. Nobody would connect him to the BMW, not for a little while. He could put some serious distance between himself and the FBI insects.

He could save himself easily. He just had to keep driving.

Volovoi shut the car off. Pulled out his cell phone and called a contact at the docks. "I need an out," he said, "Tonight."

"Give me a moment," the contact replied. A moment passed, and the contact came back. "The APL *Brazil*," he told Volovoi. "Sails midnight for Rotterdam. Good?"

Volovoi checked his watch. A quarter to ten. He would have to hurry, but he could make it.

"I'll be there," he said, and ended the call. Then he climbed out of the car.

There were police everywhere. NYPD cruisers, unmarked sedans, FBI Yukons, even a helicopter. They were searching, Volovoi realized. Somehow they'd traced the Dragon here.

Only a fool would stick around.

Volovoi checked his pistol again. Shoved it into his waistband, hidden, and crossed the sidewalk to the DuPont's front doors, every sense in his head screaming at him to turn around. He didn't. He couldn't.

Volovoi knew the Dragon would not rest while he was still alive. He would not forgive his partner's debts, nor his betrayal. Lloyd was dead. The Manhattan project was ruined. The Dragon would carry the grudge to his grave, and if he couldn't find Volovoi, he would take out his anger on Volovoi's family.

Well, so be it. Volovoi would send the Dragon to his grave a little early.

He walked into the DuPont. Slipped past the doorman, who barely looked up from his paperback novel. Entered an open elevator and pressed the button for the Dragon's floor, checked his pistol again as the doors slid closed, and waited as the elevator slowly climbed skyward.

133

IRINA MILOSOVICI SAT in the FBI conference room, watching a TV screen play the news in a corner. Beside her sat the translator, and across the table, the American family—Nancy Stevens, a teenage daughter about Catalina's age, and a young boy. Sometimes Agent Mathers came in, offered everyone coffee or sandwiches or a fast-food hamburger. Then he was out again, and Irina caught glimpses of him through the doorway, walking this way and that with an urgency she couldn't help but find attractive.

He'd hooked her with that little bit of tortured Romanian, she knew, though he'd later confessed (through Maria, the translator) that he'd spent a couple hours memorizing the phrase as he worked to find her.

"Figured you'd feel a little lost," he said. "Maybe it'd make you feel better to hear something in your own language."

She'd laughed again. Told Maria to tell him his accent needed work, and watched his face break into a wide smile as Maria relayed the joke. He'd brought her back to the office, brought her Maria, brought her food and water and a bandage for the scrape on her knee, brought her everything he could think of to make her feel comfortable.

But he couldn't bring her Catalina. She was still out there. She still belonged to the Dragon.

> > >

NANCY STEVENS'S DAUGHTER WAS WATCHING Irina from across the conference room. She was a pretty blond girl, so American. The kind of girl who appears on a magazine cover. She studied Irina with unabashed curiosity.

The girl said something to Maria, who nodded. Then the girl looked at Irina again. "You're the girl who escaped," she said. Maria translated. "The girl who was kidnapped. What's your name?"

Irina hesitated. "Irina," she said. "Irina Milosovici."

"I'm Andrea Stevens," she said. "Nice to meet you."

Irina met her eyes. "And you," she tried in English.

"Is it true you and your sister came here in a box?" Andrea asked.

Nancy Stevens, beside her, shushed her. Apologized to Irina, to Maria.

"It's okay," Irina said. "Yes. I was taken from my home in Bucharest."

"How did they kidnap you?"

Irina closed her eyes. "I always wanted to go to America," she said. "They promised me a job, as a model. There was an American man who promised to handle everything."

"And then he put you in the box."

She exhaled. "Yes."

"Why?"

Before Irina could answer, Nancy Stevens said something to her, sharp. Andrea spun, replied in kind, a teenager's quick temper. Catalina had the same; watching Andrea made Irina's heart ache for her sister.

Andrea and her mother argued for a minute. Then Nancy said something that made Andrea blush and look away, look down at the table. "Sorry," she told Irina. "I didn't mean to be rude."

"It's okay," Irina said.

Andrea was silent a beat. "My dad is going to solve this case," she said finally. "He's in New Jersey right now, catching the bad guys. He's really good."

Irina studied the girl's face, her earnest expression. Could see more of her mother's features, but the little boy, he had his dad's face, his kind eyes. Nancy Stevens had a beautiful family.

"My dad rescued me once," Andrea said. "From a bad guy. He's a really good cop. He'll get your sister back."

Irina forced a smile at the girl. She had no doubt Agent Stevens was good. Probably he was a wonderful father. But he'd sent his family to hide here all the same. He, too, was afraid of the man called the Dragon.

Irina shivered and cast her eyes to the table. The Dragon was a monster. Even the police were afraid of him. Poor sweet Catalina didn't stand a chance.

134

SHE COULDN'T REACH the knife.

The Dragon was on top of her again. His hands were all over her body, pawing at her, squeezing. He slapped at her. Swore at her. He hadn't tried to have sex with her, yet. From what Catalina could tell, he couldn't.

"Fucking Volovoi," he muttered. "Fucking little bitch."

He would kill her, she knew. He was getting frustrated, and he would take it out on her. He would take the knife and stab her, and that would be the end. It would be the end of her life, and the end of Dorina's, and the others. Everybody would die.

She had to get away.

The Dragon was struggling with the clasp of her bra. Catalina lifted her head from the pillows. Beside her, she could see the nightstand, the mountain of drugs. The Dragon sniffed, fumbled, swore again. He was clumsy and awkward.

She could see the knife where it lay on the table, beside the cocaine, unguarded and tantalizingly close. It wasn't close enough, though. She would never reach it.

Catalina reached anyway. She didn't touch the knife. Couldn't. But she came back with cocaine, a fistful of white powder. She flung into the Dragon's eyes. The Dragon reared back, coughing, grabbing at his face, and Catalina scrabbled from underneath him. Reached again for the knife.

This time, she grabbed it.

The Dragon was swearing above her, sneezing, his eyes filled with tears. Catalina spun, and lunged with the knife. Plunged it deep into his stomach. The Dragon screamed, doubled over. Struck out with his fists.

Catalina dodged him. Wrenched the knife out and came at him again, thrusting the knife in his stomach, wanting to puke at how easily it slid in. The Dragon screamed as she stabbed him. Swung his arms, wild and blind.

Catalina stabbed him until she couldn't do it anymore. Let him slump against the bed, let him fall, clumsily, to the floor.

She fumbled in the closet. Found a T-shirt and pulled it over herself. Then she ran, gripping the bloody knife in her hand.

135

"NYPD FOUND THE phone in a parking garage on Lexington," LePlavy told Stevens as Windermere sped the Charger out of the Lincoln Tunnel. "Backseat of a town car with phony registration. No sign of Catalina Milosovici or anyone else."

So where the hell is he? Stevens thought. "Can we canvass the area?"

"Already doing it," LePlavy said. "It's a full-scale manhunt. It's the middle of Manhattan, though, Agent Stevens. Even in an eight-block radius, there's more people than Wichita, Kansas."

Stevens watched the city fly by outside the Charger's windows. "Tell them to keep looking," he told LePlavy. "This is our best goddamn shot."

136

THE ELEVATOR DOORS slid open. Volovoi stepped out of the car and into the hallway. The hallway was quiet.

He gripped the pistol in his right hand as he walked down the hall. Thought again of his nieces. Of the police cars outside.

He would kill the Dragon quickly. He would kill the little girl, too; he would have to. Then he would escape. Nobody would catch on.

Volovoi reached the Dragon's door. Raised his pistol and aimed at the lock. Before he could pull the trigger, the door flew open.

The girl. Catalina Milosovici. She wore nothing but an oversized T-shirt, and in her hand she carried the Dragon's bloody knife. She ran headlong into Volovoi, collided and bounced off him. Fell to the floor. The knife scattered away.

Volovoi stared at her. At the knife. Wondered if she'd done his work for him. No matter; he'd find out soon enough. The girl stared back from the floor. He watched her eyes go wide as he leveled the pistol at her.

"It's nothing personal," he told her. "It's not prudent to leave witnesses."

He could see her jaw working. He could see the frustration in her eyes. No doubt, she'd been brave. She'd been courageous. She'd disarmed the Dragon and managed to escape, and now—now this. Now she would die, because she was unlucky.

Volovoi thought about his nieces. Forced himself to shake the girl's gaze. Tightened his finger on the trigger.

Before he could shoot, though, someone else pulled a trigger. Gunfire exploded, loud, a hammer pounding. Bullets tore through the wall around Volovoi, courtesy of the Dragon, who'd emerged at the end of a long hallway, holding a machine pistol. The Dragon was bloody. His shirt was unbuttoned, his belt undone. Volovoi ducked away, amazed at his good luck. The Dragon's bullets had missed him somehow. He had survived.

He had to kill the Dragon.

The girl was scrambling backward, back into the apartment. Volovoi ignored her. Dove for cover as the Dragon let off another round of bullets. Volovoi raised his pistol and fired back, heard the Dragon laughing.

"You've betrayed me, Andrei," the Dragon said. "You've taken my goodwill and my money and you stabbed me in the back."

Volovoi ducked behind a leather couch. Knew it would provide no protection if the Dragon advanced. He fired another couple of shots. "Your goodwill," he said. "You strangled my operation. You forced me into this cause of action."

The floorboards creaked. Shadows moved on the wall. The Dragon was advancing. And he was still laughing.

"Why did you kill Lloyd?" the Dragon said. "He could have made us both rich, Andrei. What were you thinking?"

"He could have, but he didn't," Volovoi replied. "He found out about the failure of my New Jersey operation, and he decided to opt out of our arrangement. I killed him before he could tell you he'd changed his mind."

"And then you came to kill me," the Dragon said.

Volovoi peered over the couch, his pistol hot in his hand. Heard the Dragon shuffling down the hall, heard his breathing. The little girl had stabbed him. From the sounds of it, he was hurt bad.

Good, Volovoi thought. *The police will be here, soon. I have to get out of here*

"This doesn't have to end this way, Andrei," the Dragon called out. "Our partnership was a good one. Surely we can come to an agreement."

Volovoi said nothing. If he didn't kill the Dragon quickly, the police would arrive. There would be no escape. There would only be prison, or death.

"I only want the girl," the Dragon said. "Leave me the girl, and you can go in peace. You have my word, I will forgive your betrayal."

Volovoi looked to the doorway. The girl was gone. "The girl is gone," he said. He tried to stand. Couldn't. Stared down at his clothing and saw bloody holes, ragged, three of them. The Dragon's bullets hadn't missed after all.

He felt weak suddenly. Forgot about standing. Slumped back down to the floor and studied his bloody fingers as the Dragon came out of the hallway. The Dragon looked from Volovoi to the empty doorway. Raised his machine pistol and aimed at Volovoi's face.

"So long, Andrei," he said. Then he grinned and pulled the trigger.

Nothing happened.

Outside, in the hallway, an elevator door dinged.

"Your lucky day," the Dragon said, dropping his spent clip to the floor and hurrying after the girl instead. Volovoi raised his pistol from the floor. Tried to aim at the Dragon, was too slow. Too weak. He could hear police sirens now. He lay his head down and closed his eyes.

137

SHE HAD TO run. She had to run now.

She'd retrieved the knife she'd dropped when the silent man came through the door. Crawled toward the doorway as the man fought with the Dragon, praying they didn't see her, or notice she was gone. She heard more gunshots behind her. It sounded like the world ending.

The door splintered above her head. Catalina wrenched it open as the men fired again. She didn't know who they were shooting at. She hoped it wasn't her. She threw herself out the door and landed in the hallway, all plush carpet and red and gold. It was a maze. She couldn't remember where to go.

The men would come for her. They both wanted to kill her. *Make a decision.* Catalina pictured the apartment in her head, the windows. Tried to remember the way she'd arrived. Couldn't remember. No time. She just ran. She ran left.

A bank of elevators, around the corner. Catalina pressed the call button. Waited. Waited. Realized she should have found the stairwell. Realized the stairwell was behind her, back toward the Dragon's door.

Ding.

The elevator door slid open. Nobody inside. Catalina hurried in, clutching the knife to her chest. Pressed the first-floor button, then the "close door" arrows. Heard footsteps in the hallway like thunder. Watched the door slowly close and urged it to close quicker.

It slid shut just as the Dragon arrived. He clawed at the door, pounded. Swore in frustration. Catalina screamed. Then the elevator was dropping.

The elevator was mirrors. Catalina studied herself, her clumsy makeup, her oversized T-shirt. Her hair was unkempt, and there was blood on her hands and on the knife. The pervert's blood. The Dragon's blood.

The elevator dropped toward street level. Catalina waited. Caught her breath. Prayed the car made it to the ground floor before the Dragon caught up with her again.

138

LEPLAVY CALLED BACK as Windermere sped the Charger up Madison Avenue.

"Looks like Catalina left a message on the phone," he told Stevens. "Something in Romanian. *Parca Strada balaur.* Apologies if my pronunciation is shitty."

"Parca Stradă balaur." Stevens looked out through the windshield. Around him, Manhattan rose, crowded and crazy and chaotic. "What does it mean?"

"According to Google Translate, it means 'Park Avenue dragon,' in Romanian," LePlavy said. "And I don' t think that's the name of a Chinese restaurant."

"I think you're right," Stevens told LePlavy. He ended the call. "Park Avenue, and hurry," he told Windermere. "It's our lucky night."

139

PAVEL DEMETRIOU CLUTCHED his wound as he hurried down the stairs, cursing the girl all the way to the bottom. Cursing Andrei Volovoi, too, and anyone else he could think of.

Ironic that the bitch had stabbed him. Poetic justice. He'd intended to carve her pretty face himself when he had finished with her. Instead, she'd ambushed him. Wounded him. Cut him.

She would not stop him.

Demetriou paused on a landing. Leaned against a railing to catch his breath. He felt dizzy, light-headed. There was a lot of blood, but he ignored it. One little bitch wouldn't slow the Dragon. Neither would Andrei Volovoi, or the fucking FBI, for that matter. He pushed himself off the wall. Reloaded his machine pistol and then reached for the vial around his neck. Unscrewed it and poured himself a bump of cocaine, inhaled until he saw fireworks behind his eyes.

He would track down the girl. He would drag her out of the building and escape New York with her, regroup. He would kill her eventually, after he'd enjoyed her. After he'd repaid her for the trouble her family had caused him.

The cocaine helped. Demetriou hurried down the stairs. Ignored his wounds, pushed them from his mind. Barely felt the exertion. He made the main floor and burst through the fire doors and into the lobby. Looked around. The lobby was quiet. A doorman sat behind a desk by the front doors, reading a paperback. Otherwise, nothing. No movement. No sounds.

DING.

The elevator. Demetriou spun as the doors slid open, raised the TEC-9. But the elevator was empty. No girl.

He stared at the empty car for a moment. Studied the numbers above the second elevator's closed doors. That car was climbing, from the first floor, skyward. Demetriou crossed the lobby to the doorman. "A girl," he said. "A little girl. Did you see her?"

The doorman looked up. "Beg your pardon?"

Demetriou leveled the gun at him. "A little fucking girl. Did you see her?"

The man shook his head. "No," he said. "No, man, I swear to God."

Demetriou shot him anyway. The sound echoed through the lobby, half deafening. Demetriou let the doorman slump to the ground. Then he walked back to the elevator and considered the empty car, thinking.

140

CATALINA STARED OUT at the hallway, confused. She'd pressed the first-floor button in the elevator, but the doors had opened on a hallway identical to the Dragon's upstairs. There were doors to apartments. A thick carpet. Soft lighting. No escape to the street.

The apartment closest to her was apartment 112. Beside it, 113, and so on. This was the first floor, she realized. The lobby must be below her. She was still one floor too high.

The elevator doors started to slide closed. Catalina reached for the L button, then thought better of it. Instead, she slipped out into the hallway. Too much time had wasted. The Dragon might be waiting for her in the lobby already.

She could hide. She could knock on an apartment door until somebody answered, then burst in and hide until the police came. But that could take hours. She couldn't speak any English. Probably the men had friends in the building. They might take her to the Dragon themselves.

She needed to get out of the building. The Dragon wouldn't follow her into the streets, and even if he did, she could lose him. New York was huge. And this building was deadly.

She crept down the hall, her knife at the ready, felt her stomach turn as she remembered how easily it had cut through the maniac's flesh.

She came to the fire exit. Opened the door slowly and listened. No sounds. Nothing. She slipped into the stairwell, peered up through the center, then down. Saw no hands on the railing. Heard no footsteps coming for her.

Cautiously, Catalina descended. Reached the lobby level, the heavy steel fire door. There was a window, a porthole to the lobby. She stood on her toes and peeked through it. Saw nothing. The lobby, pristine and deserted. The elevators.

She pushed the door open and slipped through. Hugged the wall to the side of the doorway, and looked out and saw the front doors, the dark night beyond. Cars and pedestrians, almost within reach.

He's not here, she thought. *He's gone. Run five meters and you're safe*. Then she saw the smear of blood behind the doorman's front desk.

Shit.

Nothing moved in the lobby. The doorman was gone. Somewhere, a clock ticked, earth-shatteringly loud. The Dragon had been here, Catalina knew. Now he was gone.

She crept out of the alcove and hurried for the doors. Made it halfway before she felt him behind her.

"*Tårfå*," he muttered. *Whore*. His hand gripped her shoulder and he wrenched her back toward him.

141

VOLOVOI PULLED HIMSELF off the hardwood, struggling to slow the flow of blood from his wounds.

Pavel had shot him three times in the stomach. The wounds bled black. They burned, a blinding-hot fiery pain. His shoulder ached where Bogdan Urzica had shot him at the gas station. It seemed like years ago.

The apartment was silent around him. The walls were strafed with shrapnel from Pavel's gun, the furniture shredded. Catalina Milosovici was gone. The Dragon had chased after her. The apartment was empty.

Volovoi couldn't hear the police yet, but he knew they were coming. Somebody would report the gunshots. The NYPD would arrive. Sooner or later, they'd make the connection, and then the FBI would show up, and if Volovoi didn't die, he would spend the rest of his life in jail.

This was okay, Volovoi decided. This was not the worst-case scenario.

The Dragon was the worst-case scenario.

He'd been stabbed. Catalina Milosovici had somehow overpowered him, put a knife in him. She'd managed to escape. But the Dragon wasn't dead. And as long as the Dragon survived, Volovoi couldn't rest. Not with his family still out in the world. Not with his nieces at risk.

Volovoi pushed himself to his feet. Propped himself against the couch and gathered his strength. In a closet by the front door, he found a couple shirts, a coat. He tore a shirt to shreds, wrapped it around his torso. Pulled the jacket over top and clutched it around him. Held his pistol tight and hoped he had the strength to point it at the Dragon when he saw the chance.

Leaning against the wall with his good shoulder, Volovoi limped toward the Dragon's ruined door. Edged out into the hallway and saw nothing, no curious neighbors, no onlookers, no cops. Not yet.

Perfect.

He struggled into the hall. Made his way down the corridor. He felt better now, a little, now that he was upright. Now that he had a goal in mind.

He would find the Dragon. He would kill the Dragon. Then, if he had any strength left, he would figure out a way to get out of this city.

Volovoi reached the elevators. Pressed the call button and waited, fighting waves of nausea and dizziness, that fire-poker pain in his belly. The elevator arrived. Volovoi slipped inside. Leaned against the mirrored walls and pressed the button for the lobby. He was leaking all over the polished floor. More blood. Big deal.

The elevator door closed. The car dropped toward the lobby. *Find the Dragon*, he told himself. *Kill him. And get the hell out of Manhattan.*

142

IN THE CHARGER, the siren screaming, lights flashing, Windermere's foot to the floor.

Stevens checked his phone. "Shots fired, Seventy-seventh and Park," he said. "Someplace called the DuPont."

Windermere glanced at him as she slalomed through traffic. "Where the hell are we now?"

"Madison and—" Stevens strained for a glimpse of a street sign. "Sixty-first. Better step on it, Carla."

"It's stepped on," Windermere said, urging the car faster. "So help me, Stevens, it's stepped on."

143

THE DRAGON GRIPPED onto Catalina's shoulder. "Not so fucking fast."

She spun at him with the knife. Felt resistance, just slight, as the blade sliced his hand. Beyond him, she could see the open elevator door. Realized he'd been hiding there, waiting for her.

No time to think about that now.

The Dragon howled as the knife cut him. Released his grip. Catalina shook free and ran for the doorway.

The glass door exploded ahead of her. The gunshot echoed through the lobby. Catalina kept running. Felt her bare feet crunch on broken glass. Felt the shards slice her skin. She didn't slow down. She couldn't.

She zagged just as he fired again. Slipped, caught her balance, stumbled out through the ruined doorway. The Dragon fired some more, shattering a window on a parked car in front of her, triggering the car's alarm. Her feet were on fire now. Every step was a fresh agony.

There were sirens. She could hear them in the air, but she knew they wouldn't help her in time. Catalina ducked away from the doorway. Ran down the street toward an intersection in the distance, the Dragon's heavy footsteps behind her. His ragged breathing.

He fired again. This shot barely missed. Catalina ducked and kept running.

144

WINDERMERE SCREAMED THE Charger up to Seventy-seventh and Park, slowed as she reached the intersection.

"Where am I going?" she asked Stevens. "Which one's the DuPont?"

Stevens scanned the rows of tall apartment buildings lining Park

Avenue, their doorways marked by covered awnings jutting out to the sidewalk. He couldn't see a name anywhere.

Then Windermere punched the gas. "Whoa," he said. "Find it?"

"I figure it's the one with the shot-up front glass," she said, steering the car through the intersection. "And the bloody thug staggering out the doorway."

Stevens reached for his Glock, his heart already pounding. Across the intersection, an imposing brick high-rise. A girl running barefoot on the sidewalk, a man chasing behind her. A tall, terrifying man with a black, wiry beard and a big pistol. The Dragon?

Windermere pointed. "Is that little sister?"

Stevens grit his teeth. "Sure looks like it."

The girl ran for the street corner. The Dragon raised his pistol, murder in his eyes. Windermere squealed the Charger to a skidding stop. The Dragon didn't take his eye off the girl.

Stevens was on the pavement before Windermere stopped the car. Drew his Glock and fired at the gunman, quick. Too quick. The shot missed. The gunman didn't blink. Drew a bead on Catalina Milosovici and fired again, a deadly barrage.

Stevens didn't check to see if the gunman hit his target. He pulled the trigger again twice, a double tap. This time the gunman paid attention. He staggered backward, clutching his wounds, his eyes searching for the shooter.

Stevens let him find him. Watched the gunman's eyes darken as he registered his face. Watched his mouth curl in a frustrated snarl, watched him spin the gun toward him.

Stevens shot him again. This time, the gunman fell.

Stevens hurried across to the sidewalk, covered the man with his

Glock, ran to him, kicked his gun away and stood overtop, breathing hard, wanting to say something, something to really underline what an evil piece of shit the guy was.

So long, you evil piece of shit, something like that.

But the gunman's eyes were lifeless, his blood soaking the pavement, and Stevens had something else on his mind. "The girl," he asked Windermere. "Catalina. Where'd she go?"

Windermere spun toward the nearest intersection, Seventy-seventh Street. Stevens followed her gaze. The girl had been hoofing it that way when last seen, when the gunman had fired his last shot. Stevens hadn't stopped to see if the man had hit his target, had been focused on putting him down.

Now, though, he looked again. Saw nothing. Empty space. Shot up or not, Catalina Milosovici was gone.

145

VOLOVOI RODE THE elevator to the lobby. Saw the carnage as soon as the doors slid open. The doorman lying dead behind his desk. The shattered front entrance, bloody footprints in the shrapnel glass. More blood on the walls, on the marble floor, a massacre site. But no sign of the Dragon or the girl.

Outside, police sirens. Flashing lights. Volovoi limped into the lobby and eyed the empty doorway, saw two FBI agents standing over a body on the sidewalk, gesturing down the street. It was the Dragon's body. The fool had chased Catalina Milosovici right into their bullets.

Volovoi ducked out of the doorway as more police cruisers screamed to a halt outside on Park Avenue. The cavalry was arriving. The Dragon was dead. The police would have the neighborhood in lockdown soon enough.

His pistol was hot in his hand, slick with blood and sweat. Volovoi contemplated his escape. His next move. His last move, perhaps.

He could go out shooting. Step into the doorway and raise the pistol and attempt to kill as many of the FBI insects as he possibly could, blast a path to the BMW at the curb and try to muscle his way out through the cordon of police cars. No doubt, the FBI agents and their NYPD companions would cut him down where he stood. There were too many of them. The BMW was parked too far away. It would not be a prudent course of action.

And anyway, the Dragon was dead. Volovoi felt a sudden freedom, a weight lifted from his chest. He imagined his life without the gangster watching over his shoulder, without the bastard's hand in his wallet. A life without worry. A second chance.

Volovoi realized he didn't want to die, not tonight. He wanted to get the hell out of Manhattan and try again.

He turned away from the front doors. Crossed the marble floor to an interior doorway, and followed a long, narrow hall through the bowels of the building to a rear exit and a quiet, tree-lined courtyard. He was limping. His heart was a runaway train. He was bleeding everywhere, and he was dizzy as shit. He would slip free from the police cordons. He would hijack a car. He would find a way out of Manhattan.

He would fucking survive.

Wouldn't he?

Volovoi navigated the courtyard, past the high-rises that neighbored the DuPont and back through the shadows and away from the sirens and the shouting and the chaos, until the courtyard dog-legged and he came to a little gate and, beyond it, Seventy-seventh Street.

He pushed the gate open. Stepped out onto Seventy-seventh Street, a narrow, leafy roadway lined with parked cars and off-duty ambulances. There was a hospital, he remembered, a few buildings down. Nurses and bandages and medicine—and he, outside, with serious wounds, and no time to tend to them now.

The street was quiet. To his right, on Park Avenue, hell was breaking loose. Police cars screamed up. Voices shouted. High above, a helicopter. But Seventy-seventh Street was dark, and the noises were muted. Volovoi stood in the shadows and surveyed the block. Then he heard her.

Thin, gasping breathing. Feet slapping the sidewalk. A hushed cry of pain with almost every step. The sounds of a scared teenage girl, a girl who'd walked on broken glass to escape her captors.

Catalina Milosovici was across the street, in the shadows, barely twenty feet away.

Volovoi watched her, had an idea. The girl had been trouble for him for days. Now she would be his ticket to freedom, his hostage. He hoisted the pistol and clutched the jacket around his wounds. Started across the street to intercept her.

146

Stevens and Windermere left the remains of Andrei Volovoi in the hands of the NYPD uniforms now arriving on-scene. Pistols in hand, they ran for Seventy-seventh.

Be okay, Stevens urged Catalina as he searched the Park Avenue sidewalk for any sign of her. *Just hold out. You're almost safe.*

At least the girl wasn't bleeding out beneath a parked car on Park. Stevens and Windermere reached Seventy-seventh Street with no sign of her, and Stevens hoped that meant Volovoi hadn't shot her. Meant she was still alive, still okay.

"Catalina," he called down the street. No response. "Shit," he said, turning to Windermere. "You see her?"

Windermere squinted into the darkness. Then he heard her gasp, and followed her eyes to the sidewalk.

Blood. Fresh blood.

Shit.

147

HER FEET WERE killing her.

Every step felt like a hundred more knives. The sidewalk was gritty and hard, her feet bloody and raw. Catalina wanted to scream. She kept quiet. She knew the Dragon would find her.

She stopped in the shadows to try and wipe the grit from her feet. Tried to tear the hem of the T-shirt to make some kind of protection. The fabric was thin, but it wouldn't tear. Her hands were slick with blood. She was shaking with fear.

She had to keep moving.

She crept out of the shadows and hurried down the block. There were ambulances beside her, dark and empty. A bright light up ahead, a red cross. A hospital. They would have police there probably. They would protect her.

The light seemed miles away. She heard voices behind her, police sirens. She didn't dare look back. Didn't dare turn around. She moved forward. Kept running. Fought to reach the light.

A police car pulled up to the hospital entrance. A police officer got out, a fat man with a mustache, a kind-looking man. Catalina ran toward him. "*Halp*," she cried out. "*Halp me, please.*"

The police officer stiffened and reached for his gun. Saw her emerge from the shadows, and picked up the radio on his collar instead. Then the world blew up behind her.

The cop's eyes went wide. He looked down at his shirt, at the crimson blossoms that had appeared on his blues. Catalina threw herself sideways as more shots burst out. This was a different gun than the Dragon's; it was louder, slower, but more powerful. A big weapon. Deadly. Catalina crawled between an ambulance and the police officer's cruiser, heard gunshots echo on the building walls around her.

The shooter was behind her. She could hear him approaching, knew she couldn't stay still. She gripped the knife tight and contemplated an ambush. Knew she didn't stand a chance against his gun.

Quiet as she could, she crept toward the street. Dodged around the police cruiser, her head down, her knees scraping the pavement. She reached the front of the car and glanced back as the shooter lurched forward, steadying himself against the ambulance.

It was not the devil-faced Dragon. It was the other man. The silent one. Volovoi.

She wondered what had happened to the Dragon, if he was still hunting her, too. She imagined both men stalking her on this narrow, dark street. Imagined escaping the Dragon only to wind up in the arms of this other man.

Behind the silent man, far up the street, police lights and sirens. Loud shouting. She'd heard gunshots behind her as she'd run from the apartment building. A police car screeching to a halt. Maybe the police had killed the Dragon. Maybe only Volovoi remained.

If that was the case, then Volovoi was the only man who knew how to save the other girls. If he died, Dorina and the others would disappear. They would suffer the fate she'd escaped, with men as evil as the Dragon.

She would have to disarm him. Knock his gun away, and force

him to tell her where the Dragon had moved the girls. She would have to hurt him.

Volovoi was coming closer. The police car sagged from his weight as he leaned on it, limping his way out into the street. Catalina crouched as low as she could, realized too late she was as good as naked in the light from the hospital doors. He would see her instantly. There would be no surprise.

She pulled herself to her feet. Heard Volovoi's breath catch as he saw her, heard his pistol boom again. Then she was running.

148

STEVENS WAS HALFWAY down the block when the shooting started. He ducked behind a car as muzzle flashes lit up the dark block. Felt Windermere slam down beside him.

"Another shooter," she said. "Where the hell'd he come from?"

Stevens peered over the car. "Wherever it was, he brought a hell of a gun."

They searched the darkness for the shooter. Saw shadows moving against a patch of bright light up ahead.

"He wasn't shooting at us," Windermere said, "was he?"

Stevens shook his head. "Don't think so."

She was already running. "What are we waiting for?"

149

CATALINA RAN, ZAGGING into the shadows, her feet screaming again. Ahead was a busy intersection, more light. Behind her, the silent man.

He'd stopped shooting. The policeman lay dead in front of her, and up the street, where she'd come from, were more voices, shouting, more sirens. The silent man, though, Volovoi, had stopped shooting.

Maybe he'd run out of bullets.

Catalina ducked behind another parked car and peeked back at him. He stood on the sidewalk, unsteady, his breathing slow and ragged. He barely moved. He was injured, she realized. He looked close to death. He would die from his wounds, or he would lurch all the way to that next crowded intersection, and a police officer would see him and shoot him there. All she had to do was stay hidden a few minutes longer and fate would run its course. She was free.

Her parents were safe. Irina was safe.

Catalina Milosovici was safe.

But Dorina wasn't.

The other girls weren't.

Catalina stood. Her feet burned beneath her. Her legs ached. Her knees bled. She steadied herself on the parked car, careful not to make noise. Gripped the knife in her hand and inched out of the shadows.

> > >

VOLOVOI LEANED AGAINST A PARKED Buick and gripped his pistol. Tried to focus his eyes where the light caught the slick steel. His vision was blurry; his whole brain unfocused. He was hurt worse than he'd thought. He needed a rest.

The police were everywhere now. He'd given away his position when he'd shot the city cop, and now the whole circus was coming. NYPD. FBI. A helicopter roared by overhead, its searchlight painting the whole street with light.

He would die here, he realized. The Dragon was dead and his nieces were alive. Surely that should be enough.

Fast footsteps behind him, the police approaching. Volovoi thought about going out shooting, about taking down as many police officers as he could before their bullets felled him. He thought about raising the pistol to his mouth and eating his last bullet instead. He was tired. His thoughts were slow and foggy. He was still mulling the question when Catalina Milosovici stepped out of the shadows.

"Not so fast." She had the Dragon's knife gripped tight in her hand. "Don't you die yet, *bulangiu.*"

150

CATALINA ADVANCED ON Volovoi, her knife at the ready. He was holding his big pistol, but it dangled from his hand, useless. He was in no condition to use it.

Volovoi looked at her sadly. Looked up the block as red and blue light filled the shadows. The police would be here in seconds, she knew. They would take the man away, or they would kill him. They would not know how to find Dorina.

"Don't you die," she said, holding up the knife, showing him the long blade. "Don't you die until I say you can go."

Volovoi didn't answer, and she saw something different in his eyes, something like regret. For a moment, she slowed her advance. Then she shook it off. She'd believed the thug who'd kept her in the box was human, too, and he'd tried to kill her in the end.

"The other girls," she said. "Tell me where they are, or I'll stab your guts out."

Volovoi exhaled. He slumped against the parked car and didn't say anything.

Catalina held up the knife. "Tell me," she said. "Tell me where they are, or I'll hurt you, you coward."

But Volovoi didn't answer. He dropped his pistol. Then he dropped to the ground.

Catalina flew at him. Landed on top of him, pinned him to the ground. He was weak now. He was minutes from death. She felt use-less, consumed by frustration.

"Tell me," she said, hammering his chest with her fists. *"Tell me, tell me, tell me."*

> > >

VOLOVOI BARELY FELT THE GIRL'S punches. She was shouting in his face, questions about the other women. Pavel's collection of prizes.

They would die in their warehouse, he knew. Tomas would abandon them to save his own skin, would leave them locked in the basement until they all starved to death. They would die, every one of them, and at last the Dragon's Manhattan project would be finished.

The girl held her knife to his cheek. "I'll hurt you," she told him. "You're not dead yet."

There was determination in her eyes. Anger and urgency, and be-hind it all, fear. She was barely more than a child. She should have been playing with dolls, or walking her little dog, or whatever else it was teenage girls did. Instead, he'd put her into the box. He'd brought her here. He'd turned her from a child into this angry ball of fury and desperation, itching to kill him.

Volovoi pictured Veronika and Adriana, one last time. Imagined their innocence stolen away. Felt a sudden sickness as he realized that no matter how many Dragons died, how many Volovois, there would always be more men to take their place. There would always be pred-ators lusting after his nieces. And he wouldn't be around to protect them.

He looked up at Catalina Milosovici. Wondered if she would ever regain what he'd stolen from her. Felt his energy slipping away, and closed his eyes.

"The warehouse," he told her. "The girls are in the warehouse."

> > >

CATALINA FELT VOLOVOI DYING. She pressed the knife harder against his skin. "What warehouse?" she said. "Where is the warehouse? *Where are the other girls?*"

Volovoi opened his mouth. Spat, burbled blood, tried to speak. Catalina pressed her ear to his mouth. Strained desperately to hear the man's answers.

She never got the chance.

Suddenly there were arms around her, picking her up and sweeping her away from the man. Police officers. A man. She fought him, kicked at him, screamed, struggled to free herself from his grip. But the cop was bigger than she was, and much stronger, and he carried her away swiftly and spoke English to her, words she gathered were supposed to be soothing.

"Let me go, you big dumb oaf," she told him in Romanian, but he ignored her cries. Kept pulling her away.

Volovoi coughed blood on the sidewalk. He made a choking sound, spasmed and went limp again, and then she knew he was gone. He was dead, and Catalina could do nothing but rage at the cop who held her, whose stupidity had just killed thirty girls.

No matter how much she kicked and punched, though, how hard she struggled, the cop wouldn't release her. He wouldn't let her go.

151

"JESUS." WINDERMERE WATCHED the paramedic apply antiseptic to the scratches and claw marks on Stevens's face. "That girl had some fight to her, huh?"

Stevens winced from a fresh sting. "Poor thing," he said. "Probably didn't even realize I was one of the good guys."

"Probably feels the same as her sister, figures all men are evil," Windermere said. "I just wonder what those bastards put her through."

"Guess we'll find out." Stevens looked across the sidewalk to the DuPont, the shattered front door, the tabloid news photographers lining the sidewalk, angling for a good shot of the first gunman's body. "Soon as the translator arrives."

They'd locked Catalina Milosovici in the back of a patrol car, for her own protection. She'd struggled, fought like a cornered animal until they got her in the backseat, and then something seemed to break inside her and she collapsed and cried, bitter and angry. Now, her tears gone, she sat morose and sullen, staring at her hands in the back of the cruiser, unresponsive to any offer of food, drink, or first aid.

"Her feet were torn to shreds," Stevens said.

Windermere nodded. "She's a fighter. I wonder what she was planning to do to Volovoi."

"Seemed like she was ready to carve out his eye."

She made a face. "Gruesome. What do you think she was telling him?"

Stevens didn't answer. Couldn't. Something about the girl wasn't really jiving for him yet. She'd fought harder than a girl who was lost and traumatized. She'd fought like he'd interrupted her somehow.

Probably she was just angry. The NYPD had guys in an apartment upstairs, said there were mountains of cocaine, guns, blood everywhere. Too early to tell just how the puzzle fit together, but Catalina was probably just trying to even the score.

Maybe.

Stevens let the paramedic fix him up, clean his wounds, apply a few bandages. Windermere watched. "You better hope those don't scar," she said. "Ruin your movie star looks."

Stevens laughed. "Chicks dig scars," he said. "At least that's what I've heard."

"Nancy tell you that?"

"No," he said, "but she put up with me for this long, and I don't figure I could get much uglier now."

She eyed him appraisingly. "That poor woman."

Movement behind them. Stevens turned to find a man studying them. He wore glasses and tweed—a professor. "Excuse me, agents," he said.

Stevens and Windermere swapped glances. "Yeah?"

"I'm Dr. Fidatov," he said. "The translator. I've just talked to Catalina, and I think there's something you both should know."

Stevens looked at Catalina's patrol car. The girl stared out at them, her eyes dark and inscrutable.

"Okay," Windermere said. "What's up?"

Fidatov cleared his throat. Fiddled with his jacket. "She said she was trying to get information when you pulled her away from the dead man," he said. "She seems to think you ruined her chance to save them."

"'Them,'" Stevens said. "Who's them? The girls in the box? Tell her we're on it. We tracked her container to the rest of the buyers. The women are safe."

Fidatov shook his head. "The other girls," he said. "The rest of the Dragon's New York captives. They're trapped in a warehouse somewhere, and according to Catalina, only the dead men could find them."

152

"COME ON," WINDERMERE said. "Come on, come on, *come on*."

From the other side of the apartment, Stevens watched her search and felt her frustration. With Fidatov's help, they'd pressed Catalina Milosovici for information. They'd found out the man they'd killed in front of the DuPont was indeed Pavel Demetriou, the gangster who called himself the Dragon. They'd found out about his lavish apartment upstairs. But the girl had only shaken her head when they asked her about the lost shipment.

"I didn't see the other girls after the Dragon took me," she said. "He never brought me to his warehouse." She glared at Stevens. "And this oaf pulled me off Volovoi before I could get any answers."

He told himself she was wrong. Andrei Volovoi was seconds from death. He was beyond saving anyone. No way he'd have given up the girls' location, no matter what Catalina did to him.

Still, though. Thirty young girls abandoned somewhere, and maybe—*maybe*—Catalina Milosovici could have convinced Andrei Volovoi to give her more information. Maybe he *had* consigned them to die.

"No," Windermere said. "Bullshit. We'll find these girls, Stevens. They're not gone yet."

But they'd searched the apartment and found nothing. Found drugs, a duffel bag full of guns, but nothing to point the way to the rest of the girls. No records. No phone numbers, even. If the Dragon had written down anything about his operation, he wasn't storing it here.

"What about Demetriou's cell phone," Stevens said. "He had to visit the warehouse at some point, right? Maybe he made a call and we can trace the GPS location back."

"His provider will want a warrant," Windermere said. "And even if they cooperate, they probably come back with like a million locations this Dragon guy called from, Stevens. Those girls will be long dead before we find them."

"Try it anyway," Stevens said. "I'll find us something better."

She walked into the kitchen, her phone to her ear, and Stevens turned to the window again. Far below, police lights flashed blue and red on the walls of neighboring apartment buildings.

Stevens felt a dead kind of numbness in his body. Thirty desperate women. Girls. And he was letting them die.

He would never forgive himself.

Shut up, he told himself. *Fight it off. There's still time.*

Then he thought of something, just as Windermere came back into the room, shaking her head. "The Dragon owns this place," he said. "I mean, this is his home, right?"

"Sure seems that way," Windermere said. "But his name's not on the deed, partner. It's another shell corporation."

"Of course it is," Stevens said. "But what else do they own?"

"Good question," Windermere said, reaching for her phone again. "Let's find out."

153

"MANHATTAN NUCLEAR." Windermere pocketed her phone. "They have a lease on this apartment and—" She grinned across the apartment at Stevens. "—they own a warehouse in the East Village, Avenue A."

Stevens felt his heart quicken, the numbness dissipate. "Hot damn," he said. "That's gotta be the place, right?"

"Gotta be." Windermere was heading for the elevator. "Let's go."

154

LEPLAVY MET THEM in Alphabet City.

"Here's the Manhattan Nuclear warehouse," he said, leading them toward a plain brick building in the middle of the block. "Used to be a clothing manufacturer, but they sold out. Manhattan Nuclear bought the place about a year ago now."

"Building a beachhead," Stevens said. "So they could take over New York."

They circled around the rear of the building, followed an alley into an open parking lot, a loading bay, a back door. A gray Bentley parked to one side, a little out of place. "HRT guys are stuck in traffic," LePlavy told them. "Going to be a little while, another half hour, maybe."

"Forget it," Windermere told him, drawing her weapon. "If these girls aren't in here, we need to cross this place off our list and keep moving." She looked at Stevens. "You coming, partner?"

Stevens drew his own weapon. "Yup."

Windermere marched up the stairs to the loading bay. Rapped on the back door. "FBI," she called, "and the Minnesota Bureau of Criminal Apprehension. Open up, or face the consequences."

Silence. She tried the door. It was unlocked.

"Slow," Stevens told her. "Slow and steady."

"Slow and steady," Windermere said. She pushed the door open.

The lights were on. The place smelled musty. She looked down at the floor. "Oh, snap."

Blood on the floor, and lots of it. A body, an older man, well dressed, his throat slit, his eyes wide. "Shit," Stevens said. "Who—"

Then the shooting started. Four or five shots, fast, from inside the warehouse. Two guns. The doorframe splintered above Windermere's head and she ducked away. *"Shit."*

Stevens spotted the shooter, big and ugly, his bald head gleaming bright as a beacon. Stevens drew aim, pulled the trigger, caught the guy with a shot to the leg. The thug howled, grabbed his thigh. Stumbled back from the door and disappeared out of sight.

Stevens started through the door. Windermere held him back. "Let me take this, partner," she told him. "No way your wife lets me live if you get shot again."

Stevens made to argue, knew from Windermere's expression that he'd never win. Reluctantly, he stepped back, let her creep through the door, her gun drawn. Watched her duck into the warehouse and followed quickly behind.

It was an antechamber, a loading area. A little room to one side, an office, and a bigger room at the front of the warehouse, most of it hidden. Windermere started toward the big room. Stevens spread out, followed behind her, searching the shadows, hardly daring to breathe.

Then the world exploded ahead of him. Stevens dove for cover, the floor and the walls going to shit around him. Too much action to return fire, and the guy's bullets were coming damn close. Stevens kept his head down, watched as Windermere leveled her Glock in the gunman's direction. Watched her exhale, cold as winter, and pull the trigger once, then again.

The gunfire stopped. The warehouse went silent again.

Windermere picked herself up. Examined the pattern of bullet holes above Stevens's head. "Well, shit, partner," she said. "I guess we found the right place."

155

THEY SEARCHED THE warehouse. The main floor first, a vast open space clogged with empty boxes and broken furniture, detritus. The manufacturing floor, dusty and abandoned.

Just off the main room was a bathroom. Traces of white powder on the sink. Cocaine. There was a small office, too, bottles of high-end booze and a futon bed. Dirty sheets. More cocaine. Condoms.

"Someone's been spending time here, anyway," Stevens said.

Windermere nodded. "So where the hell are the girls?"

Stevens walked back out to the main room. Studied the floor, the walls. There was a discolored patch of wall, freshly repainted. Stevens walked over and pressed on it, felt it give. A fresh panel of drywall, about four feet wide. Stevens traced the outline of the panel, pulled it away, found a heavy wooden door behind, a big padlock.

"Shit," he said. "A key. Bolt cutters. Anything."

"Watch out." Windermere pushed him aside, raised her Glock. Stevens ducked away, heard the gunshot, the splinter of steel. "Boom," Windermere said, reholstering her gun. "Who needs keys?"

They cleared the shards of lock free and unlatched the door. Then they looked at each other. "Ready, partner?" Windermere said.

"Hurry," Stevens told her. "For God's sake."

She pulled the latch clear and swung open the door. A dark passage. A basement stairwell. *Bingo,* Stevens thought. *Here's the mother lode.*

The stairs were creaky. They were creepy. The basement smelled of must and mildew and stale urine and worse. Stevens took the steps slow, kept his hand at his holster. Hit the bottom and stopped cold.

"Holy," he said. "Holy shit."

A low ceiling. Dim lighting. More boxes. And girls everywhere.

Teenagers, all of them, every girl in a short dress and heels, heavy makeup. They huddled together beneath bare lightbulbs, the last of the Dragon's human cargo. Stevens stared at them, couldn't move at first, couldn't help them. Just stood there and thought about his daughter, and felt suddenly, overwhelmingly, tired.

156

CATALINA DIDN'T HUG her big sister the moment they were reunited. She slapped her.

"You are a stupid cow," she said, flailing against Irina's upturned arms. "A stupid, gullible, *selfish* cow."

The FBI agent held her arms. Pulled her away. "You nearly got us killed," Catalina told her sister. "Mother and father, too. And for what? So you could be famous in this stupid country?"

Irina lowered her arms. Said nothing, just looked at her sister, skinny and anxious and exhausted, and Catalina instantly felt guilty. Ashamed. She relaxed her body, felt the FBI agent release his grip on her. "I'm sorry," she said.

It had been two long days since the FBI agents had pulled her away from the Dragon's body. Catalina had spent them in an FBI building somewhere in New York City, though she hadn't gone willingly.

She'd argued with the police for hours and hours. Forced the translator, Dr. Fidatov, to harass the cops for her, until he was sick and tired and refused to relay one more demand. So she kicked him out, demanded a new translator. Fidatov had stuck around, though. He moaned and cursed and muttered under his breath, but he didn't leave her.

And why would he? He knew the situation was dire. Thirty girls abandoned in the Dragon's warehouse, and the FBI wanted to feed her milk and cookies and talk about her feelings? Madness. She'd refused them. Hadn't talked. Had shaken off all but one of their cookies, until a tired-looking FBI agent came into the room and told her the girls were alive.

"All of them," Fidatov translated. "The FBI found the warehouse in the East Village."

"And they're alive," Catalina said. "Dorina is alive?"

"They're all alive. Every one of them. The FBI tracked them all down, thanks to you. So now you can cooperate, yes?"

Catalina felt like a chunk of concrete had been lifted from her chest. The girls were safe. Dorina was safe. Her parents, the FBI assured her, were safe. Even Irina was fine.

Fidatov watched her. The FBI agent stood at the door, an eyebrow raised. They wanted her cooperation. But Catalina wasn't ready to give it.

"No," she told the translator. "I want my sister."

> > >

IT TOOK ANOTHER DAY FOR the FBI to fly Irina to New York. By this point, Catalina had given up her hunger strike, but she had no time, still, for the army of analysts who paraded through her room, asking how she felt and how afraid she'd been, whether she'd had any dreams.

"My sister," she told them all. "I want to see my sister."

She'd waited, impatient. She dreamed of Irina, not of the bearded devil. He was dead, and so was his flat-faced friend. She knew it. She'd seen it. They couldn't hurt her anymore.

So, no, she wasn't afraid. She just missed her sister.

And then, the next day, the door to her little interview room opened, and the FBI agent ushered Irina in. She was pretty as ever, far prettier than Catalina, and she appeared far less pale, far less hungry than Catalina felt.

And suddenly, Catalina felt mad.

It was Irina who had done this, who had wanted so badly to be famous in America. It was concern for Irina and her stupid dreams that had brought Catalina to this country in the first place, to the box, to the brink of death. And now she was here, well-fed and tanned, and Catalina wanted to slap her.

So she did.

She slapped her sister until she felt stupid. Then she slunk back and caught her breath, aware of the FBI agent's eyes on her. She looked down at the floor. "I'm sorry," she said.

Then she said it again, because Irina was crying. And she'd wriggled free of the FBI agent, and then she really *was* hugging her sister, and feeling awful for being such a cow.

Irina hugged her back. "*I'm* sorry," she said. "I'm the one who's sorry, Catya."

And Catalina felt her defenses crumble, and then she was crying, too. Like a useless emotional little girl.

Shut up. You can cry now. After all of this, you're allowed to cry.

So they cried. They cried until they were out of tears, and then they pulled themselves apart and dried their eyes, and Catalina told Irina about Bogdan and Nikolai, Andrei Volovoi and the Dragon, and Irina told Catalina about Mathers and Nancy Stevens and Maria. And when Irina was finished, she regarded the small interview room and made a face.

"I don't know why I believed them," she said. "The men in Bucharest. This is not paradise."

"This?" Catalina said, gesturing to the room. "No, it certainly is not."

"Not just here," Irina said. "America. What's so special? I miss Mother and Father. I want to go home."

Catalina nodded. "I want to go with you."

157

MATHERS WAS WAITING in the arrivals area at Minneapolis–Saint Paul International. Windermere glanced at Stevens and sighed. "Until next time, partner."

Stevens followed her eyes. "Ah," he said "Back to reality. You going to be okay?"

"'Course I will," she told him. "I'd rather go home to my crummy love life than to your daughter's rampant hormones."

"Christ." Stevens made a face. "What am I going to do, Carla?"

"Talk to her," she said. "She's a smart girl. You make sure she's making good decisions, and then you get out of her way. You can't postpone the inevitable."

"I can try."

"You'll fail." She hugged him. "I'll see you tomorrow. Harris wants us in bright and early, start cleaning up the rest of the Dragon's buyers. Maybe working with Interpol to chase down that Mike bastard."

Stevens hugged her back. "Sure," he said. "Bright and early."

"Gonna be another needle-and-haystack gig. Get some rest."

Stevens shook Mathers's hand, shot a wave to them both. Shouldered his carry-on and disappeared into the crowd of passengers walking out of the terminal. Windermere watched him go. Then she turned back to Mathers. "Hey."

Mathers gave her a half-smile. "Hey."

She looked around the terminal, avoiding his eyes. She'd been thinking about this moment for days now, half dreading it, the other half counting down the minutes. Now she was here, *he* was here, and she didn't know what to say.

"So you tracked down Irina," she said finally. "Someone said you even learned some Romanian."

Mathers grinned. "They tell me my accent's atrocious," he said. "Listen." He said something unintelligible.

"Sounded okay to me," she said, shrugging.

He reached for her bag. "Just the carry-on?"

"Yeah," she said. Let him lift it and carry it toward the exit.

> > >

SHE LET HIM DRIVE HER home. Let him park in a visitor stall and carry her bag up to her condo. She unlocked the door and let him follow her in, let him crack a beer for her, let him pour it, let him bring her the glass in the living room. Then he sat, not beside her on the couch, but in the easy chair she never used, the chair she figured would be good for socializing if she ever grew up and got any real friends.

"So?" he said, leaning forward, hands clasped.

"So." She drank her beer. "So, I don't know, Mathers."

"I'm sorry I fucked up your case," he said.

She nodded. "I know."

"And I'm sorry I made everything complicated, with work and stuff. I know it's the last thing you need."

She drank some more beer. "I know."

"And—" He exhaled. Stood and walked to the window, rubbing his hands together. "I'm sorry about all of this. The emotional stuff. You said you don't want a boyfriend, I should have listened. Not fair that I pushed you into something you don't want."

She could feel his eyes on her. Knew he'd been saving this up, rehearsing it probably. Knew it wasn't easy to say.

But she couldn't look at him. She wanted to, but she just couldn't. "I know," she said. She drank again. "It's fine, Derek."

"'Fine.'" Mathers stared at her a moment. "Okay," he said finally. "So I'll just go."

Windermere closed her eyes. Contemplated the thought of her empty apartment, night falling, nobody to talk to. The thought of Mathers somewhere far away, pulling some badge bunny out of a bar. Contemplated him happy with somebody else, and her alone and empty in this soulless apartment.

She heard Mathers sigh again, heard his footsteps cross the living room toward the door. And now she wasn't seeing herself in her mind anymore, or Mathers. She was seeing the terrified teenage girls climbing out of the basement in Alphabet City, the dark-eyed women in the box on the freighter, in the brothels in Billings and Duluth.

She was seeing Irina Milosovici, Catalina, their thin faces, their haunted eyes. And she knew she didn't want to be alone.

"Don't go," she said without opening her eyes. "Mathers. Please."

There was a pause from the door. Windermere waited, didn't dare to breathe. Could feel his eyes on her, could almost read the thoughts running through his head.

The pause stretched for miles. She felt her heart pounding. Then the floorboards creaked and Mathers was beside her. She opened her eyes and let him hold her.

158

STEVENS CAUGHT A cab back to Saint Paul. Sat in the backseat with the window down, the sun and the wind on his face, and realized he was glad to be home.

The cabbie let him off behind his red Cherokee, still dirty with road dust from the trip to lake country. The passenger seats were littered with candy bar wrappers, old comic books—the kids still hadn't cleaned up from the drive.

Nancy's Taurus wasn't around. At work, he figured. Give him a chance to clean up a little, shave, get some dinner going and surprise her when she came home.

He was thinking about it, trying to plan a decent meal, as he walked up the front steps and unlocked the door, as he kicked off his shoes, said hi to the dog, and walked into the kitchen, where Andrea sat on the counter, drinking a soda and talking to Calvin, who stood by the back door.

Stevens thought the kid was going to make a run for it. His eyes went wide, and he turned to Andrea, searching for a lifeline. Andrea gave her dad a look like a popped balloon. She slid down from the counter. "Okay, Dad," she said. "Calvin's just leaving."

She tried to slip past him. Stevens held out his hand. "Hold up," he said. "I just got home. You haven't seen me in days. This is how you say hello?"

She rolled her eyes. "Hi, Dad. Can we go now?"

Stevens let her pass. Watched her disappear through the front hall with Calvin. *This is not how this is supposed to be,* he thought. He straightened. "Calvin."

A pause. Then reluctant footsteps. The kid poked his head through the doorway. "Mr. S.?"

"Come in here a second," he said. Andrea appeared at the doorway, and he shook his head. "Not you, daughter. Just Calvin."

Calvin glanced back at Andrea once. Then, slowly, he shuffled into the room. "Yeah?"

Stevens ran through every mean-dad cliché he could think of. Wondered which dad he should be. Calvin stood waiting, hands in the pocket of his cargo shorts, eyes downcast. "Look," Stevens said, "I don't like this any more than you do, but it's gotta be done, understand?"

Calvin nodded. "Yes, sir."

"I don't want to be a hard-ass. Not here. I play cop all day. The last thing I need is to be a policeman at home." He paused. "That's my wife's job."

Calvin nodded again. "Okay."

"Look at me, son."

Calvin looked up. He was a young kid. Gangly and awkward-looking, a little bit of acne and an unfortunate blush. Probably worked up every ounce of courage just to ask Andrea out. "Good," Stevens said. "Now, what's your business with my daughter?"

"Sir?"

"Your business, Calvin. Your intentions." Stevens eyed the kid. "What are you hoping to achieve here?"

Calvin studied the floor again. "I don't know," he said. "I never thought about it. Andrea's just cool, is all."

"You like lots of girls, Calvin?"

From the hallway, Andrea exhaled, loud. Stevens ignored her. Calvin blushed redder. "No, sir," he said. "Not really."

"Have lots of girlfriends? Are you some kind of player?"

"Me?" Calvin laughed. "You have the wrong guy, Mr. S."

"Okay, then," Stevens said. "So you like Andrea. What do you like about her, exactly?"

"She's, I dunno—she's smart," Calvin said. "And she's funny." He looked up at Stevens. "Really, she is. She's the funniest girl in our grade. And she doesn't take any shit—I mean crap. Sorry."

Stevens waved him off. "Go on."

"And, I don't know, she likes cool stuff," Calvin said. "She likes to do cool things."

"Like fool around in the living room when her parents aren't home."

Stevens thought the kid might die in front of him. *"No,"* he said. "Like go for bike rides and stuff. Watch old movies. Cool stuff. A lot of girls are just into makeup and hair." He looked pleadingly at Stevens. "That was just the one time, I swear. I'll never—you don't have to worry—never again—"

"Forget it," Stevens said. "Andrea, get in here."

Another long beat. Then Andrea came in. She stood beside Calvin and stared at her father, her mouth set, her eyes defiant, and Stevens again wondered when he'd become the enemy.

"First of all," he said. He coughed. "First of all, I know you guys are going to fool around, okay? I'm not stupid, and you're not twelve anymore. I know this."

Andrea grimaced. "Mortifying. So, so mortifying."

"You gotta know, though, that this is tough for me. I see things out there that turn my stomach, Andrea. I see people using each other. Hurting each other. I don't want that for you. For either of you."

He regarded them both. Andrea's eyes were still hard, but her posture had softened. Calvin still looked like the kid in the principal's office.

"Just make good decisions," Stevens said. "You know what I mean. Don't rush into something just because everyone else is doing it. Use protection. And for God's sake, don't make it all about sex. This stuff is way better when there's feelings behind it, trust me."

"*Gross,*" Andrea said.

"Whatever," Stevens told her. "'Gross' is walking in on your daughter and her boyfriend playing grab-ass. I don't want that, and neither do you. So just, you know, be smart. If you expect to be treated like an adult when it comes to your relationship with Calvin, be ready to act like an adult when it comes to your mother and me. Be respectful to us, and we'll try to be accommodating back, okay?"

"Fine," Andrea said. "Fine. Okay. Can I go?"

"Not yet," he said.

She made another face. "*Dad.*"

"I just got home from a terrible case," he told her. "Give your old dad a hug and tell him you'll be all right."

Andrea hesitated. Glanced at Calvin and then gave up and came to Stevens, wrapped him in a bear hug. "I'm glad you're home," she said into his shirt. "I'm glad you saved those girls."

Stevens hugged her back. Felt, suddenly, like he *was* home. Like everything, just then, was all right in the world. "I missed you, kiddo," he told her. He gave her one more squeeze. "Now get out of here," he said. "Go play outside or something. We're making your boyfriend uncomfortable."

Andrea rolled her eyes. "He's not my *boyfriend*, Dad." Then she was out the door, Calvin trailing behind, and Stevens listened to the sound of their footsteps through the hall and out the front door, heard their laughter as they ran down the steps into the yard.

Home, he thought. *At last.*

ACKNOWLEDGMENTS

I feel immensely blessed to have an agent who is willing to knuckle down and get her hands dirty when there's work to be done. This book owes so much to Stacia Decker; her wisdom, encouragement, and editorial acumen brought these characters, and this story, to life.

A heartfelt thanks, also, to Neil Nyren, the best editor in the business, and to Ivan Held, Katie Grinch, Sara Minnich, Christopher Nelson, Rob Sternitzky, and everyone at Putnam, whose faith and enthusiasm has enabled me to take Stevens and Windermere places I never would have dared imagine.

Thanks to the booksellers who've stood behind my odd-couple pair of crime fighters for four books, and to the readers who stay up to the wee hours, flipping these pages. Your support is inspirational and humbling in equal measure; you make me feel like a rock star.

Thanks to my friends, old and new, near and far, whose love and kindness carries me forward even on the toughest days.

And thanks, always and forever, to my family.